THE TROUBADOUR'S QUEST

Angela Hunt

Tyndale House Publishers, Inc.
Wheaton, Illinois

Library of Congress Cataloging-in-Publication Data

Hunt, Angela Elwell,   date
   The troubadour's quest / Angela Elwell Hunt.
      p.   cm. — (The Theyn chronicles : [bk. 2])
      ISBN 0-8423-1287-0
      1. Man-woman relationships—Europe—Fiction.   2. Middle Ages—
History—Fiction.   3. Troubadours—Fiction.   I. Title.
II. Series: Hunt, Angela Elwell, date   Theyn chronicles : [bk. 2].
PS3558.U46747T76   1993   93-40904
813'.54—dc20   r942

Printed in the United States of America

99 98 97 96 95 94
10 9   8   7   6   5   4   3   2   1

AUTHOR'S NOTE

Would you recognize true love if it were staring you in the face?
Maybe, and maybe not . . .

Readers familiar with *Afton of Margate Castle* will recognize
Gislebert as the troubadour who abandoned his quest for the
lovely Nadine at the conclusion of the first book of The Theyn
Chronicles.

In this second book, Gislebert is no longer needed at Margate
Castle, for Afton and Calhoun are happily married and the parents
of twin baby boys. With strange stirrings in his heart, Gislebert
realizes he wants a family of his own, so he sets out to find the
girl he hasn't seen in twelve years, the beautiful and chaste Nadine.

Throughout his noble, dangerous, and lengthy journey,
Gislebert only wants to be loved. And, like most of us, Gislebert
learns that love in its purest form demands sacrifice and submission.

The adventure of *The Troubadour's Quest* offers a passport
to the castles and courts of medieval England and France as well
as to the desperate dungeons of old French prisons. Like Don
Quixote of Cervantes' tale, Gislebert risks his life as he pursues an
ideal only to find God has supported him with that ideal all along.

But discovery lies in the journey.

Angela E. Hunt

HISTORICAL NOTE

The twelfth-century church, from which the modern Catholic church is descended, was the universal church—the only organized church in society. Most medieval men and women were illiterate and could not read the Word of God for themselves. So the priests and monks of the church took on the role of intercessor for all mankind. The clergy saw themselves as the mouth of the people and believed that their piety ensured the people's salvation.

A few people, regarded by the church clergy as heretics, refused to accept intercessors (which included not only the priests but Mary and the saints as well) and aimed to communicate directly with the Holy Spirit and secure their own salvation.

But then, as today, men and women in all circumstances were confronted with the truth of God's plan of salvation and the choice of whether to accept the Savior or reject him.

TABLE OF CONTENTS

MARGATE CASTLE

You will seek me and find me
when you seek me
with all your heart.

JEREMIAH 29:13

ONE

From the doorway of the great hall of Margate Castle, Gislebert the troubadour watched the tender family scene before him, and his heart twisted in pain. Calhoun, his best friend and companion since adolescence, lounged carelessly in a chair. His dark blue eyes followed the movements of his wife, Afton, who held twin babes at her breasts. Afton's mother, the aged Corba, hovered near in pride, hoping to be of service. "The babes look as much like you as they do my Afton," Corba told Calhoun—Lord Calhoun now, Gislebert reminded himself.

"Do you think so?" Afton asked, her natural loveliness enhanced by the soft glow of maternal pride. She turned from one tiny face to the other. "I thought they looked a bit like you, Mother."

Corba's leathery face lit up with pleasure, and her few remaining teeth gleamed in the firelight. Calhoun leaned toward the babies and caught sight of Gislebert in the doorway. "What say you, my friend?" he asked, reaching out to caress his son's tender cheek. "What do you think about Margate's newest heirs?"

Despite his desire to remain aloof, Gislebert blinked nervously. How could he tell the truth about the babies? The sight of those little boys tormented his soul and brought tears to his eyes, and Calhoun would never understand why. Gislebert had sincerely rejoiced at his friend's good fortune, and for a while, before the babies were born, he had thought he could remain at Margate forever. But lately, Margate's pleasures had become torturous.

"They are beautiful babies," he answered gruffly, aware that Calhoun, Afton, and Corba waited for words of approval. In truth, the babies were most handsome, worthy of a song or poem the finest a troubadour could offer. But Gislebert would not be the one to write such a song. The babies lay too close to his heart. He loved the twin boys as if they were his own; but they were not, and the sight of them was enough to drive Gislebert mad.

He turned his face away from the loving scene at the fireplace. His countenance would surely give him away, and Calhoun would be by his side in a moment, asking if something troubled him. But how could he explain his feelings to a man who had everything?

Calhoun had struggled, of course, as they all had, in the difficult days when Perceval of Margate held the manor in his conniving grasp. And, like Gislebert, Calhoun had lived as a man without a family, having lost his father, brother, and lately, his mother. Both men had been alone in the world.

But there the similarities ended. Calhoun had claimed the love of his life, and that love had borne him two fine sons. Gislebert had been content to stand on the periphery and watch, and as he stood now in the shadows of the great hall, his traitorous eyes turned again to spy on the blissful domestic scene before him.

Together Calhoun and Afton had grown in their love and in their devotion to God. Gislebert, too, had come to love the God who had so richly blessed his friends, had even pledged his life to the pursuit of God as he was manifested in love—he would sing of such love, he would dream of it, he would live for it—until he had eased the aching emptiness that filled his heart every time he looked at Calhoun and Afton.

As he feared, Calhoun was watching him with one eyebrow raised.

"Mama, will you take Alard?" Afton said, offering one baby to Corba. "He's a greedy little thing, and he always eats more quickly than his brother."

"But Albert is the thoughtful one," Corba countered, taking Alard from Afton's arms. "Look at that expression on his face—he's a thinker, there be no doubt of it."

"Speaking of thinkers," Calhoun said, his eyes fastened firmly on Gislebert's face, "I sense that Gislebert has something on his mind. Speak, Gislebert, for you are among friends."

Gislebert smiled politely, then glanced down at the scarred wooden floor under his feet. By heaven, were his eyes betraying him with tears? He commanded his face to harden in resolve. "I was merely rejoicing in your good fortune, my friends," he said simply, glancing up quickly to see if Calhoun doubted his words.

Apparently he did not. Calhoun relaxed in his chair and raised a tankard in Gislebert's direction. "Then take your ease and sit with us a while," he said, nodding cheerfully. "Spring is in the air, dear friend, and the long winter is nearly over. This is the time for rejoicing."

"Hear! Hear!" Afton agreed. She wrapped Albert in his blanket.

"One in my lowly position cannot argue with the earl of Margate," Gislebert answered, making an effort to keep his voice light. He turned a careful smile upon Afton. "And one would never argue with the lovely Afton. But I'd like to take my leave of you now. Night falls, and I am tired."

He bowed again and left the room.

His feet crunched along the gravel of the castle courtyard as he walked from the castle keep, and even though the wind blew cold, he could sense the moist breath of spring. He drew his cloak about him and unconsciously turned to make a wide arc around the spot where, just months before, the mighty Perceval of Margate had fallen to his death from an upper window. He would never come through this courtyard without seeing Perceval stretched out there, never walk through the great hall without remembering the bloody day when Stephen, king of all England, had counted the dead of Margate.

Too many had died on that day, but none had died at Gislebert's hand. While Calhoun had scaled the castle walls and claimed his victory, Gislebert had lingered in the shadows, afraid for his life. He had always been thus: afraid, cowardly, weak.

At that day's end, God—and King Stephen—had awarded Calhoun love, loyalty, and honor. *But you received and deserved nothing,* Gislebert thought bitterly. *In twenty-five years of living, you have won neither home, nor family, nor love.*

The wind moaned softly as it blew through the courtyard, and Gislebert lifted his eyes to the top of the castle wall. Once his heart had stirred him to leave these walls, when a young girl had visited and smiled upon him. A lifetime ago he had left Margate to search for her, but loyalty to Afton and Calhoun had brought him back. Surely now the law of love demanded that he answer another loyalty. Surely the time had come to leave Margate again, to search for the girl Nadine.

He stopped abruptly in midstep and looked up at the huge stone towers that guarded the entrance to Margate Castle. The pair of knights on duty nodded absently in his direction, doubtless recognizing him in the dim light by his brightly colored tunic. *You are no threat, for you wear the colors of a woman,* Gislebert chided himself sternly. *And you hide behind Calhoun's protection, like his servants. You tell stories of bravery and love and loyalty, yet your tales are of others' deeds, never your own. For you are not brave; you have not won a woman's love, and what do you really know of loyalty? Have you ever given all for another?*

A third knight stepped out of the stone garrison, his silver mesh hauberk gleaming in the gathering darkness. The knight glanced curiously at Gislebert. "Good eve," the fellow offered, his hand reflexively going to the hilt of his sword when Gislebert did not immediately reply.

Gislebert shook himself from his thoughts. "Be at rest; I am Gislebert, the troubadour," he said, raising a hand in the knight's direction. He attempted a smile and waved toward the sky where the moon had begun to rise. "The beauty of the night sky made me take leave of myself."

The knight grunted and spat on the ground. "I've heard that your kind was prone to flights of fancy," he said, adjusting his helmet. "Be off to your house, then. Many a foolish man has been mistakenly killed in the dark of night."

"Aye," Gislebert agreed, nodding as the knight's words echoed in his ears. He gritted his teeth and resumed his walk across the courtyard. *You are not of his kind,* he thought. *You are a wastrel, a jester, a fool. Only the strength and name of the valiant Calhoun preserves you.*

He stopped suddenly as the tall gates of the castle swung open to allow a pair of patrolling knights access to the road that led through Margate village. Gislebert had been down that road several times before, but each time he had returned, drawn back to Margate by an irresistible force that entwined his fate with Calhoun's.

Now he paused, as though listening to some inner urging. And then he nodded. *Aye, Lord God, so be it,* he prayed. *It is time to cut those cords. If I would be a man, I must leave this place and these people for all time. I must stand on my own merits, if I have any, and find the place—and the love—God would have for me.* He jerked open the door to his small house, tossed off his cloak, and sank wearily onto his narrow bed. He would leave, and soon, before his jealousy matured into resentment and bitterness. But how would he explain himself to Calhoun?

"Good morning, Gislebert," Calhoun said, looking up in surprise as Gislebert met him in the courtyard. "I was on my way to select a horse for Afton. Will I see you at dinner?"

"No . . . actually, I wanted to speak with you," Gislebert answered, falling into the rhythm of Calhoun's long strides toward the stable. "I'll just walk with you, if you don't mind."

"Has anyone offended you?" Calhoun said, frowning. "I know the knights are often disorderly, but if one of them has been disrespectful to you, I'll—"

"No, my concerns have nothing to do with the knights." Gislebert waved the matter aside. "And my thoughts can wait. Why does Afton need a new horse?"

Calhoun's face brightened as it always did when he spoke of his wife. "I want a more gentle creature for her now that she has borne my sons. The steward received three new mares yesterday, and I want to look them over."

The pungent smells of hay and manure struck Gislebert forcefully when they entered the barn, and Calhoun laughed at Gislebert's expression. "Relax, my friend. You should learn more about animals to balance your knowledge of men," Calhoun said, pulling a pair of leather gloves from a hook on the wall. "I will teach you. Did you know a fine horse exhibits the qualities of four animals?" he asked as he pulled on his gloves.

"Truly?" Gislebert asked dryly, raising an eyebrow in skepticism. "I beg of you, sir, please explain."

Calhoun laughed and waved at Josson, the steward, who held the reins of a tall white horse. Two other horses, a black and a bay, waited in nearby stalls. "An excellent horse exhibits three qualities of a fox," Calhoun said, looking carefully at the white horse's head. "Short, straight ears, good hair, and a strong tail full of hair." He grasped the horse's halter firmly with one hand and, with the other, lifted the horse's lip to examine its teeth.

"This horse is a beauty," Josson offered, bowing slightly. "Sure to please Lady Afton."

"Perhaps," Calhoun said, standing back. "But a good horse must also have four qualities of a hare: a lean head, wariness in the eye, light movement, and speed." He turned to Josson. "Have you ridden this animal?"

Josson shook his head. "No, my lord."

"Saddle all three," he said. "You, Gislebert, and I will ride."

Calhoun strode purposefully toward the stalls as Josson rushed to obey. "The third animal?" Gislebert asked.

"Four qualities of an ox," Calhoun answered, pointing to the bay. He stepped inside the stall and rubbed his hand expertly over the animal's winter-heavy coat. "A broad chest, a vast belly, large eyes that stand out from the head, and low-jointedness."

Gislebert let his eyes rove over the horse, trying to see what made one animal more valuable than another. It was difficult, for all horses looked much the same to him.

"Three qualities of an ass," Calhoun went on, leaning on the stall gate. He pointed toward the third horse, a tall animal with slender legs and a beautiful ebony coat. "Good feet, a strong backbone, and a gentle spirit."

Expertly opening the mouth of the black horse, Calhoun called to Josson, "This will be my lady's horse, Josson, for she's a three-year-old and still conformable to training. The bay is six, if I'm a day."

"How can you tell?" Gislebert asked, following Calhoun into the stall.

Calhoun lifted the horse's lip and pried the animal's teeth apart as the mare jerked her head in protest. "At three, these three teeth in the front become larger than the others," Calhoun explained. "At six, the fangs have hollow bottoms, and there's a mark at the bottom of the hollow. The white mare has worn her fangs down; they're flat and even. She's seven, I'd wager, and I'll not buy a horse that's halfway to the grave already."

They moved out of the stall so Josson could saddle the last horse, and Calhoun sighed in satisfaction as he pulled his gloves from his hands. "I'll take the bay and the black. These mares will be fine additions to our stables," he said, glancing around. "My Arabian stallion and the black mare will produce offspring as fine as my own boys."

Abruptly, Gislebert told Calhoun he was leaving.

"I wish I understood why you feel you must leave," Afton whispered, her breath warm in his ear. She retreated from the gentle embrace she had given him and stood back, her

9

dark gray eyes genuinely troubled. "You are like a brother to us, and we wish you would not go."

"It is not for us to hold him," Calhoun answered, stepping forward. He clasped Gislebert firmly by the shoulders and embraced him quickly. "God go with you, my friend, and keep you in his grace. You will always have a place of honor at my table."

"Thank you," Gislebert answered, a film of tears blurring his vision despite his best intentions.

"Have you everything you need for your journey?" Afton interjected. "Enough clothing? A warm cloak? Calhoun, can't we send an escort of knights to see him safely to his destination?"

Gislebert held up his hand in protest. "I have no destination," he said, smiling at the gentle lady who had ruled his days in recent months. "I am seeking . . . ," he faltered, ". . . myself, my place in God's service, and the girl Nadine, who has been in my thoughts for many years. I do not know where I will find her, but it is time I sought her."

"There is one thing I can offer to aid you," Calhoun said, motioning to a boy who stood near the stable. The boy darted inside the building and returned in a moment, leading the new black mare by the bridle. Beautifully outfitted, the mare wore a sturdy saddle and a handsome leather bridle.

Calhoun smiled as Gislebert stammered his protests. "Nonsense. Afton insists you have the horse. It is a fine animal, and even if you accept, we will forever remain in your debt."

Practicality silenced Gislebert. A horse would make his journey swifter. "I thank you," he said finally, when he was sure his voice was under control. He gathered his bag of belongings and walked stiffly to the horse.

Afton noticed the small bag, and her eyes filled with pity. "Is there nothing else you want?" she said, looking sorrowfully at the bag into which he had placed only paper, quills, a bottle of ink, and his lute. "We have so much to offer. . . ." She paused, biting her lip.

10

"You have given more than enough," Gislebert answered, mounting. Calhoun slipped his arm around Afton as Gislebert took the reins from the groom and turned to face Lord Calhoun one last time.

"I salute you, sir," Calhoun said. He extended his free arm to Gislebert.

Gislebert returned the salute. "And I, you," he said. "May God preserve you both."

He was about to urge the horse forward when a startled cry stopped him. "Wait!" Afton cried, breaking free of her husband's embrace. Running forward, she caught the stirrup of the mare and pulled a gleaming dagger from the voluminous sleeve of her gown. "Take this, Gislebert," she said, thrusting the handle of the dagger toward him. "The roads are fraught with danger, and the country is filled with thieves and enemies of the king. If you will not carry a sword, at least carry this to defend yourself."

Gislebert shook his head slowly. "Thank you, lady, but no," he said firmly. "A dagger in my possession would come to no good. I am a man of words, not of action, and I trust my life into God's hands."

Afton lowered the dagger in disappointment, and Calhoun stepped forward and took it from her. "Aye, then, Gislebert, may God protect you," he said. "Go with grace."

Gislebert loosened the reins, kicked his mare, and cantered quickly away through the twin towers of Margate Castle.

TWO

As the sun set over the western horizon, Gislebert paused in the doorway of the drab hospice and looked out over the road to Faversham. A few remaining travelers scurried to reach the hospice shelter, clutching their meager cloaks about them as the night wind blew chill. These most recent arrivals, like the handful of other travelers who paused here for rest and refreshment, were tired, hungry, and tense from the rigors of travel.

A gentle tug on his sleeve drew his attention. The balding monk who ran the hospice stood there. "If you please, Troubadour, can we have a song to quiet our guests?" he asked, bowing awkwardly. Gislebert nodded in reply. The monk turned and passed through the crowd, motioning for women to make their beds on the floor to his left; men settled on his right. Gislebert picked up his lute and strummed it lightly.

The sound worked its magic over the group, and soon all were settled and quiet in anticipation of the music to follow. Runny-nosed children huddled with their mothers, listening hungrily for a song, and the men leaned their backs to the wall, sternly watching over their wives and little ones. Gislebert took a breath and began to sing:

There was a lady of the North Country,
Had been a bride, now a widow was she,
And she had lovely daughters three.
Fa la la la, fa la la la ra re.

There was a knight of noble worth
Which also lived in the North.
The knight, of courage stout and brave,
A wife he did desire to have.

He knocked at the ladies' gate
One evening when it was late.
The eldest sister let him in,
And pinned the door with a silver pin.

The second sister she made his bed,
And laid soft pillows under his head.
The youngest daughter that same night,
She sang to sleep this gallant knight.

And in the morning, when it was day,
These words to him did the youngest say:
"Now that you have met us three—
I pray, sir knight, will you marry me?"
The young brave knight to her replied,
"Thy suit, fair maid, shall not be denied.
If thou canst answer me questions three,
This very day will I marry thee."
"Kind sir, in love, O then," quoth she,
"Tell me what your questions be."

"O what is longer than the way,
Or what is deeper than the sea?
Or what is louder than the horn,
Or what is sharper than a thorn?
Or what is greener than the grass,
Or what is worse than Mother Eve was?"

"O love is longer than the way,
And hell is deeper than the sea.
And thunder is louder than the horn,
And hunger is sharper than a thorn.

13

And poison is greener than the grass,
And the devil worse than Mother Eve was."

When she these questions answered had,
The knight became exceeding glad.
And having truly tried her wit,
He much commended her for it.
And after, as it is verified,
He made of her his lovely bride.

So now, fair maidens all, adieu,
This song I dedicate to you.
I wish that you may constant prove
Unto the man that you do love.

The air in the room was hot and still, but no one moved during the song of the knight and his riddle of love. When Gislebert finished and laid his lute to rest, one heavy woman wiped a tear from her eye and called out, "That's truly movin', it is."

The monk came forward to say prayers over the group. Gislebert put his lute away in his bag and moved toward the rough wooden table at the back of the room. After prayers, as the travelers spread their cloaks and prepared for sleep, the monk brought Gislebert a bowl of soup and a small loaf of hard brown bread. "Though we'd be pleased to hear more of God and less of knights and their ladies," the monk whispered, shaking his head in rueful amusement, "that tale wasn't as brash as others I've heard in these parts."

"Thank you, Father." Gislebert accepted the meal gratefully. The monk left to settle a squabble between two women, and Gislebert was glad for the chance to sit alone and think. He took a bite of the brown bread and chewed thoughtfully. Three weeks he had been on the road, journeying from Margate to Eastry and now to Faversham, and at every hospice and village he had asked the same question. Each time he had received a negative reply, so he braced himself for the worst and silently waved his hand to catch the monk's attention again.

When the holy priest had quieted the women and stood again before him, Gislebert asked the one question on his mind: "Father, have you news of a Lady Jehannenton? She has not been in these parts for over a dozen years, but she used to visit Margate on occasion. She is a kinsman to the king."

The monk folded his hands politely. "And what is she to you, my son?"

Gislebert blushed. "The lady herself is nothing to me. I have traveled many miles in search of one of the lady's maids—a girl called Nadine."

The priest rubbed his chin and nodded slowly. "You seek a girl you have not seen in over twelve years? Do you expect to ask for her hand in marriage, or—" He paused and inclined his head slightly. "Have you a darker purpose in your heart?"

"No, Father!" Gislebert looked up in horror. "My intentions are entirely honorable. I know nothing but love for the lady and, with God's help, would make her my wife. I know she may have married, but until I know, I cannot rest."

The priest sank slowly onto a stool behind him. "You speak as though your destiny lies in your love for a young girl," he said, again scratching the rough stubble on his chin. "A peculiar destiny, is it not, my son?"

"It is no more peculiar for a man to seek his destiny in love than it is for a monk to seek his in God," Gislebert answered, his temper rising. He paused to let his words sink into the stubborn monk's heart. "If Lady Jehannenton yet lives," he went on, "it is likely my Nadine is still employed in her service. I would find her, offer her my love, and hear her answer."

"And if she is married—or dead?"

Gislebert flushed. "It will be as God wills."

The priest nodded slightly. "You answer well, young man. You give a good account of yourself, but I cannot help you. I have not seen or heard of a Lady Jehannenton in these parts. Surely there are folk in London who would know of her, since she is a relative of the king's."

"Thank you," Gislebert said, looking down at his soup. "I am on my way to London."

"Be careful on your way," the priest whispered, leaning closer to Gislebert. "The road is full of blackguards who defy the king's curfew and peace. Yesterday an entire family was slain for the gold brooches on their cloaks."

"Then you need not worry, Father, God travels with me. Besides, I am simply dressed and carry no valuables," Gislebert replied.

"Still, my son, be cautious," the priest warned. "A man whose destiny lies in love is not likely to be wary of those who find their purpose in doing evil."

The priest's words rang in Gislebert's ears for several days after their encounter, but he had no trouble with thieves or errant knights on the roadway. Perhaps it was because he was decently dressed or mounted on a fine horse, he reasoned, or perhaps he traveled safely merely because he avoided darkness and dangerous side roads.

He watched his fellow travelers carefully, however, when the road to Gillingham became thick with people headed to the annual spring fair at Lord William's castle. When the crowd grew so dense that riding his horse became treacherous, Gislebert decided it was better to walk than worry about stepping on a poor villein child's foot.

His mare daintily picked her way through the crowd to a stream that babbled beside the road. Gislebert dismounted and let the horse drink deeply. Life could be most unfair, he thought, watching the impoverished villeins and villagers who trooped by him in their tattered woolen garments. Why should he ride while they walked holes into their boots? His clothing, though plain and unadorned, was whole and dyed in colors only noblemen could afford, and his leather shoes were still shiny and fresh from the cobbler's bench.

A crack of a branch caught his attention, and he glanced up into a tree that hung over the road. Apparently Gislebert was not the only traveler who had chosen to rest. A boy sat high in the tree, surveying the crowd with sharp eyes. He was a thin child, with knobby knees that protruded from a tattered brown tunic, and the rough belt tied about his middle accentuated a gaunt waistline. The boy's brown hair flew out from his head in silky tangles; his brown eyes darted among the people below like a hungry sparrow's. Though he sat still, there was something in the boy's countenance that reminded Gislebert of a cat ready to pounce.

The fair, Gislebert mused. *The boy's probably just excited about the fair.* He smiled, remembering his first fair. It had been on the grounds of Margate Castle, when he and Calhoun had returned from Calhoun's training as a knight. Like Lord William of Gillingham, whose generosity the crowd celebrated today, Lord Perceval had thrown open his fields, and Gislebert had been amazed at the treasures on display. This fair at Gillingham was certainly no different; it brought people from miles around to buy, sell, and gawk at wonders and riches from around the world.

Gislebert's mare finished drinking and began to munch on the sweet green stalks that lined the bank of the creek. Gislebert looped the end of the reins loosely around a broken tree branch and let the mare eat. His own stomach growled, and he inhaled quickly in an effort to quiet its rumbling. It had been hours since he had eaten, and the thought of the fair's food merchants set his mouth to watering. At the fair he would see and smell roasted duck, beef, lamb, venison, and other game from the king's forest, as well as breads, cakes, and sweetmeats. Perhaps there would even be a feast—food free for the asking.

But there was something of far greater interest to him than the food—and that was the information he hoped to gather. With merchants from so many different areas, surely one would know of his lady.

God, grant that it may be so.

A sudden movement from across the sea of people caught his attention. The new golden spring leaves of the tree bobbed as the boy swung down from his perch. He dropped into the crowd right behind a well-fed man and his wife, who were loaded with goods for the fair. The scent of the freshly baked bread in the man's pushcart wafted even to Gislebert, and he stood on tiptoe to see what the boy would do next.

Behind the baker and his wife, the boy moved forward in sync with the woman's steps and appeared to be judging the swing of the large lidded basket on her arm. Without sound or warning, the rascal flipped the lid and snatched a loaf of bread from the basket with the ease of a professional pickpocket. Gislebert gasped in amazement.

Practically dancing in glee, the boy darted to the side of the road near Gislebert's hiding place and perched on a fallen log. He had his face buried in the loaf, gobbling like a pig, when Gislebert caught him by the arm. "Hey!" the boy cried, forgetting his indignation long enough to sink his teeth afresh into the baker's loaf. With his cheeks loaded like a squirrel's, the boy chewed rapidly. "What do you think you're doing, disturbin' a boy's breakfast?"

Gislebert made an effort to stifle a laugh. This urchin had pluck! "I'm trying to help you," he told his prisoner, keeping his hand resolutely tightened around the boy's arm. "I saw what you did, and while I don't blame you for thinking of food if you're hungry, I can show you a better way to fill your belly."

"Oh yeah?" the boy sneered, ripping off another huge bite of bread with his teeth. He chewed furiously, casting quick, wary glances toward the troubadour in between bites. Gislebert couldn't help smiling—the boy reminded him of the cat at Margate who was forever losing his birds to the dogs.

"Yes," Gislebert answered. "If I release your arm, do you promise not to run away from me?"

"Do you promise not to turn me over to the lord's men?" the boy countered, taking another ravenous bite.

"Yes, and I won't take your bread, either, so quit stuffing yourself like a pig," Gislebert answered. "Do we have a deal?" The boy nodded, his wild brown hair falling into his eyes, and Gislebert released his grip on the boy's thin arm. "There," Gislebert said, smiling pleasantly. "Perhaps we can help each other, you and I. My name is Gislebert, and I'm a troubadour. Through all my travels, I've never yet had to steal my dinner, and if we improve your manners, you won't have to steal yours, either. What's your name?"

"What's it to you?"

"I just want to know."

"Jonas." The boy nervously wiped his mouth with the back of his hand as though he hadn't intended to answer.

Gislebert nodded approvingly. "A nice name. Where are your parents, Jonas?"

The boy tried to leap from his seat, but Gislebert caught the boy's arm again and held him tight. "It is not safe for you to be alone in this mob, Jonas. Where are your parents?"

"'Aven't got any!"

"Then who is your master?"

"'Aven't got one of them, neither!"

"Surely you're not alone out here?"

"So what if I am?" The boy's face flushed with color, and his huge brown eyes glittered with anger. "Why are you lordin' yourself over one such as me? Turn me over to the lord or let me go, but I'll not be staying with the likes of you! I'm fifteen and old enough to take care of myself!"

"I just wanted to help you, that's all," Gislebert replied, releasing the boy. He turned toward his horse, expecting to hear the sound of the boy thrashing through the greenery in a wild escape, but all remained silent behind him. Gislebert smiled and silently congratulated himself. If the boy wasn't running, something had intrigued him. Something in his words must have reached the poor boy's soul. . . .

"Where'd you get that horse?" The boy's words dispelled the warm glow of pride in Gislebert's heart. The boy was intrigued by the horse, nothing else, and was probably planning to steal the creature if luck presented him with the opportunity.

"The horse was a gift from a friend," Gislebert said, swinging himself up into the saddle.

"Go on!" the boy cried, disbelieving.

Gislebert nodded. "It's true. You might say the horse was a reward for my loyalty in friendship. I can be a very loyal friend."

The boy cocked his head, but still he did not run. After a moment he spoke again: "Where'd you say you was from?" he asked, putting out a tentative hand to stroke the horse's neck.

"I didn't say," Gislebert replied, gathering the reins in his hands. "I care more about where I'm going, and now I'm going to the fair to sing and entertain and try to gather some information." The mare took a step forward, but Gislebert pulled back on the reins. "You're welcome to come along, if you wish."

The boy teetered on one foot and then the other.

"Are you coming or not?" Gislebert asked again, extending his hand to the boy on the ground. The boy's eyes grew wide—something in the gesture seemed to spook him.

"No, I'm not coming with you!" the boy retorted, retreating back into the crowd. "And don't try to catch me, either."

In a twinkling he was deep in the crowd of villagers, and after a moment, Gislebert lost sight of him.

The skinny troubadour was as big a fool as all the others, for he had taken one look at her shorn hair and short tunic and taken her for a boy. Adele waited until the troubadour had urged his horse forward through the low brush on the side of the road, then she scampered out from behind the concealing gooseberry bush and followed. The man Gislebert seemed gentle enough, for all that he had interrupted a perfect snitching, and his eyes were not at all threatening. But still Adele was wary. The one lesson she had learned in her short life was to trust no one.

Ahead on the road, now within sight, rose the imposing gray walls of Lord William's Castle at Gillingham. The thick walls of stone squatted stubbornly in the emerald green of the wide spring field, and Adele lifted her chin in unconscious contempt for the man who hid within the massive pile of stone and timber. What kind of life could be lived in such a prison? How much better it was to be free to go wherever she wanted! Adele imagined the noble Lord William sitting in a skyless, sunless room with only a smoking chimney for comfort. If she had to be entombed within a castle or stone house to be warm and fed, Adele preferred cold and near-starvation.

She had once lived in a house, poor though it was. But in exchange for the meager roof above her head, she had to endure harsh words, back-breaking work, and the constant threat of her father's fist. Life had promised to hold little else for her, particularly since her father waited impatiently for the day when she matured into womanhood so she could be married to some villein even harsher than he. To escape this fate, Adele had devised a plan so simple that it took her breath away. She would run away and become a boy. Boys were free. They did not have to marry; they said what they thought and were not beaten for their boldness. So when the first buds of spring appeared on the oak tree outside her small hut, Adele had become Jonas. She slipped into one of her father's cast-off tunics, belted it securely about her waist, walked out the door of her hut, and vowed never to return.

She had been on the road for three weeks when she heard about the Gillingham fair, and she had joined with the crowd in eager anticipation. Now that the crowd was within sight of the castle, the villagers and villeins dispersed into the green fields outside the castle walls. Adele made a mental note that the tall troubadour on the dark horse rode toward the castle drawbridge. Undoubtedly, the man would shelter his horse in Lord William's stable while he visited the fair. Perhaps later, with a little timing and good fortune, Adele could convince the guard at the castle stable that the troubadour had sent her to fetch the horse. What was his name again? "Gislebert," Adele whispered softly. She practiced it again and again as she walked through the green field, imitating the man's cultured accent.

It wouldn't do to approach the stable too quickly, however. Adele sprinted toward the long row of rough wooden tables where the servants of Gillingham were spreading the lord's feast for his villeins and visitors. A traditional boon granted by the lord to those who worked his fields, the spring feast was also Lord William's gracious gesture of hospitality to all who visited the fair. Women in graceful blue robes with golden cloaks held basins of water for guests to wash their hands in before eating, but Adele rushed by the women in search of an empty place at a table where dinner was already being served.

An empty trencher lay on the table between a toothless villein and a young girl, and Adele did not hesitate to take her seat between them. She nodded politely, first to the elderly man, then to the girl, but saved her attention for the food piled in bowls at the center of the table. The lord's best lay there—black puddings, sausages, venison, and beef. Spicy sauces of vinegar, verjuice, and wine stood in stone bowls, and Adele licked her lips in anticipation.

"It is quite a feast, is it not?" the girl to her right remarked shyly, and Adele nodded absently in reply. She fingered the trencher of day-old bread before her and frowned as the old man on her left drew back in distaste at the sight of her dirty hands. "Couldn't you find time to wash?" the man asked, reluctantly passing a bowl of pottage to Adele.

"No," Adele answered, roughly grabbing the bowl from his hands. "There is only time to eat, for I'm starving." The man's bony jaw dropped as Adele filled her trencher with food, and though the villein and the peasant girl stared at her fixedly as she shoveled the food in, Adele did not pause until she had devoured every bite her starving stomach could hold.

Even in the ordinary spring festival usually granted by a lord to his villeins, Lord William had found a sure money-making

scheme. In addition to the ever-present demands upon his
feudal serfs, he also demanded a tithe from all merchants
who participated in his carnival. Fortunately, the merchants
considered the price a small one, and they came from towns
far and wide, even as far away as France and Italy, to ply
their wares to the villagers and villeins from several surrounding manors.

Gislebert wandered through the fair, carrying his lute
and singing his songs, bartering, not for trinkets or treasures, but for information. At every booth he stopped and
gently inquired whether or not the traveling merchant knew
a Lady Jehannenton, and though he had not yet had a posi-
tive answer to that question, he had learned much.

The ivory merchant had news that King Stephen resided
now in London—and, he whispered confidentially, even the
loyal Londoners were growing weary of the king's fickle
promises. "The king surrounds himself now with Flemish
mercenaries," one plump polyp of a man complained.
"Those loyal to the crown wait for weeks to gain access to
his presence, and if a lord displeases him—" The man whistled. "Well, let's just say he's likely to take the nobleman's
lands and bestow them on someone he deems more fitting."

The French silk merchant in the next booth told
Gislebert about a permanent fair established by Thibaut the
Great in Champagne. "I'd be there now, but for my pilgrim-
age to Canterbury," the merchant explained in fluent French.

"A permanent fair?" Gislebert exclaimed, grateful that
his courtly training included lessons in French. "What must
that be like? Do the nobles approve?"

"*Oui,*" the merchant answered. "They make more own-
ing a tenth of a busy merchant than all of a poor villein. You
should see the Champagne fairs, my friend. It is all this"—
he spread his hands wide at the activity around them—"and
much more. It is, as they say in some parts, a *véritable cité.*"

A woman in purple moved in to haggle over the price of a
silken robe, so Gislebert thanked the merchant and moved on
through the throng, nearly tripping over a squealing pig led

by a village boy. The air was thick with the bicker and babble of bargaining, and suddenly Gislebert longed for peace. The merchant stalls around him would not be quiet for several hours, and over in the west field, a group of monks performed a play for villeins and their children. The dinner tables beckoned in the east. Sniffing happily at the pleasant aromas of Lord William's dinner, Gislebert walked toward the feast.

Many had eaten by the time he arrived, and several of the bowls of food stood empty. A maid scurried to his side as he sat down at an empty table, however, and offered him a trencher and a bowl of pottage. "I'm sorry, sir, that we have not better," she said, apologizing for her offering. "The meat pottages have been eaten, and the freshwater fish—"

"It is all right," Gislebert answered, smiling up at her. She was a pretty girl, with long blonde hair carefully plaited down her back. Her eyes were blue like the tunic she wore, and suddenly a memory ruffled through his mind like wind on water. Nadine's eyes had locked with his once—had those eyes been blue or green? Since she was beauty itself, surely they were blue. And the shape of her mouth—were her lips gently curved like this girl's, or more full?

"Sir?" The girl had reddened, and Gislebert looked down at the table in embarrassment.

"I'm sorry; I didn't mean to stare at you." He looked up and smiled apologetically at the maid. "But I am on a journey to seek my love, and for an instant you reminded me of her."

The girl lowered her eyes. Her dark lashes fluttered against her cheek, and Gislebert found himself fascinated by the sight of them. "If you need anything, sir, you have but to ask." When Gislebert did not respond, she turned from him and moved away.

"Now I need nothing," Gislebert answered, when she could no longer hear him. "For you have given me a glimpse of my beloved. Nadine—eyes of blue, hair of gold, lips of rose—please, God, may she yet be waiting for me!"

THREE

The crowd thinned before nightfall, and those who lived nearby journeyed in groups back to their homes. The merchants built small campfires in the open spaces behind their booths, and the knights of Gillingham patrolled the fairgrounds in pairs. Gislebert had spent the afternoon strumming his lute and singing love songs in the shade of an oak tree, and although he had earned a small sum for his efforts, he had not sung for profit. He had sung for Nadine.

In the simple serving girl he had seen a striking example of feminine beauty, and surely Nadine surpassed that lowly damsel! He could not recall his love's face, but he remembered that she had been striking, even as a girl. How much more beautiful must she be now that maturity had brought a woman's curve to her form and softness to her face! The servant's eyes had been blue, but Nadine's eyes would be bluer. Had the servant's hair been fair? Nadine's was certainly golden. And even though the girl of Gillingham had possessed a pleasing shape, Gislebert knew that Nadine's fair skin and form would bring men to their knees.

This compelling vision of Nadine burned in his heart and brain. *Lord God, I must find her, and soon, for surely every man within a hundred miles of where she lives desires her. Love burns painfully within my breast; love compells me to seek your will—for you are love, and you will guide me safely to my lady.*

He walked aimlessly over the grounds for an hour until

the sun had set and his heart had quieted. Then an insane notion gripped him. Why not leave now and travel through the night to seek his lady? After a few hours on the road, Nadine would be hours nearer.

But the voice of common sense drowned out his mad schemes. The king's curfew limited travel after dark, and his horse slept safely in Lord William's stable. He must stay here.

But where? Other men made camp with their companions, but Gislebert had no companions and no prospects for a safe night's sleep. Desperate for an answer, he thought suddenly of the stable—why not sleep in the hay near his horse? He could get a fresh start early in the morning and be away from Gillingham even as the sun rose.

Gislebert skirted the fields and found the road, then walked slowly toward the castle in the darkness. No one else walked the road, but three knights stood guard at the lowered drawbridge. As he listened to their laughter and howling, Gislebert realized that these three had drunk too much of the lord's celebration ale. He paused for a moment, barely outside the dim circle of light from the torch one of the knights carried, and debated whether or not he should continue with his plan.

Coward, his inner voice chided him. *Though these are not the knights of Margate, still they will respect you if you confront them and demand passage.*

Not so, a conflicting voice warned. *For they are drunk and do not know you. Leave them alone, and sleep in the fields like the mouse you are.*

He took a step back, retreating from the men, and his shuffling foot caught a stone and set it skipping across the road. One of the knights, a heavyset man in the blue and white surcoat of Gillingham, spied him in the faint light.

"Who goes there?" the knight called, swaying unsteadily on his feet. Another giggled in the darkness, and the third, a tall fellow with a body built for action, stomped forward to meet Gislebert. The metal of his armor clanked with each step.

"Be you friend or foe?" the tall guard yelled hoarsely. Gislebert clenched his lute in nervous anticipation. He had grown up with knights, had faithfully served Calhoun in his knightly training, but never had he found any use for men who prided themselves on blunt, mindless toughness. Too often that toughness degenerated into cruelty.

He found his voice and formed an answer: "I am Gislebert, late from Margate Castle in the service of Lord Calhoun," he answered, deliberately deepening his voice. "I have a mare in Lord William's stable—"

"What'd you say?" the giggling guard asked, clanking unsteadily forward behind the other two knights. "You, frail troubadour, have a mare in our lord's stable?"

The other knights laughed uproariously, and Gislebert stiffened. "Aye, a black mare," he said, lifting his chin. "And, by your leave, I'd like to see her."

"I can't believe you own such an animal. Mayhap you plan to steal our lord's mare." The giggling knight ceased laughing. He drew his sword and stepped between his two fellows. "By heaven, such deception won't be allowed!" he said, his voice thick. He sliced the air with the razor-sharp blade and swayed unsteadily. The other two guards laughed and supported him as he squinted and pointed the sword toward Gislebert's throat. "Tell me again, man, what business you have within my master's gate."

"My mare—*mine*," Gislebert enunciated clearly, "is inside the stable. She wears the sign of Margate Castle; there can be no mistake of her owner."

"I'm sure your little filly is fine," the tallest knight answered. "Just let her be until morning."

Gislebert paused. This was his chance to back away, to leave the three knights to their drunken jests. But if things were to be different, was this not the heaven-sent time to begin? Perhaps God was testing him. If he was to prove himself worthy of Nadine's love, he must show himself a man and confront brutes such as these. Chivalry demanded that he stand up for himself. Surely any man of mettle would do the same.

"If you please, sirs," he said firmly, clearing his throat. "I want my horse. I am a gentleman, and I intend no harm to anyone in the castle."

"Oh, he's a gentleman, now is he?" sneered the heavyset guard. "How gentle are you, fellow?"

Before Gislebert could utter a word in protest, the heavy guard nodded to his companions, and in unison they came forward, clasped Gislebert firmly by the arms, and lifted him off his feet. "Oh, he's a light one," the giddy guard slurred. The heavyset guard snatched the lute from Gislebert's hand and moved out of the way as the duo carried Gislebert over the drawbridge and into the stone barbican. "We could hang him off the tower and let him flap like a scarecrow, if you've a mind to hauling him up there."

"Too much trouble," the tall knight grumbled. His broad fist clenched Gislebert's arm like a vise. "Let's just hang him up here in the entry and be done with him."

An iron hook protruded from the barbican wall six feet from the ground, and as Gislebert sputtered in protest, the two knights lifted him up and onto the hook. The rough iron cut through his tunic, and Gislebert screeched in pain as the hook scraped the tender flesh along his spine. After an excruciating moment, the hook slid beneath his leather belt and held him fast. He swung there like a pike pulled from the stream, his long legs dangling in space.

The third knight gave a strum on the lute, laughed, and tossed it at Gislebert's feet. Then the knights turned away without looking back, one drunkenly throwing his arm about the other.

Gislebert's leather belt strained under his weight and threatened to cut off his breath. For a moment he thrashed around, vainly trying to reach his belt to unclasp it. But the movement only made the belt draw tighter. At last he gave up and sighed, first in relief that they had done no worse to him, then in shame. Which was worse, he wondered—to accept a beating from the hands of vaunted knights, or to be exhibited like a helpless rag doll for all the world to see? For in the morning, all of Lord William's household would see him and would doubtless hear the tale of the hapless troubadour who could not command respect even from a trio of drunken knights. By noontime the nobles would be regaled with the tale in a song, and by Sunday the villagers would whisper the story in church.

Gislebert groaned. If the traveling merchants in the fields heard the story, in less than a month his shame would be spread throughout the kingdoms of the civilized world.

Hanging his head in mortification, Gislebert prayed that Nadine lay beyond the realm of his disgrace.

From her hiding place in the dark, Adele had watched the confrontation with interest. The skinny man was no match for the three guards, yet after only a brief hesitation he had approached them with an almost foolish degree of boldness. What was it, Adele wondered, that gave the man such confidence? He had nothing in his looks to recommend him, for though he was not offensive in appearance, his skin was too pale for beauty and his body too thin for strength. He rode a horse as fine as any great lord's, yet he had bought nothing at the fair. She had followed him closely, and all the troubadour had done was wander among the merchants and then sit and sing his silly songs of love.

Adele crept along the edge of the castle moat, careful to remain in the darkness. A few more hours, a few more drinks, and the guards would pass out on the walkway. Adele sat in the shadows and waited. Time, Adele had learned, was her friend.

The guards snorted and laughed and talked and drank. By the time the moon had climbed halfway across the sky, the three knights snored on the ground, their heads turned toward the heavens and their mouths open. Adele pursed her lips and crept forward until she reached the edge of the drawbridge, then scampered over the rough wood on her hands and knees so that her worn shoes made no sound. In a moment she stood in the barbican, the stone hallway that led to the castle courtyard. By the dim glow of a torch she saw the troubadour hanging from the wall like a hunting trophy.

Adele laughed quietly, and the troubadour jerked at the sound but said nothing. She stood in front of the man and placed her hands on her hips as she had often seen boys do as they taunted one another. "I suppose you still want to give me a lesson about survival in the world."

The troubadour scowled. "Is it not enough that three drunken knights will lose their heads for manhandling me? Am I to be pestered by a common rat chaser as well?"

Adele shook her head and made clucking noises. "I don't think you are in a position to scold me," she said, deepening her voice. "If you were a wise man, you'd be asking for my help."

The man rolled his eyes to heaven.

"Of course, if you'd rather I went on my way—" She picked up the lute and turned her back as if to go.

"No, help me, please. If you could just stand over here, I could brace my feet on your shoulders and push off this cursed hook."

Adele did a little dance, moving slowly toward the trapped troubadour. "Hurry," the man hissed, jerking his head toward the pile of sleeping knights. "Before they wake from their sleep and hang you up beside me!"

"They'd have to catch me first," Adele answered. Reaching the wall, she laid the lute gently on the ground, turned her back to the man, and bent over, bracing her hands on her knees. She felt the troubadour's feet on her back, then a mighty push sent Adele flying across the stone passageway. The man fell to the stone walkway, but he was free.

"Ouch!" Adele said, rubbing her back. "You're heavy."

"Stop complaining," the troubadour whispered, standing to his feet and wiping the dust from his hands. He snatched up the lute and moved quickly down the barbican toward the castle courtyard. "Now come with me, or you'll feel the imprint of a knight's boot against your back. Hurry!"

Adele hesitated only a moment, then followed the troubadour into the darkness.

Gislebert squinted in the courtyard, hugging the walls and the safety of shadow they afforded. The moon had risen high in the night sky, and he did not know how many, if any, knights were patrolling Gillingham's courtyard. He was only going to take his own horse; still, knights were by nature and experience suspicious of any stranger who stirred under cover of darkness. Under the provisions of the king's curfew, a knight was expected to aim his bow and shoot at anything that moved, so law-abiding citizens stayed in their homes while darkness and evil roamed outside.

Gislebert could see that the small service door to the stable stood open. He dashed across the open space of the courtyard without incident and gratefully slipped into the warm, horsey air of the stable. He waited a moment for his eyes to adjust to the darkness, then groaned as he realized that his mission would be difficult, if not impossible. What a fool he had been! How could he find a black horse in a dark, crowded stable at night?

"Which horse is yours?" The boy's voice at his elbow made Gislebert jump.

"Shhh," Gislebert cautioned. He closed his eyes and leaned against the stable wall in exasperation. "I don't know. I can't tell these animals apart."

"I'll find your horse, if you can find your saddle," the boy answered, stepping forward in the darkness.

"Wait—Jonas?" Gislebert whispered. "That is your name, right?" Gislebert thought the boy nodded. "How can you find my horse? I can't."

"I know what I see, and I've seen your horse," Jonas answered cryptically. "Trust me, Troubadour, and I'll get you out of here. But if you value your saddle, you'll have to fetch it yourself."

Gislebert let the boy go, then fumbled forward in the darkness until he found a door to the tack room. Inside, it was relatively easy to identify his own saddle and bridle in the darkness, for only one saddle had a rough bag of belongings tied to it. He felt the woolen bag—yes, his parchments and quills remained inside.

He shoved his lute into the bag and lugged the heavy saddle out of the tack room. Gislebert waited until he heard the steady clomp of a horse's hooves. Jonas appeared astride the animal in a small square of moonlight thrown through an open window. His dark eyes danced with pride. "I told you I'd find her," he said, lifting his chin.

"How did you do it?" Gislebert asked, truly astonished. His horse whinnied in recognition and nuzzled Gislebert's hand in search of the treat he usually brought her at morning.

Jonas shrugged. "I know what I see," he answered, slipping from the horse's broad back. "Now saddle her, Troubadour, and let's away. Your three friends at the gate won't sleep forever."

Gislebert felt his stomach knotting as the horse left the soft ground of the courtyard and clopped over the stone floor of the castle barbican. Ahead of him, the three guards still slept by the side of the road, but they dozed fitfully, snoring and rumbling.

Boom. Boom. The horse's front hooves struck the wooden drawbridge, and Gislebert winced. *Boom. Boom.* Unavoidable noise. Gislebert pulled back on the reins and stopped the horse on the drawbridge as the heavyset guard stirred.

"What was that?" he muttered, punching his neighbor. "Did you hear something?"

Gislebert held his breath. The mare snorted in impatience.

"There!" the guard called, scrambling awkwardly to his feet. "There's someone on the bridge!"

Confusion reigned as the guards cursed and leaped to their feet, and Gislebert's heart pounded. "Go!" Jonas whispered in his ear. "Don't just sit there!"

But Gislebert was frozen in indecision. How could he advance, with three drunken swordsmen blocking the road?

"The master will have our heads for leaving the draw-bridge down," one guard said, and Gislebert recognized the nasal voice of the guard who had been giggling. He was no longer laughing.

"Halt, there! Who are you and what is your business?" the tallest guard demanded. Gislebert felt a disturbing sense of déjà vu. Was he to be hung up again, or would they simply kill him this time, as punishment for stealing a horse?

"It is—," Gislebert began, but suddenly Jonas let loose a bloodcurdling scream. The mare spooked and reared back, flailing the air with her front legs. Startled into action, the guards ran forward. One caught the horse's bridle and Gislebert found himself surrounded—the tall guard on his left and the heavy knight on his right.

Gislebert felt his stomach churn, an old and familiar sensation from his childhood days. He was going to be sick, right here on a Gillingham guard. He wiped his mouth with the back of his hand and tried to moisten his dry lips.

"It's the scarecrow," the tall guard snickered, squinting at Gislebert through bloodshot eyes. "He has escaped us!"

"Not yet, he hasn't," the heavy knight replied, pointing his sword at Gislebert's chest. "Down from there, man, or I'll run you through for disturbing the peace of Gillingham!"

Gislebert automatically removed his foot from the stirrup, but Jonas punched him roughly from behind. As Gislebert turned to look back in confusion, he heard a hacking sound, a splattering of spittle on the tall guard's face, an oath, a curse, and a scream. The mare rose again. The reins swung from the hands of the third startled knight, and sensing her freedom, the mare sprinted forward, eager to be off the noisy drawbridge.

Gislebert let her run, giving the animal her head as she galloped up the dark road. He struggled to keep his balance as his foot flapped free of the stirrup. Gislebert realized that his heart pounded with every step of the mare's hooves. Behind him, Jonas clung like a burr to Gislebert's cloak and shattered the silence of the night with his laughter.

LONDON

*The king's heart is
in the hand of the Lord:
he directs it like a watercourse
wherever he pleases.*

PROVERBS 21:1

FOUR

As they flew over the dark Gillingham road, Gislebert bent low over his saddle to dodge overhanging tree branches and prayed that the horse would not trip in the darkness. When he was quite certain no pursuing hoofbeats echoed in the distance, Gislebert let the mare slow to a walk. The hard fist of fear in his stomach began to relax.

The horse snorted impatiently, her blood still racing, but Gislebert clucked soothingly and bent to pat the animal's neck. The smell of rain was in the air, and thunder rumbled in the distance.

"There," Jonas said, pointing to a scraggly stand of pines off the road. Gislebert obeyed and pointed the horse toward the trees. Doubtless he, the boy, and the horse would all be wet and miserable before the night was over.

The mare stopped underneath the branches, and the boy slipped from her back before Gislebert could even remove his foot from the stirrup. He felt weak-kneed and stiff as he lowered himself to the ground, but the boy Jonas raised his hands and spun under the trees in a crazy little dance, as if the thrill of flight had endowed him with a burst of vitality. "What are you doing?" Gislebert snapped, shifting on his feet as he tried to regain his composure. "We only have a short while before the rain begins. Make your bed, or something, while I tend to the horse."

The boy abruptly stopped dancing. Placing his hands on his hips, he turned on Gislebert with a sudden flash of defensive spirit: "I don't have to obey you. After all, if it weren't for me, you would still be hanging like a door knocker in Lord William's castle."

Gislebert felt his temper flare, and he whirled to face the urchin who alternately amused and frustrated him. "So be it. I owe you thanks for your help, and I give it freely. But now we're as good as dead if we ever encounter a knight of Gillingham. I'm sure I could have explained myself—"

"You can't explain anything to a drunken knight," the boy answered, turning resolutely and walking toward the road. He took three steps and stopped.

"Where are you going?" Gislebert pulled the saddle from the horse. "There's nothing within miles of here. You may sleep on the horse's blanket, if you like."

"It's your blanket," the boy answered, not turning his head.

"I will sleep on my cloak," Gislebert answered. He tossed the blanket to the ground and waited.

Finally the boy spoke, without looking at Gislebert, in a voice that was very firm for one so young: "If you want me to go, I will. If you want me to stay, I might." He turned, and the mischievous gleam was back in his dark eyes. "But it seems to me that you need someone to help you, Troubadour. The world is more than songs and nobles and ladies, I can assure you."

"I don't need your help," Gislebert answered, forcing himself to laugh as if the idea greatly amused him. "But you're welcome to stay with me if you adhere to my rules."

"Truly?" The words were laced with sarcasm, and the boy marched forward until he was within eight inches of Gislebert's face. Glaring up into the troubadour's eyes, the boy took a deep breath. "I have a few rules of my own, Troubadour."

Gislebert met the boy's gaze directly. "My rules are simple for they are, in truth, God's rules: no lying and no stealing. We are honest men doing honest work, for such the Lord can honor."

"I doubt God will honor such as you or me, Troubadour. I have yet to see any sign that God knows—or cares—that we even exist," the boy responded dourly.

"Of course he cares," Gislebert responded impatiently.

The boy pushed his bottom lip forward in thought. "What if we starve?"

"We won't." Gislebert undid the brooch at his neck and pulled the cloak from his back. He spread it on the ground and sat down, but still the boy did not move or answer. "Do you agree?" Gislebert finally asked. "If you steal one thing, or tell me an untruth, you will not be welcome in my company."

The boy's expression was inscrutable, but he nodded slightly. "Agreed," he said simply.

"Good. Then loosen the mare's bridle and tie her to a branch, will you? We have to sleep if we're to travel tomorrow."

The boy took a step toward the horse, then turned again to Gislebert, wagging his finger in rebuke. "You are quick, Troubadour, but haven't you forgotten *my* rules?"

Gislebert turned weary eyes on the boy. "What rules?" he sighed, drawing his cloak about him.

A fragile vulnerability appeared in the boy's eyes as he steadfastly held a warning finger in front of Gislebert's face. "Never, under penalty of death—"

"What?" Gislebert asked, annoyed.

"Never touch me," Jonas finished. "If you do, I'll kill you."

The fear of insects and the rustle of the trees kept Gislebert far from sleep. Every breath of the wind brought some new tickle to Gislebert's neck or ear, and he grew weary of slapping at bugs and leaves. Sitting up in frustration, he hugged his knees and realized that the sky had brightened in the east.

The boy's breathing had slowed and deepened, and Gislebert studied his new companion in the early dawn light. Without cover or pillow, the boy slept on the saddle blanket as easily as a puppy on his master's rug. "Apparently the outdoors suits you," Gislebert muttered to the sleeping boy. "Whereas I would give anything to sleep in a feather bed."

Gislebert wondered at the boy's pitifully frail form. He had seemed bigger and more imposing while awake. Now, naked of bravado and bluster, the boy's face was simple, with pronounced cheekbones and a sharp, clear chin. His shaggy hair, mingled now with leaves and wind, might yet prove to be lustrous; his thin body could be fed and supported. *How came you to be alone in these woods?* Gislebert wondered. *And what makes you hate the human touch? Believe me, little friend, I understand more than you think I do.*

Against his own wishes, Gislebert's dark imaginings led him back to the time when he had left Margate at fourteen. As a young man trying to make his way in the world, he had been approached by a merchant who, Gislebert learned, befriended him only for the sake of committing unspeakable perversion. Gislebert had escaped, barely, and had run from the man's house as if the devil himself gave chase.

The memory made him tremble with fear and self-loathing even now, and Gislebert clutched his cloak more closely about him. Such things were unnatural, corrupt, and since that day, Gislebert had never borne another man's touch easily.

Did a similar experience lie behind Jonas's warning that Gislebert should not touch him? A wave of compassion swept through the troubadour's heart. When he had run from the decrepit merchant at Reigate, for months he had blamed himself for the entire shame. His naivete had persuaded him to accompany the merchant; his ambition had driven him to flatter the man. Surely something in his manner, words, or body had suggested that he, Gislebert, would be open to the attentions of another man.

Even now, Gislebert felt his cheeks burn. He had never spoken of that day to anyone, especially not to Calhoun, and the memories had lain deeply buried until this past hour. If similar memories haunted Jonas, then Gislebert would prove to be a valuable friend indeed. He would protect the boy, with his life if necessary, so that Jonas, too, could find release in forgetfulness. *May God guide us both, little friend. And as I learn what it is to be a man, so will I teach you, little friend,* Gislebert thought. *In teaching, I will become more of a man for my Nadine.*

The brightening sky was darkened by gray clouds from the west, and thunder cracked overhead. As the first raindrops brushed Gislebert's cheek, he curled into a tight ball and covered his head with his cloak. He knew that he should not offer even to share his covering with Jonas. A man could protect, shelter, and comfort a woman, but it would be insulting and perverse to do these things for another man. Such was the price of honor, and such were the terms of chivalric manhood.

The heavy rains blew by them, and Gislebert awoke from a short sleep to find his clothing and cloak damp, but not soaked. He was chilled to the core of his bones, however, and as the sun climbed higher, he squinted gratefully into its warmth. The boy had already risen. The saddle blanket lay empty, and soon the rustle of undergrowth signaled the boy's arrival. "There's a creek down the hill over there," Jonas said, pointing over his shoulder. "If you want to wash up, go down. I'll water the horse."

The faint beginnings of a smile crossed the boy's face, and Gislebert suddenly realized that the boy's helpfulness could be a trap. "I'll bring the horse down," Gislebert said, staggering to his feet. He felt very stiff, and ten years older than he had the day before. "You bring the blanket and saddle, if you can carry it the distance."

"I can carry it," the boy grumbled, lifting the wet blanket from the ground.

The water of the stream was clear and cold, and Gislebert knelt at the edge of the creek and carefully splashed his face. He felt as though he had been dipped in ice, but the mare drank deeply, oblivious to the cold. Jonas slung the blanket over her back. The heavy saddle, however, wasn't so easy, and the boy struggled to hoist the weight up and onto the mare.

Gislebert restrained a smile. The bracing water had cleared the cobwebs from his brain, and he sat back on his haunches and watched the clouds blow across the early morning sky. "So," he called to the boy, who still struggled with the saddle, "have you no family, Jonas?"

Jonas let the saddle fall to the ground, and suspicion flickered in his eyes. Then he shrugged. "My mother died at my birth," he said, getting a better grip on the wide saddle. He gave a mighty heave and hoisted it above his head, then set the saddle atop the horse. Coolly indifferent to his triumph, he stooped low to fasten the saddle girth and continued his thought. "And my father may be yet dead or alive. I don't know."

"Don't you care?"

Jonas shook his head and squinted at Gislebert from between the horse's legs. "No. The truth is—and it really is the truth—I don't care where or what he is."

"What village did you come from?"

"I'll not tell you." Jonas swung himself into the saddle, the stirrups hanging well below his feet. "Can we shorten these things for me?"

"No." Gislebert sighed in exasperation. "I won't make you go back to your village, if that's what you're thinking. If you're really fifteen—" He cast a sharp glance in Jonas's direction.

"I am," Jonas answered.

"Well, if you are, then you're old enough to be on your own," Gislebert went on. "I was only fourteen when I left Margate Castle for the first time. I traveled alone for years, then served in the court of King Stephen."

"Now look who's lying!"

Gislebert grinned and hung his head modestly. "No, truly, I did. That's where I'm headed now. I'm going to London to ask the king for news of Lady Jehannenton, who employs the maid I love. I'm going to find her, win her, and marry her."

Jonas pulled his mouth in at the corners, as if he would laugh, and Gislebert frowned. "I didn't really expect you to understand, but I'm quite serious."

"It's just—" Jonas bit his lip in an effort to stop a smile. "I'm sorry, really I am, but I just can't imagine you winning the hand of a noble lady."

"Why not?" Gislebert demanded, jumping to his feet in indignation.

"Because you're not—" Jonas giggled. "I'm sorry, Troubadour, but you are not handsome in the way women count beauty. Your skin is too red, your chin too narrow, and your nose could slice cheese. Noble women may choose from the most valiant of all knights—those with broad shoulders, strong arms, and large hands." Jonas threw back his head and twittered, pointing at Gislebert. "What woman would have you?" he crowed, nearly falling from the horse in his laughter.

Gislebert gritted his teeth and strode forward, grasping the reins of the horse. "A fine woman will see beyond the mere outward appearance and realize the value within," he answered, struggling to keep his tone dignified. "Honor, loyalty, faith, and truth count for more than a creamy complexion and bulging muscles. And while we're on the subject, you scrawny rat-child, what would *you* know about beauty? Your manners are deplorable, your tongue common, and your looks—"

Jonas stopped laughing and fell silent. Gislebert suddenly wished he hadn't spoken. *God, will you never gain control of my temper?* The boy had spoken honestly; Gislebert had long known that he was not the kind of man who turned women's heads in desire or admiration.

Gislebert fumbled with the belt at his waist. "Forgive me, boy. You speak truly, and I do believe," he said, making an effort to lighten his voice, "that while I may be a lost cause, you may go far in improving your appearance with a little more food in your belly, a little less grime on

43

your neck, and a bit more gentility in your speech." He smiled up at Jonas, careful to show that his anger had passed. "Shall we journey to London?"

Jonas nodded, sliding toward the back of the saddle, and Gislebert checked to make sure his bag of belongings was still securely tied to the saddle. He had his lute, his parchments, his pens, and a companion—surely all a man needed to travel in safety and confidence.

The horse trotted softly over the dirt road to Gravesend, and Jonas's speech was accented by the mare's choppy gait. "You know, your trouble is that you think too much and talk too little," Jonas babbled as they rode. "Last night, you announced yourself to those guards as if you were the king himself. That approach will never hold sway with a knight. First, you must *lower* yourself and make them feel important."

"Knights *are* important," groused Gislebert, turning his head sideways so Jonas could catch his words. "Trust me. I served as a page to knights in my childhood, and I know what advantages and opportunities they are given."

"Why didn't you become a knight?" Jonas asked, leaning forward.

Gislebert gave Jonas a dry, one-sided smile. "Swordplay is not in my nature. My father was a knight and left me at Warwick for training as he went off to fight on the expedition of God in the Holy Land. He never returned." Gislebert shrugged and ducked under a low-hanging branch on the road. "I served as page to Lord Calhoun of Margate as he trained for knighthood, and when he returned home, I went with him. At Margate I learned the skills of the troubadour, and that has been my calling ever since."

Jonas nodded thoughtfully, and Gislebert went on. "It was during my days at Margate that Cupid's arrow struck deep in my heart. Lady Jehannenton visited the estate, and one of her maids, a girl called Nadine, looked at me and forthwith captured my heart. My body and soul, however,

were not free to leave Margate for months, and when at last
I finally did leave, I . . . "

His voice trailed away, and Jonas tapped his shoulder.
"I'm listening," the boy prodded. "Go on."

Gislebert cleared his throat. "I was sidetracked by my
obligations to a friend," he answered. "The lord and lady of
Margate are my family now, I suppose, but twelve years has
passed since I saw Nadine. The time has come to seek my
own life and my own love."

"Twelve years is a long time," Jonas observed dryly.

"'Many waters cannot quench love, neither can the
floods drown it,'" Gislebert quoted. "The Scriptures. I
learned that truth as a child."

"So you are going to London—"

"To ask news of Lady Jehannenton and my Nadine,"
Gislebert finished simply. "I served in King Stephen's court
some months ago, and we parted as friends. I believe he will
grant me a boon, for the sake of the love he holds toward me."

"And if he don't?"

Gislebert turned slightly in the saddle. "Then I shall take
lessons from you, my young friend. How would you recommend approaching a king? By lowering myself, as I should
have done before those three drunken knights?"

"You think too much and talk too little," Jonas repeated
eagerly. "You should have flattered those knights and told
them that you face a hard lord yourself—"

Gislebert chuckled. "You forget, young friend, that I
have no lord. My only masters are God, the king—and my
love for Nadine."

"Whatever . . . " Jonas waved Gislebert's comments
away. "But if you make the knights feel pleased with themselves, they will grant favors. I was going to ask them a favor
myself last night, but you got in my way."

"You were going to approach them?" Gislebert asked,
raising an eyebrow. "For what purpose?"

"To steal your horse," Jonas answered simply. "I would
have done it, too, if I hadn't had to rescue you."

FIVE

Their stomachs were about to turn inside out with hunger by the time they reached the village of Gravesend, and Gislebert agreed with Jonas that their first priority should be finding food. "But we will eat my way," he said, his voice firm. "No stealing loaves from the baker or fish from a mill trap."

Jonas's scraggly, brown hair fell into his eyes as he shook his head. "When your way fails and we perish with hunger, we will see whose way is best," he grumbled, settling back on the horse.

They entered the walled village slowly, nodding in a friendly manner at the townspeople they met. "What do you suppose they think we are?" Jonas whispered in Gislebert's ear. "Our horse is too fine to be a villager's, yet you, Troubadour, are obviously no lord."

"And you, field rat, are obviously no nobleman's son," Gislebert answered carelessly. "I think I shall take your advice about asking favors. We shall tell anyone who asks that we are in the service of a hard and powerful lord—"

"I thought you said we were not to lie," Jonas interrupted.

"Love is my powerful and hard master," Gislebert whispered in reply, nodding slowly to a man who approached from the miller's gate. "We are not lying."

The pleasant-faced miller greeted them with a polite bow. "Wot brings you to Gravesend?" he asked, giving Gislebert, Jonas, and the horse a careful scrutiny.

"I am Gislebert, and this is my companion, Jonas."
Gislebert smiled politely. "We come with tales of adventure
and love from Gillingham and wonder if we might share
them with the lord of these parts."

"You aren't from these parts, then, or you'd know there
is no lord of Gravesend," the miller answered, standing
proudly erect. "Gravesend is a duly chartered borough that
owes its allegiance only to the king himself."

Gislebert doffed his cap. "My congratulations to you,
sir. Where, then, might we exchange our news and song
for a meal? The lad and I are famished from our long journey."

The miller smiled and pointed down the road toward a
drab, mud-colored hut. "There," he said, nodding in his
eagerness. "My wife cooks for the blacksmith and the mill
workers. Ye'd be welcome at our table."

Gislebert nodded his thanks, and together he and Jonas
rode the mare to dinner.

> *O what is longer than the way,*
> *Or what is deeper than the sea?*
> *Or what is louder than the horn,*
> *Or what is sharper than a thorn?*
> *Or what is greener than the grass,*
> *Or what is worse than Mother Eve was?*
>
> *O love is longer than the way,*
> *And hell is deeper than the sea.*
> *And thunder is louder than the horn,*
> *And hunger is sharper than a thorn.*
> *And poison is greener than the grass,*
> *And the devil worse than Mother Eve was.*
>
> *So now, fair maidens all, adieu,*
> *This song I dedicate to you.*
> *I wish that you may constant prove*
> *Unto the man that you do love.*

Gislebert stilled the strings of the lute and bowed his head. The two women present—Gislebert could not call them ladies, since they still had dirt from the fields under their fingernails—clapped enthusiastically, and the miller and his workers raised their tankards in acknowledgment. The smith grunted his appreciation and wiped a dribble from his chin—a complimentary salute, Gislebert decided, since the man had paused from shoveling food into his mouth.

"Well done, sir," the miller's wife simpered, wiping a tear from her plump cheek. "'Twas a song worthy of the king himself."

"Thank you," Gislebert said, bowing with exaggerated politeness. He put his lute down on the rough table and hoped they wouldn't ask for an encore—the food had been filling and would quiet his stomach's rumbling for yet another day, but it had been heavy, tasteless fare, hardly worthy of another song.

"I want to know—" The smith's gruff voice broke the vein of chatter among the women, and instantly the room stilled. "I want to know of this *companion,*" the smith said, his dark features twisting toward Jonas in a maddening leer. Jonas froze, his hand gripping his spoon, and Gislebert could hear his own heart thumping as the man pointed a hairy finger at the boy. "Why do you travel with a maid dressed as a man?" The smith turned to Gislebert with the knowing look one man of the world gives another. "What sort of evil are *you* trying to hide?"

Jonas sprang from his place so quickly that his stool toppled over with a crash. "I'll thank you, sir," Jonas muttered, his voice and hands trembling, "to-to—"

"Amend your last question," Gislebert finished, standing with Jonas. "Jonas is a worthy lad, my companion, and my friend. A more gentle man would not have remarked on his appearance, but would have judged him as a young man of exceptional talent and character."

The smith continued to stare at Gislebert in mingled defiance and stupidity, and the smith's wife cleared her throat nervously. "Um, what does the lad do?" she asked, lacing her fingers together. "You have sung for your meal, Troubadour, but how may *he* entertain us?"

Gislebert twisted his hands awkwardly, inwardly regretting his rash words. But Jonas did not hesitate. "I'll show you what I do," he said, stepping purposefully to the fireplace. He bent to pick up a half-charred stick, turned to the plastered wall, and, using the charred wood as an implement, began to draw. In deft movements, he sketched the miller's prettily plump wife, then drew a reasonable likeness of the miller. The blacksmith's wife he drew next, in stark angular lines. Then Jonas boldly drew a sinister representation of the smith, complete with the shadowy sneer that hovered about the man's heavy mouth.

When he had finished, Jonas threw down the stick and stepped away from the wall. "It is magnificent," the miller's wife cried, clapping her little hands together. "Look, husband, at how well he has captured me!"

The smith and his wife were not so thrilled, however; Gislebert recognized the discontent in their eyes. "Jonas, I believe it is time we took our leave," he said, gathering his bag and lute. He bowed to the miller's wife. "Thank you, madame, for your hospitality. God's grace to you all." Before the company could protest, Gislebert ushered Jonas out the door.

They rode in silence for an hour, then Gislebert cleared his throat and dared to speak. "God has given you a great talent, my young friend. If you seek to honor him with it, mayhap he will—"

"God has nothing to do with me," the boy answered.

"Come now, surely you won't blame your surly mood on God. I'm sorry about the blacksmith's remark, and I know what you must be feeling. I was a scrawny child myself, and my greatest fear was that someone would think I looked—" He paused, but there was no other way to say it.

"Womanish. The other pages and squires teased me unmercifully until Calhoun befriended me."

"It's all right," Jonas answered in a flat, inflectionless voice. "I don't care what other people say or think. I am just happy to be free."

"Free?" Gislebert laughed and shifted in the saddle. "Who is truly free? All men, Jonas, have bonds that enslave them, and we accept these bonds readily in the name of love. We are bound by love to God, that we might serve and honor him. We are bound by love to friends, family, king and country, women. . . ." His voice trailed off as he wistfully thought of Nadine, and he made an effort to collect himself. "Anyway, I know of no man who considers himself truly free."

"What about the king?" Jonas asked, with honest surprise in his voice. "He can do anything he wants, so he is the freest of men. If I were king, I'd kill all those who had hurt me, and—"

The boy stopped abruptly, and when he did not continue, Gislebert nodded thoughtfully. "You say these things because you are filled with the passion of youth," he corrected gently. "The king considers himself the most trapped of men. With power comes a luxurious sort of slavery. The king is bound not only to his wife and son and throne, but to an entire country—indeed, even to the world. Of all the men I have known, the king is the least free."

"If power results in bondage, then you and I, Troubadour, are of all men *most* free," Jonas answered, a teasing note in his voice.

Gislebert shook his head and sighed. "No, Jonas. Would that it were so. But I am trapped by the bonds of love. I am compelled to search for my Nadine, and when I find her, I shall be driven to place my life in her hands. As her love, I would reply with my life to all imputations made against her; I would answer in combat all charges opposing her. I would rescue her if she were assaulted, search for her if she were lost, and redeem her if she were captured. If she were tested, I would stand beside her. If she were insulted, humiliated, or tortured, I would avenge her. If she were ever taken prisoner, I would post bail for her—"

"You are a fool, Troubadour."

"No," Gislebert answered. "Of all men, I am the least free. When I find my Nadine, I will swear to love, honor, and obey her without question and without hesitation for as long as I live. All that God has given me, I will impart to her. That, my young friend, is the price love demands, and that is what I will freely give."

Gislebert sighed, content in his vision and his dream of love, and nearly slipped from the saddle when Jonas yelped and abruptly kicked the mare. "Night falls," Jonas interrupted as Gislebert drew a breath to scold him. "If we do not make the next village by sunset, we will sleep again out in the forest. And while I do not mind the forest, Troubadour, you are too spoiled to last more than a fortnight out of doors."

"Look who speaks," Gislebert answered, urging the mare forward with his heels. "A boy no stronger than a feather!"

"Ah, but a boy smarter than you are," Jonas answered.

Gislebert admitted that the boy was right about their need for shelter and allowed the mare to break into a canter. As the horse pitched forward, the abrupt touch of the boy's hand on his back startled him for an instant, then he relaxed. Jonas only held on for safety's sake, yet the weight of the boy's touch warmed Gislebert's heart. Surely a link had formed between them, just as a similar bond had been forged years before when Calhoun had been the elder protector and Gislebert the child.

Gislebert whooped a forgotten war cry and kicked the mare into a gallop.

Over the next few weeks Jonas and Gislebert fell into a comfortable pattern. In every village they entered, they inquired first about Lady Jehannenton and then about the master of the village. Invariably they would be told that Lady

Jehannenton had not passed through in recent memory, and just as surely they would be invited to dinner with the village master—for troubadours and travelers were important sources of news and gossip.

Over dinner, Gislebert regaled his highborn hosts with stories of Margate, Gillingham, and the surrounding towns, by turns arousing, amusing, or astounding his hosts. After dinner he would draw out his lute and sing songs of love and chivalric pursuit. Though other troubadours often amused their companies with ribald songs of naughty behavior, Gislebert would not entertain such thoughts or sing such songs. If a song was not pure enough to be sung before Nadine, the queen of his heart, it was not worthy of being sung.

As an additional favor for their hosts, while Gislebert sang, Jonas would draw the hosts or other dinner guests in "pleasing sketches and gentle likenesses," as Gislebert had instructed. The boy's talent was truly remarkable, and Gislebert began to understand what the boy had meant when he said, "I saw it, and I know it." The Creator had given Jonas an almost magical eye that kept exact records of facial images. The boy had but to look at a subject, then turn to a blank sheet of parchment. The picture would fly from his mind to the paper in amazingly few strokes of coal or ink.

Spring had fully greened when they discovered that their reputations traveled faster than they. Upon entering the villages of Northfleet, Swanscombe, Dartford, Greenwich, and Southwark, Gislebert and Jonas were welcomed immediately at the city gates, and the earls of Greenwich and Southwark even had parchment, ink, and pens ready for Jonas.

The rewards of life on the road were plenteous. Gislebert and Jonas found themselves invited to bountiful meals, treated with honor and respect, and even presented handsome tunics and fur-lined cloaks worthy of the most powerful nobles. The attention was flattering, too. Gislebert's name was known and honored by the foremost lords of the land, and the ladies especially doted on Jonas, finding in his excellent and gentle portraits of them excuses to kiss his cheek. Their attentions he bore with equanimity, without pleasure or anger.

"I do not understand why you threatened me with death for touching you, but you allowed the lady Elfgiva to kiss your cheek and rumple your hair," Gislebert remarked dryly one afternoon as they rode from Dartford. "Can it be that you are developing a fondness for the ladies?"

"I'll thank you to keep your observations to yourself," Jonas replied saucily. "And my warning still stands: touch me, and I'll leave you, Troubadour, and then where will you be?"

When the earl of Greenwich offered Gislebert a permanent position at his manor, the troubadour realized that he and Jonas had become a unique and valuable team. As a troubadour, he modestly admitted, he was but one among many excellent fellows. But in partnership with Jonas, they were unequaled as after-dinner entertainment.

"You know, we could make a good living at this," Gislebert remarked casually to Jonas as they left Greenwich.

"Why don't we?" Jonas answered lightly. Gislebert merely shook his head and laughed in reply. The obvious answer hung like a cloud between them: Nadine.

Their destination and mission were part of their spreading reputation. "Hark, be you Gislebert and Jonas, troubadour and artist?" the guard at the gate of Westminster called from the top of the wall as they rode to the city gate. "We have heard of you, but we have no news of a Lady Jehannenton."

Gislebert reined in the horse and doffed his cap to the man. "Then perhaps you know that we seek an audience with the king. Is he in residence at the palace?"

"Heavens above, no," the gatekeeper replied, shaking his head. "Since the trouble arose with Empress Matilda, the king stays at the Tower of London."

Gislebert frowned. "We have come out of our way," he said, glancing back at Jonas. "We were nearer the tower when we were at Southwark."

"Stay the night with us," the gatekeeper said, moving to

open the city gate. "We have heard of your skill on the lute, Master Gislebert, and my wife would give even her hair for a portrait from your young protégé."

Gislebert had to stifle a smile. "All right, sir," he replied. "If you will shelter us for the night, we will pass the evening with you. But tomorrow we ride for the tower, for we must meet with the king."

"So be it," the gatekeeper replied. The gate swung open, and Gislebert and Jonas passed through into Westminster.

There were forty that night at supper, which was a sturdy meal of venison in a thick pottage that tasted ever so slightly of an iron kitchen kettle. Gislebert ate slowly, looking carefully around the long table in the city garrison. Soon, perhaps, he and Jonas would again enjoy decent food. Everything from their comfort to their futures depended upon Gislebert's place in the king's good graces.

The men and women of Westminster were a cheerful lot, conscious of their city's significance in two arenas: government and gospel. The royal palace of Westminster rose above the bank of the Thames, and Jonas had gasped in admiration and wonder at the sight of the building's outwork and bastions. Echoing the splendor of the palace, even the houses of common men in Westminster were spacious and splendid compared to the tiny mud and timber houses of the country villages.

Every monarch since William the Conqueror had been crowned in Westminster Abbey—which, Gislebert told Jonas proudly, had stood since 1065 and was rumored actually to have been founded by a Saxon king in 616. "Here," Gislebert said, motioning with a slice of bread to the city that lay just outside the garrison's open window, "are all Englishmen's fates tied together, Jonas. For here the king and the bishops eat, sleep, and make decisions."

"Except when there's a war on," a silver-haired woman interrupted, her face prim and forbidding. "The king has deserted us in favor of the Tower of London, where they say he's better protected." Her shrug and attitude made it clear that she resented the implication that Westminster could not insure the king's safety.

"How goes the struggle with Empress Matilda's force?" Gislebert asked politely, knowing that the struggle between King Stephen and Empress Matilda of Anjou was a major concern of all who were connected to the king.

"Bah! 'Twas the worst thing we ever did, accepting Stephen over Matilda," the woman replied. She apparently enjoyed the startled silence her words produced. "We should have known that a man who would pledge allegiance to Henry's daughter and then claim the throne for himself was not God's anointed for the throne."

"So you'd want to be ruled by a woman, then?" a vigorous, elfin man argued. "Why, no man would be able to stomach such a thing—"

"Why not?" the woman snarled in reply. "Matilda's proved her mettle in battle, hasn't she? She's the daughter of King Henry, isn't she? She's as royal as Stephen, if not more so."

The elfin man stood and clenched his fist, and Gislebert raised his hand to interrupt what threatened to become an ugly scene at the table. "Would you rather continue on in this war?" Gislebert interrupted, nodding politely to the short man. "King Stephen is my crowned sovereign and my friend, but I hope peace is within his reach, even if it requires compromise. For months now our beloved England has been ripped asunder in this bloody conflict. Lords turn against their neighbors, the manors have been ravaged and burned, and the barons in the outlying lands wield the law according to their own ideas of justice. This, my friends, is not England. It is barely civilization."

"There is but one throne," the short man muttered, sinking into his seat, "and two cannot sit on it."

"Unless they be married," the woman pointed out, giggling. "But since the empress has a husband, and the king his own wife—"

"There is little to be done about it," the gatekeeper

55

interrupted, his voice booming through the room and silencing all others. He looked carefully at Gislebert, and trouble stirred the darkness of his eyes. "You have seen more of the land than we," the gatekeeper acknowledged. "But we have seen more of Stephen than you, my friend. While he is a brave and affable fellow, he is a terrible king."

"His word is more changeable than the weather," a richly dressed merchant spoke up. "One moment he calls a man friend, the next he takes the man's estate and gives it to another."

A monk rapped gently on the table top for attention, and when every man and woman looked at him, he spoke. "The king has exhibited this mutability with the church as well. One month he attacks the holy bishops; the next he begs the Holy Father for favors." The monk shook his head. "They say Matilda's forces are drawing even closer as we speak, and I do not know whether to pray for their victory or their defeat."

"Is this true?" the gatekeeper asked, leaning toward Gislebert. "In your travels outside London, what have you seen of Empress Matilda's forces?"

Gislebert shook his head. "Nothing, friends. But I cannot give you assurance because Jonas and I have been traveling only in the southeast. We do not know what dangers are afoot in the south and west."

The gatekeeper grunted softly. "It is possible that Matilda of Anjou sleeps less than ten miles from here tonight," he said, staring blankly over the edge of the table. "If only Stephen had the courage of that woman!"

"He has the courage, my friend," Gislebert said, standing to his feet. "What Stephen lacks is Matilda's righteous anger." He smiled pleasantly at the assembled company and motioned for Jonas to follow him. "If you will excuse us, good sirs and gentle ladies, my friend and I are ready for sleep. We must travel in the early morning."

He and Jonas bowed, then left the room.

SIX

The Tower of London lay only two miles from Westminster. Gislebert announced that they would not leave immediately for the tower, but instead ride through the city so Jonas could see the delights of the royal palace. Adele tried to contain her enthusiasm and amazement, but she couldn't help gasping in awe and wonder at the sight of so many grand buildings in so small a space. "There is . . . so much!" she exclaimed, looking carefully at the artistic buildings around her.

"Wait until you see London," Gislebert answered, urging the mare to pick up her pace on the road. "Twenty-five thousand people live within the city walls; there is not another city quite like it."

They rode for a time in silence. Adele sat relaxed on the back of the saddle, her arms hanging limply at her side and her face upturned to the warm sun. She closed her eyes, luxuriating in the warmth of the yellow day that had blossomed peacefully before her.

When she opened her eyes a few minutes later, she was surprised to see the imposing stone walls of London. "What is this place?" she whispered, her hand seeking the solidity of Gislebert's back for reassurance.

"This is the western Ludgate," the troubadour answered, tossing the words over his shoulder. "This gate is just one of seven." Gislebert's voice rang faintly with the know-it-all tone that Adele found annoying, and she frowned as he continued: "London is nothing like the little villages we've visited thus far, is it?"

Adele did not answer, but swiveled her eyes up and around, trying to see everything at once. Like a magnet, the massive wall that surrounded the city drew her eyes upward. Gislebert must have experienced the same effect, for he casually mentioned that much of the London wall had stood since the time of the Romans. The idea that she was riding on ancient ground brought Adele a shiver of delight. What ancient tales these walls could tell, if only they could speak!

A small abbey church of timber and stone stood just inside the city walls and offered travelers spiritual refreshment or rest for the night. Adele breathed a silent sigh of relief when Gislebert did not stop there. He had offered his prayers for success that morning as they set out; indeed, he had recited the same prayers every morning that Adele had known him. Why should he beg God *again* for news of Nadine?

As they rode eastward toward the Tower of London, Adele noted that there were few undeveloped areas in King Stephen's London. A swampy stretch of land along the river remained free of buildings, and occasionally she spied an unexploited meadow. But along the ancient wagon roads and donkey trails, sturdy timber-framed houses with walls of wattle and daub had sprung up like clover. Smoke from the central wood fires rose lazily through holes in the thatched roofs, and the wooden shutters of every house were open to admit sunlight and fresh air. Occasionally Adele spied a stone house surrounded with spacious gardens, but those homes obviously belonged to the wealthy, not the average Londoner.

Most amazing was the business district. Shops of gold- and silversmiths paneled one street, the shops of candle-makers another. The millers and blacksmiths built their homes and businesses by the river's edge; cloth merchants lined the streets one block northward, while hay merchants pulled their wagons through the market, where sheep and pigs roamed freely. Wine sellers' shops dotted the city indiscriminately, as did the churches.

"It's like a fair!" Adele exclaimed, forgetting to deepen her voice.

Gislebert laughed. "Aye," he agreed. "A permanent fair." The tiny shops bore small signs above their doors, and open windows displayed the goods being sold, while the craftsmen worked busily in the back. "Londoners live by buying and selling," Gislebert warned. "So watch your step, young friend, or you may find you've bartered yourself into debt."

Adele looked around with interest. What if Gislebert were to find his Nadine here in the hustle and bustle of London? She had known all along that one day she must say good-bye to this man who had befriended her. Perhaps they would part this week, even today. If she had to stand alone again, London seemed a promising place to begin a new life.

"London is a large and proud city," Gislebert said, brushing wind-blown hair from his eyes as the mare carefully picked her way through the milling crowds of the narrow streets. "The Romans established a settlement here and built the first bridge over the Thames River. London has since been destroyed by fire. The Vikings laid her flat once, but she will always be the heart of Britain."

"So many people!" Adele gasped, lifting her legs farther up the horse's flank as the city pressed in upon them. The winding street where they rode was crowded by other horsemen, vendors with donkey-pulled carts, and work-worn women, who scurried by with buckets dangling from poles balanced across their shoulders.

Adele crinkled her nose. Here, deep in the marketplace where animals and men crowded each other, the smell of horse and donkey droppings mingled freely with the scent of baking food from nearby kitchens. At one point the mare stopped her determined march forward and snorted nervously at the press of noisy people around them. As Gislebert calmed the animal, Adele reconsidered making London her home.

Above all, she desired freedom, and how could you be free if you couldn't walk from one corner to another?

The crowd eased, and they progressed down the street called Thames until Adele felt Gislebert pull back on the reins. In front of them stood the Tower of London, bordered on the west by the city and on the south by the mighty Thames River. Behind the tower, like a strong arm around a beloved woman, a mighty section of the old Roman wall stood protectively.

But the tower itself was most imposing. A tall, rectangular building of three stories, its four corners were topped with towers and graceful turrets. "The king . . . ," Adele ventured, and Gislebert nodded.

"The king lives there when he is not at the Palace of Westminster," Gislebert explained. "Here we will find our answers, young Jonas."

"*You* will find *your* answers," Adele corrected him. *And perhaps it will be here,* she thought, *that I will say good-bye to you, troubadour Gislebert. It might be difficult, but I shall manage.*

Gislebert urged the horse forward to meet the king's guard at the tower entrance.

Gislebert gave his name and his purpose to a knight of the Constable of the Tower, then settled back on the uncomfortable bench to which he and Jonas had been assigned. "Our stay here will be short, but important," Gislebert whispered to Jonas, deepening his voice so that Jonas would listen carefully. "Your manners, my friend, leave much to be desired. Your speech is rough, and that we can correct. But you must be careful to do what I do in all things."

"What if you do the wrong thing?" Jonas asked impertinently. "You don't know everything, Troubadour."

"I know noblemen and knights," Gislebert answered. "Bow as I bow, speak only when spoken to, and keep your hands and face clean. We're not in the fields now—we're in the king's own palace."

Jonas scowled, and Gislebert turned his face away, determined to make the best of things. They waited for an hour in silence, then the knight returned. "You will be given quarters with the soldiers of the Constable of the Tower," the knight replied. "Your message will be taken to the king in time, and we will bring you word regarding His Highness's disposition toward you."

Gislebert nodded and gestured toward Jonas. "And my companion? and my horse?"

The knight glanced for a moment at Jonas, then turned again to Gislebert. "Your horse will be stabled, and your companion may remain with you."

"My thanks to you," Gislebert said, bowing from the waist. From the corner of his eye, he saw Jonas hesitantly imitate his bow, then they followed the knight from the tower gate office to the first floor of the tower itself.

"I think," Adele whispered as she followed Gislebert into the large chamber where the servants and squires of the royal knights were busily engaged in readying their masters for dinner, "that it is time to take my leave of you, Troubadour." She kept her eyes to the floor and sank onto a nearby wooden stool, hoping to keep out of sight.

Gislebert dropped his bag of belongings to the floor and turned to her in surprise. "Leave now?" he asked, incredulity ringing in his voice. "When we are so close to finding the answers we seek?"

"They are your answers to your quest," she replied, hardly daring to look up at him. She did not know why she wanted to cry, but if she did, he would think her a fool, or crazy.

"But you, little friend, have been through so much with me! I have always imagined that you would follow me to find Nadine and that you would somehow become part of our household. To part now, like this, with our goals unanswered—"

A sob escaped her, and Gislebert seemed startled by the

sound. He sank to one knee beside her and glanced warily over his shoulder to be sure that none of the royal knights observed the spectacle.

"I am sorry," Adele said, wiping an unmanly tear from her cheek. "But I do not belong here, among these men, and I feel most awkward. I need freedom, Troubadour, open sky and stars! This stone fortress is not for me."

"We will pause here but a few days," Gislebert protested. He raised his right hand. "On an oath, I swear it. We will soon leave this place and journey onward to find Nadine. When I have found her, I will make a home, and you will have a place in it, Jonas."

Adele ran her hands through her hair, bringing the ragged locks down over her face. Her emotions were too powerful, her confusion about her feelings for the troubadour too unsettling. Only one as blindly in love as Gislebert would fail to see her torment, and the rational side of her nature commanded her to leave, to hasten on her way.

But her heart hung on his words. He had promised a home, with room for her. She had never known the joys of home as Gislebert described them. He had spoken often of Margate, of Calhoun and Afton and the dear babies, and the vision had often comforted her as she had lain awake while Gislebert snored near her. Could she have a place in such a home? If it meant acting and dressing as a man forever, wouldn't such a home be worth the price of self-denial?

A burly knight across the room barked an order for his servant to bring his sword, and Gislebert was distracted by the rough sound. "They are a stormy breed, these knights," he admitted, turning again to Adele, "and I am not comfortable in their company, either. But if you can bear them for a few days, we will be on our way." He paused, and his eyes searched her face so intently that she had to look away.

"I will remain with you," she murmured, her voice a low whisper. "But these men . . ." Her voice trailed away.

"Ignore them if at all possible, and spend your time drawing," Gislebert suggested. "We can ask for parchments and ink, and you can sketch the knights for their entertainment."

"No." Adele shook her head, imagining a hundred inquiring male eyes peering at her. "I will not draw for these rough men."

"Then bide your time patiently, for the king will call for us as soon as he hears my name," Gislebert predicted. "We were friends once, he and I."

Adele turned to look out a narrow window. "Your fanciful stories have gone to your head," she answered, resting her chin in her hand even as she resigned herself to staying with him. "We will most likely be murdered in our sleep by a drunken knight. If the king does not call for us within three days, Troubadour, I will leave you and this place."

Gislebert raised an eyebrow. "No, you won't, young Jonas. God has decreed for each of us a place; my place is with Nadine, and yours is in our household." He lifted a finger, and something danced in the depths of his dark brown eyes. "You will see, young friend, what your tear today has bought. I offer my friendship forever, until our lives end. As Calhoun stood by me, so I will stand by you in loyalty, love, and honor until God calls you away. Together we shall journey to our destinies, side by side, as friends."

"You'll journey to madness if you continue to talk so," Adele answered, wiping her face on her sleeve to cover her embarrassment. She sniffed and smiled up at Gislebert. "And I'll not accompany you on that journey."

They ate with the men of the king's military household, the *mesnie,* and Gislebert had to admit that even he felt out of place among so many rugged and scarred knights. He and Jonas slipped quietly into empty places at the end of a long row of tables and partook of the food before them without comment. The knights nearest them, thankfully, chose to ignore the two puny men in dusty robes.

When the meal was done, both Gislebert and Jonas relaxed. They took a walk through the courtyard, and Gislebert noticed that the warm day seemed to bring out the color in Jonas's cheeks. "If you like, we could go down to the river for a swim," he suggested, laughing. "We haven't had a bath in weeks, you know."

Jonas halted in midstep, and his eyes fell to the ground. "I cannot swim," he answered, not looking up. "I do not like the river."

"Nonsense," Gislebert answered, waving his hand. "We can find a quiet, shallow spot and splash our cares away." He smiled and tried to catch Jonas's eye. The boy didn't look up, and Gislebert lowered his head to peer into Jonas's face. "Come on, boy, doesn't that sound like a fetching idea?"

Jonas threw his arms up, his hands clenched into fists. "No, it does not," he hissed, stepping away from Gislebert. "You are always making plans for me, Troubadour, and I want nothing to do with them. Leave me alone!"

"You forget," Gislebert replied, his own anger flaring within him, "that *you* chose to ride with *me*. You have attached yourself to me and my cause like a leech, and I find myself responsible for you—"

"You don't have to look out for me!" Jonas's face grew red and blotchy with anger. "I release you from your precious vow of loyalty! I can leave now—"

Words apparently failed him, for the boy broke off and sprinted toward the gate of the tower.

"Leave, then!" Gislebert shouted, amazed at the sudden declaration of war between them. The boy continued to run. Gislebert let him go, then stormed angrily about in the courtyard for five minutes, kicking up dust in frustration. Why had God burdened him with the care of this young scamp? At last he muttered an oath and ran after Jonas. The boy was only a child, after all, and unused to the ways of courtly life.

He found Jonas sitting on the bank of the river, tracks of tears shining on his dusty face. His brown eyes were troubled as though he had been wounded, and Gislebert could not understand why the boy suffered.

He sighed and sank onto the ground by Jonas's side. They sat for a moment in silence, then Gislebert spoke: "I'm sorry, Jonas, for whatever upset you," he said, shaking his head. "You don't have to take a bath in the river. You don't *ever* have to take a bath, if that will make you happy. I will not make plans for you. You are free to do what you will."

Jonas didn't answer, but sniffed, so Gislebert went on. "Soon I shall find my Nadine and build a life with her, and I want to know that you are safe, Jonas. We have . . . grown *close* in our days together, and I would not leave you alone in the world. But you are free, if that's what you want to be."

"I can take care of myself," Jonas muttered, his voice quiet and stubborn. "I only came with you, Troubadour, to teach you how to survive."

"And yet sometimes I am the teacher," Gislebert reminded him. "You are a child of the country, probably the offspring of a villein—"

Jonas cried aloud in indignation. "I know more of the world than you do," he cried, his voice breaking. "I know that I shall survive, and can survive, with or without you, Troubadour!"

"I don't doubt your word," Gislebert answered, casually throwing his arm about the boy's slender shoulders. Jonas stiffened, and Gislebert paused, then patted the boy sympathetically and dropped his arm as he stood to his feet. "Let's return to our quarters," Gislebert suggested. "We don't want to miss the king's summons, do we?"

Jonas pouted for another full day, neither speaking to nor looking at Gislebert, but walked and thought alone. After trying—and failing—to engage Jonas at the dinner table, Gislebert watched the boy leave, then put down his fork and sighed in frustration. The knight who ate at his left hand smiled. "Your brother has a sullen temper, does he not?"

Gislebert shook his head and chuckled. "The boy is not my brother. He is a—" *What?* Gislebert could not find the

65

word. Jonas had become more than a companion, but Gislebert wondered if they were truly friends. "He is," Gislebert continued, "sometimes like my right arm, but more often a thorn in my side."

The knight laughed in agreement. "Young ones often give us trouble. I, myself, have two sons in training at York."

"Congratulations," Gislebert answered. "You must be very proud."

The knight shrugged. "I have only done what is expected of me. When I die, whether tomorrow or ten years from now, the name Edmund of Tisbury will not be remembered. Only those who strive toward greatness and achieve it will leave a mark on this earth."

Gislebert studied the knight Edmund as he spoke. The man's silvery hair still bore a tinge of the brown it had once been; the crescent-shaped bags of flesh under his eyes had once been firm. In what battle had the knight received the scar upon his cheek, and in what duel had the man's nose been rendered crooked?

"I see by your face that you have served ably and well," Gislebert said softly. "Surely there are many who will remember your name. You have sons, your lord is the king himself, and you had a wife, so you have found love. Does life offer anything more?"

"I left my sons at York because I have no property or name to bequeath them," Edmund answered. "They bear me no love. My king does not know me, and my wife hated me. Our marriage was arranged, and if my wife could have killed my sons in the womb, she would have. She had no pleasure in them or in me."

Gislebert lowered his eyes from the knight's face. Such a woeful tale was not unusual, he knew, but surely love would have changed everything! Why had the knight not wooed and won his wife's love? Why had he not pursued his sons' hearts?

Gislebert opened his mouth to ask, but a royal page entered the hall and raised his hand for silence. "A message from His Royal Highness Stephen to one Gislebert of Margate," the page announced, staring steadfastly ahead.

Gislebert drew in his breath. It had happened. The king had heard his name and remembered him. "I am Gislebert," he called, standing to his feet.

The page nodded solemnly to Gislebert. "Make yourself ready and prepare to be escorted into the royal presence. The king sends his love and regard and invites you to dine with him."

The old knight looked with new appreciation at Gislebert. "It would seem I have been in the company of someone of importance," he said, bowing his head gently. "Forgive me if I have spoken my thoughts too freely."

Gislebert laid his hand on Edmund's shoulder. "You have done yourself a service, sir," he answered. "For it is not too late to seek love, if you will devote yourself to its attainment. As for me, love's fulfillment stands just beyond my reach. Wish me well, Sir Edmund, and pray that all goes well as I stand before the king."

"I will," Edmund answered.

Gislebert looked about for Jonas, but the boy had left the great hall. *How unfortunate that he chooses to pout at this hour,* Gislebert thought as he washed his hands and face in a bowl that stood near a window. *The thorn in my side has loosened himself at precisely the wrong time.* The water stilled, and he regarded his watery reflection to make certain that the face he would present to the king was clean and honest.

Gislebert dried his face and hands, straightened his tunic, and nodded to the page, who led the way upstairs to the royal apartments.

SEVEN

Gislebert of Margate—" King Stephen's stentorian voice filled the upstairs chamber, where he sat in an ornate wooden chair surrounded by fawning nobles. "What brings you to London?"

Gislebert fell to one knee and bowed deeply, then stood and looked up at his king. His knees twitched nervously, so he made an extra effort to calm his voice. "May God's grace save you, my king. I have left Margate, Your Highness, on a mission to seek the Lady Jehannenton who visited there several years ago."

The king's handsome face creased in a thoughtful frown. "Has Calhoun of Margate business with this Lady Jehannenton? Why does he send you, a troubadour, instead of one of his knights? Are you to sing her an invitation to Margate, perhaps?"

The king looked to his nobles for appreciation of his wit, and they laughed merrily. Gislebert, however, shook his head. "I am on a personal mission, Your Majesty, that I am hesitant to discuss in so great a company."

Stephen ran his hand through his thinning hair and studied Gislebert carefully. "We would know of this matter, in private, Gislebert," he said, crossing his legs casually. "And you will tell us of this personal mission later. But for now, we cannot dismiss our guests, and dinner is almost ready. Will you dine with us and give us a song afterward?"

Even though he had already eaten, it would be

unthinkable to refuse. Gislebert nodded and bowed. Stephen stood and motioned for Gislebert to stand beside him as the company proceeded to the great hall for dinner.

"How come you, Gislebert, to be traveling alone?" the king asked as they walked, lowering his voice. "Did not Calhoun send you with an escort?"

Gislebert shook his head again. "Lord Calhoun offered, my king, but I preferred to travel alone, until I befriended a young man. Jonas, a boy of fifteen, travels as my companion."

"And he does not desire to dine with us?"

"He is . . ." Gislebert paused and forced a smile. "He is restless with youth, my liege, and I do not know where he is."

Stephen nodded to two knights who stood at the door of the hall. "Find the boy Jonas and bring him to dinner," he commanded, waving the knights away. Stephen then took his place at the head table and turned to his assembled guests. "Good evening, gentlemen," he said, spreading his arms. "Let us eat."

Adele thought her heart would leave her chest when the two royal knights entered the chamber where she lay on her straw mattress. When they approached and demanded to know whether she was Jonas, companion to the man Gislebert, the room swirled, and Adele feared she would faint.

One of the knights laughed at her fear, and the other grabbed her arm and pulled her to her feet. "You're going to dinner with the king," the second knight said, pushing Adele toward a doorway. "But you're to wash up first. Hurry! The king waits."

Adele stepped to the basin of water by a window and splashed her face and trembling hands, pausing to check the water for her reflection. All seemed to be in order—she was, as usual, as plain and common as any boy. "I am ready," she finally said, deepening her voice, and the two knights led her upstairs to the king's banquet.

Adele had never seen anything like the king's banquet

room. Long tables stood at the sides and back of the room, while richly embroidered tapestries in hues of red, blue, and gold covered the walls. Knights in surcoats emblazoned with the Lion of England stood guard at each doorway, the hilts of their jeweled swords gleaming from sheaths at their sides.

And the table! Serving women kept the bowls of food hot and in plentiful supply, and the knives and spoons, which lay alongside the trenchers, were beautifully worked in silver and gold. Tall golden goblets stood in front of each diner's place, and as Adele took her place beside Gislebert at a long table, she wondered that people could bring them-selves to actually use such beautiful instruments.

A servant paused at Adele's side after she had been seated, and Gislebert elbowed her tactfully. "Wash your hands," he whispered in a low voice.

"I already did," Adele whispered back.

"Do it *again,*" Gislebert repeated firmly. Adele turned without further comment and washed her hands in the silver-plated bowl. "Now pick up your spoon and eat," Gislebert instructed. Adele obeyed without complaint. It did not matter that they had just eaten—the food at Stephen's table was an entirely different experience. Such an abundance and variety of dishes, and such seasonings! Adele knew she would have been satisfied merely to sit and breathe in the aroma of the king's food, but she ate heartily and did not hesitate to sample any dish that passed by her trencher.

After her initial fascination with the food passed, Adele looked around and tried to make sense of her surroundings. The men who lounged around these tables were not military, for even though several had jeweled swords at their sides, they wore no armor. All of them except her and Gislebert wore expressions of self-importance and pompousness.

Three men were set apart from the others at a raised table at the front of the room. The man on the left wore the costly robes of an archbishop or other high-ranking cleric, and a gold cross hung above his breast. The middle-aged man on the right wore simple, elegant robes, but creases of worry lined his face. Between these two, a majestic fellow sat upright, smiling indulgently at his fellows. His cloak of deep red was held at his shoulders by a jeweled string of gold. Adele knew this handsome man had to be King Stephen of England.

The king was not as old as Adele had imagined—probably only in his mid-forties, even though his hair had thinned considerably and his legs appeared frail under his purple tunic. Throughout dinner the king's hands fiddled nervously with his spoon and the narrow stem of his goblet, even though he smiled and joked often with his dinner companions. His face was pleasant, with laugh lines around his eyes and mouth. Adele thought the king might be a likeable fellow, if one could ever really know a king.

When all had eaten, the king clapped his hands, and the room stilled instantly. "We have with us today Gislebert of Margate, a most excellent and entertaining troubadour," the king announced. "Gislebert, will you give us a song? Today we have a most pressing need of cheer and good tidings."

A servant had been sent to fetch Gislebert's lute, and the troubadour bowed, picked up his instrument, and moved from his seat at the table to the center of the room. While the nobles drank and picked the morsels of their dinner from their teeth, Adele listened, entranced, to Gislebert's songs. But today he did not play the familiar love songs she had heard before. Instead, he sang witty political satires filled with references that Adele did not understand.

In this setting she observed a new aspect of the troubadour's personality. Though it was his nature to be quiet and reflective, here he adopted a noisy, bold demeanor and cackled outrageously at his own jokes while the king and his nobles roared in appreciation. For their praise and applause, Gislebert nodded and bowed, bobbing like a cork upon the water. Adele remained uncomfortably still in her chair, not liking what she saw.

As the king's guests clamored for an encore, the

troubadour's gaze locked with hers. He must have seen reproach in her eyes, for he stood straight before his audience and put his hand to his throat as if he would speak. The offensive attitude he had adopted was gone, discarded as easily as he might have removed an ill-fitting tunic.

"I beg your pardon, my King and gentle men," Gislebert said, his cheeks reddening as the sea of eyes turned to him. "The songs I have sung for you today might have been sung by any troubadour. But I have not been true to myself, nor to a vow I once made. Mine is not the way of the careless knight, nor the ribald jester. Mine is the way of chivalry, of the purest, most noble love God has ever designed."

He looked at Adele again with something like an apology in his eyes, then he bowed before the group and raised his lute again. "Before I leave you, I would give you the 'Riddle of the Knight,'" Gislebert said, launching into his favorite song of romance. Adele had heard it so often that she knew all the words, and she murmured them to herself as Gislebert sang the story of the maid and the traveling knight.

After Gislebert's song, the servants cleared the tables, and the men broke up into small groups for games and gambling. One group of nobles played "hot cockles," and from the security of Gislebert's side, Adele watched in horrified amazement as a group of nobles blindfolded one of their own and asked him to kneel on the hard floor. The other players took turns striking the man full force in the face or across his cheek, and the blindfolded player, often with blood dripping from his nose, had to identify his attacker or face another blow.

Adele was even more surprised by the circle of men who gambled with dice, for two of them wore the brown robes of monks. They gathered in a corner and took turns throwing the dice, exclaiming or groaning as the dice rolled money into new hands.

Adele feared she and Gislebert would be drawn into one of these games, and she tugged impatiently on his sleeve as the men milled about them. "I do not like this place, Troubadour," she whispered, glancing nervously around lest someone should pay her undue attention.

"Nor do I," Gislebert answered. "These men are rough and of the world—"

"Is that why you sang those horrid songs?"

Gislebert thrust his chin out stubbornly. "You don't understand, Jonas. I know these men. I know what they like and what they expect. If I sang only of love and beauty, they would think me less than a man—"

"So you did what they want and were not true to yourself or your God. Never have I heard such songs from you—"

"Be quiet," Gislebert hissed. He smiled politely at a nobleman who came up to thank him for the entertainment, and when the man had passed, he turned once again to Adele. "I was wrong; I forgot myself. I admitted as much. But this is the king's court, Jonas!"

Adele pushed her hair back from her eyes, the better to glare at him. "So we do things differently here, do we? All right then, Troubadour. And to think I almost liked you!"

She was about to stalk away, but Gislebert's hand caught her tunic. She turned to speak in anger, but her words froze on her lips when she saw His Highness King Stephen standing in front of them.

"Come, Gislebert and companion," the king said, clapping Gislebert affectionately on the back. "We would hear now of this personal mission which brings you to us."

Gislebert bowed and tugged resolutely on Adele's sleeve so that she was forced to follow him and the king from the great hall into the royal chamber. The king settled himself into his carved chair, the only chair in the room, and Gislebert and Adele stood before him. "Speak freely," the king said, clasping his hands together. His dark blue eyes regarded Gislebert earnestly. "How can we be of help to you, my friend?"

Gislebert wasted no time with pleasantries. "Your Highness, several years ago, Cupid's bow struck my heart with love for a girl called Nadine. She is a lady-in-waiting for Lady Jehannenton, and I have sought her for many years, but without success. Since the Lady Jehannenton is a distant kinswoman of yours, I hoped you could give me news about her."

The king nodded thoughtfully. "Were you on this search, good Gislebert, when you came to our court nearly two years ago?"

Gislebert nodded. "I was younger then and less determined, but yes, I sought her even then."

"Yet you stayed in our court for some months, and you have been at Margate Castle for many years more."

"I owed allegiance to you, my King, and to Calhoun, my friend."

"And did your passion and intention diminish during this time?"

"No, sire. It has increased steadily, especially since—"

"Since when?"

Gislebert faltered, and his face flooded with color, but he continued: "Since the birth of Calhoun's sons, my liege. I could not bear . . ." Gislebert struggled to contain his emotions, and Adele stared in amazement at the troubadour, for never had she seen him close to tears.

"I could not bear my jealous heart, for I desire love, and a wife, and sons of my own. God knows these are the desires of my heart, and if he wills, I will seek them, though I die in the quest."

The king nodded in sympathy. "These desires are only natural," he said. "I am king of all England, yet the love I bear for my wife is greater than all other loves. And my own son, Eustace, gives me unspeakable joy."

The king loosened his hands and idly rubbed the carving on his chair, and Gislebert took advantage of the moment to press his question: "Then can you tell me, Your Highness, where I can find Lady Jehannenton? For surely there I will find my Nadine."

Stephen looked up, and Adele thought a wall had come up behind his eyes. "If your passion has built through the months of searching for her, a few weeks more may help your suit," the king answered. "Tarry here in London with us, Gislebert; you and your companion are welcome. We will seek out the whereabouts of Lady Jehannenton, and we will grant your request. But until the news reaches us, we will enjoy your company."

His words were not an offer, but a command, and Gislebert murmured thanks as he stepped forward to kiss the king's hand. As he turned to leave, however, pretense fled from his face, and Adele saw deep and bitter disappointment revealed there.

Adele and Gislebert were moved from the knights' quarters and given a luxurious room on the second floor of the tower. Adele found herself forgiving the king for extending their stay in London. "Feathers! I never expected this!" she crowed, rolling on her feather mattress. "And the food, Troubadour! Two huge meals every day! You never told me it would be like this!"

"It will be like this for only a few precious days," Gislebert said, casting a warning look in Adele's direction. "As soon as the king's scout returns with news of Lady Jehannenton, we will be on our way."

"What scout?" Adele asked, rolling onto her stomach to get a better look at him. "I didn't hear anything about a scout. How do you know the king has sent one?"

"How else will he find the news he seeks?" Gislebert snapped, lifting his hands in an emphatic gesture. "King Stephen is my friend, and he will do all he can to aid me."

"As long as you aid him, too," Adele countered. "I think he keeps you here for entertainment. I think he will keep you here for years to come—you will sing at dinners, and suppers, and royal banquets. . . ."

Gislebert picked up a pillow and threw it at her; she promptly threw it back. Adele then grabbed her own pillow and hit Gislebert over the head, and soon their argument had diffused into a lighthearted pillow fight. She danced around the room as she pelted him, loving his mild threats and reveling in the rare sound of his laughter, until his pillow hit her, hard, in the center of her chest. She fell back upon the floor, gasping as her face reddened. She could not draw a breath.

"Are you all right?" Gislebert asked, leaning over Adele. "By heaven, boy, if you can't handle a pillow's blow, how do you ever intend to survive a knight's?"

Adele's eyes filled with tears, and she turned her back to Gislebert, her chest gradually relaxing enough so that she could breathe. It had been like this before, when her father's blows had knocked her across the room and stolen her breath. "Stay away from me," she croaked, her voice ending in a girlish sob. "I told you never to touch me."

"I didn't touch you," Gislebert answered, coming closer. "And I did not intend to do you harm. Let me see if you're all right." He tugged gently on the sleeve of her tunic, and Adele leaped to her feet and shielded herself with her hands.

"Stay away!" she screamed hoarsely, her body trembling like a frightened animal's. "Stay away from me!"

Gislebert flung his hands helplessly into the air, then left the room, slamming the door behind him. Adele bit her lip and finally threw herself on her mattress and surrendered to the torrent of tears that begged for release.

EIGHT

Every noon, after dinner, Gislebert sang for the king's guests, and after the recreation Gislebert loitered in the great hall, hoping for a private word with the king. Sometimes he caught King Stephen as he made his way from the hall to his chamber. Occasionally he overtook him in the winding stairwell; one time he halted Stephen as His Highness was about to enter the royal lavatory. Each time Gislebert asked for news of Lady Jehannenton, and each time the king replied that he had heard nothing.

Spring became summer, and summer glared hot and blue, reminding Gislebert that each sunrise brought another day in which Nadine might marry—or die—or move farther away from him. Impatience gnawed at him the way a dog chews on a worn bone, but there was nothing he could do but wait. *That is the problem of dealing with the king,* Gislebert thought one afternoon when Stephen stalled him yet again. *If you place all into the king's hands, there it must remain.*

Jonas, Gislebert noticed, adapted surprisingly well to the tower routine. The boy seemed more reserved and less inclined to speak than he had been in their wanderings, but the good food and wine of the king put meat on the boy's bones and brought color to his cheeks. When not walking alone in the courtyard of the tower, Jonas spent his time in their small room, drawing pictures of those who had graced the table at the king's banquets.

One morning while Jonas walked outside, Gislebert riffled through the boy's drawings and came upon a series of disturbing sketches. A stout, beefy-faced man glared at some undefined object or person in each of the dark drawings, and Gislebert felt his skin crawl as he studied them. The curve of the man's cheek and the cut of his jaw seemed vaguely familiar, but his hard and pitiless eyes were those of a stranger. Gislebert replaced the pictures and sat quietly for some time, wondering how and when Jonas had known him.

The hot morning sun brought beads of perspiration to Adele's forehead, and she pushed her heavy hair away from her face. Her cloak hung hot and heavy about her shoulders and chest, but she was too wary of discovery to walk in the courtyard without it. The knights were too involved with their training and patrols to pay a mere boy any attention. The noblemen thought her beneath them, and although the serving women occasionally cast a curious glance her way, they were aware of the great gulf between servants and free men. No one in the tower had really paid much attention to her, for she was of no social significance. But there was always a possibility that someone with sharp eyes might see through her disguise.

The gray-green waters of the Thames beckoned her to walk on the strip of vacant land at the river's edge. The sun fell upon her face like a benediction, and the breeze from the river ruffled her hair. Gislebert had lately been snappish and irritable, frustrated with his lack of success with the king. Adele found her daily walks a wonderful escape from the troubadour's surliness. "Yes," Adele breathed, enjoying the peace of the warm morning, "freedom can be good."

She had walked a good distance from the tower when the sky in the west filled with gray clouds, and the dull rumble of thunder warned her of an approaching summer storm. Somewhere in the distance a dog howled mournfully at the change of weather. Adele slowed her walk, knowing she would have to soon turn around.

A heavy hand caught her, whirled her around, and threw her to the ground near the edge of the river embankment. Before she could rise to her feet, a stranger fell upon her, his ponderous weight holding her to the ground. His dark eyes shone menacingly from the depths of his hooded cloak, and a scream clawed in her throat. "I knew it," he snarled, his voice lilting with an accent she couldn't place. "No boy could be as fair as you are, my pretty."

"Let me go, please, just let me go," she whispered frantically, grasping wildly with her free arm for something with which she could ward off her attacker. But in one sure movement her assailant grabbed both her wrists in one broad hand and pinned her arms to the ground behind her head. Her lips were smothered by his sour mouth, and the roaring of blood filled her ears so that she could hear nothing else, not even the rush of the river.

She closed her eyes, and for an instant she was back in the mud house of her birth. Her father held her arms with one hand and rigorously applied his leather strap with the other. She had borne it then, but she had been a child, a slave. She would not bear such violence now! She focused her energies and bit the cheek of the man who loomed above her. When he uttered an oath and partially lifted himself from her, she pulled her face away from his gruesome mouth. "No!" she screamed. "You won't touch me!"

With energy brought on by the mad rush of fear, she lifted her leg and kneed the man in the groin. As he groaned and curled in pain, Adele drew her legs up tightly against her chest, planted them firmly against her attacker's broad belly, and kicked as hard as she could.

The force of the blow wasn't enough to lift him off her, but it did knock the breath from his body. The man balanced himself upright on one knee, struggling to breathe, and Adele scooted out from under him like a scurrying crab. As his angry eyes shone out from the darkness of his cloak, she rushed at him in fury, knocking her startled attacker off the embankment and into the rushing water of the Thames.

Breathless and trembling, she watched the dark cloak skim the surface of the water, then vanish beneath the river's choppy waves.

Gislebert let the heavy oak door to their small room slam shut behind him and flung his lute onto his mattress, not caring if he damaged the instrument. "Still no news," he muttered, raising his eyes in exasperation to the ceiling. "God, did I not ask you today to work your will?"

When Jonas did not offer a wry comment, Gislebert looked down in surprise. The boy sat on his mattress, his cloak covered with river sand, his face awash with tears. "What happened?" Gislebert demanded, thinking the boy had been in a fight.

Jonas shook his head. "I cannot stay here, and you must not," the boy told Gislebert as tears coursed openly down his thin cheeks. "The king stalls you, Troubadour, and takes advantage of your trusting nature. If you are a man, you must act!"

Gislebert stepped back. "If you are a man, you would not express yourself through tears," he said, offended by the truth in Jonas's words. "Dry your eyes, then speak to me. You are nearly a man grown, and grown men do not cry over nothing."

"I do not cry over nothing." Jonas paused, wiping his nose on his sleeve. "I killed a man this morning."

Gislebert laughed, and when Jonas did not confess to the joke, the troubadour's knees buckled, and he sank to the floor. The boy's story could not be true, but there was nothing in Jonas's manner or appearance to suggest that he was lying. *By heaven,* the thought swept crazily through Gislebert's mind, *Jonas has kept his bloody vow.*

"Who?" Gislebert whispered hoarsely.

Jonas shook his head. "I do not know. It does not matter. I acted in self-defense, and the man drowned in the river. But his body will surface somewhere, sometime, and we must leave here, Gislebert!"

Gislebert turned his back to the boy and held his head in his hands. Jonas was right, on every account. The king had been stalling Gislebert—and the body would surface. If Jonas had killed a nobleman, or even a knight, questions would be asked and answered, perhaps with the boy's life.

"I will speak to the king tonight," Gislebert said, muttering in the low voice he reserved for dreaded subjects. "I will demand an answer. We will hear what he has to say, and we will be on our way."

Gislebert asked for a private audience with the king after supper and was surprised when it was readily granted. As the sun sank in the west, the troubadour was ushered into the king's private chamber on the upper floor of the tower. He felt very small in the large, high-ceilinged room.

"What can we do for you, friend Gislebert?" Stephen asked, smiling broadly at the troubadour from his favorite chair. "Are you not enjoying your time here with us?"

"The time in your royal presence has been a privilege and honor," Gislebert said, bowing. "But I must ask you again for the boon which brought me to you weeks ago. Surely, if you are king of England, you have acquired some knowledge of Lady Jehannenton and where she is. If you have not, I have decided to undertake the journey on my own."

The corner of Stephen's mouth twitched in a half-smile. "Ah, so Gislebert has realized that we have kept him here for his company alone," he answered, his voice rumbling through the chamber. "In truth, friend, we received news of this lady only last month. The south and west, as you know, are under control of Matilda of Anjou's forces, and there was no sure word from any of those barons."

"But you have received word?"

The king nodded slowly and with regret. "Your Lady Jehannenton resides now away from the fighting, since she is aged and does not wish to be part of the conflict. She has established a house in France, outside St. Denis."

Gislebert felt his heart soar within him. Lady Jehannenton still lived, and in France! "Did you by chance . . ." Gislebert hated to voice the question, for if the answer should prove false . . .

King Stephen read the unspoken thought. "We have it on good authority that the Lady Jehannenton lives with two maids, one called Melusina and the other called Nadine," Stephen replied. "Both are unmarried, and both are devoted in service to her. It is also reported that the Lady Jehannenton has bequeathed her considerable lands and estates to them equally."

The king smiled and leaned forward, clasping his hands. "So, Gislebert, you have the good fortune to not only fall in love with a beautiful woman but an heiress, too. Best wishes, my friend, on your journey. We will grant you leave to depart in three days time, and we will ask only one thing of you."

"Anything, sire." Gislebert looked toward the high ceiling and closed his eyes in gratitude. In exchange for the news he had just received, he would have promised anything, even his firstborn son.

"When you find your love . . ." The king paused. "If she will not have you, Gislebert, promise us on an oath that you will return to us and serve us for the rest of our life. We are growing old, good friend, and your songs and laughter have done much to encourage us in these difficult times. Greater still, sometimes we think you are the only man in this entire castle who is not politically ambitious."

"My liege, I swear it," Gislebert said, kneeling before the king's chair. He placed his hand over Stephen's. "Though I pray you will find another to dispel your troubles and lighten your heart."

"Thank you," Stephen said, settling back into his chair. "Have the servants gather whatever you need for your journey, and take three days to prepare gifts, choose fine robes, and select two of the best horses in my stable. We will send a half dozen of our finest knights to safely escort you to the English coast."

As Gislebert stood to go, the king held out his hand.

"By the way, Gislebert, do you know anything of one called Jean de Honfleur? He was to visit us with his brother, but he failed to make his appearance this afternoon."

Gislebert hid a thick swallow in his throat and made an effort to smile. "No, Your Highness, I have not met him."

Stephen shrugged. "'Tis no matter. The man was a villain; he has sought to molest every woman within the walls of this city. He probably sleeps tonight with a harlot's dagger in his filthy heart."

Gislebert suspected then that Jean de Honfleur was the man Jonas had pushed into the river and was certain that terror and guilt were clearly revealed upon his own face. But Stephen smiled at the troubadour's discomfiture and held up his hand as if to bestow a blessing.

"What is this fear in your eyes, Troubadour? Does the journey frighten you, or the aspect of facing your love?"

"'There is no fear in love,'" Gislebert quoted the familiar Scripture he had learned as a boy. "If I am afraid, perhaps it is because I face the unknown."

"Aye," the king said, nodding. "The future is frightening, friend Gislebert. Even we are apprehensive about the future."

The king paused, and Gislebert thought suddenly that Stephen looked old and tired. "I do not know if we will meet again, my friend."

"By God's grace, we will," Gislebert said, bowing his head.

"Then rise and go your way," the king murmured. "Go with God, Gislebert, and find this one you love more than your king."

THE WHITE TOWER

O Lord, the God who saves me,
day and night I cry out before you.
May my prayer come before you;
turn your ear to my cry.
For my soul is full of trouble
and my life draws near the grave.
I am counted among those
who go down to the pit;
I am like a man without strength.
I call to you, O Lord, every day;
I spread out my hands to you.

PSALM 88:1-4, 9

NINE

Stunned, Gislebert walked down the circular steps from the royal apartments. He had asked and received news that Nadine was alive, well, and yet unmarried. In three short days, he would be on his way to her, bearing gifts and the blessing of the king. Such bounty was more than he had dared hope for. The king's unexpected beneficence made the tedious weeks of waiting worthwhile.

He felt himself grinning like a crazy man. In less than a month's time, if the journey went well, he would kneel at the feet of his exquisite Nadine and offer his heart. She would recognize the purity of his love. She would then extend her hand, and they would be wed.

Gislebert paused in the narrow stairwell and leaned against the smooth stone of the wall to lift a prayer heavenward. "Does any man have a right to be so happy, God? Among the noblemen above and the knights below, surely not one is happier or more content than I, Gislebert of Margate! His heart flooded with the wonderful sense of going home, even though he did not exactly know where home was or how he would find it. But home was wherever Nadine was. Home was love and security. Home would be his final resting place.

He resumed his walk down the steep stairs and remembered Jonas's resolute determination to leave London. *The boy will be happy now,* he thought, *and we can put the horrors of the past behind us.* His brows knitted in a momentary frown. Whatever had happened to the boy here could be forgotten.

If Jonas had indeed pushed Jean de Honfleur into the river, the man's body would certainly drift out with the tidal current and might never surface. If it did, it would likely rise among peasants who would give it a swift burial and forget the matter.

Yes, Gislebert told himself, whatever had happened in the past could be wiped away in the loving home he and Nadine would make.

Jonas nodded with resolute satisfaction when Gislebert announced that they would leave in three days' time, and his eyes widened when Gislebert offhandedly remarked that they were to leave on royal horses, with a mounted escort, and in new robes, gifts of bounty from the king. "So much for us?" Jonas asked, his voice squeaking in unbelief.

"We have won the king's favor, young friend," Gislebert said, settling back onto his mattress and smiling in satisfaction. "The king gave all freely, with only one promise from me."

"And that was?"

Gislebert shrugged. "If the lady Nadine refuses my offer of love, I am to return to London and serve in Stephen's court for the rest of his days."

"A life sentence!" Jonas's eyes flashed a warning. "Be careful, Troubadour! The king seeks to own you yet."

Gislebert smiled broadly. "That is one vow I will not have to keep, young Jonas. As surely as the sun shines outside today, the lady Nadine will recognize my heart of love and be compelled to answer it. She is a woman of discretion, valor, and gracious beauty, and her noble heart will know and honor mine though a thousand other hearts lie at her feet."

Gislebert picked up his lute and strummed it gently. "Though ten thousand hearts in love do shine, my loving heart will yet claim thine," he sang, improvising a melody.

Jonas scowled. "Your poetry suffers, Troubadour, even as your love grows wearisome. I am sick to death of hearing about it."

"Then stuff your ears with wool, for I shall sing all night long," Gislebert answered, strumming the lute again. "I

shall compose a thousand songs to my Nadine, one for every
night I have lived without her. I shall praise her eyes, her
hair, her smile, even the tiny instep of her foot."

Jonas lifted the blanket on his mattress and covered himself. "May God have mercy," he mumbled through the
dense wool, lying down to sleep. "And may these next three
days pass more quickly than any I have known."

Adele slept fitfully and awoke the next morning with a curious feeling in the pit of her stomach. Vivid memories of her
attacker came crowding back. She steeled herself to face
them and told herself that the man in the cloak surely lay
miles from London. Perhaps his vile carcass floated even
now in the great North Sea the troubadour had told her
about. He would not return to haunt her, at least not within
three days. Soon she and the troubadour would be safely
away from this place with its unsettling memories.

She lay still on her mattress, reassuring herself by listening for the regular clatter and clamor of castle life, and sat
up abruptly when she realized new sounds filled the early
morning air. A miaowing wail from one of the servant's children floated from one of the lodges on the grounds, and the
wind caught voices, murmurs, whispers, and the startled
whinny of horses. A creeping uneasiness rose from the bottom of her heart.

"Troubadour," she whispered, crawling over to shake
Gislebert's shoulder. "Wake up! Some trouble is surely stirring!"

She left the sleepy troubadour and crept to the narrow
slitted window in their room. Outside, the sun had barely
risen in the east, but already a sizable company of knights in
Stephen's white and gold had donned their armor and
mounted their sturdy war horses. They stood in the courtyard, tense and ready, awaiting an order—to do what?

Gislebert had not moved. Adele reached behind her and
tugged on his foot. "Awaken, Troubadour, and tell me what
trouble stirs below."

Gislebert grunted in reply and blinked rapidly. When he saw Adele by the window, he wrapped his woolen blanket around his shoulders and sat up to peer over her head at the scene below. "'Tis strange," he murmured. "Perhaps Matilda's knights are in the area, or perhaps the king is equipping a new force to venture into the countryside."

"Shouldn't we find out?" Adele asked, her nerves tightening. "If there is trouble abroad, is it wise for us to journey toward France?"

Gislebert shook his head as if annoyed. "I'm sure it's nothing, Jonas. A military exercise or something similar. But I have a friend among the knights. I can go down and ask what's afoot."

Adele kept a careful watch at the window as Gislebert shuffled about the chamber, pulling on his leggings and shoes. After he had gone, Adele pinned her cloak about her shoulders and slipped out of the room to find her own answers. She feared that the troubadour's heart might mislead his head, and she knew their lives might be greatly affected by whatever stirred at the Tower of London.

"Well, dearie, I don't mind telling you, but there's trouble outside the city," Laudine whispered. The pretty scullery maid put down her tray and leaned closer to whisper into Adele's ear: "The sergeant at arms woke the king in the middle of the night with news that Empress Matilda and her brother Robert are at Croydon and comin' this way. They'll be here soon enough if the king doesn't do something."

"Matilda's coming from the south?" Adele whispered, her stomach tightening. "That's the way to France, right?"

The blonde maid made a face. "Of course it is, silly. Where do you think Matilda's from?"

"I didn't know," Adele whispered dully.

Laudine tilted her head and pity filled her blue eyes. "You are a sorry one, aren't you?" she whispered. "Uneducated and poor, nothing but a scared little girl under that man's cloak."

Adele stepped back, stung, and Laudine placed a

callused hand on her shoulder. "Now, don't you worry, dearie. If you and the troubadour think to hide your love by traveling as two men, well, we've had worse scandals here at the tower. But I can see right through you. You can't fool another woman about such things."

Adele drew in her breath. "You can tell?" she whispered.

"Aye." The maid nodded. "You can cut your hair and wear a man's clothes and hide what little nature has given you—" She glanced quickly over Adele's slim body. "But it's clear to me that you are a girl. So why does the troubadour scheme to hide you? There's no shame in a troubadour wedding a common girl."

"He's not hiding me," Adele answered, looking at the floor. "I'm hiding myself."

The maid's eyes flew open for an instant, then she tilted her head back and laughed. "He thinks you a boy? What a fool he is!" Her laughter cascaded through the room, and Adele looked about nervously in fear that someone would hear. Laudine finally stopped laughing and wiped a tear from her eye.

"You are wrong about the troubadour," Adele answered stubbornly. "He's not a fool. He's just . . . blind. He's so in love with another woman that he doesn't even notice me."

"He is twice a fool then," Laudine answered, gathering dishes on her tray. "But don't you worry, dear heart, I'll keep your secret. Though I really think—" She lowered her voice, and Adele had to strain to hear her. "Any man with sense would see the love that's shining from your eyes."

The maid lifted her tray. Adele stammered, "T-t-that's a foolish thought; I love him not." But Laudine only laughed and walked away.

Gislebert returned to the room in a sullen mood and did not immediately share his report. Adele guessed the reason for his bad humor, but she kept quiet and absorbed herself in sketching a portrait of Laudine. Matilda's attack had come at a most inconvenient time for the lovesick troubadour, but with the recent turn of events, something in Adele melted in relief. Their departure would be delayed. Though she did not like living in the tower with the knights and dreaded the possibility that her attacker's body might be fished from the Thames, still, if the knights and the king were called away, the tower would be safe and bearable. Most important, every day they remained in London delayed Gislebert's reunion with Nadine.

Laudine's comments had astonished her. The maid had been amazingly accurate in her identification of Adele as a woman but completely mistaken in claiming to see love from Adele for the troubadour. Adele found that idea truly laughable.

Adele put down her sketch and nervously chewed her thumbnail. For some reason, her disguise was not working as well as it had in months past. The man in the cloak had guessed her femininity, and Laudine had clearly seen it. Had others? the king? the other nobles? Several times she had felt the curious eyes of others upon her, but she always drew back into shadows or pulled her cap more closely around her head. Her shapeless tunic easily disguised her budding figure, and she carefully kept her voice low and quietly modulated. What had given her away?

No matter what the others had seen, she was certain the troubadour did not suspect her true gender. If he had thought her anything but the boy she pretended to be, honor and loyalty to Nadine would have compelled him to part company with her. His heart and mind had room for only one female, and Nadine occupied that place.

Why do I stay with him? Adele asked herself, listening to his mournful attempts at a song as he sat behind her. *I do not desire his heart, or his kiss, or his bed, and yet, to be without his company*—she winced as she tore a hangnail from her thumb. He was a habit, like washing her hands or chewing her nails. A habit that might bring her pain, but one she *could not* live without.

"I love thee, I love thee, with a love that will not die,"

Gislebert sang, and Adele quietly covered her ears. In the past when he had sung of the perfect, holy, and pure Nadine, Adele had doubted that the woman actually existed. Surely Nadine was a figment of the troubadour's overactive imagination, a composite of all the women he had ever admired. But King Stephen had confirmed Gislebert's dreams, and every word of praise the troubadour uttered now for Nadine convinced Adele that she must leave him.

Though a home with him and Nadine would be safe and secure, she could not imagine herself sharing his company or fellowship with another woman. But she couldn't leave now! Her heart sank at the idea. What would she do without him? He had become so much to her—father, brother, and friend.

Unwillingly, she pushed aside the portrait of Laudine and began to sketch the troubadour's face. She drew his narrow mouth, which regularly upbraided her for her shortcomings, his dark eyes, which praised her few virtues and talents, and his bushy brows, which were quick to lift in unspoken rebuke. How well she had come to know this face! How well she could read him!

She heard him stop singing and sigh, and she hastily pushed the sketch under her mattress. *It is a good thing my troubadour is blind,* she thought, sensing his attention as he put down his lute and came near, *or honor would demand that he leave me as he has forsaken all other women in the name of his love.*

She knew he was probably trying to gather the strength to tell her their departure would be delayed, but he sat gloomily and stared idly at the drawings in her lap. She did not speak, allowing him to collect his thoughts, and a silent gray rain began to fall outside. A mist chilled their room, and from the courtyard, a trumpet blew.

Gislebert finally spoke. "If you would turn to see, Jonas, our royal king goes out in full battle dress to fight his cousin, Empress Matilda of Anjou. One day you might wish to tell your children of the sight."

Adele continued sketching the portrait of Laudine and did not look up. "If it is such a momentous occasion," she said dryly, lowering her voice, "why don't you look, Troubadour? Surely such a day is worthy of a song."

Gislebert threw himself on his mattress. "I cannot," he answered simply. "My cause and quest for Nadine have been swallowed up in the king's battle. I can only wait and hope that our royal benefactor prevails."

"It will be as God wills," Adele answered, quietly hoping that God's will would include keeping her with Gislebert for a while longer.

Several days passed with no word from the battle. The skeleton crew of knights and servants at the Tower of London kept a careful eye on the southern horizon, but no riders in white and gold surcoats appeared, and refugees from the region of battle spoke only of fierce fighting. Finally, on the fifth day of waiting, Gislebert heard a cry in the courtyard and flew to the window. "A party of mounted knights approaches from the south," a young squire yelled, running toward the tower to take the news to the very young and very old knights who were not fit to fight.

An officer of the Constable of the Tower stepped forward and intercepted the boy. "Be it Stephen and his men?" he asked, his gruff voice echoing through the stillness of the empty courtyard.

The squire slowly shook his head. "The knights wear red and white surcoats," he answered.

Gislebert could see the officer's shoulders sag, but the man lifted his chin in determination and walked to a bell mounted on a timber. Mournfully, resolutely, the bell chimed out the news that Stephen of Blois, once king of England, had surely been defeated.

"What does it mean, Troubadour?" Jonas asked, placing a hand on his shoulder.

Gislebert jumped at the boy's touch; he had forgotten that the lad stood by his side.

"It means that we are now prisoners of Empress Matilda of Anjou," he answered, still looking out the window. A cloud of dust had begun to swirl on the southern horizon; Matilda's men would be arriving at any moment. From the size of the cloud, the empress brought a large contingent of knights with her.

Gislebert stood upright and flexed his jaw. Of all the situations he had ever imagined for himself, he had never seriously considered that he would spend time in prison. Calhoun had been imprisoned for twelve long years in Outremer, and most knights were incarcerated at one time or another for infractions of the law or misconduct. But what place would a troubadour have in a dungeon? And why, when his goal had been so close, had God allowed Matilda to crush his hopes and dreams?

"Why, God?" he muttered clenching his fists. "I have tried to do right and seek only truth and love. For this you send me to prison?"

Gislebert swallowed hard and turned away from the window. "Drink, Jonas, and eat if any food remains," he said, his voice oddly calm and detached. "For in a moment we shall be in Empress Matilda's hands and at her mercy."

He looked into Jonas's eyes, and the naked fear he saw there unsettled him.

They waited: Gislebert, calmly, and Jonas, frantically. Jonas drank the last of the water. He ate every scrap of bread remaining on the tray Laudine had brought from the kitchen. He bundled his parchments and tossed them into the fireplace where they blazed in momentary fury. While Jonas buzzed about the room in panic, Gislebert watched the arrival of several hundred of Matilda's troops, clad in red and white surcoats. *Red for love of God and white for purity,* Gislebert thought as he watched the knights canter into the courtyard. *But in my experience, the knight who wears red uses piety to disguise evil intentions.* The knights' triumphant cries and the blinding reflection of the sun from their shields brought tears to his eyes.

The courtyard became a sea of red and white, then the ocean parted for Empress Matilda herself. She rode through her knights on a lavishly decorated war horse, and Gislebert noted in surprise that the empress did not wear a woman's robes but was dressed from head to toe in the chain mesh armor of a knight. She wore a solid red tunic over her hauberk and carried a heavy sword in her right hand, its hilt encrusted with emeralds. An arrogantly handsome woman with a narrow waist, wide hips, and a regal carriage, she might have have been anywhere from thirty to fifty years old, so unlined was her face.

A group of startled London businessmen had hastily convened in the courtyard, and when Empress Matilda dismounted from her royal horse, three of the leaders of London stepped forward and bowed before her on one knee. What they murmured to the victorious empress Gislebert could not hear, but Matilda's reply rang clearly through the sultry air: "Go at once, and bring me the stores of gold and silver and whatever you have of value in your storerooms," she demanded, lifting her chin imperiously. "I have taken London today, and I intend to possess it thoroughly."

She moved through the men without so much as a backward glance and directed her sergeant at arms to open the doors of the tower to her. "Now it begins," Gislebert said, looking toward his pale, young friend. "Fasten your belt, Jonas, and determine that you will not waver. Be a man today, and remember that Matilda is neither a man nor God's anointed king."

TEN

With Stephen held prisoner in an obscure castle far from London, Matilda took a most thorough possession of the Tower of London. All who were found therein, including Jonas and Gislebert, were consigned to the largest lower chamber until Matilda's sergeants had dispatched, either by death or release, all the tower's former inhabitants.

The chamber was dim, cool, and crowded with Stephen's loyal servants when Gislebert and Jonas first entered, and there was little room for movement. The room's high ceiling and narrow, slitted windows provided adequate ventilation, however, for the room was not designed to be a prison. Gislebert told Jonas to sit and relax; they would certainly be released in time.

In less than two days, Matilda's sergeants had eased the crowding in the lower chamber. All who had been part of Stephen's military force—all knights, guards, and sergeants—were taken out and summarily hanged. Gislebert clambered up on to a bale of hay and watched out the window as his friend Edmund of Tisbury limped out to the gallows on the hill. "I promise I will remember your name," Gislebert whispered softly at the window as the old knight placed his head into the noose. "We will not forget the valiant men who died here today."

After the executions of the military force, all who had been part of the royal household staff—the cooks, maids, scribes, and servants—were released to return to their old jobs after they had taken an oath of loyalty to Matilda. Only those who fell into no clear category remained in the lower chamber prison, Gislebert and Jonas among them. Also imprisoned were several villeins Stephen had kept in chains, an earl—Lord Chapman—who had happened to be visiting the palace at the time of Matilda's overthrow, two monks, a silk merchant, a contortionist from the East, and a solitary knight called Jerome.

Gislebert studied the knight carefully, trying to understand why this man had not been executed with the others of Stephen's force. He put the question to Jonas one night as they sat on a rough bench and ate their daily meal of bread and gruel. "Why is this knight Jerome still among us?" Gislebert whispered, studying the man as he chewed his ration of dark brown bread. "If Matilda is sworn to rid the land of Stephen's knights, why does this man still live?"

Jonas shrugged, but his dark eyes went momentarily to Jerome's swarthy face. "Do we know he is one of Stephen's knights? He wears a blue surcoat, not the colors of the king."

"Others were killed simply because they did not wear Matilda's red," Gislebert countered. The noble Lord Chapman cast a disapproving glance at Gislebert, and the troubadour lowered his voice. "Why was this knight spared? Could he be among the Knights Templar or some other holy order?"

"Perhaps he was spared for his good looks alone," Jonas quipped, giving a lopsided grin. Gislebert stared at the boy, and Jonas squinted in amusement. "Think, Troubadour, about any woman other than your Nadine," he said, leaning close to whisper in Gislebert's ear. "The Empress Matilda is a woman, after all, and this man Jerome is more handsome than most. Or did you not observe the way the women servants twittered and sighed when he walked by?"

"I did not notice," Gislebert grumbled, turning his attention back to his gruel. But he *had* noticed, and he grudgingly admitted that Jerome would fit any maid's definition of handsome. With his chiseled features and muscular body, Jerome had caused a stir among the maids before they were removed from the lower chamber prison. *Which of his features made feminine hearts flutter?* Gislebert wondered. Was it his dark eyes, or the thick, brown hair tied loosely at the nape of his neck? Perhaps his appeal lay in the air of insolence that surrounded him, a devil-may-care attitude that set him apart from the other frightened prisoners. . . .

Jerome sat alone on a stool in a darkened corner of the large room, and Gislebert felt his face flush with color when the knight looked up and caught his gaze. "Talk, Troubadour, and tell me why you find my face so interesting," the knight demanded in a dark, liquid voice that hinted at restrained power and contained the tiniest trace of a French accent. The quiet sounds of men at dinner ceased, and all in the room waited for Gislebert's answer.

"It is nothing," Gislebert answered, looking quickly away. His stomach churned nervously in the silence, and for a moment he thought he would be sick. The mere presence of the sullen knight elicited nervous flutterings from the troubadour's chest.

"I won't hurt you, if that's what you fear, little man," Jerome continued, smiling with cruel confidence. "Though I could snap you in two and devour you for breakfast, that would do nothing to further my release from Matilda's prison, would it?"

Gislebert could find no words to reply, and he stirred his bowl as if he hadn't heard. Fortunately, the grinning Chinese contortionist distracted the knight by scurrying over. "You strong man, no?" he asked, bowing rapidly to Jerome. "You fight for me, maybe, if my head goes chop chop?"

"I fight for no one," Jerome answered lazily. He rose from his place and walked wordlessly over to one of the monks. The monk slowly raised his head, and Jerome answered the question on the man's round face with two words: "I'm hungry." Without protest, the monk handed over his chunk of rough bread, and Jerome walked back to his stool, ripping the bread with his teeth as he passed by Gislebert and Jonas.

Gislebert counted seven days that he and Jonas had awakened in the tower's lower chamber, and every day had been much the same. Morning found them stiff, sore, and exhausted from shivering on the damp stone floor. Gislebert's flesh, which had never been plentiful, sagged loosely from his bones, and his knees and shoulders developed bruises from his restless tossing and turning on the hard floor.

All the prisoners rose with the sun, but each one waited his turn to drink from a dipper in the bucket of water that stood near the wooden door, then journeyed to the dark corner of the room where hay had been strewn to serve as a lavatory. The intensely offensive smell of that place threatened to make Gislebert ill, but every morning he took his turn there, holding his breath and praying that Calhoun would somehow hear of his plight and intervene for him.

After all had made their solitary trips to the lavatory, they took their accustomed places in the large room and began another day of waiting upon Matilda's favor. The monks passed their time in prayer. The Chinese contortionist spent hours stretching himself into bizarre positions and exhibited a most uncivilized fondness for wearing as few garments as possible. Lord Chapman wearied himself and his cellmates by complaining about the hardships that had been thrust upon him, and the silk merchant fretted constantly about his shop in London—he was certain Matilda's men had sacked or burned it. The knight Jerome brooded in his corner and often appeared to sleep.

Jonas never complained but sat silently near Gislebert, his eyes wide and his cloak drawn protectively around him even in the heat of the afternoon. The boy's sharp tongue grew still and quiet, particularly when Jerome was near, and Gislebert became increasingly aware that the boy had come to depend upon him. Jonas would not fetch his dinner unless Gislebert preceded him. He would not lie down to rest unless Gislebert made his bed nearby. Why, Gislebert wondered, had prison reduced a cocky, worldly wise urchin to simple dependence?

Gislebert and his companions were held in the lower chamber's first storage room, a large room that had formerly been used as a place of lodging for Stephen's knights and their squires. Beyond them lay a second, smaller chamber where five of Stephen's prisoners languished in chains. Glancing through their open doorway one day as a guard brought their daily gruel, Gislebert shuddered at the sight of them. Shackled by heavy chains fastened to the wall, they were a wide-eyed, dirty lot whose spirits appeared as weak as their flesh. Gislebert wondered how they survived. *May God help us if that is to be our eventual fate,* Gislebert thought. *Surely it is better to die a quick death than die little by little here in confinement.*

Suddenly he understood, with pulse-pounding clarity, why simple freedom was so important to Jonas. The boy was not sophisticated or skilled enough to verbalize the concept fully, but Gislebert recognized that somehow Jonas instinctively knew that with slavery—and its acceptance— came defeat and death. Only in freedom could one truly live.

Gislebert treated Jonas more carefully after that realization, quite certain that the boy's fierce spirit had led him to run away from a demanding lord. What could the boy be but a villein and therefore bound to the land and whoever owned it? But Jonas, unlike thousands of others born into the peasant class, had rebelled against such slavery and exchanged a life of servitude for one of considerable danger and risk. Gislebert reasoned that Jonas's unusual fear of Jerome stemmed from the harsh cruelty of knights employed to keep villeins under the lord's strong hand, so the troubadour resolved to protect the boy as best he could.

It would not be easy, for every fragment of the troubadour's being longed to leave the prison and fly to France, where Nadine waited. How distracting was this boy's claim upon his affections! Yet he had sworn faithfulness and friendship, and something akin to brotherly love stirred in the troubadour's breast as he watched the young boy sleep in his favorite corner near the high window. A narrow shaft of sunlight shone on Jonas's face, and Gislebert marveled at the purity of the boy's delicate features. What would that face look like after months of imprisonment? If the boy's spirit had been so dulled in only a week, what would become of him in a year's time?

For Jonas's health and Gislebert's sanity, they would have to escape or be released soon. Day after day Gislebert searched for a plan to win their freedom, but all seemed hopeless. Of course, he could step to the door and create a row to gain attention, but Matilda's attention could be more dangerous than Matilda's neglect. What would become of them when the empress had time enough on her hands to sift through the relics left behind by Stephen? What would she do with a troubadour who lived only for the love of faraway Nadine? Would her woman's heart excuse his love and free him, or would her battle-hardened mettle condemn him as a fool and send him to his grave?

Gislebert unfolded his lanky frame and crept on his hands and knees toward the round-faced monk. The man's eyes were closed, either in light sleep or prayer, and as Gislebert knelt beside him, he saw that stubbled growth was already beginning to fill in the tonsured spot on the top of the holy man's head.

"Father," Gislebert whispered, so that Jonas would not awaken, "does God care what ordinary men do? If we ask him for help in this hour of need, will he hear and answer? Or does he reserve his ears and attention for kings and holy men alone? I have been praying, Father, with all my energy, and it seems that my prayers go no farther Godward than the wooden beams above us."

The monk opened his eyes and nodded thoughtfully. He did not look at Gislebert but pressed his fingertips together as if praying. "It is a good question, my friend, and one that can best be answered by another question: Does God hear and care when a sparrow falls to the ground? The Holy Scriptures tell us that he does, so I cannot doubt that he hears the call of every single man."

"And woman, too?" Gislebert asked, thinking of Nadine. "If a woman is lonely for love and asks God to reveal the way of honorable and true love to her, will God answer?"

The monk smiled. "Though woman is less than man and the instrument of man's downfall, still, surely she is of more worth than a sparrow. Yes, my friend, I believe that God hears even the prayers of a woman."

"Good." Gislebert closed his eyes and leaned his head against the cold smoothness of stone behind him. *God,* he prayed silently, *hear this prayer, and mark it today. Wherever Nadine is, preserve her life for me, and preserve mine for her, until we meet and I can tell her of my love. I do not beg for my life, God, but for love. May I know it before I die, Most Holy God, and may I be worthy of its fullness.*

Almost as an afterthought, he added: *And may Jonas's life be preserved, as well. May he prosper and find a love as fulfilling and noble as the love I bear Nadine.*

A sag-bellied rat skittered across his arm, but Jerome made no movement to swat it away. Pretending to sleep had certain advantages, for while others thought him asleep they had divulged aspects of themselves that were most interesting. His sharp ears had heard, for instance, of the deal between Lord Chapman and the silk merchant. His eyes had seen the rotund monk stash more than his share of food in his sleeves when he thought no one else was looking.

Jerome knew that the skinny troubadour pined for the love of some faraway woman, and that the pale boy called Jonas often cried aloud in his sleep. Jerome heard the older priest receive the midnight confession of the silk merchant, who was having an affair with a woman not his wife, and he saw the Chinese contortionist quietly draw long pins from his tunic and stick them into his flesh.

Jerome knew all their secrets, yet there remained one mystery no one had addressed. Days before Matilda had arrived and ordered them all into this chamber, his brother,

Jean de Honfleur, had vanished from the grounds of King Stephen's tower. Except for Stephen's absent knights, every man who had been in the tower had been herded immediately into this chamber, and Jerome thought the chances were good that someone in this company knew something of his missing brother.

He and Jean had journeyed from France together to meet with Stephen and had arrived at the tower only hours before his elder brother disappeared. Jean was excited about the possibility of meeting with Stephen and winning the king's promise to go to war against Louis, the weak, young king who cared more for building churches than maintaining his army.

They were to meet with the king after dinner, and Jean had laughingly remarked that he had time to find a wench— or two—before meeting the king. "When my appetites have been satisfied," he had said, pulling on his cloak and winking mischievously at Jerome, "I will be a better and stronger man to face Stephen. Then we shall wage war, my brother, and win back those lands which were lost by our father's stupidity."

"Go easy on these English wenches," Jerome had warned him. "They are not so eager to please as our own French women."

"They will be eager for me," Jean had prophesied, pulling his cloak over his head. "I will be back in an hour."

The hour came and went, and Jerome had walked over every inch of the tower property, searching in vain for a sign of Jean. The king's guards had been alerted and a search conducted, but nothing was ever found.

Jerome rolled over on the hard stone floor of the lower chamber and clenched his fist in silent frustration. Jean was surely lost, but Jean had always been too pragmatic and direct. Now Jerome stood alone to face the world and balance the scales that had tilted against him. If he was to regain the lands and power that were his birthright, he would have to do it alone—and by more subtle strategies.

ELEVEN

They passed a month in prison, but still Matilda had no time for Gislebert and Jonas. Lord Chapman and the silk merchant were released after paying handsomely for their freedom. The two monks were returned to their abbey, but still the contortionist, Jerome, Gislebert, and Jonas languished in the basement of the Tower of London. As the months passed, summer faded into autumn, and the chilly dampness made the prisoners' teeth chatter until their bodies were limp with exhaustion. But Matilda's priorities apparently did not include dealing with penniless prisoners.

The daily news came from Laudine and other maids, who brought food to the prisoners in late afternoon. Gislebert found Laudine's visit the one bright spot in the day, for she was not only pleasant and comforting, but a very pretty woman. And, he noticed uncomfortably, he was not alone in appreciating her sunny beauty. Whenever the women approached, Jerome left his darkened corner and stepped forward, eliciting, Gislebert noted wryly, a definite flutter among the maids. But Laudine brushed off the knight's attentions, reserving her concern for Gislebert and Jonas.

No tidbit of gossip was too small. One afternoon Laudine reported that a contingent of notable men had come to see Matilda, including the king of Scotland, the bishop of Winchester, and Matilda's brother, Richard, the earl of Gloucester. "They came in respectfully, and all bowed before her on bended knee," Laudine told Gislebert, her blue eyes wide.

"And just when they opened their mouths to speak, the empress stood and ordered them to leave. Even now, I hear she's preparing an attack on the castle of the bishop of Winchester."

"She is nothing like the gentle Stephen," Jonas remarked softly. "Can it be true that they are related?"

"She is a frightful witch," Laudine whispered, "and she'll have my head if it's told that I've said so. The Londoners, who were tired of Stephen and stood ready to give her a chance, would now run her out of England if they could. She is nothing but sharp and—" Laudine searched for the right phrase. "—a trollop in men's armor."

"She is a woman scorned," Gislebert said softly. "Stephen pledged his allegiance to her while Henry lived, then took her father's throne without hesitation."

"That's no excuse for her mannish and demanding manner," Laudine answered, raising her pert nose higher into the air. She gathered her dishes and paused at the door, swiveling her eyes toward Jonas. "A woman doesn't have to behave like a man to be loved."

The next day the basement prisoners rose eagerly when keys jingled at the lock, then stepped back in surprise as four knights in armor pushed their way into the room, followed by the Empress Matilda. She had chosen to dress in a long red fur-trimmed tunic instead of armor, but still her air and appearance were daunting. Instinctively all four prisoners bowed before her. Watching warily from under his hooded cap, Gislebert saw her eyes sweep the room in disdain, and her nostrils flared at the foul smell.

"Look up," she snapped, stamping her foot upon the stone floor. "I would see your faces."

One of the guards by her side put out a hand to jerk Gislebert's chin upward, but Matilda abruptly slapped the knight's shoulder with a rolled-up parchment. "It is enough," she said, looking at Gislebert's face with interest. She unrolled the parchment in her hand and studied it curiously. "It is a remarkable likeness," she said at last.

Her gown rustled stiffly as she moved to stand before Gislebert. "Who are you, and what is your position?" she demanded, her tones clipped and curt. "Speak, man, or I'll have your tongue cut out."

"I am Gislebert and a troubadour," he answered quickly, embarrassed that he seemed to lack the strength to look this woman in the eye. He blinked, fighting the jitters that rose in his stomach. He had never encountered a woman as fearsome as this. What if he fainted?

"Gislebert, I am holding a portrait with your likeness," the empress said, unfurling the parchment before his eyes. "Do you recognize it? Who is the artist?"

Gislebert frowned. The work was obviously Jonas's, but when had the boy sketched him? The portrait was not as rough or crude as the lad's other work but finely detailed, carefully done, and for an instant Gislebert felt as though he were looking into a magic mirror that forgave physical imperfections and shortcomings.

Matilda tapped her foot impatiently as he pondered whether or not to speak, then he heard Jonas's gentle voice from behind him: "I am the artist, Your Highness."

Matilda cocked her head, the rich auburn of her hair gleaming in the slanted sunlight from a window. She moved toward Jonas, and Gislebert could hear a grudging respect in her words: "You do fine work. What is your name, and how came you to be in Stephen's castle?"

If the boy was nervous, he did not show it. "I am Jonas, companion and friend of Gislebert the troubadour. We came to London only to ask a boon of the king and were preparing to go when—"

"When we liberated this castle," Matilda finished the sentence for him. She studied Jonas closely. "How old are you— Jonas, is it?"

"Sixteen, I think, Your Highness."

Matilda looked once again at the parchment, then at Gislebert. She nodded quickly to the guard at her right hand. "Bring the young one, clean him up, and have him in my chamber in an hour. Him—" She pointed to the contortionist, who bobbed in an unending bow before her. "Execute him immediately. I have no use for foolish entertainments, and he is likely a spy. Him—" She pointed at Jerome. "I will interview upstairs. And him—" She pointed at Gislebert, and he felt his heart stop beating for an instant. "He may remain here, as long as the boy Jonas is engaged. See to it."

The guards saluted her, and Matilda swept from the room, bellowing for her knights to hurry. One knight jerked Jonas to his feet and pushed him out the door in Matilda's wake, while wails and screeching from the Chinese contortionist filled the air until another knight's sword cut off his breath and dispatched the man to heaven or hell. Jerome cast a contemptuous glance at the knight who came for him but walked willingly out of the chamber before the knight's drawn sword. For the first time in more than a month, Gislebert found himself alone.

He sank to his knees as the heavy wooden door slammed shut and the key turned in the lock. "Oh God," he whispered, "what has this day brought?" Covering his head with his hands, he lowered his forehead to the floor, overcome with hopelessness and despair. Untried and naive Jonas, the troubadour's closest friend, now stood alone in what had to be the most dangerous and unstable court in the world. And he, Gislebert, remained miles away from where his hopes and dreams lay.

Adele felt a whisper of terror run through her as two stout female servants took charge of her and escorted her to an upstairs lavatory with a tall, wooden bathtub. As Adele clung desperately to her filthy cloak and tattered tunic, she heard the familiar voice of Laudine from the doorway: "Quick, good friends, to the kitchens! The empress sends me to take care of this lad, and you are needed below. The cook has prepared too much berry pie!"

The two servants left without protest, and Adele nearly

collapsed in relief as Laudine took charge and turned the cock so that water poured into the tall tub. "There's a stepping stool behind the tub, and ye must climb down inside," the maid instructed, smiling quietly at the astonished look on Adele's face. "It's only water, girl, and it won't hurt you."

"I must climb inside?" Adele questioned, not sure she had heard correctly.

"That's right; take off those filthy things and get inside," Laudine repeated. "And be quick about it. We must scrub your face and hands and comb your hair. I have time to cut it, if you are still intent on masquerading as a boy."

Adele hesitated, then moved toward the step stool. "Cut it, then," she said, ripping the old filthy tunic from her body. She shuddered as she tossed the foul garment aside and looked at her skin, mottled from dirt and a creeping rash.

"You must wash first," Laudine said, placing a wet cloth on the edge of the tall tub. She cast an appraising glance over Adele. "If any girl was ever able to pass for a boy, you're the one," she said simply, shaking out a new tunic. "What are you going to do when you develop? When you come into the way of women and begin to bleed?"

Adele grimaced as the cold water hit her body but took only a moment to hug herself before reaching for the wet cloth. "I don't know what I'm going to do," she answered, scrubbing her skin until it turned pink. "Sometimes I forget that I am a woman. God has stalled my womanhood thus far. Perhaps he has taken it from me."

"I don't think that is possible," Laudine answered, a wry smile on her face. "As the sun rises and sets according to God's design, so you will begin to bleed, and you will develop a woman's body and a woman's desires. And I'd be so bold as to say you will either marry that troubadour or take your leave of him."

"No!" Adele's hand came sharply down on the wooden edge of the tub, and Laudine jumped at the unexpected force of the blow. "Things are perfectly fine the way they are," Adele muttered through clenched teeth. "Now, have you a clean garment for me? And a blade for cutting my hair?"

"I have better than that," Laudine answered, pulling a pair of scissors from her apron pocket. She crossed her arms and waited patiently as Adele climbed out of the tub.

An hour later Adele stood clean and freshly shorn before the Empress Matilda in Stephen's tapestried chamber. "Jonas, companion of a troubadour and artist extraordinaire," Matilda said, extending her hand but not rising from her chair. "Come forward and kneel before me."

Adele stepped forward three steps and knelt on the hard wooden floor. "Now, Jonas, while you kneel before me, swear that you will render to me service greater than that you gave to Stephen of Blois."

Adele stammered. "I-I gave no service to Stephen."

"Good." The empress waved her hand. "We will not trouble with vows of loyalty, for you are but a child, no matter how talented. What I want from you, Jonas, is a portrait. I have defeated and captured my enemy and move soon to conquer the last pockets of resistance in the country. I want my likeness to remain behind in this tower, a portrait suitable for the ages."

Matilda gave Adele a fixed and meaningless smile, and Adele tried to repress a shudder. Something cold lay behind the empress's eyes, a bitterness that shone through the woman's attempt at graciousness.

"You will begin now, and let my servants know what you need," Matilda said simply. "Do not fail to please me, Jonas."

"You are French, are you not?" Matilda asked, her steely eyes burning into Jerome's. The setting sun threw long shadows across the dimly lit private chamber where a table, a bed, and a chair awaited the empress's use. Except for a maid and two knights, he was quite alone with the empress. "Answer me, monsieur, for I have no patience with fools."

"I am," he answered, meeting her fierce gaze with his own. He threw back his head and raked her with a fiercely possessive look, knowing that she would order him killed if his glance displeased her. But there was something in her look and posture . . .

A little smile played around the corners of her mouth, and Jerome knew he had won. He could almost feel her thoughts, her desire for a man who appreciated her, one who would not bow and scrape before her merciless demands. "What am I to do with you?" she asked coyly.

"I could be of much use," he said, arching a bushy brow. "I could tell you much about your prisoners and your knights, for I am most observant."

"I can tell you are." She snapped her fingers and gestured for the guards and maid to leave the room. When they had gone, she stepped forward and stood eye-to-eye with her prisoner.

"What is it you desire of me, Queen Matilda?" he asked, his voice heavy and hoarse.

Her head snapped back, her eyes glinting in displeasure. "Don't call me that. I am not that despised queen. I am *Matildis Imperatrix Henrici Regis filia et Anglorum Domina.*"

Matilda, empress, daughter of King Henry, and Lady of the English . . .

He could have kicked himself. What a fool! He forced a rueful smile to his face and hung his head like a scolded puppy. "I beg your forgiveness, my empress. For a moment I thought of the other Matilda, realizing the irony that Stephen faces two Matildas—one who loved and married him, the other, who will surely best him and reclaim her rightful throne."

"And of the two, which do you love?"

He raised his eyes to hers again and met her fierce gaze without flinching. "The mightier Matilda, my empress."

Her eyes relented. "What have you to tell me, monsieur?" she asked. "Speak freely, and perhaps I can arrange for an hour or two of freedom for you."

"You could take the bonds from my hands, but I will never be free as long as you are in the room," he whispered caressingly.

"What news have you?"

"One of your servants," he whispered, "one who took your vow of loyalty, openly calls you a witch. Though I do not doubt her word, for you have bewitched me in the space of a heartbeat."

"The servant's name?" the empress whispered, her face coming nearer.

"Laudine," he answered, closing his eyes as her lips met his.

She could have drawn a hundred portraits of the empress without ever visiting her chamber again, so indelibly had that haughty image been impressed upon her brain. But Adele began and did not finish a score of sketches so that she would be called for again. Perhaps, she hoped, she could overhear or impart some information that would result in gaining their freedom. Even if she did not, as Matilda's artist, she was granted favors.

Her arms were loaded with blankets when she returned to their basement cell. How grateful the troubadour would be! It had been so long since he had smiled. It would be wonderful to bring him joy, even in this small gesture. And although she sorrowed for the contortionist who had unfairly lost his life, she found hope in the thought that she and the troubadour would once again be alone and free to share their thoughts.

But Gislebert was not alone when she returned. Jerome had also been restored to their prison. And he, too, had returned with a token from the upstairs chambers. On the floor between Gislebert and Jerome lay a wooden cask, which he and Gislebert had apparently drained.

The guard locked the door behind her, and Gislebert staggered to his feet as she approached. "You ought to try this, Jonas, you really ought to," Gislebert babbled, staggering toward her with a gourd as she threw the precious blankets on the floor. "This ale warms the toes and even the nose."

He laughed, delighted with his own pitiful rhyme, and

Adele looked up at him with contempt. How had Jerome and Gislebert become drinking companions?

She glanced toward the knight, whose eyes were smug and sated as he sipped from the wooden gourd in his hand. His hair shone black in the fading light, and something in his attitude disturbed her. A warning bell rang in her memory.

"Gislebert," she said, turning purposefully from Jerome. She took the troubadour's arm and pushed on his shoulder until he sat upon the floor. "You're drunk."

"Not really," Gislebert answered in a carelessly drunken reply. He grinned up at her with reddened eyes. "Not on ale, anyway. If I'm drunk on anything, I'm drunk on love. I've been telling Jerome"—he hiccupped—"about my beautiful Nadine."

"The beautiful *heiress* Nadine," Jerome corrected, pausing to gulp noisily from his gourd. He smacked his lips. "The rich and beautiful Nadine."

"Thatisher." Gislebert slurred his words together. "And soon I'm going to leave here and find my love, and we'll be happy together. I've never known my father, you know, nor my mother—never had a sister, or a brother—"

Gislebert tilted his head back and sang, his voice echoing among the rafters of the beamed roof: "Though such great torments I have known, through you alone, I'd rather die for your harsh sake, than from another pleasure take."

"Bravo!" Jerome lifted his gourd and drank. Adele turned aside and pulled a blanket from the pile on the floor. As she unfolded it to make her bed, she silently heaped epithets upon the troubadour's name. *Let him spend the night in drunken regard of his Nadine,* she thought, jerking the blanket over the floor to a space far from the troubadour. *If Matilda orders him killed tomorrow, life will be much simpler.*

The red-eyed maid who came to fetch Adele the next morning wept into her apron when Adele asked for Laudine. "She's dead," the girl whispered, pausing to blow her nose.

"Don't ask me why, but the empress asked specifically for Laudine last night, then had her killed. Her body's hanging outside from the gallows."

Adele's heart went into sudden shock. Laudine executed? Why? The maid read the question on Adele's face and shook her head in reply. "We don't understand what happened. Someone said the empress accused Laudine of calling her a witch, but how did Her Highness hear that? Laudine would never say such a thing to the empress."

Adele glanced quickly at the sleeping forms of Gislebert and Jerome. Laudine had spoken freely with them about Matilda and had used the very word *witch* to describe the empress. But surely neither Gislebert nor Jerome would speak ill of the maid. Adele shivered and drew her cloak more closely about her as she stepped into the hall and allowed the maid to lock the door behind her. Whatever happened in this castle, one thing was certain—Matilda had eyes and ears in all corners.

Adele had hoped to gain the trust of the empress and win freedom for herself and Gislebert, but her hopes vanished one afternoon when Matilda called for her sergeants and abruptly ordered "Jonas" back to the basement. "She is planning something too important for the ears of a mere artist," Adele told Gislebert upon her return. "Something is definitely afoot in the castle, but I don't know what it is."

"Matilda hopes to strengthen her position," Jerome called from across the room, his powerful voice startling both Adele and Gislebert. Usually he remained aloof from their conversations, and apart from the evening when he had plied Gislebert with ale, he had never expressed interest in their affairs. His sudden entrance into their discussion was unusual.

"You are obviously a military man," Gislebert said, bowing respectfully to Jerome. "What say you of the situation? We know so little, cut off as we are."

"We are not cut off. We are at the center of the world, Troubadour," Jerome answered, his glance clearly revealing his contempt for one who thought so little of Matilda's tower. "The empress has conquered London, and now she will move to conquer the castle that resists at Winchester. The empress controls England, Anjou, and soon will solidify her kingdom into one great whole."

"You speak very well of one who holds you prisoner," Adele muttered.

Gislebert paid no attention to her comment. "Surely Matilda rides for Winchester soon," Gislebert whispered, turning to Adele. He lowered his voice. "She will leave the castle—do you understand, Jonas? It may be that we can find a chance to escape!"

"I wouldn't make any plans," Jerome interrupted, obviously overhearing Gislebert's frantic whisper. Disdain and contempt shone from his eyes as he glanced at them. "Empress Matilda of Anjou should not be underestimated."

"And how would you know so much about her?" Adele countered, but Jerome only smiled in reply and drew his cloak about him.

A pair of knights removed Jerome from their chamber the next day, and when the sun set without the knight's return, Gislebert's suspicions were confirmed. "Jerome is the lowest sort of scoundrel, and we did wrong to ever honor him with the name 'knight,'" he remarked, staring absently at the ceiling as he lay in the dark.

"What?" Jonas asked, his voice heavy with fatigue.

"Jerome is without loyalty and without honor," Gislebert went on. "A mere mercenary. The people of London complained when Stephen hired Flemish mercenaries to fight his battles, but Matilda has obviously resorted to the same practice."

"A mercenary?" Jonas's cloak rustled as the boy sat up. "What's a mercenary?"

"A hired warrior," Gislebert replied, bitterness spilling into his voice. "A man who is skilled with the sword, the axe, and the lance but who assumes his role without pledging his life and honor in service as the code of chivalry demands. Such a man is dangerous, for he bears loyalty only to himself."

Jonas did not reply for a moment, then the boy spoke again in the darkness: "You think Jerome has sold himself to Matilda?"

"I'm sure of it," Gislebert answered. "Matilda needs men now for the siege of the castle at Winchester. Unless I am sorely mistaken, Jerome will ride tomorrow with Matilda's forces."

"So with his service, he earns his freedom?" Jonas asked, sleep still heavy in his voice.

"Aye," Gislebert answered. "And it is not the first time he has offered his service for the empress. She would not trust him unless he had first proved himself."

"How could he do that?" Jonas's voice seemed closer now, and Gislebert knew the boy had turned to face him in the dark. "He's been imprisoned, just like us, for all these many days."

"He was taken out on one occasion," Gislebert answered. "After hearing our conversations with Laudine. I fear he bought the favor of the empress with the blood of that pretty maid."

Jonas gasped. "Laudine?" he asked, his voice squeaking girlishly, as it always did when he was frightened.

"We should thank God that he did not destroy us as well, my little friend," Gislebert added. "For he was here as a spy, of that I am convinced. Be glad that we are rid of him."

"But, Troubadour, you cannot *prove* these things! Surely you could be wrong. It could all be a horrible coincidence."

"True," Gislebert admitted. "But I have seen more of court politics than you, young friend. Why are you so upset? You have never liked Jerome."

"No. He reminded me of something—and he frightened me."

Gislebert sighed in the darkness. "Well, he's gone now.

Say your prayers, Jonas, and put Jerome from your mind. If God has not forgotten us, we shall need him in the days ahead."

When Matilda and her army rode for Winchester the next day, as Gislebert had predicted, she left only a handful of knights to secure the Tower of London. Save for those knights, all who remained at the tower sighed in relief.

The empress and her knights had scarcely been gone an hour when Gislebert and Jonas heard the babble of excited voices in the courtyard. The sun had not yet risen overhead when a breathless maid brought them news. Stephen's wife, Queen Matilda of England, rode in the country outside London raising a force of knights still loyal to the king. There were reports that the queen planned to besiege the besiegers of Winchester.

"The battle of the Matildas," Gislebert crowed, clapping his hands in delight when the maid had gone. "Oh, may God send me sweet inspiration! What a song this will make!"

"The song will be good only if it ends in our freedom," Jonas groused, sitting on the floor with his back against the sturdy wall of their prison. "Will Stephen's queen send troops to liberate the tower?"

"We are of minor importance," Gislebert answered, waving Jonas's concern aside. "The future of our nation will be decided in this time, young friend."

"And we will see nothing of it," Jonas grumbled, lowering his head in his hands.

Gislebert paused. Sitting thus, with his head resting on his slender hands, Jonas looked very frail and very thin. Gislebert frowned. Had these days of imprisonment made the boy ill?

"Perhaps we should think of plotting an escape," Gislebert said, revising his opinion. "No matter which Matilda returns to claim power, there will be confusion at the tower in the days to come."

"I hope so," Jonas mumbled. "I am sick to death of this place."

The words brought a chill to Gislebert's heart.

The battle raged for days, and every afternoon when the maid brought their meal, she lowered her voice beyond the guard's hearing and relayed the latest news from Winchester. The Empress Matilda's force was strong, she reported. And the bishop of Winchester had stood in danger of losing his castle, but a runner had escaped with a plea for help. Queen Matilda's force, composed mainly of faithful Londoners, numbered a thousand strong and now held the empress's army trapped between the front lines and the castle walls of Winchester.

"The occupiers of the castle flung out firebrands, burning down the greater part of the surrounding village," the maid told them, rattling off her message as quickly as she could. "Two abbeys are gone, but the monks praise God for their sacrifice. Still, the townspeople are suffering. Stephen's forces guard the roads, so the townspeople are wanting for provisions. Many are starving. They do not know how much longer they can hold out."

A week later the maid returned with brighter news. "Empress Matilda's brother, the earl of Gloucester, thought to distract Stephen's army by fortifying the Abbey of Wherwell, six miles from Winchester," she said, keeping her voice low. "But King Stephen's army, led by Queen Matilda herself, attacked vigorously on every side and compelled the earl's men to take refuge in the church."

"How dreadful," Jonas whispered. "Fighting in a church?"

The maid nodded. "They say it was indeed a dreadful and wretched sight, savage armed men raging about in a house of prayer. The virgin nuns had to leave their cloisters as the roofs burned around their heads."

"But the outcome," Gislebert pressed. "Has the final outcome been determined?"

"The Empress Matilda's army was routed," she whispered. "The earl of Gloucester was himself taken captive by Queen Matilda, and it is said he will be exchanged for Stephen's liberty. The empress, though, escaped with a handful of men still loyal to her."

"So what happens now?" Jonas asked, his eyes wary. "Who holds this tower? Whose prisoners are we?"

"A handful of knights, like this brute behind me, still hold this tower." The maid jerked her head toward the red-and-white clothed knight who loitered in the doorway. "But if Stephen is crowned again, the king will be coming here shortly, and you can wager there won't be a red-and-white surcoat within twenty miles of this place."

Gislebert sighed with satisfaction as he took his bowl of gruel from her tray. "It is nearly over, young friend," he said, looking down at Jonas. "Soon we'll be on our way to France, and the fresh air will do you good, I think. You have grown thin in our time here, and I'd wager a girl in any country village could outwrestle you."

Jonas looked at him sharply, frowning, and Gislebert made a mental note not to tease his young charge again.

TWELVE

As the sun struggled to rise three days later, a cloud of dust rose from the courtyard and filtered into the basement window where Gislebert and Jonas were imprisoned. Gislebert saw the unusual dusty haze, heard the commotion, and ran to the window, climbing on top of a bale of hay to see which army stirred in the courtyard beyond.

A few moments later, one of the maids turned the key in the lock and shoved the door open with a powerful push. "Freedom!" she cried, tossing the keys into the room. "The crown was restored to Stephen yesterday at Canterbury. Empress Matilda's knights have left the tower, and all political prisoners are free!"

Jonas sat up and rubbed the sleep from his eyes. "What?" he asked, squinting in the unexpected burst of light from the open door. "Did you say *free?*"

"We're free! Praise be to God, we are free!" Gislebert echoed, turning to him. He was startled to feel tears welling up in his eyes, and on an impulse he rushed to Jonas and embraced the boy. Jonas stiffened and threw his own arms up protectively in front of his chest, but he did not seem to be angry when Gislebert released him.

"What are we doing here, then?" Jonas asked, rising to his feet. He brushed dirt from his cloak and tunic. "Let's leave this place! But first—" He turned to the maid. "Is there any chance we might find fresh clothing? Mine is not so bad, but the troubadour stinks."

The girl laughed merrily, tossing her head back, and curt-seyed to them in an extravagant gesture. "But of course," she said, opening her arms and pointing toward the hall that led to freedom. "Just come upstairs, and you'll have a bath, fresh clothing, and whatever you need."

"I don't know about the bath," Jonas said, suddenly pulling back. "I had one a few weeks ago. But the troubadour—"

"I know, I stink," Gislebert said, leading the way out of the room. "A bath would please me, fair maiden, and so would a new tunic. You see, I have an appointment with my destiny in France, and I really must be on my way."

"Let's away, *today,* Troubadour," Adele insisted, watching Gislebert twirl for the tenth time in his new tunic and cloak. The deep burgundy of the cloak complemented the troubadour's auburn hair, and Adele thought Gislebert was enjoying the maid's attention entirely too much.

"Let's pause a moment," Gislebert said, holding up a finger. "If you will recall, Jonas, we were only three days away from our journey into France when the king left to fight Empress Matilda's forces in the south. Do you not remember that Stephen had promised us horses, gifts, and finer clothes than these? If we pause and wait here yet a while, mayhap Stephen will remember his promise."

Gislebert winked at Adele and twirled his index finger in the air. "How would you prefer to travel to St. Denis? On foot, like a mere villein, or on a fine horse, loaded with presents?"

"I care nothing for horses or presents," Adele grumbled, certain that the troubadour had lost his sanity. "I want to be *away* from this place. Freedom! Don't you know what that means? If we stay here, we are exchanging the empress for a king. We will not be free."

Gislebert ignored Adele, studying instead the buckles on his new shoes.

"Think of it this way, Troubadour," Adele argued, moving closer to Gislebert. "You have waited years to find your Nadine. How can you stand to wait even a single day more?"

"I will love her more tomorrow than yesterday," Gislebert answered, smoothing the new stockings that covered his scrawny legs. "And the longer we tarry, the greater love I will have to offer her."

"You have lost your mind," Adele shouted, throwing her hands into the air in exasperation.

Gislebert suddenly grew serious and caught Adele's hand. "No, I have not," he whispered intensely, his breath hot in her face. "I understand, my naive friend, more than you think I do. I know the world and the ways of it, and I know His Highness the king. He is an insecure man, fawned upon by many and liked by few. He counts me among his friends, and if I leave without assuring him of my fealty and accepting his regard, I place my soul—*our* very lives—in danger. Try to understand."

Adele wrested her hand from Gislebert's grasp but did not argue. No, she did not understand politics or why they had to remain in London. Every fiber of her being wanted nothing more than to run far away from the city's confining walls and troubling dark waters.

Gislebert eventually compromised. Jonas insisted they leave the royal tower, which they did, but Gislebert was adamant that they remain in London until the king's arrival.

The king returned on a frosty day in early October, but the biting weather and threat of sleet did nothing to dampen the enthusiasm of the London crowd. Trumpeters heralded the king's return, and Jonas and Gislebert were among the tumultuous throng that welcomed the king back into the city. "London grew tired of Stephen in six years, but wearied of Empress Matilda in six weeks," one merchant joked. "All hail, the lesser of two evils!"

The king entered the city from the Tower Postern gate, and Gislebert and Jonas climbed a rickety ladder to the top of the old Roman wall to watch the procession. Battle-scarred knights, weary from the recent struggle, traveled first in the procession, and behind them followed pack horses richly bedecked with spoils of war: furs, jewels, gold and silver tankards, and relics taken from the ill-fated abbey at Wherwell. Behind the treasure rode the grim knights of Matilda's captive army, their red-and-white surcoats permanently stained with the blood and dirt of war. War wagons rumbled forth, carrying catapults and battering rams, and finally, on a white horse, rode Stephen of Blois, king of England.

The victorious king rode proudly, his thinning hair hidden by the regal crown on his head, but his beard shone with more silver than when Gislebert had last stood before him. As the king waved and nodded to the cheering populace, Jonas remarked that Stephen looked tired.

Gislebert was about to agree when a familiar face among the knights who rode behind the king caught his eye. "Look," Gislebert cried, grasping Jonas's arm. "There! Behind the king! Is that not Jerome?"

Jonas looked and nodded slowly as Jerome, now clad in a surcoat of Stephen's gold and white, turned impassive eyes upon them—and smiled. As Gislebert and Jonas watched in stunned horror, Jerome spurred his horse and broke from the line of knights until he rode by Stephen's side. Leaning toward the king, he said something so startling that Stephen reined in his horse and raised his hand for silence.

The crowd stilled. A wild wind hooted across the silent gathering, and the knights behind the king telegraphed questioning glances. Jerome clasped the wide rim of his saddle and leaned forward, his face a mask of expectation.

"It has come to our attention that men we once knew as friends have turned to our enemy," Stephen said, sadness ringing in his voice. "Sir Jerome, of late from valiant duty at Wherwell, can produce evidence of this treachery and treason. We denounce to you, friends and fellow men of London, and demand the lives of the troubadour called Gislebert, and the boy Jonas!"

With a sweep of his arm, Stephen pointed directly at Gislebert and Jonas, and a wave of despair swept over the troubadour. *This can't be happening,* he thought, certain that at any moment he would be shaken from a bad dream. What lies had Jerome told the king? And for what purpose?

"We must flee, Gislebert!" Jonas was shaking him, screeching in his ear. The eyes of the crowd turned to look up to the wall where they stood, but fortunately, the ladder they had used stood on the other side of the wall.

Jonas grabbed Gislebert's arm and pulled him toward the ladder. "Hurry, or they'll tear us apart!" Jonas cried, nearly pushing Gislebert off the wall. "Down the ladder, or we're dead!"

Gislebert shook himself free of his stupor and scrambled down the ladder as quickly as his thin legs would carry him.

They ran. Only the wall held the fervently patriotic crowd from tearing them apart, and as they ran, Adele stripped the rich burgundy cloak from Gislebert's shoulders and dropped it in the street, along with the soft blue cloak she wore. Though she felt half-dressed and uncomfortably exposed in only a tunic, she knew that all of London searched for a man and a boy, one in a burgundy cloak, and one in blue. Losing the cloaks was infinitely preferable to being identified as Stephen's traitors.

They finally paused from their flight behind a stable that stood on the river's edge. Adele shuddered as she glanced at the dark, choppy waters. An unpleasant memory beckoned, but she turned her back to the Thames and pushed the troubador into a pile of straw scattered along the stable's wall.

Dropping to the ground, Gislebert still wore a look of dumb stupefaction on his face. Adele grabbed his thin shoulders and shook him gently. "Troubadour, we are doomed if we remain here, do you understand?" she demanded, looking deep into his eyes. "Jerome has foiled us. You cannot go back to the tower; you *cannot* meet with the king. Stephen thinks you a traitor, and Jerome will be able to prove his point."

"How?" Gislebert's brown eyes were honestly confused. "What harm did we do? We were in *prison!*"

"I drew portraits of the empress," Adele explained carefully, as if to a dim-witted child, "portraits that still remain behind in the tower. Have men not been killed for less?"

Gislebert nodded slowly, and Adele blinked in disbelief as twin tears quivered on his lower lashes. "I have nothing now to offer my Nadine," he whispered. "No favor of the king, no presents, no fine horses, no—"

"You have your loving heart, remember?" When Gislebert did not answer, Adele sighed and sank into the straw next to him. His shoulder was cold upon hers, and she leaned closer to comfort him. "You always said that a loving and sincere heart was worth more than anything in the world," she reminded him gently. "Remember your song? 'Oh, what is longer than the way . . . ?'"

"'Or what is deeper than the sea?'" Gislebert echoed. "'Or what is louder than the horn, or what is sharper than a thorn? Or what is greener than the grass, or what is worse than Mother Eve was?'"

He did not continue, and Adele took a breath and softly sang, "'O love is longer than the way, and hell is deeper than the sea. And thunder is louder than the horn, and hunger is sharper than a thorn. And poison is greener than the grass, and the devil worse than Mother Eve was.'"

"Love is longer than the way, Troubadour," Adele said softly, feeling him turn slightly so that his head fell upon her shoulder. She let it rest there and gently ran her fingers through his hair. "We've felt hunger, you and I, and we've seen hell, and poison, and the devil himself in Jerome."

Gislebert did not answer, but she felt his head move in a gentle nod. "We shall overcome, you and I," she whispered softly, smelling the sweet perfume of his hair. "So sleep, Troubadour. Tomorrow we shall find love's way and walk in it."

The dim light of dawn surrounded them when Gislebert awoke in the hay. For a moment he could not remember where he was or what had brought him to such a place. But with one look at Jonas, the boy's tunic dirtied with mud from their frantic flight through the streets, the horrific memory came back with startling clarity. Jerome had poisoned King Stephen against them! But for what purpose? Gislebert could find none, for he had done the knight no wrong and had nothing Jerome could possibly wish to take.

He found himself blushing when he remembered his infantile need for comfort hours before. He had shown every weakness. He had wept in Jonas's embrace, and the young boy had actually comforted him. Had he really displayed such an abysmal and unmanly lack of strength?

He heard Jonas stir and made an effort to keep his eyes from the boy's face. "Last night should not be spoken of," he said, pretending to adjust his leggings. "I behaved most unseemly. A man should be—stronger than tears."

Jonas did not answer, and Gislebert finally glanced toward the boy. Did a tear glimmer on his cheek? Gislebert looked away in embarrassment until the lad had time to collect himself.

"What you say is true," Jonas finally muttered, his voice low and gruff. "We shall not speak of it again."

Gislebert scooted forward in the hay and looked at the landscape about them. "Well, what do we do?" he asked. "We cannot stay in London, and we probably should not remain in England."

"No," Jonas agreed. "We should be off."

"Stephen's men travel far and fast," Gislebert continued, thinking aloud. "As we go to France—"

"Do we dare go?" Jonas interrupted. "All who know you know that you seek Nadine in St. Denis."

"I must go; it is my destiny," Gislebert answered calmly. "Even if I am to die there, still I must go."

Jonas sighed but did not argue.

"As we go to France, perhaps we should disguise ourselves," Gislebert suggested. "New names, new professions.

Men do not know our faces, but we are known throughout the country as Gislebert and Jonas, troubadour and artist."

"What would you have us be?" Jonas asked, sliding forward until he sat by Gislebert's side. "I could be known as Jonas the pickpocket."

Gislebert shook his head and rumpled the boy's hair affectionately. "No. I will be Ahearn, a scribe and expert in horses," he said, gesturing grandly in the air. "I have learned a few things about horses. Perhaps I can take a temporary position with a nobleman journeying to France."

"And me?" Jonas asked, looking toward the horizon.

"You are an artist," Gislebert murmured. "Have you any other talents?"

Jonas shook his head, and Gislebert chewed his bottom lip thoughtfully. "I know one sure disguise," Jonas suggested shyly. "And I am willing to do it, though it involves great sacrifice on my part."

Gislebert lifted an eyebrow. "Truly?"

"Truly." Jonas sighed deeply. "I will be Adele, the wife of Ahearn, the scribe and expert in horses."

Gislebert sat speechless for a moment, then threw back his head and laughed until tears coursed down his face.

While he laughed, Jonas thrust his lower lip forward in a pout. "I don't see why it is so funny," he argued, kicking the ground with his foot. "I am the one making the sacrifice, after all."

"I am sorry," Gislebert said, clapping Jonas squarely on the back. "It is just that you are the last person I would have thought willing to dress as a woman. But you are right, young friend; it is a good disguise. Why shouldn't the artist Jonas become Adele? As for being my wife—"

"I told you once, if you touch me, I will kill you," Jonas said, raising his fists in mock defense.

Gislebert threw up his hands protectively. "Believe me, Jonas, a man in woman's clothing holds no attraction for me."

They crept out of the city along the eroding riverbank at low tide, then walked in darkness on the forest road to the hospice at Bromley. Before they approached the hospice, Gislebert bade Adele hide in the forest while he approached the building and begged for a few cast-off garments of women's clothing.

When he returned, Adele stepped behind a bush and cast her leggings and short tunic away. It felt strange to wear a woman's long tunic again. She had not worn a woman's garment in more than a year. Somehow, though, a woman's tunic felt right. Draping the rough woolen cloak about her head and shoulders, she half-regretted her rash decision to throw off the blue cloak she had acquired in London. She pushed her hair back from her forehead, bit her lips to make them red, and wiped the smudges of dirt from her cheeks.

When she was sure the troubadour would not run from her in horror, she stepped from behind the bushes. "Ahearn of Bromley, meet your wife, Adele," she said lightly, using her natural voice.

Gislebert turned, and Adele knew she would never forget the expression the moonlight revealed upon his face. For an instant it was as though he beheld Nadine, the object of his passion. His eyes widened, his pupils darkened, and his lips parted in an expression halfway between wonder and pleasure.

After a moment he tilted his head and laughed, breaking the spell. "By heaven," he murmured, regarding her carefully, "this disguise will work! None who see you will doubt that you are a woman!"

"That's the idea," she growled, lowering her voice. Gislebert whooped in pleasure, the sound of his laughter echoing among the trees. "Come, my wife," he said, taking her arm, "and let us enter the hospice as Adele and Ahearn. I am no longer a troubadour, but a scribe and horseman."

"Perhaps you had better conceal your passion for horses," Adele replied lightly, "at least until you acquire one, dear husband."

SOUTHWICK CASTLE

Those who pursue us are at our heels;
we are weary and find no rest.

LAMENTATIONS 5:5

THIRTEEN

Adele inhaled deeply of the crisply cool morning air as she and Gislebert stepped from the porch of the hospice to the road. "Thus it begins," she whispered, not caring if Gislebert should hear, "our journey as husband and wife."

Apparently he did hear, for he chuckled and gave her a lopsided grin. "Don't grow too accustomed to your role, *Adele,*" he said, punching her arm with masculine familiarity. "For as soon as we reach France, you'll be able to put those womanish things aside." He paused and watched his breath steam in the chilly air. "I don't know how you can stand to wear a woman's dress."

"Though it suits me not, a woman's tunic is preferable to hanging," Adele answered, pulling the skimpy fabric of the worn cloak more closely about her shorn head.

In truth, her tunic gave no comfort, for the good monk at the hospice had been as frugal with his donation of clothing as he was with the pottage he had scrupulously doled out for their supper. Under the long tunic she wore no undergarments, and the tunic itself offered little protection from the biting autumn wind. The yards of rough cloth that passed for a cloak could have sheltered her body, but Adele felt it more important to gather the fabric about her head and shoulders to hide her unfeminine hair.

Despite her discomfort and a nagging soreness in her throat, she did not complain, but thrust her cold hands into her sleeves and tried to keep pace with Gislebert, who set out as if he would walk to France in a day.

A smudge of sun dappled through the cloud cover overhead as they passed the fields of a small village. The villagers lined the fields, sowing garlic and beans, and they returned Gislebert's friendly salute with frankly curious stares.

"Look at them—they're staring at us," Gislebert muttered. "You look foolish, Jonas. They know you are a man."

"They wonder who we are, that's all," Adele answered, growing impatient with Gislebert's paranoia.

"You make a foolish woman," Gislebert grumbled, and Adele felt her heart sink. She hadn't expected him to think her beautiful, but did she really look as ugly as he made her feel? Aside from that first night when he had gazed upon her in wonder and amazement, he rarely turned to her now except to remark that her long skirts were slowing her down or that the veil on her head had cut off her common sense.

"Jonas, I am hungry," Gislebert said suddenly, glancing at the villagers around him. "But without my song and your art, we have nothing to offer in exchange for a meal." He drew his lips into a tight smile. "How do the poor eat, Jonas, when there is no bread or meat to be stolen?"

His question stung, but Adele ignored the slight and jerked her head toward the fringe of forest beyond the cultivated fields. "In the hedgerows we could find hips, haws, wild berries, and nuts," she said quietly. "Perhaps even wild apples or plums."

"A delightful idea," Gislebert answered, his eyes shining at her with newfound respect. "I'm delighted you know these things."

Adele shrugged. "I ate nothing but the forest's bounty for weeks, Troubadour."

"I forget," Gislebert answered, stepping off the road and leading the way toward the forest. "Let us pray that this forest provides us with a worthy breakfast."

They took an hour to search for and gather a complete

meal, but they found berries, wild apples, and even a walnut tree. Adele showed Gislebert how to crack the nuts between the wooden soles of his shoes and marveled that the troubadour, so confident in the court of a king, stood helpless in the forest. She ate quietly, her belly rumbling with appreciation, and she realized that she was more hungry than she had ever been in her life. The ravenous appetite of youth had awakened within her, and she continued eating even after Gislebert had eaten his fill.

"Come, we must go on," Gislebert said, brushing leaves from his tunic. Adele grabbed two wild apples and stuffed them into her sleeves, then looked up to see Gislebert laughing at her. "You're hiding those in the wrong place," he said, arching an eyebrow. "If you would be a woman, Jonas, hide them at your bosom."

Adele felt herself blushing. She led the way out of the woods so the troubadour would not see her red face.

For days they continued their southward trek toward France, walking by day, eating what the forest had to offer, and resting at night either in a roadside hospice or at the base of a tree in the woods. When necessity forced them to sleep in the forest, Adele found that she was no longer the self-sufficient and careless youngster she had once been. Only months before, she had not cared what dangers lurked about her, but now she slept lightly, hearing every sound and imagining terrors that might attack or separate her from Gislebert.

Nighttime brought fever, too, and coughing fits that left her weak. She was frightened, fearing that the noise would alert some wild animal to their presence. The pitiless cold wind raged over them. Freezing rains chilled them to the bone, and their meatless diet left both Adele and Gislebert weak and tired.

The wind blew unbearably bitter one night as she and Gislebert sought shelter in the woods. The bone-numbing cold left them helpless and weary, and Adele thought she would drop from fatigue when Gislebert pointed to a narrow strip of earth between two fallen trees. "The trees will shelter us," he called as the bawling wind snatched his words away.

The troubadour crawled into the sheltered niche and opened his arms to help her into the space. She lay down beside him, her back to his chest, their bodies pressed together in the tight crevice. Before she could wonder at the strangeness of it all, the blackness of exhaustion claimed her.

She awakened later and felt hot, as though her skin and mouth burned. The ground lay as a cold slab beneath her. The wind howled like a demon above them, and she shivered. The troubadour's eyes were closed in sleep, and she turned and slipped her arms around him for comfort. He did not jerk away, but pulled her into the shelter of his arms. Warmed by Gislebert's presence, Adele slept.

Gislebert awakened to a vague and unexpected sensation. Surely some kind angel had warmed him in a dream; perhaps Nadine's spirit had come to encircle him in her arms. His consciousness still clouded in sleep, he smiled in gratitude and slowly opened his eyes.

Nadine did not lie upon his arm. Jonas did.

Gislebert's first impulse dictated that he leap up and away, for never would he knowingly sleep in the arms of another man! If a friend lay dying, a comrade might embrace him, but this—

He lifted his left arm from Jonas's waist. The boy lay still, his face pale, his lips slightly blue, and Gislebert thought he might be able to remove himself entirely without waking the boy. This circumstance would not be spoken of, nor would it be repeated. From this day forward Gislebert would sleep far away, no matter what the weather.

He tried to remove his right arm from under the boy's head and grimaced as Jonas's head fell to the ground with a dull sound. Still the boy did not awaken, and Gislebert breathed a sigh of relief. But an afterthought struck him: *Why hadn't the boy moved? Jonas was a light sleeper, a restless mover, and he had not stirred—*

Gislebert held his hand over the boy's nose and felt no movement of air. He pressed his ear over the boy's heart and heard only the faintest of sounds. Panicked, Gislebert gathered Jonas in his arms and staggered through the frozen forest to the road. The dark road lay stark and bleak like a battlefield, sentries of leafless trees lining the road, but nothing else moved. Gislebert gripped the boy more securely in his arms and began to run as fast as his weakened legs would carry him, calling hoarsely for help.

A Saxon peasant clearing a nearby field heard the troubadour's cries and walked slowly to the road as Gislebert stopped and panted to catch his breath. "My friend—my wife," Gislebert gasped, lowering Jonas to the brown grass at the side of the road. "She is barely breathing, my friend. Can we get her to a warm shelter?"

Without a word, the peasant nodded and strode resolutely toward his small house beyond the field, where an ox waited in a pen. The man seemed to take forever to return, and Gislebert squirmed in frustration on the road. Jonas still did not move, and Gislebert withdrew in horror when he reached out to touch the boy's hand. Jonas's flesh was as cold as a dead man's.

"The village is an hour from here, but the monks operate a shelter outside the city," the man explained when he returned with the ox hitched to an oxcart. Gislebert lifted Jonas into the small wooden cart; the peasant goaded the ox with a sharpened stick.

"She has not been very well," Gislebert said as the beast grumbled and began to move forward. "We have urgent business in France, and we want to cross the channel before winter."

"You will not make it with a sick woman, my friend," the peasant replied, nodding sagely. "But you could leave her at the hospice. The monks will care for her until you return."

Gislebert glanced down at Jonas's pale face. The warmth of the sun seemed to bring out a little color in the boy's cheeks, but still he did not stir. "I cannot leave my . . . wife," Gislebert said slowly, reaching into the cart to pick up one of the boy's cold hands. Rubbing it between his own as he walked, he murmured again, "I cannot leave her."

The peasant rang the bell at the hospice, and within minutes a short, balding monk answered the summons. He raised his eyebrows in a silent question, and the peasant offered an explanation by jerking his thumb toward the oxcart. "It's my wife," Gislebert said, shifting his weight awkwardly as the monk and peasant communicated silently. "She's ill."

The peasant turned to Gislebert as the monk went back into the small building. "These priests have taken a vow of silence until the Feast of All Saints and All Souls," he said. "You can talk to them all you like, but don't expect an answer."

"All Saints," Gislebert whispered. "Is it nearly November already?"

"Aye," the peasant replied, nodding to the two monks who scurried from the hospice gate. "If you want to reach France before winter, my friend, you had better be off soon. You're at Burgess Hill, and the coast is a two days' journey from here. Are you sure you don't want to leave your wife with the good fathers?"

Gislebert looked down the road. Jonas would understand if he did leave and would probably urge him onward. And who but God knew that Jonas was not nearly dead already? The boy was a mere skeleton. Perhaps these frail efforts had come too late.

But you made a promise, a vow of friendship, he reminded himself. He had sworn to make a home for this boy, and he would do it.

"No, I cannot leave," he said, turning again to the peasant. He bowed to the monks. "Holy fathers, will you help me carry my wife inside? She is not heavy." He looked at the peasant, wishing he had a coin or something of value to give the man. "I cannot repay you for your kindness," he said, bowing with as much dignity as he could muster.

The peasant's homely face collapsed into a complex set of wrinkles as he smiled. "Only those with too many possessions worry about rewards and such," he said, turning his ox northward. "For those of us who haven't enough to eat, a word of thanks is enough. God speed your journey, good sir."

Gislebert waved until the man had disappeared down the road, then he followed the monks as they carried Jonas into the hospice.

The hospice was like many others Gislebert and Jonas had visited—a small, mud-walled house with four distinct corners: one for the sick, one for the monks, one for men, and one for women. Smoke stung Gislebert's eyes as he entered the room, for the fire at the central hearth had been laid with green wood and ventilation was poor. Standing at the fire, a toothless old woman stirred a boiling cauldron that smelled of vegetables and gristly meat. "Good day to you, sir," she said, bowing with exaggerated politeness to Gislebert. "Wot brings you to us while it is yet day?"

"My wife is ill," Gislebert said, nodding to Jonas, who had been placed on a straw mattress in the corner intended for those with sickness. One of the monks found a rough wool blanket and covered him. The other monk made the sign of the cross over the boy's pale face and moved his lips in silent prayer.

The old woman walked to where Jonas lay and sniffed the air over the boy. "It's bad," she said after a minute, her hooked nose crinkling in distaste. "We'll be lucky if the fathers can pull her through."

Gislebert sniffed the air, too, but could smell only the boiled herbs and smoke from the hearth. "Is there no doctor?" he asked, lowering himself to the packed earthen floor by Jonas's bed. "No one who knows medicine?"

The hag laughed, spittle flying from her gums. "Wot's to pay him with?" she cackled, throwing back her head. "For all your fine speech, sir, you look as penniless as a chicken. How's a chicken going to hire a doctor?"

Gislebert frowned, and the old woman moved closer. "But never ye worry, sir, for I've a knowledge of herbs, I do. I've got mandrakes aplenty to help your little wife, and my husband the barber showed me how to do bloodletting before he passed on, God rest 'im. The fathers will pray, and you won't have to pay, so don't you worry, sir, not one little bit."

The hospice filled up every night with weary travelers, most of them poor, and emptied out every morning. Gislebert left Jonas's side only when the ammoniac smell of sweat and urine became unbearable. Then he would step outside into the frosty fresh air, breathe deeply for a few moments, and return to the boy's bed.

Gislebert had never felt so helpless and alone. For the first time in his life he had no lord to beg for aid and protection, and his weary eyes regarded the poor peasants around him in a new and compassionate light.

In quiet moments he sat by Jonas's bedside and prayed dull, repetitive prayers for help and health. *Is this trial a punishment for some sin I've committed?* he wondered in prayer. *If so, show me, God, that I may mend my ways and follow the path of divine love once again.*

But no inner voice replied—no miracles occurred. Gislebert dropped his eyes to the dark earthen floor and wondered if God heard his prayers at all.

He felt feeble, too, when it came to medicine, for he knew less than a scullery maid about how to tend the sick. When the old hag applied leeches to Jonas's wrist and throat, Gislebert said nothing but bit his tongue and prayed the cure would work. The boy had grown steadily paler and weaker, save for feverishly bright spots on his haggard cheeks. He stirred only in wild coughing fits. His breathing, which grew more ragged as the days progressed, disturbed other travelers, and only those who were exhausted or afraid to face the cold tarried long at the hospice at Burgess Hill.

The old woman brought barley water and other strange concoctions from the cauldron over her fire, but Jonas could not eat or drink on his own. The old woman remedied the problem by propping the boy's mouth open and sponging nourishment into his mouth until he swallowed reflexively. Gislebert bit his knuckles nervously. Never had he seen anyone grow so sick.

One afternoon when the old woman ripped a bloody bloated leech from the tender flesh at Jonas's frail wrist, Gislebert stood and drove his fist into his palm. "I must do something," he cried, pacing around the room. "Your medicines do nothing, old woman. Surely there is a doctor in these parts who can help."

The woman bent lower over Jonas and wiped a trail of drool from his chin. "Lord Galbert of Southwick employs a doctor at the castle," she replied reluctantly. "But wot will you pay 'im with, sir?"

"My life, if necessary," Gislebert answered, crossing the room with purposeful strides. He grabbed a rough cloak from a hook by the door and paused before stepping out into the cold. "Watch her carefully," he said, casting a steady glare upon the old woman. "Even if she dies before I return, don't move her from her place."

Gislebert walked at a breathless pace for five hours before the gentle hills of the southern coast parted enough for him to glimpse Southwick Castle. His heart skipped a beat, for behind the mighty castle shone the gentle blue-silver sea of the English Channel. "So close!" he murmured to himself, his teeth chattering in the cold. "So close, and yet Nadine stays far from my reach."

He picked up his pace, conscious that the sun fell steadily in the west, and studied the earl of Southwick's castle. This fortress stood short and sturdy compared to the elevated towers of Margate, and yet Gislebert was certain that Southwick could not be taken easily. Its towers boasted the new round design that left no blind corners behind which attackers might hide, and regularly spaced arrow loops dotted the top of the wall as if part of an aesthetic design. The mighty castle wall, or *chemise,* enclosed a large piece of property, and the earl's blue-and-gold standard fluttered freely from the tallest tower.

"Virtue and heavenly trust," Gislebert whispered to himself, interpreting the meaning of the earl's colors. "May your standard be true, Lord Galbert."

When a mounted knight thundered up from behind, Gislebert found himself nearly frozen and barely able to turn and bow as propriety demanded. "Who are you, and what is your business?" the knight growled, his hand on his lance.

"I am Ahearn of Bromley, and I journey to France," Gislebert replied. "But that is not my business here. My wife lies dying in the hospice at Burgess Hill, and I come to Southwick to beg a doctor to save her."

The knight regarded Gislebert with eagle eyes. "What sort of man are you, Ahearn? Do you carry a sword?"

"No, nor dagger," Gislebert replied, trying to open his stiff fingers. "In truth, I am a scribe and am too frozen to be of danger to anyone in the castle. I am only here to beg for my wife's life."

The knight nodded. "Follow behind me, then, man, and I'll grant you safe entrance to see the doctor," he replied. "But run quickly, for my horse is fleet."

The knight spurred his horse to a trot, and Gislebert groaned and urged his weary legs to keep up.

The occupants of Southwick Castle were busily engaged in the Feast of All Saints and All Souls, a great two-day banquet to honor the dead. When Gislebert and the knight approached the castle, the troubadour gaped in amazement as nearly twenty women and men, their tunics dyed in dark colors, rang bells as they moved through a small field outside the castle gates. "Pray for the dead," one woman chanted as Gislebert drew near. "May my husband's soul be lifted soon from purgatory to heaven."

"What are they doing in the lord's fields?" Gislebert

huffed, calling to the knight who rode before him. The villeins of Margate had never engaged in such a practice.

"Their dead are buried there," the knight explained, casting a backward glance over his shoulder. "They are too poor to pay a priest for prayers, so on this day they are allowed to pray themselves for their departed ones."

Gislebert closed his eyes and prayed that Jonas wouldn't soon be among the dead. What if the boy died even today?

The knight crossed the lowered drawbridge, and Gislebert ran after him, his feet moving in wooden repetition across the rough planks. When the knight passed through the barbican and dismounted in the courtyard, momentum carried Gislebert forward until he collapsed at the knight's feet.

"Hold there," the knight laughed, his strong hands gripping Gislebert under the arms and lifting him up. "You need a strong drink, and heat, and food."

"The doctor," Gislebert gasped, waving his hand feebly. "I must see—"

"The doctor will not go anywhere today," the knight replied, propelling Gislebert toward the garrison where other knights lounged in the doorway. "'Tis a holiday, and the priest leads us in prayers at nightfall. Perhaps tomorrow, good man."

Gislebert had not the energy to reply but collapsed on a bench in the garrison. The knight clapped him on the shoulder and called to his fellows: "Look what I dragged in, my brothers! A scribe! Will not Lord Galbert be pleased?"

The other knights raised their tankards and roared their approval, and a steaming plate of meat and a gourd of ale was placed before Gislebert. He ate greedily, like an animal, and before he knew it, he had drifted away in sleep, his belly full and his mind too weary to struggle any longer.

FOURTEEN

So, Ahearn, you are a scribe?"

Gislebert straightened himself from his bow and moistened his chapped lips before replying to the question from Lord Galbert. "Yes, sir, I am," he answered. "Fluent in English, French, and Latin, in poetry, mathematics, and—" The word *song* lingered on his lips, but Gislebert halted. If he was not careful, he would be known again as a troubadour, and even now Stephen's knights might be searching for a troubadour called Gislebert.

"And your wife is at Burgess Hill?" the earl of Southwick asked again, peering out from his chair in the cavernous great hall like a king on a throne. He was a pleasant-looking man—perhaps a bit spoiled, for he had rounded shoulders, plump hands, and a protruding belly that gave evidence of extravagant dinners and little physical labor.

Gislebert nodded politely. "Yes, sir. And I have come from there to save her life. If you could spare your doctor for a short time—"

"I have most pressing need of a scribe." The earl ran his hand thoughtfully through his stubby brown hair and regarded Gislebert carefully. "My steward, who had been with me for many years, died last week of the coughing illness. My doctor could not save him."

Lord Galbert raised an eyebrow, clearly expecting a reply, and Gislebert cleared his throat nervously. "I hold every hope for my wife's recovery," he said, pressing his fingertips together. "If you would release your doctor to travel with me to Burgess Hill—"

"You will become my scribe and steward," the earl finished, slanting a questioning glance at the troubadour. "Is that agreeable to you, Ahearn?"

Gislebert cocked his head in surprise. He had not expected such an invitation, but perhaps the earl's offer was the answer for his problems. If he was employed by the earl, he could hire the doctor. Unless Jonas was miraculously healed overnight, the boy would not be fit for winter travel. Service for the earl would grant them food, a roof over their heads, and safety within the walls of the castle.

Gislebert bowed, "I am not unaware of the honor of your invitation, my lord, but I am available to serve as your scribe for the winter only. I have an obligation in France that requires my presence in the spring."

Lord Galbert raised his hand to his chin as he thought, then turned his attention to his wife. "What say you, my Lady Wynne?" he asked, looking with affection at the regal woman who sat at his right hand.

For the first time Gislebert allowed himself to study the lady of Southwick, and he found Lady Wynne to be startlingly attractive. She wore her hair brushed back like a luminous dark halo about her head, and her face was long and elegant.

Lady Wynne nodded and gave Gislebert a gracious smile. "The idea suits me well," she said, her dark eyes moving toward her husband. "I have been much overworked of late, and this man Ahearn might train one of our own to serve as steward after he departs."

"Like you his character?" the lord asked, gesturing toward Gislebert.

Lady Wynne dimpled. "He is well behaved and well spoken," she said, inclining her head. "One would think that he had oft been in service in noble households."

Lord Galbert looked back at Gislebert and clapped his hands. "So be it, then," he said, gesturing to a knight who stood at the door. "Fetch the doctor, Sir Ingram, and horses for the party to accompany Ahearn to Burgess Hill."

The tall young knight at the door nodded and saluted. "My lord, I will."

Gislebert feared they would be too late, for the sun had nearly set when their horses thundered up the road to Burgess Hill. It had been more than twenty-four hours since he had seen Jonas, and he feared the boy had died during the night. Had he pledged himself to Lord Galbert for nothing?

But the old woman greeted him with a relaxed smile when he burst through the door, and she bent low to the ground at the sight of the knight and the doctor. "We are honored, my lords," she said, her toothless cackle irritating Gislebert. He ignored her and crossed the room to the mattress where Jonas lay.

The boy's features looked even more refined now that death's pale hand hovered near. His skin was luminescent, almost glowing. For a moment Gislebert thought that an angel lay there. The knight behind him must have received the same impression, for the man gasped. Then the doctor moved forward and rummaged in the bag at his belt. From it he withdrew a sandglass and proceeded to hold Jonas's wrist between his fingers, watching the falling sand in the glass.

"Wot's he doing?" the old woman whispered hoarsely in Gislebert's ear. He considered swatting her away as he would a fly, but instead he shook his head and said nothing.

After pausing for a moment, the doctor released Jonas's wrist, then motioned for Ingram to step forward. "Lift her," the doctor said, and Ingram gently slid his arms beneath Jonas. When the boy's body was safely above the bed, the doctor knelt and sniffed the dark yellow urine stain on the mattress.

Gislebert's nose crinkled in distaste merely from watching, and the old woman whistled in fascination. "Has she a fever every day?" the doctor asked, squinting at the hag. "And at what time of day?"

The woman shrugged. "She's hot most all the time," she said, wiping her wet nose on her sleeve. "Wot does it mean?"

The doctor motioned for Ingram to lower Jonas again to the mattress and steepled his own fingers. "The stomach," he said, pressing his lips together, "is a cauldron in which food is cooked. If it is filled too full, it will boil over and the food remains uncooked."

"There's no chance of that," Gislebert interrupted. "The b—my wife's not had a full meal in weeks."

The doctor raised an eyebrow. "Therein may lie the problem," he said. "Not enough food—not enough body heat. You see, the liver supplies the heat for the stomach's cauldron, and the humors must be kept in balance—phlegm, blood, yellow bile, and black bile. You can hear phlegm in her lungs—that's out of balance, and she's lost too much blood."

"I only bled her like I've seen the barber do," the old woman protested. "It helped other people."

"But not this girl," the doctor answered. He laid a protective hand on Jonas's forehead. "Fevers are tertian, quartan, daily, hectic, and pestilential. What kind is present can be determined by the pattern of fever, whether it occurs every third day, every fourth—"

"Every day," Gislebert interrupted. "She's had fever every day."

"Well then," the doctor said, brushing his hands together, "she has a daily hectic fever, I would imagine. Her recovery will depend upon many things, including the phases of the moon and the positions of the constellations. But with God's help and my science, we may pull your wife through this illness."

Gislebert turned bewildered eyes on the doctor. "That's it?" he asked, his voice cracking in sardonic weariness. "That's all you can do?"

"Of course not," the doctor answered, rising to his feet. "We will take her back to Southwick, where she will be put under my care. Have no fear, Ahearn, you need trouble yourself no longer."

The doctor nodded to Ingram, who lifted Jonas again. Gislebert groaned at the pitiful sight of the boy's lean body encased in the tattered tunic of a woman and put out his hand to stop the knight as the boy's body passed him. If Jonas had to die, Gislebert did not want the world to see him like this.

"Let me wrap her in a covering," Gislebert said, unfolding the blanket he had brought from Southwick. "It is too cold outside."

Adele felt warmth and heard noise before coming fully to her senses. Her feet were deliciously toasty and her forehead cool, a delightful change from the nightmare she had been living for a long, long time. Around her she heard the murmur of a woman's soft singing, and on other occasions, the nasal instruction of a man who lifted her wrist and occasionally placed a soft hand on her forehead.

There was a third voice she could not place. Masculine and gentle, it spoke in a quiet murmur to the woman, then came near to whisper in her ear: "Sleep well, beautiful Adele."

Adele? Who called her by that name? Only one man called her that, her father, and her name never passed his lips without sounding like a bawdy curse. He had called her when he was hungry, when he was thirsty, when the chickens laid too few eggs. "Adele!" he would bawl, then his face would darken and his hand reach for the strap. "Adele, come!" he would say, indicating the post she was to hug while he vented his frustrations upon her back. And if she ran from his violence, he would catch her, and the beating would be twice as bad. "Adele—"

"No!" she sat up in bed, her eyes open wide.

A raven-haired woman leaned forward in surprise, her embroidery falling from her hands. "Good! You have awakened," the woman said, a gentle smile framing her strong and beautiful face. "But rest, dear Adele, and regain your strength."

Adele allowed the woman to touch her, to push her sweat-soaked hair from her forehead. She looked down in amazement at her clothes—she wore a fine linen tunic, and her skin was clean and pink.

"I had the maids bathe and dress you," the woman said, her dusky eyes sparking with kindness. "You've been ill for a long time, my dear."

"Gisle—my husband," Adele whispered, trying to make sense of her new surroundings.

"Your husband, Ahearn, is with my husband even now," the lady replied, moving back to her seat. "You are at the Castle of Southwick, and I am Wynne, the earl's wife."

"Has my husband—" Adele clumsily gripped the material of her new tunic. "Has my husband seen me like this?"

Lady Wynne laughed. "Good gracious, no, though you are a pretty sight. When he brought you back from that horrid hospice, I took charge of you immediately. He asks for you every day, of course, but I won't let him lay a finger on you. As lady of the house, it's my job to nurse the sick." Lady Wynne smiled contentedly. "Your husband has been busy settling the affairs of Southwick. Harvest is over and done, and winter is upon us, I'm afraid. The earl hasn't given Ahearn a moment to rest."

Adele lay back on the pillow. So Gislebert hadn't seen her and probably didn't know that at least one person in this place had witnessed that she was a woman. "My husband must not know you bathed me," Adele said, shaking her head timidly. "No one must tell him."

"Protective, is he?" Lady Wynne asked, arching an elegant brow. "Do not worry, my dear, no man has seen your nakedness."

"He must not know," Adele insisted, sitting up again. "Please tell the maids—"

"No one will say anything," Lady Wynne answered, standing to smooth the blanket that covered her patient. "Now lie back and rest. Don't worry about anything."

Adele sighed and settled back into the warm comfort

of the bed. "What is this place?" she asked, shyly looking around.

"You're in a dormitory off my chamber," Lady Wynne answered, picking up her embroidery again. "The chambermaids usually sleep here, but now the room has become our infirmary." Her fine, silky eyebrows rose a trifle in delicate rebuke. "You really should rest, my dear, and collect your strength so that you can rejoin your husband."

"Rejoin him? Has he left—"

"When he's not working, he sleeps in the steward's house, a lovely little place just inside the castle walls," the lady answered. "You'll love it, little one, but I'm not letting you out of my sight until you're better. So rest, then you'll eat, and soon you'll be back in the arms of your husband."

Adele sighed in relief and withdrew into a dreamless sleep.

"How is our beautiful Adele today?"

There! That mysterious voice! Adele's eyes flew open, and she saw a slim, golden-haired knight standing at the foot of her bed. He wore a blue-and-gold surcoat that complemented his hair and golden skin, and laughter sparkled in his blue eyes as he glanced about her room. Was she dreaming? Surely not, for Lady Wynne murmured to the knight, and he bowed in reverence to her before turning once again to glance in Adele's direction.

When he saw that her eyes were open, he kissed his fingertips in delight. "*Bon Dieu!* She awakes!" he cried, his voice brimming with enthusiasm. "My lady, you did not tell me that the beautiful Adele has rejoined the land of the living."

"I did not tell *you,* but I told her husband," Lady Wynne rejoined, raising a warning with her eyes.

"And yet her husband does not come," the knight replied, grasping the wooden frame of Adele's bed. "By the sword of St. Denis, she has the most beautiful eyes I've ever seen! Do you think she hears me?"

"I'm sure she does," Lady Wynne replied, glancing up from her needlework. "She is not deaf, only sick."

"May I fetch her bowl? a blanket? May I do anything for her?" His eagerness was appealing, and Adele found a shy smile springing to her lips. The knight saw the smile, and sunshine seemed to break across his face.

"You have done more than enough," Lady Wynne replied firmly, standing to her feet. "Now be on your way, Sir Ingram, or you will give the servants more gossip than they need."

The knight called Sir Ingram grinned at Lady Wynne, blew an enthusiastic kiss to Adele, and called a final remark as he descended the stairs: "I shall continue to come, my lady, and gossip be hanged."

The doctor with the nasal voice prescribed bowls of chicken broth, the milk of pulverized almonds, and barley water mixed with figs, honey, and licorice. He came to see Adele every morning without fail and administered broths of herbs and mysterious drugs from his bag. Adele endured him, but Lady Wynne's visits brought her the most pleasure. She passed the days of her convalescence lapping up the lady's attention and gentle instruction like a kitten before milk and imagined that the kind, gracious, and beautiful Lady Wynne was the mother she had never known.

Adele confessed her daydreams one morning as Lady Wynne helped her drink from a bowl of watered-down pottage. When the lady froze at Adele's words and did not answer, Adele glibly rambled on and tried to cover her mistake. "I'm sorry if I offended you, mistress, not being highborn, but you're so kind and gentle."

"I'm not offended," Lady Wynne finally replied, two spots of color appearing in her cheeks. "It's just that you reminded me of my own loss." The lady grew silent, and Adele saw that her hands trembled. "I have one son, as you may have heard, but I lost a daughter at birth. I had wanted a little girl very badly, and neither the earl nor I have ever forgotten the heartbreak."

149

Adele reached for the lady's hand and squeezed it gently while the woman dabbed at her eyes with a handkerchief. "I'm sorry; I forget myself," Lady Wynne said, forcing a smile. "But my little girl would be about your age if she had lived."

Adele smiled and released the lady's hand. "I thank you, most sincerely," she whispered. "And I'm honored to count you as a friend. If I can be of any service to you—"

"Thank you," the lady interrupted, gently tidying the covers on Adele's bed. She grabbed the corner of the blanket that covered Adele and lifted it up, exposing Adele's thin legs. "What say you? Shall we take another walk? We must strengthen those birdlike legs of yours!"

Adele groaned in feigned reluctance but swung her legs out of the bed and began a slow and careful walk around the room.

FIFTEEN

Lady Wynne arranged a celebration for the day when the doctor pronounced Adele strong enough to return to her husband. In honor of the occasion, the lady of the manor presented Adele with a warm woolen tunic, proper undergarments, and a rich red cloak. Adele dressed herself carefully, rejoicing in the softness of the cloth. Her hair had grown past her shoulders, a most unbecoming length for a man. She had mentioned cutting it, but Lady Wynne cried out in protest, so Adele left her hair alone.

When Adele had dressed in her new clothes, Lady Wynne and Sir Ingram escorted her down the castle stairs to the great hall, where Gislebert waited with Lord Galbert. "Ah, she is a pretty wench indeed," Lord Galbert said, clapping Gislebert on the back. "No wonder you were frantic with worry about her."

Adele looked toward Gislebert but tried to avoid his eyes. He had only seen her as a reluctant woman; never had he seen her thus, in proper clothing and the glow of health. Never had she felt like this, calm and content and almost pretty, and never had she felt such a rush of emotion for the troubadour. He had stayed with her when his heart wanted to be away. He had indentured himself for her sake. Her heart quivered with gratitude, yet she worried about revealing too much of herself in her glance.

"Come on, bid your husband good morning," Lady Wynne urged.

Adele stood before the troubadour and looked up into his face. His eyes glowed with health, satisfaction, and something else—relief?

His eyebrow raised in an unspoken question, and she responded by placing her hand delicately in his. "I, Adele, rejoice to be by your side again, my husband," she said, curtseying.

Gislebert blushed while the knights around him hooted with delight, then he dropped her hand like a hot coal and nodded to Lord Galbert. "For your shelter and aid, we owe you our lives," Gislebert said, bowing low. "We will never be able to repay you."

"Just serve me until spring, Ahearn," Lord Galbert replied, waving his hand carelessly. "Be happy and prosper. That is all we ask."

Carefully guiding Adele by the elbow, Gislebert turned and led her out of the hall and down the wide steps of the castle keep. The household staff and military men cheered as the troubadour led his "bride" to the small steward's house by the castle gate. Adele looked back once—Lady Wynne beamed in approval, and sorrow covered Ingram's face like a cloud.

"I can't believe our pretense has not been discovered," Gislebert murmured through his forced smile as they walked. "Did no one discover that you are a man?"

"My disguise is still in place," Adele answered, waving timidly to the cheering servants. "You need not fear, my friend. No one at this place thinks me anything but the girl I claim to be."

Gislebert shook his head in amazement. "Our good fortune belies belief," he said, opening the door to their new home. "And surely God has led us here in his mercy, for the lord of Southwick is fair and just. All men here seem to hold favorable opinions of me. All"—he shrugged—"but one."

"And who is that, husband?" Adele asked, putting her arm about his shoulder as Gislebert obeyed tradition and prepared to carry her across the threshold of their home.

"Ingram," Gislebert answered, lifting her easily into his arms. "For some reason, he cannot stand the sight of me."

The one-room house was small but neat, furnished with a table, a bench, a hearth and fireplace, and one large bed that stood in the center of the room. Gislebert good-naturedly agreed to sleep on the floor. "You have been ill," he said, spreading his cloak on the floor of hard-packed earth.

Adele slipped out of her surcoat and sank onto the bed in her tunic, tired from the excitement of the day. Gislebert rose and came toward her. She drew in her breath, hoping that he would whisper some tender word about missing her, but he only reached over her for a pillow and smiled his thanks as he moved away.

"You do not have to sleep on the floor," Adele murmured, feeling strangely disappointed. "Some would think it bizarre if you did not sleep in the bed with me. After all, I am supposed to be your wife."

Gislebert laughed and punched his pillow as he settled down. "No, Jonas, while we are in this house, we shall be as the men we are," he answered. "Frankly, I find it more than a little bizarre that we pull off this charade so easily. It is not a story I look forward to telling my children."

Adele's cheeks burned in shame. "If that is how you feel—"

"Isn't it how you feel, too?" Gislebert yawned loudly. "After all, I would die of shame to wear a woman's dress, and I'm sure it is only the weakness of your illness that makes a woman's place bearable for you. In four or five months, though, we shall be on a ship for France, and your days as a woman will be through." His eyes gleamed toward her over the top of his pillow. "I will never forget, and will always appreciate, the sacrifice you have made for me here."

"And you for me," Adele quietly replied as darkness fell upon the room. "You could have left me at the hospice, or even here at Southwick. I know you wanted to be away to France—or have you changed your mind?"

Gislebert snorted. "No, my little friend, my heart still

yearns for Nadine and St. Denis. But I made a vow of friendship to you. Staying with you was what one friend does for another. So sleep, Jonas, and be quiet so I can dream of the face of my Nadine."

Adele turned her back to him and kicked her mattress in frustration. Closing her eyes, she concentrated all her attention on the handsome image of the knight called Ingram.

Gislebert rose with the sun and made his way out early the next morning. She sat up as he left, hugging her knees to her, and heard hoots and rowdy calls from the knights in the garrison as Gislebert passed by them. *They imagine he has enjoyed an intimate night with his long-lost wife,* she realized, her cheeks burning.

She sprang out of bed and thrust the shutters open. "Oh, Ahearn," she called loudly, darting back inside to grab his pillow. Gislebert stopped in the courtyard and stared stupidly as she tossed the pillow out the window. "The next time you sleep on the floor, Ahearn, clean up your mess before you leave!" Gislebert looked at her in bewilderment, while behind him the knights of the garrison slapped their legs in uncontrolled laughter.

"Adele!" Gislebert bellowed, stalking toward her. "What are you doing?"

"Feeling better!" she yelled back, not caring who heard. She reached outward for the knobs on the shutters and caught a glimpse of Ingram, who stood by his horse and watched her with frank longing and amusement in his eyes. She gave him a quick smile even as her fingers found the knobs, and she slammed the shutters closed while Gislebert raged outside in impotent fury.

By the time the knights had ridden out on their patrols, however, her pleasure at venting her anger evaporated, and no feeling remained but an aching emptiness. Why had she humiliated Gislebert? She could tell him— and the trusting troubadour would believe her—that she acted only to reinforce their deception, for what husband and wife did not occasionally fight?

But she knew the root of her anger went much deeper. Gislebert had hurt her because he was not willing to be close to her. Indeed, he would not even look at her as every other man in the castle did. Though she was not yet mature, still she was a woman, and at least one other man had found her beautiful! How pleasant Sir Ingram's attentions had been!

But she could not say these things to Gislebert, for he remained with her only because he thought her a homeless boy and considered himself her protector. She sank onto her bed, realizing she had but two choices: If she revealed the true cause of her anger and her womanhood, she would lose the companionship of the troubadour; if she continued in the charade of Jonas, she would keep the troubadour but not his honest affection. Neither was a fair choice, and neither answered the frustrating problem of her friendship with a man who simply could not see her for what she was.

A light tap on her door brought Adele to her feet, and words failed her when she found Lady Wynne outside her house. "My dear," Lady Wynne said, peering past Adele into the house, "how long have you been a wife? You should have been dressed and out of bed hours ago."

"I . . . ah . . . wasn't feeling well," Adele answered guiltily.

Lady Wynne stepped into the room, looked around, and eyed Adele squarely. "Confess now," she said, her dark eyes piercing through to Adele's soul. "You haven't been married long, have you? And the scribe shows you no interest, does he? What was it, an arranged marriage?"

Adele sank to her bed, amazed at the woman's intuition. "Truly, no," she answered. "We have not been married long."

"Have you come of age?" Lady Wynne pressed, sitting beside Adele. In a gentler tone she added, "Have you yet begun to bleed in the manner of women?"

Adele blushed and hung her head. "No," she whispered.

"I thought not," Lady Wynne answered, looking pointedly at Adele's flat chest. "How old are you?"

"Near sixteen," Adele mumbled.

"Time enough," Lady Wynne answered, standing to her feet. "Myself, I married at twelve, bled at fourteen, and had my son at sixteen," she said, looking around the room. She ran her palm across the table and then brushed her hands together. "Girl, I can tell you had no mother. If you want a husband to love you, dear, you must keep a clean house."

Adele lifted her head at the mention of the word *love,* and her interest did not escape Lady Wynne's attention. "Ah, so you do love the scribe," she whispered softly. "I wondered."

"No, I do not love him," Adele answered, shaking her head stubbornly. "But we are great friends. He cannot love me, you see, for his heart is filled with the image of another."

Lady Wynne slipped to her side and put a comforting arm around Adele. "My dear child, one must be taught to love," she said soothingly. "You can teach the scribe to love you, and in doing so, you will come to love him. Then you will find your home in his arms. You will have children, and we will have no more scenes like the one you gave us this morning."

Adele's eyebrows flew upward in alarm, and Lady Wynne chuckled. "Oh yes, the chambermaids talked of nothing else this morning," she said. "I dare say everyone within twenty miles of Southwick knows now that the earl's new scribe sleeps on the floor and leaves his wife alone in the bed."

Adele covered her mouth with her hand, stifling a giggle, and Lady Wynne ruffled her hair. "So get up, young lady, and learn what I shall teach you," she said, standing. She surveyed the small room. "We will begin with this house. If you hang alder leaves around the room, you'll rid the house of fleas. Hang a cord coated in honey in a corner, and the flies will alight there, then toss out the cord. Keep your home clean, and your husband will rejoice to come home and find you there."

A wave of gratitude rolled over Adele, and she fell on her face before Lady Wynne, throwing her arms about the woman's knees. "Thank you, my lady," Adele whispered, her voice failing.

A tender hand fell upon her head, and the lady's gentle words followed: "Do not fret, my dear; you have married the right man. By holy law you own your husband's body. I will teach you how to win his heart."

Gislebert grimaced every time he thought of the change in Jonas. The scene in the courtyard had been gruesome enough, even when Jonas later assured him that it was designed only to aid their disguise. But other changes in the boy were even more disturbing. Every day Jonas's speech grew more refined, his appearance more feminine, and the small steward's house had become the center of Jonas's world. To avoid a repeat of the courtyard scene, Gislebert made a point of creeping from the place while Jonas remained asleep. But in the evening he could not fail to hear Jonas's cheerful singing as the boy cleaned the table and prepared supper.

To Gislebert's chagrin, the boy had even begun to collect women's clothes. To the fine tunic and cloak given to him by Lady Wynne, the boy had added numerous tunics, cloaks, and even linen undergarments. His hair, which had never been longer than his chin, now hung loosely past his shoulders, and Gislebert thought he would faint one noon when Jonas proudly wore a woman's wimple to dinner in the lord's hall.

Gislebert blamed everything on Lady Wynne. She might be a gracious and gentle lady, much loved by the earl and well regarded by the knights, but her attentions were ruining Jonas. Gislebert thought that perhaps her attention to the boy sprang from missing her own son, Vinson, who served as a squire at another castle while he trained to be a knight. But no matter *why* the lady behaved as she did, Gislebert could do nothing to stop her destructive influence, for he was sworn to obey her.

Most frustrating to Gislebert was the thought that some-how he was to blame for the boy's predicament. Though he had at first been repulsed by the idea of Jonas dressing as a woman, still he had allowed it and perpetuated the pretense through the boy's long illness. And now with the boy firmly identified as Adele, wife of Ahearn, what could Gislebert do but continue the charade?

Gislebert knew that if he told even part of the truth—that Jonas was no woman—Lord Galbert would demand to know the entire truth and the reason for their disguise. If the entire truth were told, the earl would not only be highly offended that his trusted steward had lied to him but would be within his rights to have Jonas and Gislebert executed as enemies of the crown. He recognized the honorable and true path before him, yet Gislebert asked himself again and again, *Is it not better to continue as we are for Nadine's sake?*

For Nadine's sake he did nothing but watch the sky and wait for spring, when he and Jonas could leave Southwick and continue their journey to France. Until then Gislebert resolved to bear Jonas's increasing femininity as best he could—which meant, in practical terms, that he avoided the boy as much as possible.

"I hope you do not mind, Ahearn, but I have decided to employ Adele as a chambermaid during the Christmas festivi-ties," Lady Wynne announced at dinner as the household ate in the great hall. Gislebert was seated next to Lord Galbert at a raised table in the front of the room; each man had his wife at his side. The knights and domestic staff ate at long tables placed along the walls of the great hall, and every voice stilled as Lady Wynne made her announcement about Adele.

Gislebert swallowed a particularly stubborn piece of pork and nodded graciously at the earl's wife. "You have my blessing," he replied, aware that every ear in the hall listened eagerly for the latest development in the Ahearn-Adele mar-riage. He did not look at Jonas. "I am sure my wife will make a fine chambermaid."

"Have all the animals been butchered?" Lord Galbert asked abruptly, pausing to wave his spoon in Gislebert's direction.

"Just the animals which could not be fed through the winter," Gislebert answered. "Four cows, five sheep. I believe our stores will provide for the rest."

"I like the way he says that," Lord Galbert remarked to his wife. "*Our* stores. Tell me," he said, turning to Gislebert, "could we dissuade you from this pressing task in France? We would be honored to have you and your wife remain with us permanently. You could raise your children here at Southwick, and you have my word of honor that you will be well treated."

Gislebert grimaced at the word *children,* then cursed himself silently, for his pained expression had not gone unnoticed by Lady Wynne. That lady's gaze hardened, and she frowned in disapproval.

"No, I'm sorry, my lord, but my destiny still awaits in France." Gislebert turned away from Lady Wynne's icy stare. "But I still have two full months to serve you here."

"Maybe more, if winter weather prevails," Lord Galbert added cheerfully. "Have you hired extra servants for Christmas?"

Gislebert nodded and consulted the parchment on the table in front of him. "Two porters, one tailor, one furrier, three bakers, one butcher, two shoemakers, and two candlemakers."

"Good!" Lord Galbert beamed. He lowered his voice so that it would not reach to the other tables. "This will be a wonderful Christmas, with generosity to all. I want extra furs for all the knights, shoes for all the domestic servants, and a fine horse for my most faithful knight, Ingram. Know you anything about horses, Ahearn?"

"Of course." Gislebert smiled politely. "A good horse, my lord, has three qualities of a fox, four qualities of a hare, four qualities of an ox, and three qualities of an ass. I'll demonstrate later in the stable, if you wish."

Lord Galbert slapped his steward on the back. "By

heaven, I find favor in this man," he said, grinning mischievously. "I can't wait to hear what you mean."

As the fields of Southwick hardened in the grip of a cruel December frost, the villeins, servants, and knights of the earl turned their attention to merrymaking. Adele watched in wonder as the castle prepared for Christmas, for never had her small village reveled in the holiday as the Castle of Southwick did. All work required of the villeins was suspended on Saint Nicholas's Day, December sixth, and the hayward, the plowman, the shepherd, swineherd, and oxherd lined the great hall and waited for the annual bestowment of their perquisites: food, clothing, drink, and bundles of firewood. Each man carried his treasures home, where hungry wives and children rejoiced in the lord's bounty and blessings.

Adele helped Lady Wynne with the decoration of the castle. On the morning of the seventh of December they bundled themselves in furs and gloves and rode into the forest with Sir Ingram as their chaperon. "Look for holly, ivy, berries, bay leaves, anything green or red," Lady Wynne told Adele as she broke a cluster of red berries from a bush. She gave Adele a rare, intimate smile. "We will surround ourselves with greenery and forget the cold outside."

Adele joined in the sport eagerly and laughed when Ingram dismounted and gallantly offered his entwined hands as a step so she could reach high into a tree. She placed her foot in his palms, gripped her hand on his shoulder for balance, and he lifted her within reach of an ivy that had twined itself through the branches of an old oak. As he lowered her, she found his deep blue eyes only inches from hers. Power and hunger filled his gaze, and the sight of such raw emotion confused her. A tremor of awareness passed between them. Ingram opened his mouth as if to speak, but she placed her free hand across his parted lips.

"Thank you, sir," she said, flushing as a rush of warmth flashed over her. He placed her on solid ground, and the intensity of his eyes became so unbearable that she turned her back to him and called ahead to Lady Wynne: "My lady! Wait for me!"

Seven days before Christmas, the sound of a guard's trumpet stilled the hubbub of activity in the courtyard. "Three riders approach," the knight on the wall called to the men in the courtyard. "He carries a standard with the three lions of England!"

"Messengers from the king," Lady Wynne whispered, turning from the window in the castle's hall. Her eyes widened, and she quickly motioned for Adele and the other maids to clear their work from the table. "They will bring news, and we can only hope it is favorable."

"Surely all is well with King Stephen," Adele whispered, gathering the yarn for a tapestry into her arms. "He has been recrowned and reclaimed the throne—"

"One cannot know about such a king," Lady Wynne replied, smoothing her hair. She pinched her cheeks and turned again to the window as three knights rode through the gates of Southwick.

Lord Galbert had heard the trumpet, too, and he and Gislebert came down the stairs in a breathless rush as the ladies' maids scurried from the room. "Make haste, show them in," Lord Galbert told the two knights who stood guard at the castle doorway. He turned to his wife. "Lady, let us receive our guests. Ahearn, remain, for I may have need of you."

Adele took a seat in a far corner and noticed that Gislebert's face paled when the knights in Stephen's white-and-gold surcoats entered the room. "Greetings in the name of the king," the first knight roared, producing a rolled and sealed parchment from his surcoat. "We bring Christmas greetings from your sovereign and assurances that you remain in his favor."

"We would send the same assurances and Christmas greetings to our king," Lord Galbert answered, nodding with dignity. "But certainly the king does not send three knights for such a simple task—"

"My husband wishes to say that the king surely knows we love him and accept his love," Lady Wynne broke in smoothly, helping her husband's faltering tongue. "Is there anything else we can do for His Highness?"

"Only this," the knight replied, unrolling the parchment. "His Highness King Stephen of England wishes to know the whereabouts of certain criminals who aided the Empress Matilda in the recent uprising. Every man recorded in this document is under the sentence of death."

The knight held up the parchment and began to read: "Do you know or have you sheltered Sir Halsey of Gisors?"

"No," Lord Galbert shook his head. "As God is my witness, no."

"Lord Osmund of Pembroke?"

"No."

"The Saxon monk called Reginauld?"

"No."

"The troubadour Gislebert who travels with an artist called Jonas?"

Adele felt her heart pound and glanced at Gislebert. His knuckles whitened as they gripped the back of Lord Galbert's chair, but his face remained as expressionless as stone.

"No, my friend. I have neither seen nor employed a troubadour called Gislebert."

"The knight called Thayer?"

"No."

The reading went on for some time, and Lord Galbert shook his head at the mention of each name. When the knight had finished, he rerolled his parchment and glanced at Gislebert. "You, steward, have you knowledge of any of these traitors to the king?"

Adele held her breath as Gislebert cleared his throat. How would her ever-truthful troubadour reply?

"Sir knight, I do not know any traitors to His Highness

the king," Gislebert answered, bowing respectfully. "All in this place regard the king with love and loyalty."

"Good day, then, and Happy Christmas," the knight replied. Bowing again, the three went out, and all who remained in Southwick's great hall united in a sigh of relief.

Sixteen

The serious celebration was to begin at supper on Christmas Eve, and Adele anticipated it with more delight than she had thought possible. "Hurry, Gislebert," she said, turning from the window of their house. "The villeins have gathered outside to see the Yule log, and the lord and lady will expect us to be present. Can't you work on those figures another time?"

Gislebert looked up from his parchments and scowled as he dipped his pen into the hollowed cow's horn that held his ink. "No, it must be done now," he snapped, averting his eyes from her. "Careful accounts must be kept, for Lord Galbert knows no limit to his own generosity. I must keep him in line, so that he does not empty his own stores."

"Let him give what he wants to give," Adele answered crossly, sitting on the edge of the bed. "He is rich; he can afford—"

"On Monday, the oxherd, the plowman, and their wives were treated to dinner," Gislebert interrupted. "They consumed one and a half quarters of bread and two barrels of wine. The oxherd drank more beer than I would have believed humanly possible. The chief shepherd, his family, and the domestic staff ate dinner with the lord on Tuesday—that meal alone consisted of six sheep, one ox, three calves, and eight pounds of fat."

"So?" Adele snapped.

"That's not all," Gislebert continued, running his finger

down the page. "Six dozen fowls, twenty eggs, and ten geese. The contingent of knights from Brighton cost us hay for fifty horses and three and a half quarters of oats."

"I liked you better before you kept accounts," Adele answered sourly, her lower lip edging forward in a pout. She concentrated on enunciating clearly, the way Lady Wynne had taught her: "You were more fun as a troubadour."

"And you were more bearable as a man."

He hadn't meant to say those words, Adele knew, for he bit his lip and looked at the floor as he always did when embarrassed. More *bearable?* What did he mean?

She pressed her lips together firmly. "I only wear this guise to protect us. Have you forgotten that the king seeks our heads?"

"I have not forgotten," Gislebert answered, looking back to his parchments. He dipped his pen in the ink and made another scrawled notation.

"Then what do you mean? Why am I not *bearable?*"

Gislebert threw his pen down on the paper and slammed his hand against the table. "You dress as a woman, you walk like a woman, you speak as a woman, you even smell like a woman! You are a man—you figure it out!"

Adele could only stare dumbly as he stalked across the room, grabbed his heavy cloak from the hook on the wall, and slammed the door behind him.

"Behold the Yule log!" As the villeins and servants roared in approval, Ingram led the company of Southwick knights as they rode through the barbican. Behind their splendid horses they hauled a section of oak as long as a man and as wide as the lord's table.

"It's enormous," Adele breathed to a washer woman who stood nearby, and the woman nodded.

"It 'as to burn for twelve nights, dearie," the woman cackled. "It'd better be of a right goodly size."

The men and women of Southwick indulged in a bit of cheerful jesting as the knights unroped the log and moved to hoist it onto their shoulders. "You canna carry that," the smith called, his swarthy face alight with unusual glee. "It's bigger than all of you put together."

"About the size of your wife, then," Ingram shot back, and the crowd roared as the smith rolled his eyes in appreciation of his wife's form and the knight's wit.

"One, two, three!" Ingram called, and more than half a dozen knights braced themselves against the packed earth of the courtyard and worked the log onto their shoulders. Like a coffin they carried it up the steps of the castle keep and into the great hall, where Lady Wynne's chambermaids had cleared the mammoth fireplace.

Adele followed the crowd into the hall, wondering if anyone had noticed that her "husband" was not at her side. Probably not, since a steward's work kept him busy at all times of the day. But still, it was Christmas, and even the humblest villein and his wife rejoiced together.

Why wouldn't Gislebert stand with her—and what in the world had he meant when he said she was more bearable as a man? Had she been unduly harsh or critical? No, her conscience assured her. Lady Wynne had taught her well that a wife must be discreet and learn to hold her tongue. "It is a wife's highest calling," Lady Wynne had said, her crown of dark hair gleaming in the candlelight one evening as they waited for Gislebert and the master to return from hunting. "A wife must keep her husband's secrets. A worthy wife must be loving with her husband, moderate with her kinsmen, distant with other men, and aloof from idle men who are said to lead corrupt, amorous, or dissolute lives."

"But," Adele had interrupted, thinking of Gislebert, "can a woman not develop a friendship with certain men? Can she not have a male friend and companion?"

Lady Wynne nodded and smiled softly. "You are thinking of my friendship with Ingram, are you not?" she asked. Adele did not reply, but Lady Wynne went on with her needlework and did not look up. "It is true that we share an easy familiarity, but Ingram is like a son to me, Adele. Since my own son is far from me, Ingram eases the pain of separation I feel. But he knows his place and keeps his distance."

The lady put down her sewing and leaned forward to pat Adele's cheek. "Friendship between men and women is difficult, my dear, for it tends to become love. You may treat a man as a son, a father, a lover, or a husband, but there is little ground in between. Of course," the lady added, picking up her sewing again, "proper women treat their husbands as lovers and take no others."

The words rang in Adele's memory as Ingram moved into her view in the great hall. He stood with a torch next to the bed of twigs upon which the Yule log rested and looked to Lady Wynne for permission to light the fire. Lady Wynne raised her clear voice in a carol, and as they sang of the joys of Christ's birth, Ingram lowered his torch to the waiting kindling. Flames began to lick eagerly at the rough bark of the log.

Adele looked across the room for Gislebert and spied him at the side of Lord Galbert, who swayed drunkenly from his generous portion of celebration ale. Gislebert was holding the master's arm. Whether for support or in friendship, Adele could not tell, but his eyes met hers and flashed in recognition. She gave him a smile, and his narrow face arranged itself in a polite grin before he looked away.

What did it mean? Could he no longer see her as a friend? Adele's thoughts were disturbed by a light touch on her elbow, and when she turned, Ingram stood beside her, his deep voice ringing with the sincerity of the carol. She turned again to face the log and reluctantly joined the song.

Gislebert groaned as he rose from his bed on the floor. For all others, Christmas Day meant merriment and festivity, but it would be the most tiring day of his life. The villeins were due to arrive soon after sunrise, and the feasting would begin before the sun had risen halfway in the sky.

Gislebert counted on his fingers as he mentally listed all that had to be done. The cooks had their orders. The animals

for the feast had been butchered the day before, and all the
treasures of Southwick Castle had been polished, aired,
dusted, and arranged. Tapestries hung on every wall. Polished
mirrors shone in the entryway, and Galbert's strongbox
bulged with its store of valuable relics, coins, and jewelry.
Everything Galbert possessed of value would be put on display, so that all who served the earl of Southwick would realize his wealth.

Gislebert modestly turned his back to the bed where
Jonas lay sleeping and pulled up the long, thick hose that
covered his spindly legs. His short blue tunic was new, as
was the belt that held up his hose, and the boots that were
still too stiff to be comfortable. He groaned as he slipped
the boots on, but he would offend Galbert if he did not
wear them. As Galbert's chief steward, Gislebert must not
only display the lord's treasures, but be an example of his
generosity.

He reached for his fur-lined cloak and paused for a
moment to observe Jonas as the boy slept. Gislebert chewed
his bottom lip, wondering if he should wake him, then
decided against it. They had not talked much of late. A stab
of guilt pricked Gislebert's heart, but he had no time to
indulge his conscience. Later, when they had left this place
and Jonas had removed those silly women's clothes, they
would resume their old ways and friendship. Until then,
Gislebert did not have time to worry about young Jonas.

Adele dressed carefully in the beautiful garments that Lady
Wynne had given her for this day. "Your husband is proving
to be a difficult challenge," Lady Wynne had said, allowing
Adele to choose garments from the lady's own wardrobe.
"You have done all I have asked, and still I do not see love
from the steward's eyes. Is his heart as hard as that?"

"His heart is not hard. It is . . . preoccupied," Adele had
answered slowly, and Lady Wynne's hand had fallen upon
hers in sympathy.

"Then choose a garment that will amaze him with your

beauty," the lady replied. "And we will pray that Christmas will bring the miracle you seek."

From the lady's generous wardrobe, Adele had chosen a fine linen chemise, a long-sleeved tunic of sunny yellow, and a surcoat of bright blue. Its wide, fur-lined sleeves were rich with bright embroidery. Tassels hung from the surcoat at the shoulder. A jeweled belt accented Adele's narrow waist. As a final touch, Lady Wynne had placed a crimson cloak upon Adele's shoulders, a cloak so wide and plentiful in fabric that Adele gasped at its extravagance.

"It is too much!" she had protested, but Lady Wynne had only smiled.

"Nothing is too much for you, my little bird," the lady had replied. "Now tomorrow, for the feast, do not cover your hair with a wimple, but wear a cap, so your neck and hair will be exposed for the dancing."

When she was dressed, Adele checked her reflection in the still water of her washbasin. Despite the fine clothing, she found nothing pleasing in her appearance. Her face and neck were pale, and bones protruded at the base of her throat. She placed her hands on the belt at her waist and ran them slowly up over her rib cage to her budding breasts. She had never worn a garment this closely fitted and this revealing. She still had the appearance of a boy, but surely anyone who looked at her would see that a young woman stood before them.

She turned away from the reflection of her own troubled eyes. Did she really want Gislebert to know the truth? Her heart answered yes, but her reason railed against that answer. The troubadour still dreamed of Nadine. If she, another woman, came between him and his obsession . . .

The ringing of the bell in the courtyard called her to the feast, and she paused before the basin again, pinching her cheeks and biting her lips to make them red. Her hair, though not long, had been brushed to a glowing sheen. Her little white maiden's cap sat as a simple spot of brightness on her head but set off the fullness of her hair and contrasted nicely with her dark eyes. If Gislebert could not see her femininity today, the image of Nadine blinded him more than Adele realized.

At the invitation of the bell, the villeins and servants paraded into the castle's great hall, carrying gifts of bread, hens, and ale, which would in part provide the Christmas dinner. Land-holding villeins were led to places at the table where beef, bacon, and chicken stew waited; lesser villeins brought their own cloths, cup, and trenchers and were ushered to less bountiful tables.

As the steward's wife, Adele was seated at a "high" table. Gislebert sat next to her but did not even glance her way, so busy was he recording the offerings of the villeins and the reciprocal gifts that would be bestowed by the lord.

When all the guests had been seated, dinner was served. The food was plentiful, for Christmas at Southwick meant brawn, pudding, sauce, mustard, beef, mutton, pork, mince pies, goose, veal, turkey, cheese, apples, and nuts. With the hearty appetite of the recovering invalid, Adele ate until she felt her stomach strain against her belt. After dinner, as the Yule log roared and warmed the room, the lord's gifts were given to his vassals: chickens to the villeins, shoes to the domestic servants, fur-lined cloaks for the knights, a new tunic and leggings for Gislebert.

After Lord Galbert had announced his gifts, loaves of rare white bread were presented to all. The guests eagerly tore into them, for the lucky man or woman who found a vanilla bean hidden in the loaf was proclaimed "king" of the feast. Laughter and loud speculation filled the air as lord and peasant alike chewed and clawed their way through the loaf, until a triumphant cry interrupted the frantic searching. "I have it!" a voice shouted, and Ingram stood from the crowd, the vanilla bean upraised in his fingers.

"My friend, Sir Ingram," Lord Galbert called, standing. "You are as favored in games as you are in service." He bowed to the knight. "As king of the feast, my friend, you shall lead our festivities. What say you? Now that we have dined and exchanged gifts, what shall we do next? Games? Hunting? Hawking?"

Ingram's blue eyes swept the crowd, and Adele blushed when she felt them come to rest upon her. "My lord, as king of the feast, I decree that we shall dance," Ingram proclaimed, bowing to Lord Galbert. "Call for the musicians, clear the room, and let us make merry!"

"A fine idea," Lord Galbert agreed, extending his hand to his lady. "So it is decreed." Every man, both great and small, rose to move tables and chairs, and the women scurried to remove the serving dishes to the kitchens downstairs. Adele did her part, carrying a huge platter loaded with a well-picked over turkey carcass and was amazed at the change in the room by the time she had arrived back upstairs in the great hall. The fire blazed brightly, the floors were cleared and swept, the musicians had assembled in the upper balcony, and Lord Galbert and Lady Wynne sat in their raised chairs, Sir Ingram by Lord Galbert's side.

At a signal from Lord Galbert, a trumpet blared, and the lord stood to address the people of his manor: "Beautiful ladies and gentle men, a blessed Christmas to you all. And now, my friend Ingram, would you lead in our dance?"

"I shall." Ingram stood and stepped to the center of the room. "It would be my honor to begin the dance with the aid of the beautiful wife of Ahearn," Ingram announced boldly.

A murmur rippled through the crowd, and for an instant Adele did not realize that *she* was the desired dancing partner. But then the eyes of the company fell upon her, and the intensity of their collective attention made her cheeks burn. Surely Ingram could not mean her! She was married, and not beautiful, and—

Ingram's approach paralyzed her thoughts, and in a moment he knelt at her feet and extended his hand. "Come dance with me," he said, the rich timbre of his voice sending the nearby maids into a tizzy.

"I know not—," she protested, but before the words were out of her mouth, he had taken her hand and led her onto the floor. Other couples lined up before and behind, and quiet, gentle music began to play—music that contrasted sharply with the rapid pulse of Adele's own heart. Ingram danced with grace and power and guided her through the steps and motions of the courtly dance with ease. By the time the first song had ended, Adele felt as if she had been dancing all her life.

During the next song, a fast-moving carol, Adele found herself in a ring of women who held hands and moved clockwise, while an interior circle of men moved in an opposite direction. The dance was quick and furious. Her entire body seemed wedded to the music. Surprised to see Gislebert's face rush by in a blur, she closed her eyes as the men sped past, first Ingram, then Gislebert, then Ingram, then Gislebert. Suddenly, the music changed, and each man took the hands of the woman in front of him and danced away in a new direction. Adele looked up. Ingram's arms held her securely.

"I am too tired," she said breathlessly when the music stopped. "Please, I must sit down."

The knight led her out of the hall to a bench in the massive stone entryway. Their footsteps echoed in the stillness until Ingram seated her, then he took his place by her side. "I forgot that you have not been well," he said, running his hands through his golden hair. Adele found the gesture disturbingly attractive. "Forgive me. I assumed you were as strong as you are beautiful."

"Me? Oh no, I am not beautiful," she argued, shaking her head. "You are wrong, Ingram, and you should not say such a thing to me."

"Why not? It is true." He took her hand in his, and Adele drew in her breath when he lifted her hand to his cheek. Unbidden, her newfound femininity responded to his masculine touch, and she wished for a moment that Gislebert would behave like this.

172

"Ingram, I am a married woman!"

The knight smiled, but she read sadness in his eyes. "Do you think I cannot see the pain you feel? I know, dear Adele, that the man Ahearn is not a husband to you. Why would a man sleep on the floor with a beauty like you in his bed? Why would he ignore you, unless he chooses not to love you?"

His gaze focused on her lips. His voice grew dark and liquid, and Adele sensed his restrained power. His grip on her fingers tightened a bit and frightened her. "Though I do not understand how Ahearn can be so cold, I can ask Lord Galbert to release you from this marriage," Ingram continued, his strong body leaning into hers. "He will call a bishop, who can issue an annulment, and you will be free to marry me. Just say the word, my love, and—"

"I cannot love you," she whispered. But her words lacked conviction, and Ingram heard in them the opportunity to take her into his arms. She cried out in bewilderment and fear as his strong arms encircled her, but her cry ceased when he kissed the moist hollow of her throat.

Never before had she experienced such a feeling. She did not know that touch could be like this! Her father's touch had been harsh and brutal, as had the unwelcome attentions of the cloaked man in London. Gislebert had touched her only through incidental contact, rarely on purpose, and never with tenderness. Never had a man romanced her. Never had the tender touch of a man's lips aroused the tingling sense of delight that began to flow through her.

"You are not even married to Ahearn," Ingram whispered warmly. Adele felt herself relax and melt under his touch. His lips traveled along the side of her cheek toward her ear. "You would not be with me now if you were, for I know your virtue. I know not whether Ahearn is your brother or cousin. But I know men and women, and I know you are not husband and wife. Speak now if I am wrong." He tangled his hands in her hair, and his body tensed. "Speak now!"

"I cannot deny what you say." She pulled her head back

and looked at him steadily, and his eyes closed in relief. His hand trembled and slipped from her hair. He spread his fingers and slid his right palm across her open hand. "As I love you, I will keep your secret, if you bid me," he whispered, resting his forehead upon hers. "But is it so terribly important that the world believe you are married to that piddling fool?"

"It is very important," she murmured, as his lips made whisper-light contact with her own. "It is a matter of my life or death."

"Then I shall wait," Ingram replied, the sweet throbbing of his lips making her draw closer to him. "And upon my life, he will do a better job of pretending to be your husband."

Adele could wait no longer. Her hand went around Ingram's neck and pulled his head to hers for the kiss she had never expected to want.

SEVENTEEN

Gislebert sat well behind the dancers, the manor's scrawled ledger book on the table in front of him. Let the others feast and dance, and let Jonas scamper around like a young fool. But he had danced once, and now he had work to do. Gislebert squinted at the numbers on the page as his tired eyes blurred the notations together.

"Steward, I would speak with you."

Gislebert looked up. Ingram stood there, his hand on his sword and a strong gleam in his eye. Apparently the man had enjoyed too much of Lord Galbert's drink already—a common failure of knights. With a pint of ale in their bellies, they were ready to use anything that moved for target practice.

"I'm very busy, Ingram. Can we talk tomorrow?"

"We'll talk now," Ingram answered, coming behind the table. With his broad hand he grasped Gislebert firmly by the tunic and lifted him out of his chair. He didn't seem at all drunk now.

"What?" Gislebert squeaked.

"I know things," Ingram said, his eyes burning hotly with some newfound passion. He pulled Gislebert into a corner, away from the sight of the dancers. "I know that you aren't truly married to Adele, and—" His glare demanded silence as Gislebert opened his mouth to protest. "I know you pretend to be married to save her life. Well, Ahearn, there is no sincerity in your pretense, and even the peasants joke about you and your so-called wife. From this day forward, I want to see truth in your disguise. I want you to spend more time with her, look at her, admire her beauty, and give every indication that you are completely besotted with her."

Gislebert's gaping mouth closed. What did the knight know, and how had he learned it? Surely he did not know all, or he would know that the disguise went much deeper than a false marriage.

"I cannot and will not sleep with her," Gislebert ventured, raising a hand in defense.

"I don't want you to," Ingram answered, his hand relaxing slightly from Gislebert's neck. "For I love her, and though honor and fierce necessity prevent me from publicly declaring my devotion to her, still I will watch for her and guard her with my life, if necessary. You have wounded her, Steward, with your indifference, and a beautiful woman should feel prized and valued!"

"All right," Gislebert said, raising his hands in surrender, and the knight released him. Gislebert brushed his tunic, smoothing out the wrinkles from his rough handling, then glanced up at Ingram. "What will you do with your love?" he asked, peering keenly into the knight's face. "You are right, my friend. I do not love Adele, but another, and I am leaving Southwick in the spring. I journey to France in search of my love."

"Adele will remain here with me."

Gislebert gave the knight a rueful smile. "I am afraid, Ingram, that if Adele does not go with me, you may find that she is not *exactly* what a man wants in a wife."

"First I will ask Lord Galbert to give me leave to marry," Ingram answered, with honest dignity. "And then I will ask for her love in return. I will cherish her always and treat her as the beauty she is."

"Well," Gislebert answered, trying with difficulty to stifle the laughter that threatened to rise from his throat, "I hope you have better luck with her than I did. At times she is more stubborn and ungainly than a boy, and—"

Ingram's fist halted Gislebert's words, and the force of the blow spun the troubadour to the ground. Every nerve in his face roared in pain, and his bony back throbbed with the impact of his fall.

"If you insult her again," Ingram said, standing over Gislebert, "I will kill you. Heed my words, Ahearn, until you leave. I will be watching you."

Gislebert was glad when Jonas did not remark on the purple bruise that covered his cheek, but even so, he was faintly annoyed that the boy seemed not to notice it. Jonas returned from the Christmas feast in a thoughtful daze, and not even Gislebert's pitiful moaning could rouse the boy to conversation. Jonas simply came in, murmured hello, removed the gaudy surcoat he wore, and climbed into bed.

Gislebert made his bed on the floor and looked longingly at the mattress where Jonas lay. There was plenty of room for two, even two men, and Gislebert's aching bones demanded softness. But the thought of Ingram's face peering in through the shutter in the morning quickly banished the idea from Gislebert's mind. He laid his bruised body down upon the hard floor, grateful that none of his bones had been broken.

'Twould be quite a sight, Ingram marrying the boy, Gislebert thought to himself, a crooked smile sending fresh pain along the nerves of his cheek. *If Jonas chooses to remain behind, I'll have a bit of revenge upon Ingram after all.*

Adele awakened before sunrise the next morning and stretched luxuriously in bed, reliving again the touch of Ingram's lips upon hers. Such magic had been in his voice, his words! Was it for this lovely sensation that men and women strove past the point of reason? Was it for this feeling that Gislebert pursued Nadine?

Gislebert stirred, and Adele sat up in bed and hugged her knees. Presently the troubadour groaned and opened his eyes, and Adele noticed for the first time the huge purple and blue bruise upon his cheek.

"Troubadour! What happened to you?"

Gislebert groaned as his facial muscles twitched. "I should have known I'm not a brawler," he mumbled, sitting up. "Serves me right for mingling among men who aren't of my fine sensibilities." He winced as he turned his eyes in her direction.

"Troubadour, I would ask you a question," she said, rocking gently back and forth. "What is love? And how do you know if you have found it?"

Gislebert raised an eyebrow and made an attempt to smile as he turned to face her. "That's right, the knight Ingram fancies himself in love with Adele," he said, leaning against a leg of the table. "He even gave me a warning—I'm to act more the role of the proper husband toward Adele or the knight will have my head."

Adele drew in her breath. "Really? He said that?"

"Aye, and more," Gislebert said, gently pressing his fingertips to his bruised cheek. "He's right, though. Everyone at Southwick thinks us a genuinely odd couple."

Adele did not answer but studied the mounds her feet made under the covers.

"So," Gislebert went on, slowly raising himself from the floor, "from today until we leave, I will be a dutiful and proper husband for Adele. I will watch her and talk to her and do everything but sleep with her." He winked at Adele. "Ingram was very specific about that. Although I don't know how I'm supposed to be a husband, knowing who and what you are—"

"Am I so horrible?" Adele asked sourly.

Gislebert laughed. "As a boy, no. As a woman—" He pretended to shudder. "But I have worked out a solution. I shall imagine you are my beautiful Nadine. We shall walk together and talk together and dance together, as Nadine and Gislebert, and you may fantasize me to be any maid you wish, Jonas. It's only for two months more, of course, and then we'll take our leave of this place."

Adele didn't answer but angrily kicked the covers from her feet as Gislebert threw his cloak across his shoulders and stepped out into the freezing air. "Good morning, Ingram," she heard him call. "Had you a merry Christmas yesterday? My wife and I celebrated most joyfully and fell asleep as soon as we returned home."

The next eleven days were filled with continued Christmas festivities, dances, and enormous meals. Gislebert made a point of taking time for Jonas. He had always enjoyed the boy's company, and for a while he rationalized his role by pretending they were actors in a drama. Just as men always wore women's robes to play women's parts, so he and Jonas were playing parts for the sake of their own lives.

But Gislebert could not still his longing heart, and often it took all his will not to turn from Jonas in despair. It should be Nadine at his side, not this boy in maiden's garb.

Instead of Jonas's dark eyes he should be gazing into the clear blue eyes Nadine surely possessed; in place of the angular line of Jonas's jaw he should be admiring the soft curves of beauty that surely belonged to Nadine. Instead of the dark, full hair that shone in the candlelight, he imagined lustrous gold; instead of an elfin form, he longed to admire the voluptuous fullness he was sure his Nadine now possessed.

One night as they sat at supper in the great hall, Gislebert lost himself in his imaginings of Nadine and sighed. Ingram immediately turned in his direction, one eyebrow raised in a query, and Lady Wynne glanced sharply at Gislebert.

Gislebert jerked himself back to reality and cleared his throat. "Let us have a toast," he said, raising the golden goblet at his place. "To love—the eternal, changeless force that drives us all forward!"

"To love," Lady Wynne seconded, nodding to Adele and raising her glass in triumph.

"To love," Ingram echoed, lifting his glass while he
glared suspiciously at Gislebert.

"To love," Jonas said softly. His glass touched Gislebert's,
and they drank deeply.

The Christmas holidays brought an end not only to work
but to everyday standards of behavior and status. Lord
Galbert was unusually casual and free during the holidays,
and Lady Wynne literally let her hair escape from its confining plaits and wore it long and free over her shoulders.

Adele found herself caught up in this new freedom
and carelessness. Two men stood ready and willing to
give her attention: Gislebert, her newly devoted "husband," and Ingram, whose ever-watchful smile followed
her wherever she went. Under the pleased and indulgent
attitudes of both men, she laughed, she smiled, she followed her impulses, not caring what the troubadour
thought or might say when they were alone. She wore her
dresses long and her belt tight, enjoying her image as a
woman.

On Twelfth Day, the last day of holiday, Lord Galbert
presented Ingram with his gift: a fine black stallion. Gislebert
and Adele, standing among the crowd, watched as Ingram
fell to his knees before the lord and kissed Galbert's hand
in friendship and fealty. "Rise, Sir Ingram, my servant and
friend," Lord Galbert instructed. "Enjoy the bounty you have
earned and so richly deserve."

Ingram mounted, and the crowd stepped back as
the young knight rode the magnificent beast in a circle
around the castle keep. Chickens scattered, children ran in
glee, and the cattle, which had not yet been butchered,
protested as the stallion galloped by.

Ingram completed his circle and saluted Lord Galbert as
the stallion pranced nervously in the courtyard. "My thanks
to you, my lord," the knight said, removing his helmet in
respect. He tossed the helmet to a squire and gathered the

reins in his hands. "Might I, my lord, take one of your household for a short ride into the country?"

"Why not?" Lord Galbert answered, waving his hand generously. "Take whomever you like. The animal is yours and yours alone."

Ingram urged the horse forward until the animal stood before Adele and Gislebert. "Adele, will you do me a great honor and accompany me?" Ingram asked, his eyes shining down upon her.

"Sir, my wife!" Gislebert protested—too vigorously, Adele thought.

"Do you mind, sir?" Ingram asked, as a hundred ears listened.

Gislebert paused dramatically, and Adele knew he was purposely exaggerating his role in their little play. "In the hands of an honorable knight such as you, sir, she will be safe," Gislebert answered, bowing deeply to the knight. He stood and extended Adele's hand to Ingram, who swung her up behind him with ease. He tenderly placed her hands about his waist and then spurred the horse, and as the people of Southwick cheered, they rode out through the barbican and into the frozen countryside.

The chilly wind stung Adele's ears, and she nestled her head against Ingram's back as he rode down the long road from the castle. She had never been down this road and gasped in surprise when she lifted her head to behold a sandy stretch that extended from one horizon to the other. The wild, lonely, barren place frightened her, and she shrank against Ingram for reassurance. "What is this place?" she asked, breathless.

"The English Channel," Ingram answered, frank astonishment in his voice. He turned and placed his gloved hand on her cheek. "Beyond this, my love, is France, and beyond France, Spain. Surely you have heard of these places?"

"I have heard but never imagined anything like this," she said, breathing in the exhilarating scent of salt water and sea air.

His eyes glinted, and Adele realized that geography did

not lie uppermost in his mind. "I waited as long as I could," he said, his voice like a warm embrace in the chilly air. "But I had to see you again."

He turned from her, and Adele experienced a second of disappointment. But he only dismounted and tied the horse to the trunk of a scrubby tree. He extended his hands to her, and she slid from the saddle and fell into his arms. Laughing, he pulled her to his side as they ran along the beach, finally dropping to the sand behind a wind-blown dune covered in brown sea grasses.

"Adele," he whispered, his breath tickling her ear. "How well you were named, for you are noble and true."

She closed her eyes, not wanting to think. She did not understand this tenuous link between them, the force that made her skin crawl when he touched her, this warmth that rose from her belly even though the wind blew cold upon her face. *Is this love?* she wondered, as his hands slid over her shoulders and down her arms. She shuddered in pleasure as his lips brushed her forehead. His caress was not rough but tender. There was nothing demanding in him, only gentleness.

"Ingram," she whispered, catching his face in her hands and turning it so that she looked into his eyes. "Do you love me?"

"I do," he said, pulling free from her grasp to nuzzle her neck. "I can show you how much."

"But why?" She put her hand under his chin and again made him look at her. "What makes you love me? What makes Gisle—I mean, Ahearn love Nadine, and what makes Lord Galbert love Lady Wynne?"

Ingram slipped his arm about her and laughed. "Wiser men than I have asked that question and failed to find an answer," he said, looking deep into her eyes. "I only know that I loved you the day I saw you in that horrid hospice. As I carried you on my horse, I prayed that God would spare you for this moment, so I could tell you of my love. As you recovered, I watched you. You never complained, never cried out, never reacted in anger—"

"You do not know me well." She placed her hand gently

on his chest, keeping a space between them, but still he caressed her with his eyes.

"I know you well enough," he answered, reaching for her hand. He kissed it, then pressed it inside his surcoat, next to his skin. "Feel my heart pounding, Adele; it beats for you!" he whispered. "Next month the steward will leave, and surely then you will not need to hide as his wife. I will marry you and keep you safe, and if anyone should try to harm you, I will defend you with my life. Just say you'll be mine, dear, beautiful Adele!"

His heart beat hard against her palm and sent a wave of warmth along her arm. Did she love him? She did not know. She only knew that Gislebert did not love her, and Ingram did. She wanted to love him! She felt her heart skip as she sought to place herself on this lofty plane from which Ingram declared his love. Her lips trembled, a thrill raced through her, and she was conscious only of his nearness.

He groaned, pulling her into his arms, and she nestled into his supple strength. In Ingram she could find protection and acceptance. A small sound of wonder came from her throat as his lips found hers and claimed them.

"Come back, Adele! On an oath, I promise I will not force you!" Ingram's voice came to her on the wind, and Adele wiped tears from her cheek as she walked on the road from the beach. Her nightmare had reared its ugly head once more—the man she had thought would protect her had pressed his advantage of strength and size, and his face now bore the angry scratches of her resistance.

She heard him curse softly, then came the muffled clip-clop of the horse on the sandy road. Soon he rode next to her and extended his hand from the height of his saddle. "Come, Adele, let me take you back to the castle," Ingram said, his eyes watering in the biting wind. "May God strike me dead if I meant to hurt you."

She did not answer but staggered on, limping. She had

turned her ankle as she sprinted through the sand, trying to escape him.

"Adele, you cannot go back to the castle this way. You left with me on a simple ride, and to come back tattered and disheveled . . ." He slowed the horse to a walk and kept pace with her. "Forgive me, Adele. I was hasty in my desire for your love, but I am a man—"

"A man?" She choked on the word. "Do men always abuse the women they love?"

"What are you talking about? Come on, love, ride with me."

She did not answer but continued in silence, trying to find answers to her own confusion. She did not know this man, and yet he had awakened a desire within her that she did not know she possessed. But ultimately he wanted little more than the stranger in London had . . . than her father had on the day she ran away. When Ingram's kisses had grown too forceful, he had not listened to her protests. When his hands had fumbled with her tunic, he had ignored her pleas.

"It's an hour's walk to Southwick and a ten-minute ride," Ingram said, leaning toward her with a gentle smile. "Come and ride with me. We can forget this ever happened."

"No." She stopped in the road and cast an angry look up at him. "Go to Southwick without me, Ingram, and tell the others whatever you like. But I shall never come near you again."

"Why?" His eyes were honestly troubled. "I love you. I would not hurt you. I've sworn to protect you—"

She spat on his boot and watched his handsome face harden. "Good-bye, then," he said, a wall coming up behind his eyes as he gathered his reins. "They will raise the drawbridge at dark. Make haste or you will freeze tonight in the fields."

The knight spurred his horse and galloped down the road toward the castle, while Adele wiped from her eyes a new outpouring of angry tears.

"My lord, I am worried about my wife," Gislebert said, bowing nervously before Galbert and Wynne as they sat at supper. "Ingram returned some time ago, and there has been no sign of Adele. May I organize a search for her?"

Lady Wynne tilted her head, and her eyes shone with curiosity. "Tell me, Ahearn, if you love your wife," she asked simply.

"Of course I do," Gislebert said, stepping back as if offended. "That is why I'm begging, my lord, for a company of knights to look for her. She may be hurt, or ill, and the weather is frightful outside—"

"Did you see Ingram?" Lady Wynne persisted. "His face is scratched, and he has not smiled since his return. He says your wife refused to come back."

"I care not about his scratches," Gislebert answered. "He is a knight and can take care of himself. But my wife, my Adele—"

"Search for her yourself," Lord Galbert said, waving his hand. "You are the fool, Ahearn, for allowing Ingram to take your wife from you. My men are drunk from their revelry and in no condition to be of any use to you. Take a horse and a torch, and we will alert the guards to lower the bridge when you return."

Gislebert looked at the bleary-eyed master of the castle and nodded in stunned reply. For all his faithful service, was he to receive only a horse and a promise to lower the drawbridge?

The sun lingered just above the horizon as Gislebert returned to his house—*their* house—and filled a bag with men's clothing. He grabbed a blanket and ran for the stables, selecting an aged mare that Lord Galbert would not miss. Mounting with his supplies and a torch, he yelled for the guards to hold the drawbridge open until he had passed through.

Adele walked slowly and wept, hugging herself. Her tears flowed without explanation, her thoughts jumbled in an incoherent disorder, and her belly cramped with fear as the bitterly cold wind blew upon her. The sun hung low in the west, and she did not think of Southwick but of shelter. She limped through a ravaged field until she found a large rock to shield her from the biting wind as she rested.

A distinct wetness between her legs alarmed her, and when she rose, she discovered a spot of blood on the back of her gown. She groaned and sank to the ground in surprise. Was this an act of God for reassuming the clothes of a woman? She had begun to bleed as all women did. Now, she remembered Laudine's prediction: She would develop the full body and desires of a woman.

She wiped her eyes and hiccuped as a hysterical sob escaped her. The desires of a woman? Did women desire to be manhandled and taunted by men who claimed to love them? Surely it was better to be a man, even a monk who put aside fleshly desires and lived without love. Better to walk with Gislebert as a man than be a woman and pressured by hot-blooded knights like Ingram.

The sun slipped below the western horizon, and Adele realized that the gates of Southwick would be closed for the night. The wind had risen, and the cold had grown more bitter. Surely she would die here tonight. She wrapped her cloak around her, grateful for its warmth, and laid her head against the rock for support.

She thought she was dreaming when she heard her name. "Jonas!" a voice called in the darkness, "Jo—nas." The sound of a horse's hooves accompanied the sound, and the glare of a torch burned from the highway.

"Gislebert!" Adele answered, leaping to her unsteady feet. She hobbled toward the road, where the troubadour dismounted from a huge gray mare and ran toward her. In her excitement and gratitude, she threw her arms around him and realized, after the shock of joy had passed, that the troubadour's relief equaled her own. "Is it really you, Gislebert?" she asked. "I thought I was alone; I thought I would die. . . ."

"It is Gislebert, your loyal friend," he answered, holding the torch aloft so he could see her face. "And you will not die, Jonas. Forgive me for my foolishness and my coldness. It was too much to ask of you, this deception. We will leave Ahearn and Adele at Southwick and go on with our lives and our friendship as it was before."

He smiled in relief and gestured toward the horse. "I've brought men's clothing. From this point on we will face the world with our true faces. I'm sorry, Jonas, but when Ingram returned without you, I knew our masquerade was done and our time finished. . . ."

She held up her hand for silence. "It is behind us. I'm glad you came."

Gislebert did not answer, respecting her reticence to discuss Ingram, and turned to untie a bag of clothing from the mare's saddle. She felt her heart sink at the thought of donning the plain short tunic of a man, but she had smoothed her face by the time he turned to face her again. "Dress properly, and I'll find a sheltered place for us to sleep," Gislebert said, pulling the mare from the road. "We can have a fire, and I've brought blankets, so we'll make it through the night very well."

Adele took the bag of clothing and walked toward a dark recess among the rocks. She would find a way to hide her bleeding and her developing figure, and count on Gislebert's obsession with Nadine to keep him blind to *her* true face. If, through all that had happened this day, Gislebert still did not see her, perhaps he never would.

St. Denis

Be joyful in hope,
patient in affliction, faithful in prayer.
ROMANS 12:12

EIGHTEEN

The calm reflection of the moon on the water outside the sea captain's window should have been comforting, but Adele's heart stirred with unrest. So much had happened in the past day! Once again Gislebert had stepped in to change her life, and she had allowed it. Better this man, who regarded her with simple friendship and loyalty, than a love-crazed knight who ignored her pleas and most sacred wishes.

Gislebert and the sea captain shook hands on their deal: The mare would serve as payment for their passage across the channel. Gislebert felt no guilt for taking the animal, for he had left Southwick without the wages that had been promised for his work.

"We sail at first light tomorrow," the captain said, turning his attention to the charts on the table in front of him. "Don't be late, or we'll sail without you."

"Is there a place for lodging nearby?" Gislebert asked, leaning over the man's desk. "We will need someone to awaken us."

The captain jerked his head toward a back room where Adele could see piles of rope and mildewed sailcloth. "You can bunk down in there, if you like." His faded blue eyes regarded them with suspicion. "Unless there's some reason you'd be needing to sleep hidden. If so, I could take you out to the boat."

"No, this room will be fine," Gislebert answered,

bowing politely. "Though we come after dark, we are honest men, sir."

The captain shrugged. "I've sailed rogues, priests, ladies, and Norman noblemen under cover of darkness," he said. "It doesn't matter to me what a man's done or where he goes to hide from his crime, so long as he has money to pay for his passage."

"Then good night." Gislebert led the way toward the back room and motioned to Adele. "In here, young Jonas. It won't be as comfortable as our lodgings at Southwick, but we can bear it for one night."

Adele noticed the sailor studying her. He scratched his head as she walked past, then grunted and left the building, slamming the door behind him. "What do we do from here, Troubadour?" Adele asked, following Gislebert into the back room. She sank wearily onto a pile of sailcloth. "How are we to make our way to St. Denis? I don't speak French. We have no horse—"

"I speak the language, and many of Normandy and the other provinces speak our tongue," Gislebert replied, pulling his cloak more closely about him in the chill of the small room. "And we have walked before. We shall get by, you and I, on our wits alone. I can continue to be a scribe or sing again as a troubadour—"

"Under which name?"

Gislebert paused. "Stephen will undoubtedly have spies in France, but the laws and edicts of Stephen will not extend to that land. We will use our own names, Jonas, and the devil take Stephen's order. I am sick to death of Ahearn and Adele." The troubadour ran his hands through his hair, "Surely God frowned on us in our deception, and now that we are our true selves, I pray he will reveal his will."

Adele looked away as the troubadour sighed and lay down upon the wooden floor. "I can't believe that we are almost to France! I am glad, Jonas, that you gave us an excuse to leave Southwick early. Although this is not how I planned to make our journey, still, why should we not go now? You are well, the year is new, and my Nadine waits just across this sea."

"And what of Lord Galbert and Lady Wynne?" Adele asked softly. "I liked them. I was beginning to feel at home at Southwick."

Gislebert scowled. "They will do well without us, Jonas. I left the accounts in good order, and Lord Galbert will undoubtedly commandeer some scribe as he invoked my services months ago. As for Lady Wynne—" He laughed. "Her influence upon you was too strong, my boy. And Ingram! The force of necessity bade me come after you. If he loved you, as he said he did, I feared he would continue his suit and discover that you were not a maid at all. We have to leave now, my friend. I'm sorry if you will miss the place."

"Men's clothes are not warm enough. I am chilled to the bone," Adele interrupted, deliberately changing the subject. "Why did you not bring me my red cloak, Troubadour? It was warm and full enough for two people."

Gislebert raised up on one elbow and grinned at Adele. "Because, young Jonas, I never want to see you in woman's clothes again. Ingram's attentions for Adele gave me great concern, but worse still—"

"What?" Adele asked crossly.

"Even I was beginning to find you attractive," Gislebert answered, smiling broadly. "Now sleep, for tomorrow we rise before the sun and journey to where the beautiful Nadine waits for us."

"For you, you mean," Adele answered, turning her back to Gislebert.

"For me," Gislebert agreed. "But surely love waits for you, too, my little brother. Mayhap you will fall in love, too, with the first pretty French girl we meet."

They landed on the shores of Normandy at Le Havre, where the Seine River joined with the mighty waters of the channel. "This water," Gislebert said, his eyes glowing as he gazed inland, "will lead us to Paris, which will lead us to St. Denis. Our journey is almost at an end, Jonas."

Adele said nothing but stared across the countryside. Even in winter, the fields were green, the landscape flat, the winds milder and more temperate than they had been in England. The sun's path on the quiet river dazzled her eyes, and the countryside seemed yet virgin and unblemished. "It is beautiful," she whispered, not wanting to take her eyes from the land. "Perhaps we *will* find happiness here."

"Most certainly we will," Gislebert answered, his hand clapping her shoulder. "Now, boy, press on. We will find shelter and food for the night, and continue until we reach St. Denis. Nothing will deter our quest today."

To speed their journey and provide for their food and lodging, Gislebert resorted to his old trade as troubadour. Though he no longer had a lute but sang a cappella, still his songs were well received. He and Jonas rang the bell or announced themselves at every large manor they passed and were unanimously invited in and welcomed at dinner. While Jonas ate as if the meal were his last, Gislebert sang stories of love and regretted that he had not visited France sooner.

Inspiration visited him one night and offered a new song. Gislebert sang it in French the next day, to the delight of his hosts. The song told the tale of a boy who pretended to be a maid and found himself wooed by a handsome and valiant knight. After an enthusiastic courtship, the knight discovered the shameful pretense and left the boy out in the cold night, where he died. The song elicited laughter in the beginning, but evoked tears from men and women alike in the end.

"What new song do you sing?" Jonas asked one afternoon after Lady Nicola of Gisors sent them from her castle loaded with gifts. They rode on two handsome geldings, wore new clothes, and Gislebert carried a purse of silver hidden under his new surcoat. "What are the words? And why does that song bring us such splendid treasures?"

"You would not like it," Gislebert answered, patting the neck of his new mount. "But God inspired me to invent it. We shall reach Nadine even more quickly now, young friend."

"Why did you never sing that song in England?" Jonas persisted. "We could have used such results long ago."

Gislebert turned back to smile at his young friend. "I could never have imagined such a tale before this time," he answered. He spurred his mount, and the animal lunged forward. "Onward, Jonas!" he called over his shoulder. "We should reach shelter before nightfall."

Three weeks after their arrival in France, Gislebert and Adele rode triumphantly into the village that surrounded the Abbey of St. Denis. Adele had never seen such a town: austere and orderly, the men and women wore dark colors and hurried from place to place with their eyes habitually downcast. St. Denis stood in marked contrast to the other rowdy villages they had visited.

"What is wrong with these people?" she whispered to Gislebert as their horses carefully picked their way through the wide village streets.

Gislebert nodded respectfully to a passing monk and turned to Adele. "The town revolves around the abbey and the cathedral here. The bishop of the cathedral rules the abbey and the village. The men and women of this town place their duties to God before their own pleasures."

"And your Nadine is *here?*" Adele asked, raising an eyebrow.

"Lady Jehannenton is most pious, and she chooses to live here," Gislebert corrected her. "Nadine is but a servant, though a most beautiful and noble one."

Two single lines of monks proceeded from a long, narrow building, and Gislebert and Adele reined in their horses to let the monks cross the street uninterrupted.

"So where do we go from here?" Adele asked. "Perhaps

we should find lodgings—we have silver enough to pay. Then we can—"

"We will find Lady Jehannenton at all costs," Gislebert said, not even glancing in Adele's direction. "If all goes well, perhaps I shall sleep in the arms of my Nadine tonight!"

The last monk passed in front of them, and Gislebert eagerly spurred his horse forward as Adele watched him go. Had she followed him so far only to be left alone?

The house of Lady Jehannenton stood only a few feet from the walls of the abbey, and Gislebert had to ask only a single peasant woman where to find it. Surrounded by a tall stone wall, the house was effectively cut off from the village except for a sturdy oak door that served as a gate. Peering through a barred opening in the door, Gislebert saw a dignified, sturdy house of stone with shuttered windows, a generous courtyard filled with blooming flowers, and smoke ascending from the chimney.

Gislebert murmured, his heart beating strangely in his chest. His body tightened in fear, and he could scarcely breathe. "Jonas!" he called out, his voice hoarse. "I cannot move. Ring for a servant and see if we will be admitted."

Jonas slipped off his horse and walked to the gate— rather slowly, Gislebert thought. But his nerves had reached the point where anything that stalled his reunion with Nadine seemed torturous. Jonas rang the bell and waited a few moments, then Gislebert saw a woman step through the door of the house and approach the gate. A white wimple covered her head and neck, a formless black tunic her body. Surely this dowdy creature could not be Nadine! A nun, perhaps, but not Nadine.

The woman walked to the gate but did not lift her eyes toward the opening. *"Est-ce qu'il y a des hommes ici?"* she called.

Jonas looked at Gislebert in confusion, and the troubadour slid from his horse, coming to stand beside Jonas.

"Oui, il y a des hommes ici," he called, then to Jonas he whispered, "She wants to know if we are men."

The maid threw up her hands and scurried away as if frightened, and Jonas called out to stop her. "Please, good lady, we desire an audience with your mistress."

The maid paused, and Gislebert pulled eagerly on the bars at the gate. "We would see your mistress, mademoiselle. We are Gislebert and Jonas, from England, and we have journeyed many days and nights to reach this place."

The maid turned to face them, then spoke in halting English: "I am sorry, but Madame Jehannenton receives no male visitors save her priest."

"Surely she will see us," Gislebert said, smiling. "We have come so far, and I bring regards from her distant cousin, King Stephen of England."

The maid stubbornly shook her head. "It is no good, monsieur. Madame took a vow on the death of her husband, and she will see no other men. Though King Louis himself should desire to visit, he would not be allowed to pass though these gates."

"By the sword of St. Denis, mademoiselle, I don't wish to marry her! I only want to speak to her! Has she a maid, a girl called Nadine—"

The servant put up her hand in protest. "Please, monsieur, no more. None of the ladies in the household will see men, including Mesdemoiselles Nadine and Melusina, in respect for their mistress's vow. Now go your way, *s'il vous plaît.*"

She turned, her back a black wall of stone, and Gislebert slumped in defeat. "What sort of woman pledges that she will not even look upon a man?" he shouted, waving his hands in the air like a crazy man as he walked to his horse. "'Twould be nearly an impossible vow to keep."

"A loving woman who honored her husband's loyalty," Jonas answered, gathering the bridle of his horse. The boy put a foot in the stirrup and paused before mounting. "And the vow is not so difficult to keep, if the lady cloisters herself in her own home."

"What do we do now?" Gislebert leaned his forehead on his saddle and tried to think. "If they are truly cloistered in that house, there is no way in." He laughed bitterly and raised his eyes to heaven. "As long as I am a man, that is. But if I were not a man, how could I love Nadine?"

"How, indeed?" Jonas echoed. He turned his horse away from the house, then turned back to the troubadour. "Don't worry," the boy said, giving Gislebert a melancholy smile. "Your Nadine is bound by her mistress's vow only so long as the lady lives. And if your love is truly deathless, Troubadour, surely it will outlive an old woman."

Gislebert sighed in his impatience and remounted his horse. "I suppose there is nothing to do but find lodgings and employment," he said, looking around. "For I will not leave this place without accomplishing all that I came to do. At the first opportunity, though it take me years, I will offer Nadine my heart."

They gave thirty silver coins to a merchant near the cathedral, who promptly turned his wife and chickens out of his meager house and bowed as Gislebert and Adele entered. "You will find rest here," the man said, greedily clutching the silver in his hand.

"I'm sure we will," Gislebert answered gruffly. "Now, away with you, sir, for all is well."

Adele looked around and crinkled her nose in distaste. The place reeked of animals and stale smoke. Lumps of dried cow manure glowed in the shallow fire pit. "Find us a log, Gislebert, so we may have a decent fire," she said, holding her chapped hands over the glowing coals. "I may never be warm again."

"How am I to find logs when my mind is fixed on reaching Nadine?" Gislebert asked, sinking to the only stool in the room, his head in his hands. "I can see no way to reach her, Jonas, unless . . ."

"Find me a log and food, and I will help you reach Nadine," Adele replied firmly. She held up the leather flap that served as a door and pointed to the street beyond. "Go, Troubadour, and be of use, or we have come to this place to die."

"I may die of a broken heart," Gislebert mumbled, but he stood, slumping, to follow the direction of Adele's outstretched hand.

"Your heart will not break," Adele snapped, turning the full fury of her eyes upon his haggard face. "There is too much work to be done. You say you are a man—if you are, and if you would win your love, Troubadour, rouse your tongue and your hands to work."

He left without answering. In his absence, she swept the house and put things in order, boarding their horses in a stable nearby and transferring their few possessions from their saddles to their new home. The mistress of the house next door agreed to give them a bowl of pottage in exchange for a portrait, and by the time Gislebert returned with logs for the fire, the succulent aroma of food filled the house.

As Gislebert arranged the logs in the open fire pit, Adele noted with satisfaction that the troubadour's eyes had lost much of their look of hopelessness. She leaned against the wall and sighed in contentment. Though not as grand as the steward's house at Southwick, this place would serve them well. They would gather proper beds, a table, and food, and as long as Nadine was cloistered away in the stone house near the abbey, Adele could be happily content with the troubadour.

As long as Nadine . . . As usual, Nadine stood between them and happiness. Would the troubadour be able to regain his sense, or would his frustration render him an emotional invalid?

"Troubadour, you must put thoughts of Nadine behind you," she reprimanded as he moped by the fire, his head on his arms. "You will never win your love if you do not rise to your feet like a man and do something. What is love, if not a call to action?"

"What is love?" Gislebert murmured, his eyes misting. "It is an inborn suffering which causes each one to wish above all things the embraces of the other."

"What do you know of suffering?" Adele asked, looking down on him with gentle scorn. "You, who were born in a castle and reared by noblemen—"

"There is no greater torment than my love," Gislebert interrupted, tiny twin reflections of the fire shining in his eyes. "I am tormented because my love may not gain its desire. I am frightened to think that I might be wasting my efforts and my time. I fear that rumors of my love may reach my lady and harm her regard for me. I fear that Nadine may scorn my poverty and my lack of beauty."

"Men do not scorn your poverty, nor women your lack of beauty," Adele countered. "Have you not been well received in castles throughout France and England? You are a deserving man, Troubadour, and surely the lady will appreciate all you have endured to find her."

"That is my greatest fear," Gislebert whispered, his eyes focusing on Adele's. "I shudder to confess it, but as God knows my heart he knows I am often fearful of the future. What if Nadine returns my love and I experience joy abundant, only to lose her later?"

Adele shook her head and turned away. "You are a fool," she whispered. She spread her cloak on the packed earthen floor and lay down to face the fire. "Sleep well, Troubadour, for if we are to survive in this place, we must go to work."

NINETEEN

I cannot serve as a troubadour in St. Denis," Gislebert told Adele as he breakfasted on leftover pottage the next morning. "Songs require that I meditate on love, and such meditation here would drive me to madness. I shall visit the merchants and offer my services as a scribe."

"Perhaps I can find work, too," Adele said, folding her cloak carefully into a cowl around her shoulders. When she was sure that she was fully covered, she pulled her hair back with a leather strap and deliberately smudged her cheeks with dirt. "I heard yesterday that the abbot of St. Denis seeks skilled artisans."

Gislebert pulled on his boots and nodded. "'Tis a good idea. Maybe the abbot of St. Denis will need a scribe, too."

The village of St. Denis stood, in a unique way, as a picture of a particular struggle in the Christian church. Adele did not understand all the struggle entailed. She only knew there were two monasteries of St. Denis—a magnificent, impressive one inside the village walls and an austere, smaller monastery hidden in the forest half an hour's walk outside the village.

Gislebert had attempted to explain the differences between the two religious houses, but all she clearly understood was that the forest monastery was led by devout monks who did not believe in art or adornment. The Royal Abbey of St. Denis inside the city, however, held the piously preserved relics of St. Denis, St. Rustique, and St. Eleuthere, the holy martyrs of France. As the home of such worthy relics, the Cluniac monks who ran this abbey felt it their duty to adorn the buildings of the cathedral and abbey with as much gold and colorful paint as possible.

Adele had often felt uncomfortable dressed as a man, but when she and the troubadour stood at the gate of the Abbey of St. Denis, she felt like an absolute interloper. The monk on duty at the gatehouse raked his eyes over both her and Gislebert, then wordlessly pointed away from the abbey toward the great cathedral that stood just beyond the abbey gate.

"The abbot works today in the cathedral?" Gislebert asked.

The monk pressed his hands together and bowed, the bald tonsured spot on his head looking faintly ridiculous in his thick hair. Gislebert thanked him, and they went on their way.

"Why do they shave their heads?" Adele asked, trying to keep pace with Gislebert's eager, long strides. "Why are they so silent?"

"They are silent, Jonas, because the rule of St. Benedict demands frugality in all personal things, even the economy of speech," Gislebert answered. "They are tonsured at investure as a symbol: as lambs are sheared before their master, so the monks are shorn before God." The troubadour frowned. "But why do they post a young man at the gate? That, young Jonas, is unusual."

"Why?"

Gislebert's brow furrowed in thought. "Usually the Benedictine order demands that an older monk be placed there, one whose years will not permit him to wander about. But this young monk . . ."

"Perhaps the abbot fears an assault on his life," Adele joked. "The brawny strength of the younger man would prevail against any intruder."

Gislebert nodded thoughtfully at her words. "In any case, this abbot of St. Denis may be cut of a different cloth," he said, rubbing his hands together. "This may bode well for us, Jonas. A devout Benedictine would rarely employ outsiders, so perhaps there is hope for both of us."

Adele had never been inside any church save the small mud house that served as the sanctuary of God in her village. The ancient basilica of St. Denis left her breathless. Entering the wide narthex of the building, she stepped through towering wooden doors into the church's long center aisle, eclipsed in its grandeur only by the huge stone altar at the end of the nave. "It's incredible," she whispered, raising her eyes slowly to the roof, which was partially hidden by the scaffolding of construction workers. "More lofty than King Stephen's house."

"Surely it should be, for it is the house of God," Gislebert remarked, stepping past her. He saluted a workman who hurried by, and asked for the whereabouts of the abbot.

The workman grimaced and pointed past the altar. "You will find Abbot Suger back there, ranting and raving about something," the man replied in a voice heavy with an unmistakable Saxon accent.

Gislebert moved immediately forward, but Adele followed the workman. "Be you from England?" she whispered.

The man grinned so broadly that she could count five blackened teeth. "Aye, and so are many of us here. The abbot's called for workers from England, France, Italy, and Denmark. I think he'd bring workers from hades itself if a man could sculpt a decent statue."

She thanked him with her eyes and followed Gislebert down the nave.

Gislebert paused on the edge of the transept as workmen in short tunics scurried to escape the anger of an antagonistic voice. Motionless robed monks, bound by holy obedience, stood in rapt attention as the voice droned endlessly on. As Gislebert craned his neck for a better view, he finally spotted the only man imposing enough to be Abbot Suger.

He was dressed in the colorful robes of a bishop, his ponderous waistline accented by a silken belt. His plump hands flew through the air as he punctuated his words with striking gestures. Brown hair neatly framed his face and tonsure. A full brown beard lined his jaw and chin, and a look of ingrained snobbery dominated his full lips as the massive and mighty Suger berated his listeners.

"Let every man follow his own opinion," Suger bellowed at two barefoot monks who stood before him with defiance in their eyes. "You Cistercian brothers may keep your simple buildings and bare feet, but as for myself, I declare that it has always seemed right to me that everything which is most precious should above all add to the celebration of the Holy Eucharist. If golden cups, golden phials, and small golden mortars were used, in obedience to the Word of God and by the command of the prophet, to contain the blood of he-goats, calves, or red heifers, how much more should they be used to hold the blood of Jesus Christ?"

"But the holy rule of St. Benedict demands frugality and temperance in all we do," one of the barefoot monks protested. "We bring you this letter from Abbot Bernard, and he protests that the walls of this church shine, but the poor man is hungry!"

The visiting monk opened the parchment at his belt, unrolled it, and began to read: "'The church walls are clothed in gold, while the children of the church remain naked. What is gold doing in the holy place? I fear, my brother Suger, that you are more concerned with the beauty of the statues than with the virtue of the saints. The poor of St. Denis are allowed to groan in hunger, while the money that might have been spent to feed them is spent on useless luxury.'"

"Enough!" Abbot Suger held up his hand and pressed

his lips together. "Those who criticize us claim that the celebration of the Mass needs only a holy soul, a pure mind, and
faithful intention. We are certainly in complete agreement
that these are what matter above all else, but we believe that
outward ornaments and sacred chalices should serve
nowhere so much as in our worship."

The abbot lowered his voice to a conspiratorial whisper.
"Even the saints of this church speak on this subject. Whilst
I, through weakness and pusillanimity, had planned a modest altarpiece, the holy martyrs themselves procured in a
most unexpected way much gold and stones so precious that
even kings would be unlikely to own them. It was as though
they wished to tell us through their own mouths that
whether we wished it or not, they wanted the very best."

"But Abbot—" The second monk tried to intercede.

"There is no room for objection," Abbot Suger continued, his face set in his resoluteness. "Even now the saints
bring me all that we need to complete this masterful edifice;
for instance, these two here!"

Gislebert dropped his jaw as the heavily jeweled finger
of the abbot pointed through the sea of monks to him and
Jonas. "How do I know that God has not sent these two
men to me?" the abbot asked the monks. "Watch, my sons,
and see how God provides. You, with the red hair—what
gift or service do you offer to me today?"

Gislebert shifted his weight uneasily as he struggled to
find his voice. "I would serve as your scribe, sir," he said.
"I read and write French, Latin, and English and am skilled
in numbers."

Suger rolled his eyes toward the two monks. "Excellent,
and we praise God for his goodness," Suger replied, rubbing
his plump hands together. "I have had need of a scribe, and
you see, dear brothers, how God has provided. And you, in
your youth—" The abbot nodded to Jonas, "What service
or gift do *you* bring to God this day?"

Jonas cleared his throat. "I am an artisan, skilled with

pen and ink," he replied. "Though I do not know how you can use me."

"God knows," the abbot replied, nodding gravely. He lifted his hand in an emphatic gesture. "Do you see, dear brothers, how God supplies our every need? I could not turn away the gold and silver offerings he brings any more than I can deny these two men the opportunity to serve him."

Soundly defeated, the two monks bowed to the abbot and left the basilica. When the abbot was sure they had gone, his eyes fell again upon Jonas and Gislebert. "Well, you two," he said, his voice was biting and dry, "it would appear that you are now in my service. Scribe, come with me. Artist, get you to one called Abbot Robert in the court-yard. He will tell you what work is to be done."

Adele held her breath as she reluctantly searched among the working monks for Abbot Robert. She did not think she could work for a man like the bawling Suger. Better to draw sketches in the sand for scraps of bread than work for a man who did nothing but yell and proclaim his own holiness all day.

Stone masons and carpenters milled about the court-yard, all at work on enlarging the church of St. Denis. The few monks present seemed to be overseers of the work. Only one monk did not stalk around and command the workers with impunity, and Adele walked in his direction. Like the two in the cathedral, he wore no shoes, despite the cold, and sat quietly on a slab of stone, his face upraised to the warmth of the sun.

"Excuse me, Father, but I am searching for the abbot called Robert."

The monk's head jerked toward her, and Adele gasped at the sight of the man's opaque eyes. A blind monk! How came he to be working here with the masons?

"I am Abbot Robert," the man replied, his face search-ing for her. "Why do you seek me?"

Adele stepped closer. The old monk's hands and feet were blue with cold, yet he wore only a single robe belted by a short piece of rough cord. "Abbot Suger sent me to offer my services as an artist," she said. "I am skilled with pen and ink, and can portray a most realistic likeness."

The monk smiled in delight and clapped his hand over the walking stick at his side. "Sent *you,* did he? By all the powers of God, did he *see* you?"

"Y-yes," Adele stammered.

"And still he sent you." The monk laughed softly, his voice crackling with age. "And they say I am blind."

A warning bell rang in Adele's mind, but the old monk stood and put out his hand for her arm. "Come, my dear, and let me describe the job as we walk. For you, I have a singular project in mind, one that will require much time and skill."

"I am willing to learn, Holy Father."

"I will pray that God will grant you the skill," the monk replied. "And we have time for him to do it. Our abbot Suger demands a representation of the twelve apostles and our Savior in one of the chapels. It is my thought that the faces of these thirteen statues should be the faces of common men, with the exception of our holy Savior's, of course."

"Common men?" Adele halted as a mason crossed her path with a cart loaded with stone. The monk stopped in midstep as she did.

"Yes, for our Lord chose common men to walk with him," Abbot Robert answered, smiling easily. "It is my intention that you and I should journey daily into the villages and surrounding country, and find faces for each of the twelve apostles. You will sketch them, then mold them in clay." He turned to face her. "Do you understand?"

"Yes, I do," Adele answered. "But what of the face of Christ? If you don't want a common man's face . . ."

"I trust that God will show you what to do," Abbot Robert replied, his tall, spare frame moving in tandem with hers. "If you seek God's will always, my little friend, you

207

will learn to see with your heart instead of your eyes. By the way . . ." He paused and tilted his head toward her. "What is your name?"

"Jonas," Adele answered.

The monk raised an eyebrow. "Are you sure you wish to be called by a boy's name?"

"Of course," Adele answered, a thread of exasperation creeping into her voice. "What else would you call me?"

The old monk shrugged and turned his face toward the road. "That is for you to decide, my dear."

Abbot Suger claimed two all-consuming ambitions, and Gislebert soon found himself caught up in each of them. Suger's first ambition lay in strengthening and glorifying the crown of France. His second lay in rebuilding and embellishing his precious abbey at St. Denis. The Royal Abbey, the abbot regularly proclaimed, should be a symbol of the glorious and devout French nation, and Suger's oratory and impassioned pleas had won the enthusiastic support of the young King Louis VII.

As Suger's scribe, the task of recording the gifts, bestowments, and inheritances due to the abbey fell to Gislebert. From the king to the lowest peasant, all were encouraged to dig deep into their coffers to support the enterprise of rebuilding the abbey of France's patron saint. The rebuilding of the basilica had begun twenty years before Gislebert arrived in St. Denis, and every day the cathedral grew more magnificent and Suger more possessed.

"He is, in his way, a madman," Gislebert confessed to Jonas one night as they lay in the darkness. "The other day he told me that he had lain in bed pondering the right source of wood for the roof beams, and his first act of the morning was to hustle his carpenters out to the forest to consider his choice."

"He is enthusiastic, that is all," Jonas mumbled.

"He is the proudest man I have ever known," Gislebert continued. "Today he asked me to examine a verse he has composed for the front doors of the church. For twenty years he has been revising the verse!"

"Was it any good?"

Gislebert laughed. "'I, Suger, caused these things to be made,'" he quoted. He glanced over at the bundled shadow that was Jonas. "How goes your work with Abbot Robert?"

"Well enough," Jonas answered. "We found a smith that will make a remarkable Thomas. The streak of incredulity in the man's nature is evident in his face; even Abbot Robert sensed it. I drew a sketch, and tomorrow I will work on the clay mold for his face."

"How can a blind monk judge your sketch?" Gislebert asked, sitting up. He was too full of thoughts to sleep.

"He will hold the clay mask in his hands, and make a judgment then," Jonas answered, yawning. "Go to sleep, Troubadour, for we must rise with the sun tomorrow."

"And have you thought yet how to do the face of Christ?"

"No," Jonas snapped, his weariness making him impatient. "But I know the model will not be Suger."

After dressing and then breakfasting on a bit of stale bread and cheese, Gislebert bade Jonas farewell and set out for the abbey. He never walked directly there, but skirted the main road until he stood again at the gate of Lady Jehannenton's house. Every morning he peered through the barred window at the gate for a sign of life. Today nothing stirred except smoke from the chimney. But Gislebert found even that comforting, for it meant that Nadine was warm and comfortable.

"Until the day we meet," he whispered, blowing a kiss to the maiden inside the house. Then he straightened his shoulders and continued on his journey to the abbey.

"Jonas, you must do this for me!" Gislebert's face was firmly set as he pounded the table in determination.

"No! You said I should never again put on the robes of a woman!"

209

"But you didn't mind doing it before! Why should you mind now?" Gislebert reached for her hand, and Adele instinctively drew back, afraid of what he asked. Gislebert hated her as Adele; he despised the sight of her in a woman's tunic.

"Please, Jonas," Gislebert begged, his eyes filling with tears of frustration. "I've thought about it for weeks, and you can do this one thing for me. Once again, dress as a woman and visit the house of Lady Jehannenton. Talk to Nadine, discover her situation, and tell her of my love. See if she will escape for a day, even an hour, and meet me so that I may offer my heart to her."

"I won't do it. You said God would not bless deception." Adele stood to her feet and turned away so that the troubadour could not see the emotion that flooded her face. Why must he be so intent on destroying their happiness? Together they had found service, they had made a home again, and still Gislebert maintained his obsessive love for a woman he did not even know.

"How do I know God won't use a harmless ruse?" Gislebert asked. "Today I considered stealing a monk's robe and pretending to be a priest to gain entrance to the lady's house, but she would hate me for lying. Then I recalled that you make a most lovely woman, Jonas! You alone can help me. Please, do this thing for me!"

Despite her disdain for his changeable rules, something in his words made her relent.

Gislebert brought her a tunic, surcoat, and cloak of fine fabrics, and Adele felt a wave of memory sweep over her as she took off her leggings and slipped on the long woman's tunic. She could almost smell the sweet fragrance that had always surrounded Lady Wynne and could almost hear the woman's warm and husky voice.

"Are you ready yet?" Gislebert called impatiently from the courtyard. Adele closed her eyes in exasperation. She still did not know why she had agreed to do this. Lately she found herself less and less willing to deceive people. While the troubadour's "rules" of honest living had seemed foolish at first, she had to admit she now enjoyed being "honest men doing honest work." It felt . . . right.

Which only made this latest deception that much more distasteful. Besides, putting on a woman's clothes always interrupted the camaraderie between her and the troubadour; evidence of her femininity always left him distant and remote.

But today his eyes lighted joyfully at the sight of her. "Perfect," he said, kissing the tips of his fingers as she came to the doorway, fully dressed. "Now mount sidesaddle like a gentle lady, and let us make haste to the house of Lady Jehannenton."

Her foot caught in the hem of her long tunic as she tried to mount her horse, and she scowled as she yanked the offending garment out of her way. She closed her eyes and whispered a fervent prayer that this duty would be over and done with quickly.

TWENTY

Gislebert persistently rang the bell at Lady Jehannenton's gate until the sober-faced servant appeared. Before the servant had a chance to inquire whether men stood outside the gate, he called boldly: "Adele of Southwick," Gislebert said, improvising freely, "wishes an audience with Lady Jehannenton."

The maid glanced suspiciously at Gislebert, then peered through the tiny window at Adele. "We know no Adele of Southwick," the servant replied. "Be gone, monsieur."

"But Adele is a remarkable talent," Gislebert insisted, wrapping his fingers around the bars of the window. "Lady Jehannenton would be truly upset if she knew she had missed this opportunity. Adele of Southwick has sketched portraits of noble women throughout England, including the worthy Empress Matilda of Anjou."

"Truly?" The maid's brow lifted in skepticism.

"Truly." Gislebert nodded. "May God strike me dead if I am not telling the absolute truth."

The maid nodded at Adele. "Be you ze Adele of Southwick?"

"I am."

"Be you an artist, truly?"

"I am."

"I'll ask the mistress if she will see you." The maid turned and left, and Gislebert paced frantically until she reappeared. "Madame Jehannenton will see ze artist and no other," she replied, opening the gate a crack. "Monsieur, you must wait outside."

"With pleasure." Gislebert bowed gallantly as Adele swept past him into the courtyard and followed the maid into the house.

"Is she really an artist?" A tall, blonde, blue-eyed vision of loveliness spoke, and Adele felt her heart sink. If this young woman was Nadine, Gislebert's visions of beauty were uncannily accurate.

"Oui, madame," Adele answered, practicing the French phrases the troubadour had taught her. She curtsied before the young girl.

"Oh, you don't have to curtsey to me," the girl answered, blushing prettily. "Only to the mistress. I'm Melusina, Lady Jehannenton's companion."

"You live here alone?" Adele asked, pretending casual interest.

"There is one other," a calm voice answered from behind a curtain, and a slender girl of surpassing loveliness stepped into the room. Adele felt envy stab her heart— Melusina was beautiful, but this girl was stunning. Vibrant red hair flowed in a single thick braid past the lady's slender waist. Her green eyes sparkled with curiosity from a face of creamy skin, and Adele noted ruefully that not a single freckle marred the young woman's clear complexion. She wore an ivory tunic that was fitted tightly at her slender waistline and bloomed to fullness at her hips.

"You must be Nadine," Adele replied, her hands shaking. She pressed them together firmly at her waist.

"How do you know my name?" the girl asked, stroking a tiny puppy in her arms. "We have not ventured out of this house in three years."

"All who know you speak of your beauty," Adele answered. "My friend, who is very like a brother, sent me here to capture your loveliness on paper, for he would see for himself how lovely an English rose blooms in France."

Melusina giggled girlishly, and Nadine tilted her head thoughtfully. "'Twould be improper for me to offer a portrait first," she said. "What do you think, Melusina? Would a portrait bring our mistress pleasure?"

"Indeed, it would," Melusina answered. She smiled warmly at Adele. "We shall take you in at once." She paused. "Lady Jehannenton is not entirely in her right mind, but she is harmless and still a very great lady. It would pleasure all of us if you would sketch her portrait."

"I shall need parchment, pen and ink, and paint, if you can procure it," Adele said.

Nadine waved a hand at the servant who lingered in the doorway, and the girl sprinted away to fetch the required items. "Our lady will not look upon men, but there is no reason why men should not look upon her," Nadine said, gently scratching her puppy's head. "Perhaps, if we are pleased with your result, you shall do portraits of all of us."

"It would be my pleasure," Adele answered, nodding graciously and forcing a smile.

After meeting the Lady Jehannenton, Adele understood why her ladies and servant enforced the "no men" vow so vigilantly. The vow did not necessarily protect their mistress, for age and senility had advanced their irreversible decay upon her, but it did protect the populace. The wrinkled, white-haired lady hunched in the voluminous bed had a penchant for throwing things; more than once Adele ducked as a pillow sailed by her head. Most surprisingly, the lady threw things without even knowing that she threw them. Often in the middle of a thought or phrase, she would snatch an item and send it sailing from her side without missing a breath.

"We used to supply her with cats, for she likes the sound of their purring," Melusina whispered as Adele sat stiffly in a chair at the lady's bedside. "But she threw them all across the room, and one out the window. Three died, two were lamed, and when we were sure she no longer noticed their absence, we supplied her with pillows instead."

"How very strange," Adele murmured, but paused when the eagle eyes of Lady Jehannenton focused upon her.

"So you were at Southwick? Knew you the Lady Wynne and her husband, Galbert?"

Adele nodded. "Yes, my lady. I knew them both and held them in high esteem."

"And knew you their cat? And their sapphire blue cloak? Wynne had a sapphire blue cloak that sang most agreeably. One day I chatted freely with it for over an hour." Lady Jehannenton frowned. "Or was it the steward's cloak I spoke to?"

"Let me remind you, dear lady, of this woman's purpose," Nadine broke in smoothly. "She wishes to paint a portrait of you, perhaps in a garden scene, or on horseback. Would such a painting please you?"

Lady Jehannenton looked past Nadine, and her puckered face brightened in a smile. "Yes," she said, exposing her toothless gums. Her arm bent reflexively, picked up a pillow, and tossed it across the room, but no one in the chamber moved to retrieve it. "That would be lovely. Perhaps a portrait of me and you, my two girls, on a hunt."

"It shall be done," Nadine answered, nodding regally to Adele. Adele nodded in acceptance, and the maid approached with the parchments, pens, and paint Adele had requested. Walking in a wide circle around the lady's bed, the maid laid the items on a table near Adele, and Adele smoothed the parchment and studied her subject carefully.

"Did you tell her of my love? What did she say?" Gislebert demanded when Adele emerged from the gate.

Adele climbed wearily upon her horse, wishing that she could toss off her tunic and ride astride like a man. "Troubadour, I am tired and the sun is setting. We must be home before curfew."

"But she is there? She is well? Is she as beautiful as I imagined?"

Adele gathered her reins. "She is there, she is well, and

she is more beautiful than any woman I have ever seen. I will be sketching her portrait presently, and you can judge from that picture."

"Is there any hope? What must I do?"

Adele turned to face him and did not care that distaste for her task showed clearly in her face. "I am to return there every afternoon, so I will go when I have finished my work for Abbot Robert. I am commissioned to do portraits of all three ladies, maybe even more, for I believe they are desperate for companionship, even mine. When the time is right, Troubadour, I will speak of you, but not before."

"But Jonas, if it is only for my sake that you go there, why not speak to Nadine tomorrow? Then your task will be complete and I will—"

"You will wait." She urged her horse closer to the troubadour and deepened her voice. "One thing is certain, Troubadour: Melusina and Nadine will not show their faces to the world while their mistress lives, for they will not risk her displeasure. She has named them as her heirs, and her holdings are substantial."

"She is truly an heiress?" Delight played across Gislebert's face. "How good God is! King Stephen was right; my love is not only a beauty, but wealthy! See, Jonas, God always brings us the best, even when we don't desire it—"

"You listen too much to Abbot Suger," Adele replied. She jerked her horse's reins and headed toward home.

Gislebert's days were filled with frantic prayer for Nadine and frenetic work for Suger. Desperate for the completion of his cathedral and determined to maintain control over the king of France, Suger quietly served as Louis's chief advisor and pressured the king to continue in his generous and pious support of the church in France. Twenty-two-year-old Louis accepted Suger's control easily, for Suger had guided his father. And in the days of his childhood, when Louis the Young was crowned king at seventeen, with only his giddy fifteen-year-old queen Eleanor by his side, Suger's advice and guidance had been invaluable.

Under Suger's influence, the king's nickname among the people had changed from "the Young" to "the Pious," and in recent years, Louis had done little but issue proclamations that urged his people to fast, pray, and give for the completion of the new cathedral. The cathedral stood, Suger explained to any who asked, as a visible reminder to the world that France was only a fief under the king's authority by the grace of God.

Adamant that this image be presented to the king, and thus to the people, Suger had Gislebert write and publish the news that his monks had found (or forged, Gislebert privately allowed) documents in the old libraries of the abbey that linked Louis's Capetian dynasty to Charlemagne, the mighty Carolingian king of the Franks who had ruled over an empire that extended from Italy to Spain.

"Once my cathedral is completed, the kings of France will journey here, to place coins upon our gilded altar and remind themselves that they owe their fealty to God," Suger rhapsodized one afternoon, drawing plans for his new altar.

"A gilded altar, Your Grace?" Gislebert delicately questioned. "Will not your humble Cistercian brothers be offended by an overabundance of gold upon the altar?"

"May it gleam, and more," Suger replied, his careful hand adding detail to the drawing. "We shall entirely enclose the altar by placing golden panels on each side, so that it will seem to be surrounded in gold."

"It will be—quite a sight," Gislebert answered, sighing. "Visible from everywhere except the side chapels."

Suger paused. "True, Scribe, your words are true. The altar will not be visible from every aspect of the church, for it is not tall enough. What is needed is a tall masterpiece. . . ."

He rubbed his hand across his beard. "A cross!" he said, snapping his fingers. "A tall cross, at least ten cubits high.

We will decorate it with precious stones of the highest caliber, and it will gleam from every corner of the church!"

"Aye, if there is light enough," Gislebert idly remarked, scratching notes on a parchment before him.

Suger pressed his fingertips to his lips and stared thoughtfully at Gislebert. "By the blessings of God you have come to me!" he said, bringing his heavy hand down upon the table. "You inspire my thoughts, Scribe! We need light! I shall knock down the walls of the old basilica and insert windows. Light shall fill every corner of the room, and everything within shall shine in reflected glory! I, Suger, shall do it!"

The abbot clapped his hands and several monks came running from their work to implement the master's latest idea. Gislebert picked up his pen and sighed. If Suger continued in his quest for perfection, the work at the abbey might never be done.

Disgusted, Gislebert tossed his scribbled poem into the fire and watched the flames consume his unworthy words of love. A noise outside caught his attention, and he looked up in joyful anticipation when Jonas came through the door. "What news from the house of Lady Jehannenton?" he asked, his heart beating faster. "Did you speak my name to Nadine?"

"No," Jonas answered, taking the long cloak from his shoulders. "There was no opportunity. Lady Jehannenton was cross. She threw her supper tray across the room, and I spent my time today helping the maids clean up the mess."

"But is the lady well? Does she still smile upon your visits?"

"She is as well as one can be who is bedridden. My portrait of Lady Jehannenton will be finished tomorrow, and Nadine has said that I may paint her portrait next."

Jonas sighed and sank onto his mattress as if he would sleep, and Gislebert frowned. "Won't you take off that ridiculous tunic?" he asked, dipping his pen into the ink-filled horn fastened to his table.

"I put it on at your bidding, and I'm too tired to take it off," Jonas answered, rolling over on his side to sleep. "I'll dress more to your liking in the morning."

"Tomorrow morning the abbot begins his work on his jeweled cross," Gislebert replied, thoughtfully holding his pen over the parchment before him. "I find I can think of little else, and the letter of love that I would write for Nadine remains but a blank sheet."

Jonas's heavy eyes opened. "You're writing a letter to the lady?"

"Yes, since you will not speak to her of me, perhaps you should take her my letter," Gislebert answered. "It is more fitting that I speak for myself. If you will but deliver this letter, Jonas, and continue to bring me news, you may paint to your heart's content without betraying your true love."

"My true love?" Jonas's eyes widened, and Gislebert chuckled grimly.

"Yes. I have determined that the reason you don't speak on my behalf is that you have fallen in love with Nadine yourself. Why else would you go to her house, linger long, and never accomplish what I sent you to do? You were to speak to Nadine for me, young friend. And yet three weeks have passed, and you have not spoken of me at all."

Jonas raised himself up on an elbow and glared at the troubadour. "You fancy me in love with your lady? You make me laugh, Troubadour. I do not love her."

"Then why will you not speak to her?"

Jonas shrugged. "The time is not right. We are always surrounded by servants. Melusina is always with us—"

"Perhaps you love this Melusina." Gislebert held a finger aloft. "Now it begins to make sense. You do not speak to Nadine because doing so would bring an end to your time at their house. If you do not love Nadine, you must love the lady Melusina."

Jonas's eyes flashed in rebellion. "While I do find

Melusina a more worthy woman than the selfish Nadine, still I bear her no love other than that of a friend."

"You dare to call Nadine selfish?" Gislebert stood from his stool, his pulse pounding in his temple.

Jonas sat up, rising to the challenge. "She is! You do not know her, Troubadour. I see evidence of her vanity every day!"

"How dare you!" Gislebert trembled in every nerve. He put out his hands and grasped the edge of the table lest his fists pummel Jonas.

"Listen, Troubadour, and know that my words are true! I love neither Melusina nor Nadine. If you want to love either woman, you are free to do as you wish." Jonas turned away and lay back down on his mattress.

"You are incapable of love if you cannot see the beauty of character that resides in my Nadine."

"You are incapable of reason," Jonas answered, his eyes closed. "Write your letter, Troubadour, and to prove your suspicions false, I will deliver it for you. Then, if you should gain the lady's favor and meet with her, you shall discover the truth of my words."

"I will write that letter," Gislebert said, again taking his seat at the table. "And I will prove you wrong, my young friend."

Twenty-one

*M*ost honored *Nadine:*

*I have had difficulty composing this letter, for though
we met years ago on the grounds of Margate and in the
presence of Lord Perceval and Lady Endeline, you may
not remember the lonely person of Gislebert, at that time
a lowly troubadour. But in my heart since that day has
burned an awesome and consuming love for you, my lady.
I have traveled the world and endured much pain and
tribulation to write this letter to you.*

*It does not seem profitable to dwell much on the praise
of your person, for your character and beauty echo through
widely separated parts of the world. Furthermore, praise
uttered in the presence of the person praised seems to have
the appearance of clever flattery. For the present, then, it is
my intention to offer you myself and my services and to beg
earnestly that you may see fit to accept them. And I beseech
God in heaven that he may grant me his grace to do those
things which are wholly pleasing to your desire. I have in
my heart a firm and fixed ambition, not only to offer you
my services, but on your behalf to offer them to the entire
world and to serve with a humble and acceptable spirit.*

*I admit that I ask to be loved, because to live in love is
more pleasant than any other way of life in the world. I
pray that you will not refuse to love me because of the
humility of my inferior rank, although my character is of
the very best. I am employed, at present, by Abbot Suger at*

the church of St. Denis, and you may send word to him and inquire of my character.

What qualifications do I bring to you with my love? Not much in the way of beauty, I must confess. But I bring my character and my deeds, which for the last several years have been offered in your name. I have frequented the assemblies of great men and visited great courts. I am moderate in indulging in games of dice. I am quick to recount and take to heart the great deeds of men of old. While not adept in battle, I am courageous in the feats life has offered me. I am not a lover of several women; my heart has beat for you alone for years without end. I devote only a moderate amount of care to the adornment of my person and try to show myself wise, tractable, and pleasant to every man and woman I meet.

I am careful not to utter falsehoods, am not quick to make promises, and never utter foul words. I have never cheated any man with a false promise, nor do I utter harmful or shameful or mocking words against God's clergy or monks, but always render them due honor with all my strength and mind. I go to church frequently and listen gladly to those who celebrate the divine service. I have but one companion, a boy called Jonas, who depends on me as an elder brother. I have made two vows in life: one, to find you and offer my love; and two, to make a home for this boy once you and I have settled love's suit.

I hope you will find me worthy to plead in the court of Love. For the hope of the love I desire, I try to do all these things. I pray to God that he may ever increase my determination to serve you and that he may incline your mind toward me, and ever keep it so, to reward me to the extent of my deserts.

In your service, Lady, I am
Gislebert

"This man is your brother, Adele?" Nadine asked, looking up from the letter.

"A good friend, whom I love as a brother," Adele answered, dipping her brush into the small paint pot at her easel. "It was he who bade me come and paint for you. The maid has seen him at your gate."

Nadine turned to the maid, who curtsied politely. "Is he a handsome man, Vonette?"

The maid blushed and stammered for words. "Handsome? I do not think him ze handsomest man in the world, but he has a comely enough face, a thin figure—"

"He is red, and long, and skinny," Adele answered. "Not strong as knights are, and not well-fleshed as a nobleman. But he is sincere, and he has talked of nothing but his love for you ever since I have known him. Now, mademoiselle, you must turn your face to the light."

Nadine obeyed, turning her delicate profile toward the window. She said nothing, but her brow furrowed gently as she considered the letter in her hand, and Adele felt her heart sink.

"What troubles you, my young friend?" The soft voice of Abbot Robert broke through Adele's concentration on the swarthy face of the peasant before her, and she paused in mid stroke to consider her aged friend.

"Troubles? I have no troubles, Father," she replied, taking pains to insure that her voice was smooth. In her many mornings with the blind monk she had learned that little escaped him, for although his eyes did not function, his hearing, touch, taste, and smell were far more effective than the average person's.

"Do you not?" He raised his face to her, and his milky eyes cast about in her direction. "I hear trouble in your silence and vexation in the few words you have spoken to our friend Matthew who sits before us."

Adele looked up at the peasant who posed for the face of Matthew the disciple. The man blinked uncertainly. "I am sorry if I have been short with you, my friend," Adele said,

223

nodding pleasantly at the man. "It is not our intention to detain you from your work."

"Doesn't matter, so long as I receive the chicken you promised," the man replied, his smile widening at the prospect of reward.

"You shall have it within the hour," Adele replied, quickly finishing the sketch. She put her pen down and smiled at the man. "Go find the monk who tends the henhouse at the Abbey of St. Denis and tell him that you are due a chicken by the word of Abbot Robert and the artist Jonas."

"Good enough," the man answered, slipping down from the fence upon which he had perched.

As the man's footsteps receded, Abbot Robert turned to Adele once again. "I'll ask again, my friend. What troubles you? You can tell me, Jonas the artist. If my wisdom cannot provide an answer, perhaps the simple act of unburdening your soul will give you rest."

Adele sighed and leaned against the low stone wall where the monk sat. "It is love, Father," she said, keeping her voice low. "I do not understand it. What is love, after all, and why do men seek it so fervently?"

"The Scriptures say that the greatest love is demonstrated when one lays down his life for a friend," the abbot answered, folding his hands on his walking stick. "Have you experienced this degree of love, young Jonas?"

"I know not," Adele answered crossly. "There is one whom I *might* love, but he—she—looks upon me as a brother only."

"The question is not whether this person loves you," the abbot replied, "but whether or not *you* love this person. If you love, you must know it."

"Must I?" Adele answered, her voice breaking in exasperation. "I care, I know I do, but in the name of love some have forced attentions upon me that I did not seek—"

She broke off suddenly, aware that she had said too much, but the monk's smooth face did not shift in its expression. "Let us be honest with each other," the abbot said, reaching out for her hand. "I know, my dear, that you are neither a man nor the boy you pretend to be. Though I do not know why you assume the name and occupation of a man, I am sure you have a good reason."

Her momentary surprise faded into relief. Here was one who saw all, a man she could trust. "I had a good reason," she said simply. "My life depended upon my running away with a boy's name and form. I had to leave home or be killed, and what chance of survival does a girl have alone?"

"Must you still continue this charade?" the monk asked. "Surely you are of an age to marry and raise children. Your step is graceful, Jonas, your voice soft, and your character noble. Certainly there are many men who would desire to have you as wife."

"None," she said, her voice cracking. "There is only one man with whom I am well acquainted, Father, and he is the one who cares for me as a brother. But he believes me a man—"

"How could he? If he knows you well—"

"He knows Jonas, and he knows Adele. He is repulsed by Adele's form and manner," she replied, her anger spilling forth into her words. "Every afternoon I don a woman's clothes and visit the house of the lady he loves. When I stand before him as a woman, he turns from me in disgust unless I have news to share of his precious lady. He hates me as a woman, Father, he cannot—"

"'There is none so blind as he who will not see,'" the abbot quoted softly. "And you will not leave him to seek your own life?"

Adele considered the question. "Leave him?" she asked. "He would not leave me when I lay dying at Southwick. Besides, Father, he is helpless without me. He knows the ways of the world and of the noble courts, but he is helpless in the forest and the countryside. More than once, he would have died without me, and I couldn't just leave—"

"My dear, you love him," the abbot said, slowly shaking his head. "For you have done what love requires; you have sacrificed for your beloved one. You love this man, Adele, and you do him a great injustice to keep your true self hidden."

"But he loves another," Adele answered, her voice breaking. Tears streamed from her eyes, and the monk instinctively reached out and tenderly wiped them from her face.

"God will show you what you must do," Abbot Robert replied, his voice ringing in sincerity and conviction. "For God knows you, my dear, and loves you as you are."

And for a moment, Adele believed him.

He stood to his feet and held out his hand to her. "Now, my little friend, have you considered your sketch of Christ our Lord? Perhaps you should combine the best of all faces, since his was perfection and love itself."

Looking up at the unlined and gentle face of the abbot, a sudden inspiration struck Adele. "I have found the face of love," she said, taking his arm. "Never fear, Father, our project shall be completed in due time."

"Another letter?" Nadine asked as Adele entered the ladies' chamber and proffered Gislebert's latest offering for his beloved. "Have you not told this man that I am not free to accept suitors?"

"He knows," Adele answered, tossing the letter offhandedly into Nadine's lap. "And still he persists in letting you know of his love and intention."

"What's this?" Lady Jehannenton croaked from her bed. "A man in the house?"

"No, madame, no," Melusina said soothingly, rushing to the lady's bedside. "No man, my lady, only a letter. A man outside the house fancies himself in love with Nadine."

"Does he wear a red cloak?" the lady asked, her birdlike eyes searching the room.

Melusina questioned Adele with her eyes, and Adele shook her head as she pulled out her paint pots. "No, my lady, he does not," Melusina answered, ducking as the lady Jehannenton tossed a comb from her hair across the room.

"Good. Red cloaks cannot be trusted," Lady

Jehannenton warbled, waving a finger in Melusina's direction.

Nadine eased herself into a chair by the window and adjusted her braid for the portrait, a miniature likeness that was to adorn her psalter. "Be sure you capture my likeness accurately," she told Adele, her tone cold and condescending. A three-noted husky laugh escaped her, and she raised an eyebrow toward Melusina. "You know, I believe I actually remember the troubadour from Margate," she said, her eyes sparkling like chipped emeralds. "A mousy boy, with auburn hair, a long nose, and huge, crooked teeth. He followed our party around like a tiresome pup, and I was quite glad to be rid of him when we left Margate."

Like an awakening giant, anger stirred in Adele's soul, and she lowered her paintbrush and glared up at the lady in front of her. But Nadine did not notice, so intent was she on her reflection in the small looking glass she held.

"Perhaps he has grown to be a respectable man," Melusina charitably interjected.

"Perhaps," Nadine allowed, lowering the mirror. "I will write a letter myself, to Abbot Suger, and inquire about Gislebert's character and qualities. Who knows? The mousy boy may be in a position of power, for the abbot, after all, is said to rule even the king. Vonette," she called, clapping her hands for the servant, "bring me paper and pen."

Nadine turned her chilly green eyes upon Adele. "I trust you will not be disturbed if I write as you paint my image?"

"No, my lady," Adele answered, dipping her brush into her colors. "For I have thoroughly seen what manner of woman you are."

She painted for an hour, concentrating carefully to capture the complete breadth of Nadine's beauty despite her distaste for the woman. At one point Adele paused to brush her hair back from her sweaty forehead and realized with a start that her body was perspiring even though the other women sat in warm surcoats and heavy tunics. Her hands were cold and clammy; she could feel the blood rushing

from her face. The room began to spin. "Melusina," Adele
called, putting her hands to her cheeks.

"Are you all right?" Melusina asked, noticing Adele's
discomfort.

Adele shook her head, then slumped from her stool to
the floor at Melusina's feet.

For the second time in her life she awakened in a strange
bed and in a stranger's clothes. "Ze ladies bid me bathe and
dress you," Vonette explained voluntarily when Adele
opened her eyes. "It is ze morning after you fainted. Are
you feeling bettair now?"

Adele swallowed; her throat throbbed in pain. "I'm fine,
and I must go," she said, pushing herself up with her hands.
"I'm expected at the abbey."

"I would rest for ze day, if I were you," Vonette said,
smiling indulgently. "Everything can wait, can it not? Drink
my herbal tea, and you will feel much bettair. It is quiet here
in my little room, and you can rest."

Adele nodded meekly and accepted the cup Vonette
gave her. If Gislebert missed her last night, surely he would
know where to find her. She smiled gently as she tasted the
tea. Maybe the troubadour needed to miss her.

Adele had just finished a loaf of Vonette's delicious brown
bread when Nadine came into the small room, flashing a
letter. "I have heard from Abbot Suger," the girl said, pacing back and forth in the small space. "Your friend Gislebert
is a man of some respect at the abbey, and Suger writes that
he is noble and worthy of trust. Are these things true,
Adele?"

Adele nodded, the pain in her throat overcoming her
urge to speak.

"And what are your thoughts about his ability to rise in
power? If Suger dies within the next five years, will your friend
Gislebert continue in his place of powerful employment? Is it
possible that he will have a place in Louis's court?"

Adele closed her eyes and shook her head.

"Speak, you little fool!"

Adele glared at the hot-tempered beauty. "I know not what he will do, for everything in his life is centered around you," she croaked hoarsely. "If you asked him to live in a pigsty, he would. If you commanded him to seek a place in the king's court, he would do that, too. But he would not lie, cheat, or steal. He is an honorable man."

"What good is honor without ambition?" Nadine snapped crossly. The silken swish of her garments filled the room as she turned to leave. "If you're well enough, leave here, Adele. You may come and paint, but you are not welcome as a houseguest."

The afternoon had nearly passed before Gislebert heard a noise at the door. "Jonas, is that you?" he demanded, his voice harsher than he had intended. "What kept you from our house last night? Did the ladies discover your secret? Is my suit for Nadine forever lost by your deceit?"

Jonas scowled as he slowly came into the room, still dressed in his woman's clothes. By the sword of St. Denis, that boy could be infuriating!

"No," Jonas answered, slipping his long cloak from his shoulders. "Your secret is still safe, Troubadour."

Gislebert glanced suspiciously at the boy as Jonas removed the veil he wore and fell onto his mattress as if exhausted. He seemed withdrawn, and he looked paler and more tired than usual. Had he spent the night in mischief? The boy was sixteen, after all, and sixteen-year-old boys generally venture into trouble at one time or another. But no, Gislebert realized, Jonas would have no place with the village's bad boys while dressed in the clothing of a woman. Unless . . . could he be taking advantage of his hidden identity to insinuate himself with Nadine or Melusina?

Gislebert whispered a prayer that Lady Jehannenton would pass to her heavenly reward before truth revealed the deception he and Jonas had worked upon her household.

TWENTY-TWO

Spring passed into summer, summer into winter, and winter into spring again. Under the watchful and approving supervision of Abbot Robert, Jonas completed the faces of the twelve disciples and the Lord Christ. These molded faces were used as models for the master sculptors who adorned the columns inside Suger's glorious cathedral, and those master artisans had nothing but praise for Jonas's fine work.

Gislebert continued his work for Suger, rising in that vain man's estimation as no monk could. Any monk exalted enough to work for Suger would have been bound to point out that the abbot's unbounded pride was a direct contradiction to the religious vow of humility. Gislebert, however, remained silent when the abbot instructed that four likenesses of himself were to be placed in the abbey and thirteen inscriptions in his own honor were to be engraved in stone or metal and placed in various parts of the church. "He kneels at the feet of Christ on the tympanum and at the feet of the Virgin Mary in a stained-glass window in the ambulatory," Gislebert told Jonas one night as they ate bread and cheese for supper. "His name is written in the glass in letters as large as those which honor the mother of God."

Jonas giggled. "Of such pride are the ladies of Lady Jehannenton's house," the boy replied. "Now they require my hand to paint images of themselves in their chamber, in the great hall, and in the entryway. Nadine says that when the house is finally open for guests again, no house in the entire city will compare in beauty and majesty."

Gislebert cut himself another slice of cheese and cast a fond glance at the boy. Jonas had grown tall in the past year, and though the boy had not yet grown a beard, Gislebert told him not to worry—Gislebert himself had not shaved until he was twenty-one.

"Nadine is right about her house, of course," Gislebert answered, his pulse quickening as it always did at the mention of his beloved. "Did she read my letter today?"

"She read it and still insists she cannot grant you an audience," Jonas replied, wiping his mouth on a cloth napkin. "But be of good cheer, my friend. The Lady Jehannenton grows more demented with every passing day. Nadine says the lady is not far from heaven's door. Today she spent an hour conversing with her bedpost."

"At least she is surrounded by those who love her," Gislebert answered, his voice softening. "My generous Nadine! How gentle she must be to stay with the elder lady! What love her heart is capable of!"

"It's capable of loving her estate, at least," Jonas corrected. "Though I would never suggest that your precious lady seeks anything but the opportunity to do service." The boy stood, brushed a few crumbs from the table, and turned toward his mattress. "Good night, Gislebert."

Gislebert blew out their single candle on the table, and Jonas's hay mattress rustled in the darkness as the boy turned his back to the troubadour. Jonas was ever quick to point out what he perceived as faults in Nadine's character, but Gislebert dismissed them as jealous prattle. Always, he found hope in the boy's words. They had been in St. Denis more than a year, and those days would not have to be endured again. Each day that passed now brought him closer to the fateful hour when he would finally meet Nadine.

"Your Grace, some brothers from Citeaux desire a word with you."

Suger frowned in annoyance; the summons interrupted his accounting with Gislebert. He waggled his hand toward the young monk who brought the news. "Send them away. Tell them to return later."

"My abbot, they bring gems and offer them for sale."

Suger raised an eyebrow in sudden interest. "Gems?" he asked, snapping his fingers at Gislebert. "Do they bring many?"

The young monk nodded. "An abundance of precious stones: amethysts, sapphires, rubies, emeralds, and topazes. They were given as alms by the Comte Thibaud and are worth in excess of two thousand pounds. As Cistercians, the monks of Citeaux could not keep them—"

Abbot Suger waved a hand to cut off the monk. He turned gleaming eyes upon Gislebert. "Bring your pen and payment for these stones," he commanded, slipping his ponderous weight from his stool.

"How much should I bring, Your Grace?" Gislebert asked.

"Six hundred—no, four hundred pounds," Suger replied. "We will thank God for their generosity and urge them to feel grateful for four hundred. The jeweled cross will be finished after all!"

Gislebert gathered his pen, parchments, and purse and followed the abbot to the reception hall.

TWENTY-THREE

On the second Sunday in June 1144, Abbot Suger completed and consecrated the newly renovated choir of St. Denis Cathedral. With Gislebert's help and the king's blessing, Suger planned a grandiose ceremony to consecrate twenty new gilded altars in radiating chapels, an innovative design that would relieve the press of the crowd on worship days. To the elaborate ceremonies were invited the king of France, all the peers of the realm, and the archbishops and bishops from Sens, Senlis, Soissons, Chartres, Rheims, and Beauvais.

"These men will see what I have done and will take my ideas and even my artisans with them," Suger gloated, rubbing his jeweled hands together as his monks dressed him in his ceremonial robes. "They will talk of little else but our gilded altars, our great jeweled cross, our chalices, the painted sculptures, the paving, the choir stalls, and our hangings of many colors."

"It is a wonder, Your Grace," Gislebert allowed, bowing respectfully. "An incredible accomplishment that will bring glory to God and to the kings of France."

"Such was my purpose," Suger said, nodding carefully at Gislebert, "and my destiny."

The abbot claimed his gold-encrusted shepherd's crook and took his place in line behind his brother monks. He walked regally out of his house toward the church that bore his name in over a dozen inscriptions. A wry smile crossed Gislebert's face as he stood on the abbot's balcony watching the procession. He thought of the last inscription, newly engraved inside the church:

> With the new chevet attached to the old facade
> The heart of the sanctuary glows in splendor.
> That which is united in splendor, radiates in splendor
> And the magnificent work inundated with a new light
> shines.
> It is I, Suger, who have in my time enlarged this edifice.
> Under my direction it was done.

Below Gislebert, in bare feet and the humble robes of a Cistercian Benedictine, Abbot Robert clung to Adele's hand and offered praise to God for the work that had been done. "For with or without the gilding of gold," he said quietly, "the work has been accomplished to allow men and women the opportunity to come to God."

"How can you work with a man like Suger?" Adele asked, looking up into the monk's cloudy eyes. "He is so filled with himself and his fancy buildings and robes, and you are of the common man—"

"Yet we work together for one cause," Abbot Robert interrupted. Suger is a Cluniac monk; I am a common Cistercian. He lives in the village; I dwell in the forest. But we labor together to bring men to God, just as you and your friend Gislebert work together for the other's good."

Adele opened her mouth to protest, thinking that Gislebert certainly cared nothing for her, but the old abbot closed his eyes and began to chant:

> *"O Salutary Lord, Star of the Sea,*
> *Thou who art the Sun of Justice;*
> *Creator of light, ever holy,*
> *Receive our praise this day."*

Not many days after the cathedral's historic dedication, two knights clothed in the white-mantled surcoats of the Knights

Templar thundered into the village with news that rocked the quiet village of St. Denis. The knights promptly demanded an audience with Abbot Suger. Gislebert was working in the abbot's chamber when the knights were ushered in, and the abbot bade him stay.

"Your Grace," the first knight said, falling to one knee and kissing the abbot's ring. "We bring disturbing news from the Holy Land."

"What news?" the abbot asked, leaning forward in his chair.

"Zengi, the lord of the Saracens, has taken the Christian state of Edessa," the knight replied. "Our Holy Father in Rome has called for another expedition to the Holy Land, to liberate our captured kingdom in the name of Christ. He asks for your help, Your Grace, in securing the blessing of the king of France."

"Only the blessing? Our king Louis is devout and will certainly bless this effort."

The knight cleared his throat. "Actually, Your Grace, His Holiness, the pope, asks for the dual blessings of money and men. Will Louis take an oath and commit himself and his country to this new expedition for God?"

Suger stroked his beard as he carefully considered the proposition set before him. "He is not called Louis the Pious for no reason," the abbot finally replied, clasping his hands before him. "You may tell the Holy Father that I shall do my best to persuade the king."

The knights bowed, saluted the abbot, and went out. When they had gone, Gislebert ventured a comment: "Do you, sir, plan on joining the expedition?"

Suger smiled ruefully and shook his head. "No, my friend, I am too old and needed elsewhere. Our friend the king will doubtless join this expedition with enthusiasm and energy, and someone will be needed to see to the daily affairs of state. As I aided his father, so will I aid Louis, the son."

The abbot stood and rang a bell to summon the monk

who served as his messenger. "I feared that my duties were done now that the church is complete," the abbot said, his countenance quickening with a renewed fervor. "But it would appear that the Lord has other work for Suger to accomplish." The abbot turned to Gislebert and nodded, his eyes gleaming. "Within two years, I predict that Suger will be appointed regent of France in the king's absence," he said, lifting his hand in an emphatic gesture. "Born as the son of a serf, Suger will yet leave his name in history."

The news spread throughout the countryside like a plague. Within the day, every soul at the abbey knew of the disaster in the Holy Land. Within the week, every man and woman in the village had heard that the infidels had gained the upper hand in the hard-fought and bloody battle for the land of God.

Lady Jehannenton took the news with uncharacteristic silence. "Her son, her only child, died in the first expedition of God," Melusina explained to Adele on the afternoon that Vonette broke the news to the household. "This news has opened my lady's wounds and heartbreak."

Indeed, the aged lady never spoke again but retreated into a world of silence, her eyes fixed open, staring at nothing. She would not eat or sleep but stared so resolutely that Melusina was driven to wave her hand in front of the lady's face to make certain the lady still blinked, and therefore still lived. Finally, after a week Melusina called for the doctor's wife and the priest.

Adele had continued to visit the ladies' house, and she stood by quietly. The priest administered oil to the forehead of the devout lady Jehannenton as her eyes finally closed in death. Melusina burst into tears. Nadine dutifully dabbed dry eyes with a delicate lace handkerchief, and Adele was genuinely sorry to see the old woman depart from among the living. Mad though she was, the lady had never been cruel, and her simple act of designating her two maids as heirs placed her among the few women who dared to do what they wanted and not what was expected.

While Melusina wept, Nadine called Vonette to summon the hired mourners that Lady Jehannenton's rank demanded. The priest agreed to send a litter for the body, which would lie in state in the great cathedral for two days with Nadine and Melusina in attendance. At the conclusion of those days, the survivors, in their best garments, would escort the body to its final resting place in the tombs beneath the abbey. After the funeral they would feast; after the feast they would give alms to the poor; and only then would they be discharged of their duties to their late mistress.

Nadine recited the order of the next few days to the still-weeping Melusina and asked Adele if she would be willing to help them through the "trial of the coming week." Adele agreed, nodding gently, even while she realized that Gislebert's imposed exile would soon be over. Once their final duty to their mistress was done, Nadine and Melusina would be free and available heiresses, and Gislebert would be eager to claim the love he had sought throughout his life.

Adele left the women and slipped her light, summer cloak about her shoulders. Gislebert would be thrilled with the news she brought him tonight.

Gislebert lined up for the funeral feast with his fellow villagers at the gate of the late Lady Jehannenton's house. His breath came quickly, like someone about to dive into icy water, and his stomach churned when he thought that soon, on this very day, he would stand before his lady and offer his respects. She had received and read his letters. She knew his heart, and now he would see in her eyes if he had a chance to win her love.

The gate opened, and the line moved forward. He took a deep breath and plunged ahead. Jonas had chosen to remain home, and Gislebert had not thought to object, for now that Nadine's gate had been flung open by the sober hand of death, there was no need for the boy to masquerade as a woman. Gislebert could present his own suit. But as he inched forward in the line of mourners, he found himself wishing that Jonas had come along. In this nerve-racking hour, the troubadour sorely needed a friend.

Generously laden tables had been set end to end in the great hall. The villagers filed past the head table where two women sat in mourning dress, then moved to their places at the feast tables. Gislebert removed his cap and nervously fingered its brim, wondering what he should say. Perhaps a simple, "Mademoiselle, I am Gislebert," would be most eloquent at this time, for he had been writing his heart's deepest thoughts to the lady for nearly a year and a half.

When he finally found himself face-to-face with the maiden, his mind and mouth were struck dumb. Jonas had described Melusina as blonde and blue-eyed, but had been remarkably vague when pressed for details about Nadine's appearance. Gislebert was startled by the vibrance of her red hair and the crystalline shine of her emerald eyes. Her creamy complexion was perfect, her lips a thread of scarlet, her nose slender and fine. Despite the black robe of mourning she wore, every aspect of her countenance shone in sheer loveliness.

"Monsieur, surely you are Gislebert, secretary and scribe to Abbot Suger," she said, her voice like a warm caress in the chill of the room. She nodded politely and smiled gently.

"I-I am," Gislebert stammered, his flesh shriveling into a sea of goose pimples beneath his best tunic. "I am your servant."

"Thank you," Nadine replied. Then she turned graciously to greet her next guest, and Gislebert took a step forward to pay his respects to Melusina. But later he could not recall what that lady had spoken or what she had looked like. His heart and mind were filled only with the image and voice of Nadine.

"Gislebert, am I to replace you? Your mind is not with me," Suger reproved the troubadour. "We must write a letter on behalf of the king to his wife, Eleanor." Suger settled himself in his padded chair and sighed. "The girl is too vivacious to be queen and does not know how to comport herself. Even as her husband readies himself to an expedition to the Holy Land, she thinks of nothing but garden parties and royal balls."

"Can the king not control his own wife?" Gislebert asked, raising an eyebrow.

"The king hates his wife," Suger replied. "He concentrates on fulfilling God's victory in the Holy Land, and his wife complains that Louis is more monk than king." The abbot pressed his fingertips to his temples and closed his eyes. "Write, Scribe: *To my gracious queen, Eleanor, from your most humble servant, Suger.*"

Gislebert picked up his pen and recorded the abbot's words, his fingers transcribing the abbot's voice even as his mind dreamed of his own gracious lady. But a name leaped from the page into his mind, and Gislebert momentarily froze.

"Excuse me, Your Grace, did you say *Jerome?*"

Suger scowled. "It is not like you, Gislebert, to make me repeat myself. I hate to repeat myself, but I see I must." He sighed dramatically and kept speaking: "Your gracious majesty should spend more time in the company of your husband the king and less time with this upstart Jerome. Word has reached my ears that the knight is a profligate, exiled first from his own lands of Honfleur, then from King Stephen's court for treachery and devious behavior. We fail to see, gracious Queen, how his company could possibly aid your cause with the king or the people you serve."

Suger waved his hand. "Sign it with the usual pleasantries and titles," he said, rising from his chair. "And send the letter to Paris immediately by my messenger. If Eleanor does not mend her ways, I fear the king may be tempted to put her aside. And that," the abbot said, shaking his heavy head, "would never do."

Gislebert signed the letter with the abbot's usual titles, pressed the abbot's stamp into the seal, and handed it to the messenger. "To Her Highness the queen, with all haste," he instructed the monk. "And return to me once your errand is completed."

When the monk had left, Gislebert sat at his desk and nervously chewed his thumb. Could the knight Jerome mentioned in the abbot's letter be the same man who had brought King Stephen's condemnation upon his and Jonas's heads? Was the same knight now truly banished from King Stephen's court? What had happened and how?

Something else in the letter struck a familiar chord in Gislebert's memory, but although he tried to puzzle through the unsettling feeling that he had missed something, he could not. He considered asking the abbot for more details, but Suger would have construed Gislebert's questions as interest in base gossip.

In the space of three hours, the messenger monk returned, knocked quietly on Gislebert's door, and entered. "My errand is complete," he said carelessly, refusing Gislebert the deference he always bestowed upon the abbot. "I placed the letter directly into the hand of the queen."

"Was there a reply?" Gislebert asked. "Did the queen read the letter immediately?"

"Yes." The monk nodded without smiling. "She read it and laughed, and then reached out to stroke the face of a man who sat at dinner with her."

"What sort of man was this?" Gislebert asked, fear rising in his throat. "Was he a tall man and muscular, with a handsome face and dark hair? Was he called Jerome, a knight?"

"It is as you say," the monk answered. "And our queen replied that I might tell the abbot that his words were read, regarded, and rejected. She further said that I might tell the abbot that the king was of no use to her, and she preferred to surround herself with men of action." The monk looked awkwardly at the floor.

"Anything else?" Gislebert whispered, hoping the monk had finished.

"Then the knight kissed our queen most passionately, and she waved me away."

Gislebert groaned. How could he relay this message to Suger?

Jerome washed his hands in the queen's lilac-perfumed lavatory, smiling at the ease with which he had conquered Eleanor, queen of France. She had not even presented a challenge. After one look at his insistent eyes, she had dismissed her servants and fallen upon him, not caring that her husband consulted with his knights and clergymen in the next room.

Jerome flung a handful of water on his flushed face and leaned forward, his bare chest gleaming with sweat. A queen's affections might be useful, but it was clear he would gain no ground with Louis by enticing his queen. If he was to regain an estate and the honor of his family name, another tactic must be applied. And Eleanor had presented just the information he needed.

They had laughed when the blushing messenger-monk from Suger beat a hasty retreat from the room. "That Suger and his scribe send me letters every week and admonish me for misbehavior," Eleanor had said, running her finger along his shoulders. "I am deathly tired of both of them."

"Tell them to leave you alone," Jerome answered, kissing the little finger of her right hand. "Since they are monks and eager for heaven, tell them to leave us the joys of earth."

"Ah, but his scribe is not a monk, but a mousy Englishman called Gislebert," Eleanor had replied, her pretty lips forming in a beguiling pout.

"Gislebert?" Jerome felt an unexpected shock. "An Englishman?"

"Oui, my pretty one," Eleanor replied, opening her arms to him. "A tall, bony Englishman."

Jerome let his lips brush hers, then pulled away for an instant. "Eleanor, darling, is there a woman in these parts known as Nadine? An heiress who serves a lady . . ." He thought hard, remembering. ". . . a Lady Jehannenton?"

"Lady Jehannenton lived in St. Denis," Eleanor replied, skimming her hands over his shoulders. "She died last week."

Jerome could not contain a smile, and the woman in his arms was foolish enough to assume he smiled at her. "I should not speak of death with you so happy here with me," she purred in his ear. "So come now, Jerome, and let us pleasure ourselves."

"Only one thing troubles me," he said, pulling her forward so that his lips could wander up the tingling cord at the back of her neck. "I ought to visit this mourning Nadine, for I was a dear friend of Lady Jehannenton's. Could you write me a letter of introduction?"

She shivered agreeably and brought her face close to his. "Anything for you, Jerome," she whispered just before her mouth was smothered by his warm lips.

Gislebert sat alone in his house, brooding over Suger's reaction to the queen's outright refusal to heed the abbot's words. First the abbot had been shocked, then he had grown haughty. Finally the man of God had resorted to throwing a book across the room.

Gislebert could identify with that sense of frustration, for even though he had met Nadine and written her countless letters, still she had not invited him to visit at her house. Must he wait forever?

Gislebert heard the squeak of the gate in their small courtyard and lifted his head eagerly. Jonas would be eager to hear that Stephen had exiled Jerome. In one small way God had avenged their cause. But when Jonas entered, Gislebert forgot his news, so shocked was he to see the boy again in a woman's dress.

"What are you doing?" Gislebert asked, his eyes taking in the woman's tunic, surcoat, and veil. "I thought you no longer needed to visit the house of Melusina and Nadine."

"There was reason today," Jonas said, his cheeks flushed. He pulled up a rough stool and perched on its edge. "Gislebert, I assumed my woman's clothes and visited simply because I missed the ladies' company."

"I think you are in love with Melusina," Gislebert countered. "Approach her as a man! Declare yourself!"

"Never mind that," Jonas said, waving Gislebert's comments aside. "Melusina and I were having a pleasant conversation when a knight rode up to the gate. The ladies would not have admitted him, but he carried a letter of introduction from the queen!"

Gislebert felt the flesh at the base of his neck prickle. "A knight?" he whispered.

Jonas nodded. "You will never guess who—"

"Jerome," Gislebert answered, feeling weak. "Jerome, who of late has been exiled from King Stephen's court. He was in Paris, having his vile way with the queen, but why should he have visited Nadine? Unless . . ." Gislebert's mind worked feverishly, sorting through his knowledge of the swarthy knight they had known for only a few short weeks in the prison at London.

"The heiress Nadine!" Jonas answered, his eyes gleaming in the room's dim light. "Don't you remember, Troubadour? You got drunk one night and told the man everything! You told him that you loved an heiress, you told him her name, you told him of her fortune. The man is now without a country and without an estate. He must marry well, or he is nothing."

"He will soon be without the queen, as well," Gislebert muttered darkly. "For though he toys with our queen's affections, the king or Suger will have him stopped. Suger would hang the man, if he had the power."

"He toys with Nadine and Melusina, as well," Jonas answered. "I remained in the hall as the man entered, and he extended his hand to both ladies. He did not recognize me, dressed like this—" Jonas indicated the woman's tunic he wore. "But he charmed them with stories. He told them that news of their beauty had spread through the continent, and he assured them that he was the confidant of several kings and queens."

"And the ladies? How did they respond?"

"Melusina was kind, as usual, and polite. But, Troubadour, though it pains me to tell you, Nadine devoured the knight's appearance with her eyes and his stories with her heart. I fear you have a rival for her love."

Gislebert brought his fist down on the table. How cruelly life could turn! Nadine had been the sole image in his heart since his youth, and now the infamous Jerome had stalked in and swept Gislebert's pleas from her mind.

"Jonas, what am I to do?" Gislebert asked, frankly begging. A wall seemed to come up behind Jonas's eyes, and the boy shrugged. "If you love her, Troubadour, make your case with her," he replied. "Go there tomorrow at dinner, for Jerome is an invited guest, and she could not hospitably refuse you. Make your case for love and demand an answer. You must act, and quickly, for your gentle letters and simple songs will not stand against Jerome."

Gislebert knew that Jonas was right. Tomorrow he would act—and act forcefully.

TWENTY-FOUR

Vonette squirmed in the doorway to the ladies' chamber, and Nadine ignored the maid's fidgeting and smoothed her green, sleeveless tunic. The light fabric of the garment accented her shapely figure, and the shade of green matched her eyes exactly. "Is our guest here?" she asked, careful that her voice did not betray her heightened nerves. What a man she had invited for dinner! Despite the cool surcoat he wore yesterday, she had seen the muscles bulge and slide under his bronze tan as he knelt at her feet. And his eyes! He had stared at her in cool possessiveness until she blushed. After three years of avoiding men, she was ready to accept his unspoken challenge.

"Two gentlemen guests stand outside the gate," Vonette volunteered, biting her lip. "Monsieur Gislebert and Sir Jerome. Both beg to be admitted to dine with us."

Nadine sat down abruptly as despair flooded over her. From her bed, Melusina giggled. "For years you pined for gentlemen callers, and now two worthy men stand outside your gate," the blonde girl said, laughing. "What will you do, dear friend?"

"Melusina, you must help me," Nadine said, rising resolutely from her chair. "The situation need not be awkward, for you can engage Monsieur Gislebert in conversation. Be not stingy with your attentions, and perhaps, in time, he will send his odious love letters to you. In the meantime, I shall gain the love of Sir Jerome—"

"You forget, Nadine, that I have no interest in marriage, and to engage Gislebert would be most unfair. He has written you for two years, and to cast his affections aside—"

"He is nothing to me," Nadine cried, flashing into sudden fury. "I thought once that I might accept him, if the rumors are true that the king will ride for the Holy Land. With Suger as regent and Gislebert as his scribe, I would be assured a place at court, but—"

"Now that a handsome man comes with a letter from the queen, you prefer your bird in the hand to the grouse in the bush," Melusina answered curtly.

"If you're not going to help me, Melusina, get yourself to the convent now and spare me the trouble of providing shelter for your tiresome head!"

"In due time, I will go," Melusina answered stiffly, rising from her bed. "I had thought to remain with you until your marriage, but perhaps you will do better alone." She nodded at Vonette, who cowered in the doorway. "Bid the gentlemen enter, Vonette, and set places for three at dinner. I will be fasting today."

Melusina turned and swept grandly out of the chamber while Nadine seethed in silence.

Nadine believed that small animals and women made a pleasing combination, so she gathered her lapdog in her arms and smoothed the rough edges of her demeanor before she entered the hall where Gislebert and Jerome stood silent in obvious mutual animosity. "Messieurs," she said, extending her hand first to Jerome. The puppy growled, and Nadine hastily put him on the floor, then turned to give her hand to Gislebert. "What a pleasure to have you dine with me today! Melusina regrets that she cannot be present; her religious duties call her from us."

She walked gracefully behind the small table in the hall and took her place. The knight sat at her right hand, and the troubadour took the seat at her left. How was she supposed to endure this dinner? She smiled carefully and rang the bell to alert Vonette that they were ready to eat.

As Vonette brought in the food, Jerome took her right hand and clasped it tenderly in his own. "Her Majesty the queen bid me search the kingdom far and wide to see if your beauty truly surpasses all others," he said, his dark eyes gleaming against his tanned face. She felt herself being caught up in the strength and feel and sound of him . . . then somewhere in her consciousness, like a bothersome gnat, the irritating whine of the troubadour buzzed in her left ear for her attention.

"My lady," the troubadour whimpered, tugging at her tunic like a child who will not be ignored, "I would not have foisted my presence upon you except for the arduous task which has compelled my presence."

She turned and blinked at the troubadour. "Has this task anything to do with the abbot Suger or the king?"

"No, my lady. It is love which compels me to come. Love constrains me to offer all I have and might someday possess. This is not how I imagined this moment . . . but will you do me the honor of becoming my wife?"

His sudden proposal shocked her, and by the way Jerome tightened his grip on her hand, she was sure the knight was as surprised as she. "Marriage?" she breathed, not sure she had heard him correctly. Was the man a fool? Could he not see that she had given her hand to Jerome, who was twice the man in size and strength?

Gislebert slipped from his chair and knelt at her feet. "Yes, my lady, I would have your answer. I have written you faithfully throughout your long exile from society. I have loved you since the day I met you as a child. My heart is ready for your reply."

She turned expectantly to Jerome, who hesitated only for a moment. "But I, lady, offer you my hand as well, my heart, and my service as a knight in the service of God and our king. Though my love is yet newly sprung, can a new flame not burn as hotly as one which has smoldered for years?"

There, Jerome had done it. She sighed in relief and smiled. Perhaps the troublesome troubadour had done her a favor by spurring the knight on to declare his love so soon. Now she had only to eliminate Gislebert, and Jerome would be hers.

She gracefully withdrew her hand from Jerome's grasp and folded it in her lap. "Messieurs, I am not unaware of the honor you would grant me," she said, demurely lowering her eyes to the table. "But I cannot choose between two such worthy men. I shall ask God to make the decision for me and trust in his wisdom."

"Ask anything, for God approves my love," Gislebert said, leaning forward.

She cast wildly about for an idea, then smiled. Why not test the limit of their devotion?

She laced her fingers together, as primly as the noblest lady in the land. "What I ask is this: Tomorrow night each of you shall bring me an item whose value is beyond measure, something which cannot be duplicated in this world or in the world to come."

She heard Jerome draw in his breath, and she gave him a discreet sidelong glance.

"My lady," the troubadour interrupted, grasping for her hand, "I have brought you such an item already. My loving heart is priceless, and neither man nor angel can duplicate the passionate yearning which I bring to you."

She pulled her hand from his grip and held up a delicate finger. "True, Monsieur Gislebert, but who can say that Jerome's heart is not likewise precious and unique? No, the item you bring me must be something tangible, something I can wear around my neck as a badge of honor."

The troubadour rose from the floor and returned to his seat, clearly troubled, but Jerome smiled at her cheerfully. "A worthy challenge!" he said, his dark eyes holding hers. "I shall look forward to this contest, my lady, and am confident that God will reveal his holy will."

"We shall see," Nadine replied, lifting her glass first to Jerome, then to Gislebert. "Godspeed and good success to both of you. I shall greet you both again tomorrow night."

Adele remained at home waiting Gislebert's approach, her stomach tense and knotted. If the troubadour was successful in his suit, soon he would marry Nadine and move into Lady Jehannenton's house with his bride. If he failed, surely he would fall deep into despair, possibly to the point of taking his own life. Neither option held out any hope for her. She could not share Gislebert with Nadine, whom she deeply disliked. And she did not know how she could live without the troubadour.

Did she love him? For years she had denied it. But Abbot Robert had said she did, and his sightless eyes perceived far more than Gislebert ever had. But if she did love the troubadour, what was she to do with that love if Gislebert married Nadine?

Gislebert's rangy hand lifted the flap, and Adele gripped the bench beneath her for support. His eyes were neither downcast nor joyful as they sought her face, but troubled.

"What news, Troubadour?" she asked, trying not to show that her life hinged upon his words. "Shall you be married?"

"Indeed I shall," Gislebert answered, sinking onto the floor by the hearth. "To gloom and despair. Jerome has also declared his intention to be married to my Nadine."

"A woman cannot have two husbands at the same time."

"That is true," Gislebert answered. He leaned forward and rested his chin on his hand. "The lady has offered her hand and heart to the man who bestows upon her a priceless gift."

"Priceless?" Adele made a face. "Surely then, your love—"

"—is what I offered," Gislebert answered, finishing the thought for her. "But the lady wants something she can hang around her beautiful neck. Something unique, something which cannot be equaled in this world or in the world to come. What is more, she wants this object tomorrow night."

Adele did not know how to answer, and Gislebert sighed. "Jonas, my little friend, what am I to do? If this contest were to be won on sincere intentions or purity of heart, there would be no contest, for we both know what a scoundrel Jerome is. But I cannot speak of this to Nadine, for she would think that envy leads me to blacken the reputation of my rival. So I must be silent. And I must win, for I cannot live without her."

"You could," Adele argued softly. "You have lived without her for these many years, Troubadour. You could find love elsewhere if you would open your heart. My friend Abbot Robert says—"

"What do monks know about love, Jonas?" Gislebert questioned, standing to his feet. He crossed to his mattress and lay down. "Abbot Suger says that wealth and power and influence catch the eyes of both men and women. If I had but one of the gems he put into that gigantic cross of his, surely that would win the heart of my Nadine!"

"You cannot steal to win her love," Adele whispered, a warning in her voice. "God would not honor you if you stole—"

"Listen to yourself, my little beggaring thief," Gislebert said, snorting in derision. "Do you expect God to honor Jerome? He does not deserve it, but he has only to ask for a token from our flirtatious queen, and she will give him any jewel he desires. He has connections, while I—"

"You have connections you know not of," Adele answered, her cheeks burning. She stood to her feet and paused by the door. "I will do what I can to help you," she said softly, gathering her cloak. "The vow of love and friendship you once gave me compels me to do the same. Because of the love I bear toward you, Gislebert the troubadour, I offer my hand in friendship, fealty, and aid. I will do what I can to help."

She paused, but Gislebert had lowered his head into his pillow and only mumbled in reply.

"So the lady asks for a unique, priceless object she can wear around her neck?" Abbot Robert asked, his laughter breaking the nighttime stillness in the courtyard of the forest monastery. The building rose as ghostly plain stone from the fringe of trees outside the village, and his raucous laughter seemed strangely out of character for this holy, unadorned place.

"Shhhh," Adele warned, putting her finger across her lips. "It is the grand silence. Your fellow monks will think you a heretic for breaking their rules."

"Rules are made to be broken," the abbot replied, his teeth gleaming in the moonlight. "After all, did our Lord not heal on the Sabbath? If you have a problem, my dear, I am here to help whenever you need me."

"I don't know what to do," Adele continued, waving her hands helplessly. "He is miserable, Father. He weeps into his pillow like a child. His heart is valiant enough, but he is not a noble and has no riches to aid his cause—"

"And what of you?" the abbot asked, gently reaching out to lay his hand on hers. "What will you do, my daughter, if the troubadour marries his lady? You will be alone in the world, and this is an uncertain and dangerous world for a woman alone."

Adele considered. "I have been as a woman and a man in the world," she said, keeping her voice low. "I could continue as a man if Gislebert marries. Even now I fool the monks at the abbey. This morning Suger's assistant approached me about more work—something about new statues for the abbey."

"You are growing older," the monk said, shaking his head. "It is not natural for you to masquerade as a man, my child. Soon your heart will rebel at assuming such a false role. You cannot hide beneath cloaks and cowls forever."

Adele lowered her eyes and continued pacing evenly in

the safety of the monastery courtyard. The voices of Abbot
Robert's brother monks rose in the darkness as they chanted
the final office of the day and prepared for bed. Suddenly
she felt like an intruder, and she blushed. A woman had no
place in a monastery; she had no business listening to men
lift their intimate prayers to God before lying down to sleep.

"Excuse me, Father, I should go," she said, pulling away.

His hand caught her wrist before she could run, and the
abbot lifted a trembling finger: "If, dear girl, you could procure a priceless and unique treasure for your friend Gislebert
by surrendering your life, would you do it?"

She stopped and thought. Would she? Thus far her life
had been of little consequence, but if by dying she could
ease Gislebert's suffering and bring him the joy he had
sought his entire life . . .

"Yes," she answered suddenly, "I would do it."

"Meet me then, tomorrow at noon, by the well nearest
your house," the abbot said, shaking his head slowly. "I will
give you an answer then."

The sun rose to its zenith and passed a few degrees into the
west before she saw the abbot shuffling toward the well, his
tall walking stick in one hand and the other outstretched to
pat the heads of children on his way through the streets. A
black bag hung from his waist. Adele wondered what it contained, for never had she seen him vary his outfit from the
simple, woolen robe he wore day and night, year round.

"Hello, Father," she called as he came nearer, and he
smiled and continued in her direction. She took his arm and
led him to a bench near the well. "You said you would give
me an answer today," she said, gently wiping beads of perspiration from his forehead. "Did God reveal the answer to
Gislebert's dilemma in your dreams last night?"

"No, he revealed the answer to *your* dilemma," the monk
replied, smiling. He lowered himself onto the bench. "You
sprang from the Creator's hand as a lovely young woman, but
for too long you have denied your true self. Submit to God's

design, my daughter. Place your life in our Lord's hands. Until he leads you in another direction, you shall enter a convent, Adele, and serve God there with all your heart and life."

"A convent?" Adele lowered her voice. "Really, Father, I would not make a good nun. I have been too independent too long."

"All the more reason you should rest in the shelter of the heavenly Shepherd's fold," Abbot Robert replied. "You do not have to take the sacred vows. I am suggesting a time of rest and retreat until God directs your path away from that place."

"Why should God direct my pathway *to* that place?"

"Because you love the troubadour."

She pulled away, and the abbot reached out for her hand and drew her nearer. "My child, my proposal is this: I will give you an object that is both priceless and unique. It can be mounted on a chain for a lady's neck, or hung in a place of honor. I leave the fate of the object in God's hands, but of you, in payment, I require a promise."

"What promise?" She scarcely dared to breathe.

"You shall go to the nunnery outside the village walls and rest in our blessed Lord. You will be safe and sheltered. You can learn to live as a woman, and God will heal the deep wounds that scar your soul. You shall stay there until you are ready to leave or you feel God's leading to take the holy vows."

Adele sat silently, and after a pause, the abbot waved a finger in her direction. "You said you would surrender your life for such an object," he reminded her. "I will freely give it to you, and you may do with it what you will, but as payment I shall require that you place your life—and your trust—in God's hands. No more men's clothes, Jonas. No more deception. From the day you cross the convent threshold, only truth will be found in your life."

She considered his words carefully. "I was willing to die, not live as a nun," she said, placing her hand on the old monk's arm. "But I agree to your plan. Have you thought this through, dear Father? God will be losing a priceless treasure and gaining only my worthless life."

"God cannot lose anything," the abbot replied, gently patting her hand. "And he will rejoice to gain your priceless soul. Take this, Jonas, and be well."

He untied the black bag at his belt and slipped it into her hand. "Adele," she corrected, feeling the weight of the treasure in her hand. "And Adele thanks you, Father."

She was waiting at their table when Gislebert came home from the abbey, his face flushed and lined with worry. He frowned when he saw her, for she wore her woman's clothing, and he raised a single eyebrow in a silent question when he saw the black bag on the table.

"I thought you were going to throw those clothes out," he said crossly, kicking his boots off near the fire. "What have you brought now? Cosmetics? How can you sit there calmly when tonight I lose the hand of the lady I love?"

"You shall not lose her," Adele answered, unknotting the drawstring of the bag. She pulled the bag open and drew out an ovoid crystal, which she laid on the table. Carefully engraved into the underside of the crystal was a portrait of Christ on the cross. Angels hovered near in the clouds, and weeping women stood at his feet. The detail and three-dimensional relief of the work were fantastic, and Gislebert gasped in admiration as he drew near to admire it.

Adele smiled in relief. "Do you like it? Abbot Robert said it is over three hundred years old, priceless, and unique. No artisan today could duplicate its work."

"How did he—how did *you*—come upon this treasure? It is truly a masterpiece!"

"Abbot Robert has held it in safekeeping for many years. When I questioned him about the wisdom of giving it to me, he said that we could never take anything from God, but that God lends us his treasures to enjoy."

"Jonas, this is incredible." Gislebert sat on the table and held the crystal in his hands, examining it carefully. When he was satisfied that he held the extraordinary treasure that would win victory over Jerome, he put the crystal on the table and gave Adele a smile of pure joy. "I could kiss you, my little friend!"

An undeniable impulse brought Adele to her feet. Without pausing to think, she threw herself at Gislebert, bringing his lips to hers and entwining her arms about his neck. His lips opened in surprise, his body tensed, and before she could respond, he pulled away and ran toward the doorway. He thrust up his arms as if to ward evil away.

"I didn't mean it!" he said, his eyes wide in consternation. "What has come over you, boy?"

"I am not a boy; I have never been a boy," she said, rushing toward him. "Look at me, Gislebert, and know that I am a woman, truly, and that I love you. Is it possible that you could love me?"

"It cannot be!" Gislebert roared, stumbling backward along the wall to escape her embrace.

"I speak truly! I am Adele, I was born Adele. I donned the guise of Jonas only to escape the dangers that would befall a girl alone. But though I was a scrawny girl when we first met, I am a woman now. And in the time we have shared—"

"Stop!" Gislebert cried, covering his ears with his hands. He closed his eyes as though he could not bear the sight of her, and Adele's heart constricted painfully. Was he regretting the secrets he had spoken in the time they had spent together? Was the truth going to cost her what she most treasured?

"You have played me for a fool," he said at last, an icy anger edging his voice as he looked at her with clear, cold eyes. "You have compromised my honor, endangered my suite for Nadine, and lied in the basest manner possible."

"But—," she began, only to be cut off by his lifted hand.

"I told you when we met that you should never tell me an untruth, and now I find that you have deceived me in every single hour, in every moment."

"I wanted you to see the truth for yourself," she whispered, her voice breaking. "Ingram saw it. Lady Wynne saw it."

"And I am a fool because I did not see."

"You are not a fool, Gislebert, you are just so blind with your love for Nadine—"

Again he stopped her, this time by turning away angrily. He reached for the crystal on the table. "It is a good thing that I will be married soon," he said, replacing the crystal in its black bag. "Until then, you must not reveal the truth to anyone who thinks you a boy. If Nadine discovers I have been traveling with a woman, my suit is finished."

His eyes fell on Adele, and the cold light she saw there made her skin crawl. "If you care for me at all, you will remain here and remain silent. After I am married, I care not what you do."

He went to the door, lifted the leather flap, and walked out into the lengthening shadows of sunset without a pause.

Adele sank onto her mattress and sighed. It was over. She had revealed her true self, and her inmost heart, as Abbot Robert had urged her to do, but Gislebert had rejected her love. Nadine had truly captured his heart, and now Adele had provided the tool through which her own beloved troubadour would win another woman as his bride.

TWENTY-FIVE

Gislebert squinted with amusement as Jerome opened a velvet pouch and laid a string of diamonds on Nadine's lap. "Unique in this world and in the world to come," the knight said, pulling back his shoulders and lifting his granite jaw. "Priceless beyond measure, and certainly beyond anything the troubadour will offer tonight."

Nadine bowed gracefully to Jerome and entwined the string of diamonds between her fingers. Holding them to the light of the candle by her side, she murmured in pleasure. "Lovely, sir knight; they are lovely."

Honor demanded that she appear impartial, and after admiring them for a moment more, she put the diamonds back into the velvet pouch. "And you, friend Gislebert, what do you bring this night?"

Gislebert stepped forward, his heart pounding in his ears. "As I have told you before, mademoiselle, I bring you my loving heart. Nothing could be more unique or more priceless, for my heart obeys the rules of courtly love. I know a man cannot be bound by a double love, and I will forsake all others for you. I turn pale in your presence. My heart palpitates when you pass before my eyes, and I have eaten and slept little since falling in love with you. As love can deny nothing to love, I will deny you nothing your heart desires should you agree to be my wife."

"Have you an offering or not?" Jerome asked dryly, resting his hand on his sword. "Let us not waste the lady's time."

Gislebert nodded confidently. "I offer you my heart and a priceless and unique relic more precious and rare than any valuable jewels my opponent could hope to procure."

He pulled the black bag from his surcoat and unwrapped the crystal, holding it against the dark cloth so that Nadine could see the full effect of the engraving inside. The lady gasped at the sight of it, and Jerome stood in stunned silence.

"Unique in this world and in the world to come," Gislebert said, lifting the crystal so that the candle's flame shone through it and illuminated the body of Christ on the cross. "For what need will there be in heaven for pictures of our Lord's past suffering?"

Nadine nodded slowly, her hair shimmering in the light like fire. "You speak truly," she said, offering both necklace and crystal back to her guests. "And I cannot accept either gift until I accept one of you in marriage. For I have a second request and duty that my husband must fulfill. The presentation of your gifts assures me that I would be cherished in your house, but a woman must also be protected. Tomorrow night, in the courtyard of this house, you must duel for my hand. Whichever of you is the victor will be my husband."

Jerome unsheathed his sword and extended it toward her feet, saluting her. Gislebert stood by numbly. His certain victory vanished with her words, and his eager heart stilled.

"Tomorrow night, then," Jerome said, turning to face Gislebert. His jet black eyes danced in delight. "We shall meet one last time, Troubadour."

Gislebert did not go home, for another, more troubling problem waited there. He wandered instead to the lodgings of Abbot Suger at the abbey. The abbot was a man of wisdom and action, learned in the ways of the world. Perhaps he would know what Gislebert should do.

The abbey's gatekeeper assumed that Gislebert had arrived to discuss important business, for he let Gislebert in without comment and escorted him immediately to the abbot. Suger sat in his hall at supper, generous portions of food heaped in bowls around him, and he raised a bushy brow at Gislebert's appearance. "What brings you here, Scribe?" Suger said, taking a bite from a huge turkey drumstick. Around the food in his mouth, he asked, "Something that could not wait until morning?"

"It is my life that stands at risk, Your Grace," Gislebert said, bowing slightly. "The lady I love has required that I duel a knight tomorrow night. I am no knight, and I will surely fail."

Suger looked as if he would laugh, but he forced himself to swallow his food and carefully wiped his mouth with a napkin. "What is that to me, Scribe? Are you telling me that I need to employ another after tomorrow?"

"I'm asking you for help," Gislebert answered, his anger rising. "You are a priest, are you not? And my employer, and the representative of the king—"

"And in none of those capacities am I obliged to free you from a duel," the abbot replied, wiping his greasy fingers. "Since you have neither the strength nor temperament of a fighter, I suggest you hire a champion to fight for you. By the law of chivalry, you cannot be denied."

"I have no money with which to hire a champion," Gislebert answered, his cheeks growing hot. "I have only this." He pulled the bag with the crystal from his surcoat and laid the crystal on the table.

The effect was startling. Suger glanced at the crystal, then got up from his bench and fell to his knees before the table where it lay. "It is . . . breathtaking," the abbot said, closing his hands as if for prayer. "Wherever did you get this?"

Gislebert shrugged. "What does it matter? It is promised to Nadine if I win, and if I die, anyone may pluck it from my dead body."

"Whom do you fight?" the abbot asked, his eyes still fastened securely to the crystal.

"The knight Jerome, of late from England."

Suger's mouth dropped in astonishment as he regarded his scribe. "The queen's lover?"

"The same."

"Oh, my dear Gislebert, you will definitely not die," Suger said, gingerly running his finger over the smooth surface of the crystal. "I will hire the best champion in France to fight for you." The abbot whistled in appreciation for the glass upon his table. "By God, this is a most wondrous relic! Surely it is one of the Carolingian carvings, for only they knew how to engrave rock crystal in this manner."

"It's over three hundred years old," Gislebert replied. "That much I know."

"I don't care how you got it, for God supplies in miraculous ways," Suger replied, rising from his knees. "You shall give this to me, Gislebert, and I will guarantee your safety and victory in the duel tomorrow."

"But if I win, I have to give it to my beloved," Gislebert protested. "She said the victor must give something priceless and unique—something she can wear around her neck."

"Bah! A lady would much rather wear jewels than a crystal relic, trust me," Suger replied. "I will give you a string of rare emeralds that were recently given as alms by the Count de Mustique. You shall have your lady, she shall have her jewels, and I shall have this crystal. I will build a shrine to house it, and people will come from miles to pray before it in the cathedral. I, Suger, shall do it!"

Gislebert bit his lip. How could he refuse the abbot's plan?

Gislebert did not sleep that night but worked feverishly, following the abbot's urgent instructions. As soon as day dawned, the master stone masons, the architects, and the artisans were to be called. A shrine would be built for the crystal as soon as possible.

By noon, when the timid hand of a monk tugged at his sleeve, Gislebert's eyes were heavy. "Excuse me, monsieur, but the abbot begs me to introduce Ludlow, your champion, and Knox, his guardian," the monk said, extending a hand to a gentle giant who passed into the hall with a small, wiry man at his side.

"Knox, here, at your service," the small man replied, his beady eyes sweeping over Gislebert as if he would weigh the amount of silver in the troubadour's pockets. "I understand you have need of my friend, Ludlow. The abbot has procured our services for tonight."

A hulking man, Ludlow stood more than six feet tall, with a low forehead, oxlike shoulders, and arms as thick as Gislebert's waist. As the mammoth man bowed timidly, Gislebert saw that a cross had been shaved into the crown of thick, sandy hair on the man's head. Gislebert recognized the sign and made a discreet signal to engage Knox's attention.

"Your charge is an idiot?" he whispered.

Knox nodded. "A gentleman, but uneducable. He fights like a lion, however, and has never been defeated."

Gislebert nodded, then gave Ludlow a timid smile. "Well, my friend," he said, slipping from his stool and approaching the giant, who grinned at him in the innocent manner of a child, "we shall have a bit of a contest tonight, you see? You may use a sword, a mace, or a dagger—"

"A sword," Ludlow answered, nodding eagerly. "I love a good sword fight. Men run like little rabbits when my sword comes at them, for my arms are longer than most, you see. And then I stick them, just once, and they bleed. But Knox says it's all part of the sword game. Then I win, and we eat, and the other fellows go home—"

"There, there, Luddy, my boy, you shall do it again tonight," Knox interrupted, clapping Ludlow on the back. "And after, I will take you out for a nice, thick pottage, all right?"

Gislebert read disapproval in the eyes of the monk who had led the men in, and he frowned. This was not the most noble way to win a contest, but if the law allowed it, perhaps God would forgive. "Brother monk, will you take Ludlow and Knox for some dinner and perhaps for a new tunic and shoes?" Gislebert asked, reassuming his seat. "I will be with you as soon as I have completed my work."

The monk nodded and led the pair away. Gislebert sat back on his stool and frowned at the parchments before him. Would this harsh recent development tarnish his noble love for Nadine?

Jerome whistled as he sharpened his sword on the whetstone. Gislebert and the boy had escaped him in London, but he hadn't really cared. Jerome personally had borne them no ill will. He had plotted their deaths only because they could expose his traitorous service for Empress Matilda to King Stephen.

With them gone, Jerome had breathed more easily—until a scarred monk from the bloody siege at Wherwell came to Stephen's court. The cursed monk, who loved to talk more than most, had been most convincing in his tale of seeing Jerome actually remove his red and white surcoat in the heat of battle to don the white and gold of Stephen's army. "He took a dead knight's own surcoat," the priest told King Stephen, tears rolling down his cheeks. "No doubt that valiant knight was buried as a traitor, and Jerome walks in your court with honor."

Stephen's face had blackened with anger, but Jerome had made a contingency plan and escaped the tower before the guards knew he had gone. He had traveled to France under the cover of darkness, teasing or bullying his way into the hearts of women who sheltered and protected him—willingly or not.

But tomorrow he would become a wealthy and powerful man, and if the price of property and respectability was Gislebert's life, then life had led him to a surprising and delicious turn. Jerome had never dared to hope that with the large estates of Lady Jehannenton would come as ravishing a woman as Nadine, but . . .

He chuckled to himself as his blade glowed in the late

afternoon sunlight. "Such pleasures are the spoils of war," he remarked aloud, sheathing his sword. "Eh, brother Jean?"

When Gislebert, Ludlow, Knox, and Suger's representative arrived, Jerome stood ready and waiting in Nadine's courtyard.

"Good evening, friend Gislebert. Who are these you bring with you?" Nadine asked, stepping out of the house with Melusina and Vonette behind her. "Jerome comes alone to do battle for himself, but you come here with a crowd. And what of the monk? Surely he has no interest in these proceedings."

Gislebert bowed. "The monk, my lady, is a representative of Abbot Suger's. He is sent to insure that all that transpires here tonight is done in accordance with the laws of chivalry and the edicts of God."

"And the idiot?" Nadine asked, glancing at the cross-shaped emblem in Ludlow's hair.

"He is my champion," Gislebert said, nodding gravely. "I am no man of the sword, my lady, but of love. It is my right to procure a champion to fight in my place."

"Quite a champion he is, too," Knox added, stepping forward. He crossed his puny arms across his chest and glared across the courtyard at Jerome. "Undefeated. Absolutely undefeated and unconquerable."

Nadine's smile seemed to stiffen, and she leaned back to whisper in Melusina's ear. From the opposite side of the courtyard, Jerome narrowed his eyes and studied the massive sword in Ludlow's hand.

"Perhaps it would not be fair to have an idiot fight against a valiant knight," Nadine offered, the fringe of her silk tunic rustling in the evening breeze. "Have you another champion, Gislebert?"

"No other," Gislebert answered, shaking his head in genuine regret.

"You need not worry about Ludlow, mademoiselle, for he has fought sixteen times and killed sixteen opponents,"

Knox added, still glaring at Jerome. "He undertakes this battle freely and willingly—"

"My lady," Jerome interrupted, shifting uneasily from his place. Nadine cast a sharp glance at him.

"If I withdraw my suit—"

"You would withdraw?" Nadine asked, her eyes glittering catlike in the twilight. "From my hand and my favor?"

Jerome stepped forward and knelt at Nadine's feet. Gislebert thought the man's face looked pale beneath his tan. "I cannot fight an idiot, my lady—nor can I fight the monk or the troubadour. None of them are equal to my fighting skill, and I fear God would not hold me blameless for their deaths."

"So you withdraw, then?" Gislebert asked, hope rising in his heart.

"I do." Jerome stood, sheathed his sword, and bowed to Ludlow. "And I bid you good night."

He turned and stalked through the gate, while Ludlow grinned happily and Knox strutted about like a bantam rooster. The monk came forward and pulled a black prayer book from his pocket. "Present your gift, then, sir, and let's be on with it," the monk said. Gislebert moved toward the woman who would soon be his betrothed and under his protection.

"Shouldn't we go to the church?" Melusina asked, alarmed that things were proceeding so rapidly. "Is this proper?"

"Abbot Suger sent me to make sure all things were done in haste and in all propriety," the monk replied, opening his prayer book. He nodded toward Gislebert. "Continue with your gift."

Gislebert pulled the string of emeralds from his surcoat and approached Nadine, who stood as still as a statue. Melusina and Vonette retreated a respectful distance, and Gislebert found his hands shaking as he undid the clasp and held it before the white skin of his love's elegant throat.

"I always did dream that I would stand before you thus," he whispered, his words for her alone. Her thick, sooty lashes fluttered downward—probably in modesty, he thought—and she would not look at him. "I give you these in exchange for the crystal, which would have been burdensome for your beautiful neck, and I place within your hands my heart to hold forever. We shall be married here, in this place, in three days."

If she had looked up or given him any encouragement, he would have kissed her. But she did not, so Gislebert clasped the emeralds around her neck and stood at her side as tradition demanded. The monk approached and began the betrothal ceremony.

"Do you, Nadine, agree to be married to this man?"

"I do." Her voice was low, but Gislebert heard the answer and nodded for the priest to continue.

"Do you, Gislebert, agree to be married to this woman?"

"I do."

"Have you a ring?"

Gislebert fumbled at his little finger for the ring that Suger had remembered and donated at the last minute. He took Nadine's hand, which trembled as violently as his own, and gently slipped the ring over her little finger, her index finger, and then finally, her ring finger. As he settled it onto her hand, he repeated the traditional vows: "With this ring I thee wed; with this gold I thee honor; with this dowry I thee endow."

Gislebert then stood in embarrassed pride and pleasure as Nadine, the beauty of his dreams, obeyed the wedding tradition of years past and prostrated herself at his feet as her lord and master.

The next two days were a happy blur. Gislebert determined to ignore his problems with Adele, thinking only of the morning when he would walk to Nadine's gate, knock upon the door as master of the house, and take a seat by his wife at the table set for their wedding feast. Abbot Suger would be there, and Melusina and Vonette. Gislebert had even considered inviting Jerome merely to flaunt his good fortune before that undeserving and cowardly knight.

After the wedding feast—ah, then! He would take

Nadine's slender hand and lead her to their marriage bed, which would be bedecked in flowers. The wedding guests would follow into their nuptial chamber; the priest would chant prayers for their happiness and fertility, and then pronounce them married. Nadine would then be his *sponsa nova nupta,* his wife forever.

As the wedding guests left the chamber, he would place his unworthy lips on those of his bride, and she would open like a flower to his touch.

The irritation in Adele's voice broke off his reverie, but Gislebert could not be annoyed. Instead, he grinned happily at her, though she deserved a proper rebuke.

"You are too young to understand the depth of the love," Gislebert said, laughing. He pulled off one of his boots and sighed. "Tomorrow night I shall sit on my own bed, with my wife by my side."

Across the room, Adele lay on her mattress and turned her back to Gislebert. "I know, I know. I am ignorant of the glory of love," Adele parroted the words of a speech he'd given earlier. "I know only infatuation and youthful yearnings. Well, so be it. But I'd appreciate it if you would go to sleep, Troubadour, and keep your thoughts to yourself."

"Indeed I shall, for they are not fit for girlish ears," Gislebert said, his other boot thudding to the floor. He lay on his back and put his hands behind his head, contemplating his wedding night. A piece of straw poked his skin through his mattress, and Gislebert frowned. The morning after his marriage, he would destroy any and all straw mattresses in the house—nothing but a feather mattress would do for him and Nadine. *But for the first night,* Gislebert thought, grinning lazily as sleep fell upon him, *straw, hay, dust, or whatever—anything will do.*

He rose early, splashed his face in the basin of water, and pulled on his best tunic and newest surcoat. August had laid a warm shoulder of sun against his open door, and Gislebert felt that all of creation rejoiced with him.

All of creation but Adele. She had said little in the last few days. Gislebert credited her silence to embarrassed shame. She had not asked to attend the wedding; he had not invited her.

He left her sleeping and stepped out of the house. Breathing deeply, he plucked a sprig of laurel from a tree and tucked it in his cap. All in all, it was a fine day to be married.

Adele waited until the sound of Gislebert's incessant humming had faded, then she crawled out of bed and pulled her surcoat over the long tunic she slept in. It would not matter what she wore, for all in the convent wore black tunics. The day had come for her to keep her promise to the abbot. Gislebert had left this house for a new life; she would follow and leave for hers. But before she left, she would make sure that Jonas, that nonexistent boy, vanished thoroughly.

She walked around the room, slowly and methodically, piling every object that had once belonged to Jonas onto the hearth fire: his leggings, his sketches, his clay molds, his tunic, his summer cloak, his boots. The fire smoldered under the sudden load of fuel, and Adele blew on the embers until flames licked eagerly at the dry cloth and brittle parchments.

When every trace of Jonas lay in the fire pit, she pulled a square of fabric around her head and walked through the doorway of their house. She did not look back.

WESTMINSTER

Hope deferred makes the heart sick.

PROVERBS 13:12

TWENTY-SIX

No flowers adorned the gateposts. No horses waited outside the walls of the house. Gislebert felt a creeping uneasiness steal across his soul as he approached Nadine's gate. His hand reached for the bellpull, and he pulled it gently at first, lest the ladies were still asleep. After a moment, he yanked with all his might and set the bell clamoring.

When no reassuring face appeared, Gislebert squared his thin shoulders to break through the locked gate. Then Vonette opened the door of the house and hurried through the courtyard toward him. Her eyes were red from weeping, and Gislebert noticed that her fingers shook as she unfastened the latch of the gate.

"What's wrong, Vonette?" Gislebert demanded, sweeping past her into the courtyard. "Is Nadine ill?"

"No, monsieur," Vonette answered, her skirts rustling behind him as she struggled to keep up. "She is well, my lord, but she is not here."

"Not here?" Gislebert whirled around, and the maid quivered under the intensity of his gaze.

"She—last night—," Vonette stammered.

"Why don't I explain the situation to Monsieur Gislebert?" The smooth voice of Melusina called from the open door, and Gislebert turned from one girl to the other, his impatience rising with every second that Nadine did not appear. Melusina motioned for Gislebert to come into the

271

hall, and he clenched his fists as he followed her into the house. What could possibly be amiss?

Melusina led him into the great hall and motioned for Gislebert to sit in a chair beside the cold fireplace. When he had seated himself, she folded her hands at her waist and cleared her throat. "It gives me great pain to tell you this," she said, her thumbs nervously wriggling over her hands, "but last night Sir Jerome came to the house as we slept and took Nadine away."

Gislebert leapt to his feet and flashed into sudden fury. "Outrageous! Does his greed know no bounds? Does he demand a ransom?"

Melusina lowered her eyes and shook her head. "We believe he has abducted Nadine with the intention of marrying her himself."

"How do you know?" Gislebert snapped, pacing before the fireplace. "No doubt Nadine resisted—could you not have helped her? Why did you not send word for me?"

Melusina pressed her lips together. "Surely you knew that Jerome coveted the lands Nadine has inherited."

"So he stole my bride? The king shall hear of this! Vengeance will be mine, for I will see to it—"

Melusina's gentle upraised hand stopped Gislebert's frantic pacing. "Monsieur, you should also know that we are certain Nadine went willingly with the knight. She took her clothes; her bed has not been slept in, and she made no preparations for her marriage today."

Gislebert's eyes widened in disbelief. "No," he whispered, his breath catching in his throat. "She swore before God and his holy priest that she would marry me. She is my betrothed; her love is mine alone! Jerome has no right to take her!"

Melusina nodded in agreement. "You are right, monsieur, and you have behaved most nobly through these past days. I apologize for my companion. She has acted in a rash manner."

Her words scarcely reached his ears, so intent was he upon absorbing the shocking news. Only when she came forward and placed her hand on his arm did Gislebert look at Melusina again. "Because you deserve the bride you were pledged," she whispered, her smoky blue eyes brimming with compassion, "I offer myself to you in her place. I know I am not as beautiful as Nadine, but if I can ease your troubled heart, I would do so."

Her simple act of sacrifice brought Gislebert to his senses. Melusina, that beautiful and frail flower, offered herself to *him*?

Gislebert placed his hand over hers and patted it gently. "Your generosity is deeply touching," he said, looking fully into her liquid eyes, "and I am grateful for your sacrifice. But I cannot ask this of you, for I know you have planned to give your heart and service to God."

"And what of you?" she asked softly, her voice husky with pity. "What of your heart?"

"My heart has survived sorrow before, and it will survive still," Gislebert answered, as emotions swept over him— emotions that were deeper and stronger than he had ever felt before. "I know Nadine loved me, as I love her still. Jerome has bewitched her, Melusina, for he is a scoundrel and a villain. I will find him, claim my bride, and be rid of Jerome—even if I have to kill him."

"No, think again, monsieur," Melusina begged, patting his hand absently. "I do not think this plan is wise, and I pray you will abandon it. Jerome is a villain, but you are a gentle heart. And murder is not in your nature. And though I loved her like a sister, I knew her, and surely you must know that Nadine is—"

"—the most noble and true of women," Gislebert finished, stopping her words with his eyes. "Though it appears she has forsaken me, still I *must* believe in her, gentle lady. My love for her has sustained me for years, and if it dies . . ." His eyes left her face and wandered over the room, so lifeless without Nadine's shining presence. ". . . I die."

"Then I will pray for you," Melusina answered, extending her hand formally. "And I pray God will grant his wisdom as you seek his will."

Gislebert bowed and kissed her hand, then turned to leave. As he passed out of the hall, he caught sight of a miniature portrait of Nadine on a table near the door. He gasped at the lifelike image and picked up the psalter on which it had been painted.

"Was this painted by . . . ," he asked, the question pricking his heart strangely.

". . . by your friend, Adele," Melusina answered. "She painted several portraits for us, and Nadine especially asked that her psalter be painted with her image."

Gislebert turned the little book over in his hands. Nadine's small hands had handled this, had leafed through the pages during daily prayers, had offered petitions to God. . . .

"You may keep it, monsieur," Melusina said, reading his thoughts. "May it comfort your heart until you find peace. And do not worry about the wedding feast. I shall instruct Vonette to turn away any guests as they arrive."

Gislebert groaned; he had not even thought about the indignity of turning away the few friends who would arrive soon. "Thank you, mademoiselle," he answered, bowing his head to the noble Melusina. "You are most kind."

Clutching the psalter in his hand, he prowled madly through the bustling city and searched for any glimpse of Jerome or Nadine. Once or twice he caught a glimpse of red hair or a dark-haired knight, but he was always disappointed as he drew closer. Surely they were far away by now, perhaps even legally married. And to further seal his deed, Jerome had undoubtedly claimed the virgin body of Gislebert's rightful bride. The thought of Jerome's grasping hands on Nadine's creamy skin drove Gislebert into a frenzy, and he crisscrossed the city for three hours before falling exhausted onto a low stone wall near the abbey well.

What could he do? What should he do? He smacked his

forehead with the palm of his hand, trying to still his frantic thoughts, but reason lay buried under anger, pain, and shock. He needed the impartial voice of common sense, and he thought suddenly of Adele. Though his soul still stung from the humiliation of her deception, she had always held practical views. That thought brought Gislebert to his feet and propelled him toward home.

As he neared his house, his ravaged thoughts were distracted by the sight of a cloud of smoke over his neighborhood. Distraught villagers shouted at one another, and Gislebert dodged through the milling crowd until he saw someone he recognized—the tanner who lived in the house next to his. "What has happened?" Gislebert cried, grabbing the man by his tunic.

The soot-smudged tanner regarded Gislebert in a weary daze. "All is lost," he said flatly, his hands hanging limply by his side. "My house and yours. My livelihood, my chickens—"

"What of the—the boy who lived with me?" Gislebert asked, wishing the man would speak more pointedly. "Have you seen Jonas, the boy?"

The man shook his head slowly. "The fire began after sunrise," he said. "The wind carried the flames from your house to ours, and both were gone in a flash. My wife and I escaped with our lives, but I saw no one else."

Gislebert released the man and staggered toward a heap of darkened timbers and smoldering embers, all that remained of the house. The thatched roof had completely disintegrated. Gislebert dashed forward to search through the smoking remains, hoping Adele had not slept through the blaze, but the neighbors caught his tunic and held him back. "The boy, did he escape?" he cried, throwing his head back as he fought to free himself.

"We saw no boy," a woman said, struggling in English. She murmured something in French to her companion, who shook her head as well. Gislebert looked up at the hazy sky and wept openly. Adele had to be dead. If she were not, she would be standing there beside the rubble, waiting for Gislebert.

He relaxed in the grasp of the men who held him and raised his hands in a gesture of surrender. "I will not go into the fire," he told them in French. "I do not need to search for what is no more."

He had lost his love and his friend in one morning's time—what more would God demand of him? As the startled villagers pulled back in surprise, Gislebert dropped to the ground and sobbed like a woman.

Monks from Suger's abbey led him to shelter for the night, and the next morning Gislebert stood before Suger in his disheveled wedding garments. "Nothing remains of my house," Gislebert announced, folding his dirty hands in front of him. "My friend has perished in the fire. And as you have surely heard, my bride has been abducted by the knight Jerome."

"I know," Suger said, his hawkish eyes gleaming with distaste. "I am sorry this happened to you, Scribe. In fact, I had hoped Ludlow's sword would bring an end to Jerome de Honfleur."

A dim ripple ran across Gislebert's mind, but he was too tired to consider its source.

"Alas, the knight Jerome was even more cowardly than I imagined," Suger went on. "What will you do now, Gislebert?"

Gislebert cleared his throat and gathered his thoughts. "I must leave, Your Grace. I have a vow to keep. Before my journey here, I gave my word to King Stephen that if my love spurned me for any reason, I would return and serve him for the rest of his life. Therefore, sir, I must take my leave of you."

Suger arched his bushy brows. "Did I not hear that this king once issued a warrant for your death?"

Gislebert stepped back, stung. Suger had never given any sign that he knew of Gislebert's trouble in England.

"It's all right," Suger said, waving a hand as if to sweep away Gislebert's apprehension. "I know about the warrant, and I know that Jerome implicated you in a false charge. I also know, faithful scribe, that King Stephen has pardoned you."

"It does not matter whether or not I am pardoned," Gislebert answered, lowering his gaze to the floor. "If I die, I am resigned to do so, for what is life without love? If I live, I shall always hope that I will again find Nadine and liberate her from the knave who has taken her from me."

"Before you go," Suger said, easing his weight out of his chair, "as a last act, go to your desk and pay yourself wages of two hundred marks of silver. If you journey to England, you shall go in prosperity. It shall not be said that Suger's man journeyed in want and hunger."

Gislebert obeyed and filled a bag with the silver marks, which he tied inside his surcoat. "I shall be hard-pressed to find a replacement for you," Suger said, extending his hand to the troubadour.

"You, Suger, will do it," Gislebert answered smoothly. He knelt to kiss the abbot's ring, while Suger chanted a prayer and made the sign of the cross over the troubadour's head. When the abbot had finished, Gislebert stood, smiled his thanks, and left the Abbey of St. Denis.

After bargaining for a sturdy and fleet horse, he rode one last time to the ruins of the tiny house he had shared with Adele. The sun lingered in the western sky as he approached, and the slow clip-clop of his horse's hooves echoed through the narrow street as he drew near the blackened gap in the row of houses.

"Be you Gislebert?" a voice called, and the troubadour jerked his head toward the source of the sound. An aged monk waited in front of the house, his white eyes gleaming eerily through the impending dusk.

"I am," he said, his voice heavy. "And you are Abbot Robert. My friend spoke of you often."

"Jonas spoke often of you, as well," the abbot said, nodding slowly. He grasped the top of his tall walking stick and seemed to regard the ruined house in front of him. "I can smell the ashes," he said, pointing a quivering finger at the pile of rubble. "Tragedy has visited this place."

"Indeed it has," Gislebert answered, gripping his reins tightly as he regarded the ruined house. How much did the monk know? "I fear Jonas died in the blaze, Abbot. There has been no sign of him since yesterday morning, and it is unlike the boy to leave without a word."

The monk received this news in silence, then nodded curtly. "If he was so attached, Jonas must have loved you very much."

"We were close friends." Gislebert sighed. "But what use is love, Abbot, when love brings pain and treachery? I loved a woman, and awoke yesterday morning to find that my intended bride had been abducted by a villain." His weariness seemed to grow as he spoke, and he sighed audibly. "I have lost all I have loved in the space of a few hours."

The monk silently regarded this answer, and Gislebert wondered why the man did not speak.

"You have not lost love," Abbot Robert finally replied, smiling gently. "You have but to seek it, and you will find it. One day, my friend, your eyes will be opened and you will see."

Gislebert rolled his eyes in exasperation.

"You find this difficult to believe?"

Gislebert felt a curious shock at the accuracy of the monk's intuition, but he defended himself quickly. "Yes, Abbot, I do. Love has always eluded me, though I have searched for it all my life. I am a poet, a troubadour, and I know what love is supposed to be. I sought the most perfect, most holy love in the world, and when I stepped forward to claim it, it flew from my grasp. Yet its image burns brightly in my heart, and still I must seek it."

"There is but one perfect and holy love—God's love. That is the love you should seek, my son. God's love will ease the sorrow in your soul, but you must be willing to receive it."

"Go back to your prayers, old man," Gislebert snapped, losing his patience and respect in one instant. "I have followed God's precepts, and all has come to naught."

Still the abbot smiled. "I have a word from our Holy Scriptures for you, Troubadour, and it can be translated thusly: *'I know the plans I have for you,' declares the Lord, 'plans to prosper you and not to harm you, plans to give you hope and a blessed future. You will seek me and find me when you seek me with all your heart.'"*

"Farewell, Abbot Robert," Gislebert replied, snapping the reins on his horse and urging the animal forward. "When you send your prayers heavenward, greet Jonas for me."

TWENTY-SEVEN

Despite the curfew and danger from robbers and the king's patrols, Gislebert left the safety of the walls of St. Denis and rode through the night, despair equipping him with an odd sort of courage. *What have I to lose?* he asked himself, urging his horse into a steady canter. *If I die, I die, and perhaps in death Nadine and I shall meet and love again. If I live, I live yet for Nadine.*

A plan began to formulate in his mind as he rode, and he found his hopelessness and desperation evolving into two distinctly different emotions: anger toward Jerome and compassion for the captured Nadine.

The codes of chivalry demanded that he confront Jerome and avenge his honor, but Gislebert's common sense reminded him that without a champion, he would be as certain for defeat as Jerome had been before Ludlow. He needed a strong and sure defender, and he might find one in King Stephen.

Suger had said that Stephen had issued a pardon. If the abbot's words were true, the king might actually be eager to make amends for his hasty condemnation of Gislebert. Furthermore, Nadine had inherited English as well as French lands from Lady Jehannenton, and if Jerome crossed the channel to claim those lands, he would place himself in Gislebert's hands. With Stephen's blessing and a contingent of royal knights, Gislebert could find Jerome and skewer him like the undeserving dog he was.

Nadine, then, would be free from the man who had brutally stolen her lawful husband's rights. Once Gislebert had vanquished her dastardly abductor, she would bow before Gislebert in gratitude and beg to be received once again as the troubadour's promised bride.

He straightened in the saddle; his plan felt right. A sharp sound echoed through the stillness of the night, and Gislebert slowed his horse and peered through the darkness ahead. After waiting in silence for a time and hearing nothing, he eased the horse forward. Surely Jerome had slipped into Nadine's house this way and quietly stolen her away. Perhaps she lay sleeping on her bed, and he snatched her before she could call for help. She simply could not have willingly gone with a man Gislebert knew to be a liar, a traitor, and an immoral scoundrel. Nadine *had* to be ransomed and rescued, and Gislebert would secure Stephen's promise of help even if the king demanded his life in return.

As the sun rose in the east, so did Gislebert's spirits. If it took months, he would find Jerome and fight until Nadine was his lawful wife. A random voice echoed in his brain: *"I know the plans I have for you," declares the Lord, "plans to prosper you and not to harm you, plans to give you hope and a blessed future. . . . "* Gislebert smiled. "Yes, Abbot Robert," he murmured, "if God's plans match my plans, they are very good indeed."

He asked for and found shelter in the castle at Gisors, where he and Adele had been well received years before, and upon taking to his bed, Gislebert slept for two days without awakening. When he finally did rise and dress for dinner, his noble host nodded gravely. "Some great tragedy or illness has overtaken you," Lord Rainger said, his eyes frankly questioning. "I wonder if it is a story you could share with us?"

Gislebert smiled and shook his head. "I fear I cannot," he said, running his hands through his unruly hair. "For I have lost both a friend and my betrothed in these last few days. Sorrow rides upon my shoulder, Lord Rainger, and binds my tongue tightly."

"I understand," Lord Rainger replied. "Still, I would have you join us at dinner today and rest in our hospitality. I have engaged a most interesting diversion for our entertainment after the meal."

When the serving bowls had at last been cleared from the long tables, Lord Rainger clapped his hands. A dark-haired woman in a veil and long skirt entered the hall and sashayed to the center of the room. Her hair rose as a wild black cloud behind her head. As her dark eyes peered over the veil that covered her face, she raised her hands slowly, her bracelets jingling.

"What is she?" Gislebert asked, leaning toward his host.

"A Gypsy," Lord Rainger replied, smiling with satisfaction. "King Geza of Hungary seeks to rid his land of witches and those who practice the dark arts, and many have found their way to France."

"My lord, I protest!" A dark-robed man sitting with the household staff rose and bowed politely to Lord Rainger. "This is an offense in the sight of God, my lord! Surely you do not intend to invite witches to this honorable household—"

"Enough, Chaplain," Lord Rainger said, waving a languid hand at his cleric. "If she bothers you, you are dismissed."

The chaplain turned in a huff and left the hall, and Rainger's wife reached out for her husband's hand. "I tremble at her presence," Lady Nicola protested, her pretty blue eyes shining in gentle rebuke. "She is so—unnatural!"

"Nonsense, let us listen to her," her husband insisted, patting his wife's hand indulgently. "We do not believe what she says. We are merely using her for sport."

The servants and knights of Lord Rainger's household stilled as the dark-haired Gypsy twirled in a circle, her bright red shawl enveloping her form. Suddenly the woman stopped and pointed a finger at Gislebert. "Please, sir, your dream," she demanded, her voice an odd gurgle.

"Pardon?" Gislebert asked, uncomfortably aware that every eye in the room had turned to him.

"Tell me of your dream last night!" the Gypsy persisted, her dark eyes commanding his response.

Gislebert attempted to smile. "Why, 'twas nothing of consequence, if I remember." He laid his index finger alongside his head, thinking. "I dreamed that I was walking outside on a frosty morning. I was playing a lute and singing."

"Anything else?" the Gypsy persisted.

"Yes, monsieur, anything else?" Lady Nicola asked, her eyes wide with curiosity.

Gislebert frowned as the full memory of his dream returned. "The frost lay in a forest of trees, and a nightingale perched in each tree. Though I urged the birds to sing, they would not."

The Gypsy closed her eyes and nodded, then twirled slowly in the middle of the room while chanting in a tongue that Gislebert had never heard. Finally she stopped swaying and turned to Gislebert again. "The frost on the ground signifies exile to a strange country, my lord, but your wanderings will end in peace," she said, closing her eyes. "The lute that you played indicates that you will hear joyful news from an absent friend."

"A favorable reading," Lord Rainger said, nodding at Gislebert. "You are a fortunate man."

"If I believed it," Gislebert said, laughing.

But the Gypsy held up her hand to silence him. "There still remains the matter of the silent nightingales, my lord."

"And what do they portend?" Gislebert asked, raising an eyebrow. "What wonderful news do they bring?"

"Singing nightingales bring favorable news," the Gypsy answered, swaying gently to a rhythm only she heard. "One silent nightingale foretells a misunderstanding among friends. A forest of silent nightingales, sir, signifies an enormous misunderstanding, a critical error of judgment."

The Gypsy twirled again, her cloak nearly enveloping her, and the knights at a nearby table clamored for her attention. Lady Nicola leaned over to Gislebert. "Have you made such an error, my friend?" she asked. "Is this woman truly gifted, or does she use us for sport?"

"She says I have been exiled, which is true," Gislebert admitted. "But any in these parts may have known of my journey from England. She says I will hear joyful news from an absent friend, which I surely hope to hear from my king. And she says I have made a critical error of judgment, and what man has not done so at one time or another?"

"What was your critical error?" Lady Nicola asked softly as the Gypsy stopped in front of another dinner guest.

Gislebert shook his head. "I do not dare to guess at it, my lady. For now I labor in happy ignorance, deciding my own fate, and if I were to change the direction of my life at the word of this woman, what course would I then take? If a man does not know where—or when—he has done wrong, how can he judge when he has done right?"

"We have only God's Word to tell us so," the lady replied, pulling her psalter from a pocket within her surcoat.

"God's Word—and his priests," Gislebert answered, thinking of Abbot Robert.

The Gypsy's words haunted him as he rode from Gisors the next day, and Lady Nicola's question nagged at him. Had he committed a critical error? Did his fault lie in leaving Nadine unprotected? Leaving Adele asleep on the morning of the fire? In his decision to return to England?

A quiet voice from within the depths of his conscience murmured that he had been wrong to speak with the gypsy at all, for men of God had no business consulting the powers of darkness.

He found no peace, and throughout the next several days Gislebert's mind began to play tricks on him. In Sotteville, he spied a young girl with Adele's face. In Rouen, he heard Adele's voice coming from a milking girl. In men and women alike, he saw reminders of Adele: dark eyes, narrow chin, high cheekbones. The English sea captain at Le Havre remembered him and asked, "Aren't you the troubadour?" Gislebert started at the sound, for Adele had uttered the word *troubadour* with exactly the same inflection and diction.

He began to feel that the girl's spirit haunted him. Would God never cease to remind him that he had abandoned Adele? In all things regarding Nadine, he had behaved properly and according to the laws of God and love, but his friendship with Adele had splintered as the time approached for his marriage. After that awful scene when Adele revealed the truth of who she was, he should have been gentle, understanding, constant in his friendship. Instead, he had run to present Nadine with the engraved crystal; he had worked first and hardest to insure her love.

Surely that was my sin, Gislebert thought, his conscience smiting him. *Adele looked to me for everything—security, friendship, trust, even faith in God. When I left her so heartlessly, I took it all from her.*

In the bow of the tiny ship that sped him to England's shores, Gislebert fell on his knees and turned his eyes toward heaven. 'Til today, his prayers had been little more than urgent requests for the love of Nadine. He had always considered his prayers pure, his motives holy. But in the past few days, he had come to recognize his own selfishness— mayhap his own cruelty. And he saw that faith that fed only one's own soul was not faith at all.

Now his soul felt a need for cleansing, for absolution, for God's pardon.

In the only way he knew, Gislebert lifted his eyes to the turquoise sky above the English Channel and asked God's forgiveness for slighting Adele. "I confess that I placed my quest for love above the demands of friendship," Gislebert whispered, careful lest the other passengers hear him and think him mad. "And in doing so, I wronged Adele dreadfully. Indeed, most holy God, her blood may be on my hands, and for this I beg your forgiveness. Welcome her soul into your heaven, and keep her until we meet again."

There was no reply save the insistent slap of the waves against the boat, but Gislebert rose to his feet feeling strangely comforted.

"His Royal Highness King Stephen of England calls for Gislebert, the troubadour of Margate."

The royal page's call brought Gislebert to his feet, and he carefully adjusted his cloak and tunic as he followed the page into the great hall of the palace of Westminster. His tension rose with each step he took toward the faraway throne at the end of the hall, and only when he stood directly in front of the king did Gislebert relax. For the man sitting on the royal throne of England did not wear the face of anger, but of age, and weary dignity.

Stephen held forth his hand, and Gislebert knelt to kiss it. "Welcome, old and much-beloved friend," Stephen said, his voice resonating throughout the hall. "We welcome you back to Mother England's shores and pray that your journey has brought you peace."

Gislebert stood upright and looked into the tired eyes of the king. "I have sought, and found, and lost," Gislebert said. "And in honor of the vow between us, I have returned to fulfill my word, even though your anger may demand my life."

"You were pardoned long ago," Stephen answered, rubbing his silvery beard. "And I am glad you have come home, although I am not sure why you have come. Did the beautiful Nadine refuse your love?"

"A villain stole her love from me," Gislebert answered, "even though we were betrothed according to the ordinances of the church. I stand before you, my king, to beg mercy and to ask that you extend your favor and a contingent of fighting men so that I may pursue the knight Jerome if he comes ashore in England. He has wronged me once again and stolen my bride."

286

Stephen leaned forward in his seat, a glint of interest in his eyes. "The knight Jerome de Honfleur? The same knight who misrepresented you to us and has been exiled from our royal court and these lands?"

"The same, my liege."

The king spat on the floor in disgust. "We do not like to speak his name, my friend, for a worse turncoat has never walked England's shores. I shudder when I think that I nearly gave aid to him and his brother, Jean de Honfleur—do you remember when the elder brother disappeared? You were at the tower with us. I distinctly remember asking you if you had seen the man."

The floodgates of Gislebert's memory opened, and he gasped in horror as the realization hit him. Jean de Honfleur! He had disappeared from the tower on the day Adele pushed a man into the river!

"I remember, my liege," Gislebert managed to whisper.

"How did this Jerome learn of your Nadine, then?" the king asked, his eyes flickering with curiosity as he leaned back and crossed his long legs.

"While we were imprisoned at the tower together, he learned of Nadine and of her inheritance, for I could speak of little else. Within days of Lady Jehannenton's death, he arrived to press his suit with my lady. He used a profane connection with Queen Eleanor of France to press his advantage."

Stephen blinked in astonished silence, then slapped the arm of his chair. "The devil take him!" he roared, and three knights sprang forward eagerly.

"Rest, my good knights," Stephen said, raising his hand. "The devil has taken the rogue from us; the fellow breathes now in France."

"Unless he comes here to claim Nadine's inheritance," Gislebert spoke up. "If he does, I would ask to ride with your men when they locate Jerome and watch as they arrest him for his misconduct. The laws of the land, of God, and of love demand that justice be done."

Stephen's eyes narrowed; he rested his chin in his hand and leaned forward in contemplation. After several moments the king finally spoke. "Your cause is just, Gislebert," he said, shifting in his chair, "and we will do what we can to aid you. But if this scoundrel Jerome remains in France, there is nothing we can do, for he is an expatriate. If he ventures onto English shores, however, we will send men to arrest him."

Gislebert waved his hands in frustration. "But how will you know when he has landed? He may walk even now on the English lands that Nadine has inherited."

"We will alert the nobles on the surrounding estates," Stephen answered, gesturing to his scribe, who scribbled furiously on a parchment. "If Jerome dares set foot in England, we will find him and seek your justice."

"And if he does not?"

Stephen cast Gislebert a warning look, and the troubadour knew he tried the royal patience. "I promise you shall be avenged, my friend," Stephen said. "Until that time, you shall fulfill your vow to me and remain at my side and in my company."

Gislebert smoothed his face to conceal his disappointment and bowed before the king. He had regained the king's favor, but apparently the king intended to hold Gislebert to his vow. As long as he had no bride, he would be bound to the king's side.

TWENTY-EIGHT

After three years of difficult adjustment, Adele grew accustomed both to her holy female companions and her role in the convent. The abbess, Madame Marie, took a firm and supportive interest in the young woman. Adele learned to read, write, and speak French and Latin contained in the nun's prayer books.

At twenty-one, she was the picture of a genteel French lady—her face and form had changed little, but grace and confidence now shone from her eyes. And her manners had been refined to a pleasing smoothness. After stealing a forbidden glance at her reflection in the washbasin one afternoon, Adele wondered if Gislebert the troubadour would know her should he ever return to St. Denis.

Life had seemed empty and strange without his presence at first, for the atmosphere of the convent was quiet, feminine, and rarefied. Adele missed Gislebert's complaining, his unembarrassed belching, and the annoying creak of his mattress that came from his habit of jiggling his legs while he waited for sleep. She missed their conversations, their arguments—even, she admitted one lonely afternoon, his saccharine poetry of love and Nadine.

She did not grow to miss him less, but consigned her memories of their time together to another place in her mind. Often at night she would lie in her tiny curtained cubicle and close her eyes to visit that place. They would be together again on the road, laughing and singing, walking miles and miles as the wind howled around them. When she awoke the next morning in the convent, often her legs would actually ache, or she would shiver at the memory of the frosty wind even though the sun shone hot outside.

Because the troubadour still lived in her heart, she could not agree to take her vows and become a fully professed nun. Other young girls came to the convent and took their perpetual vows as young as fourteen, but Adele shook her head each time the abbess inquired whether or not God had finally spoken. "These other girls have always intended to give their lives to God, and they are following the wishes of their families," Adele tried to explain to the bishop, the priest, and the abbess whenever they asked why she refused to take her vows. "I have no family, and I do not know that God would have me stay here forever. My life is in his hands, but it is not dependent upon the nunnery."

Melusina had come to the convent shortly after Adele and readily took her vows after the year of postulancy and novitiate. That lovely girl now wore the long black robe, scapular, and confining white wimple and veil of the fully professed nuns. She had gladly endured all that the nunnery required, surrendering her inherited lands, her money, and even her beautiful golden hair for a life of simplicity, poverty, obedience, and chastity. And though they were never to speak of their past lives, Adele had first discerned that the troubadour's marriage had not taken place, when the usually serene eyes of Melusina clouded at the mention of Gislebert's name.

Abbot Robert had supplied the missing pieces of the story. When Adele heard that Gislebert had left St. Denis alone, a stab of regret pierced her heart for a moment. If she had remained with him, perhaps in time he would have come to value her love. But she had surrendered her life and will to God, and knew she would have to trust his purpose.

Abbot Robert visited her at the nunnery every week, and through him she continued her work for the cathedral of St. Denis. King Louis now fought in the Holy Land, and Suger, as he had predicted, served as regent of France in the king's absence. Still bent on self-promotion, the mighty abbot wrote two books proclaiming his work and continued to enlarge and beautify his chapels. Adele found herself busy, for the abbot constantly demanded new and more precious works of art. She continued to sketch and make clay molds for the master sculptors, and Abbot Robert joked one day that the abbey monks could not believe how well the little postulant's work matched that of the boy Jonas.

In the convent she found more freedom than she had believed possible. As a postulant, the abbess required her to perform all the religious offices and activities of the nuns. But she participated with pleasure, for she found companionship and comfort in her conversations with God. Throughout the day, as the other nuns around her recited the eight offices of Matins, Lauds, Prime, Terce, Sexts, Nones, Vespers, and Compline, she moved her lips soundlessly in prayers for the troubadour, for guidance, and for wisdom. For the first time in her life, Adele felt truly free. With her thoughts focused on God, she found a blessed release from fear and anger.

After breakfast and morning prayers, the nuns went to their work, and on the rare mornings when there were no sketches to be made, Adele headed toward a small thatched covering that served as a school for several peasant children. While their parents worked in the fields, Adele settled the children on the ground around her and taught them about the love of God. "Love is not selfish," she would tell them in French, "love is kind. Love does not change. It sacrifices for another. It compels us to do what is right."

She tousled the head of a little red-haired boy next to her and quoted her favorite Scripture: "'I have loved you with an everlasting love; I have drawn you with loving-kindness,'" she whispered, bending low to whisper in the child's ear. "'I will bring Israel back from the land of the north, he will come with weeping, he will pray as I bring him back.'"

Time passed for Gislebert and Adele in two separate countries united by a single cause: the second glorious expedition of God to Outremer, the crusader states established in the Holy Land. King Louis VII of France took the crusader's oath and led a contingent eastward. Stephen sent a generous army of knights and nobles, and the German emperor Conrad and his knights buttressed the mighty force. Though hopes were high, the group of crusaders fell prey to weather, illness, and the Turks before they even reached Outremer.

The crusaders mustered their forces at Acre, tried to regain Damascus by siege, and failed miserably. The few survivors returned home to their European castles and estates weak, wounded, and ashamed.

As the focus of kings shifted from England's civil strife to the east, Empress Matilda of Anjou withdrew her forces from England and concentrated on having her son, Henry, duke of Normandy, recognized as heir to Stephen's throne. Upon hearing the rumors, Stephen instructed all who served him to prepare his son, Eustace, for the confrontation that would undoubtedly take place in the future. Stephen's knights trained Eustace in sword fighting and jousting; Stephen's chaplain taught him history, religion, and law, and to Gislebert fell the odious task of instructing the royal son in the arts of love and marriage.

At King Stephen's court at Westminster, Gislebert stood in his small chamber and faced his adolescent pupil for the first time. "Your father has asked me to speak to you," Gislebert said, motioning for the young prince to take a seat. "It is most important that you, as son of the king, be wisely instructed in the knightly arts—"

"I am already a knight," the boy answered, scowling with the typical impatience of youth. He fell into the chair Gislebert had indicated, and his slouch communicated that he would rather be almost anywhere than in the dismally small chamber of his father's friend.

"I know, Prince Eustace," Gislebert said, pressing his hands together, "but part of the knightly arts includes knowing the tenets of courtly love. My own friend, Lord Calhoun of Margate, underwent such training at Warwick Castle as a squire, and—"

"Get on with it," Eustace growled. "I am hunting this afternoon."

Gislebert pressed his lips together. "All right, then," he said firmly. "What gifts might you freely send a lady who pleases you?"

Eustace said nothing but scowled more deeply.

Gislebert sighed. "A handkerchief, a fillet for the hair, a wreath of gold or silver, a breastpin, a mirror, a girdle, a purse, a tassel, a comb, sleeves, gloves, a ring, a picture, a washbasin, little dishes, trays, a flag, or any little gift which may be useful for the care of the person or pleasing to look at," Gislebert recited, taking a deep breath.

"But if you send a lady a ring, she ought to put it on her left hand and on her little finger because a man's life and death reside more in his little finger than in the others. Remember, my prince, that love dies if revealed too soon, so if you correspond with a lady, you should refrain from signing your own name, and you ought not to seal your letters with your own seal unless you have a secret seal known only to you and your lady. True love, my prince, will not endure if made public."

"Is that what happened to you?" Eustace sneered. "The entire court talks about the lady who escaped with a rogue rather than marry you."

His words burned like a brand in the troubadour's heart, and Gislebert turned away to compose himself before continuing. "What happened to me is not your concern," he replied over his shoulder. "Let us just say that love can drive a man to distraction and ruin and pain. Often it leads men to deadly, inescapable warfare and overthrows great cities and mighty fortresses and the safest of castles. Love can change the good fortune of wealth into the evil fortune of poverty. You, my prince, must watch yourself if you would not bring yourself and your future kingdom into ruin."

"I will watch myself," Eustace answered in a bored tone. "Now, let me go, Troubadour, for the hunt awaits me."

"Till tomorrow, then," Gislebert said, turning as the royal prince bolted out the door.

Adele pressed her face into her hands as she lay prostrate before the altar in the nun's chapel. Again Madame Marie and the bishop had asked if she would take her vows, and again she had refused. Madame Marie's face had frozen over like a glacier, and Adele feared that she had alienated her superior. Why could they not let her wait in silence and patience?

Because they fear you are wasting your life, the answer came to her. *You are a leech, taking from the convent, yet unwilling to give what it demands. You work for the nuns, pray with them, eat and sleep with them, yet you are not one of them. When they sing praises with breathless adoration, you alone keep your eyes downcast, for you cannot fully understand their fervor.*

"God, give me a sign!" she whispered, peeking through her outstretched fingers to the cross at the front of the chapel. "If I fast, and pray, and seek your will, will you give me a sign and tell me what I should do?"

The single candle on the table before the altar sputtered and went out, leaving her alone in the darkness.

The next day Adele fasted, only pretending to eat. To call attention to herself would have invited unwanted pity, so she stirred her bowl of pottage and dutifully raised her wooden spoon to her lips without partaking of food. She went about her work and prayers as usual, but all the while she begged God for an answer, for a sign.

Her answer came that afternoon. It was her turn to supervise the courtyard, and when a visitor rang the bell, she was surprised to see a young man standing at the gate. He rode a black mare like the one Gislebert had once owned. A small bag of belongings was tied to the saddle, and the fret-work of a lute was clearly visible at the top of the bag.

She gave him a polite, nunlike smile.

"Pardon me, madame, I seek rest for the night," the man said, doffing his cap.

Adele smiled and pointed down the road to the forest monastery. "There, monsieur, is a monastery. This is a nunnery, and we are not equipped to shelter men."

"Merci beaucoup," the man replied. He smiled warmly at her and mounted his horse. Dropping his reins, he pulled the lute from his bag and began to sing as his horse moved away:

> *O what is longer than the way,*
> *Or what is deeper than the sea?*
> *Or what is louder than the horn,*
> *Or what is sharper than a thorn?*
> *Or what is greener than the grass,*
> *Or what is worse than Mother Eve was?*
>
> *O love is longer than the way,*
> *And hell is deeper than the sea.*
> *And thunder is louder than the horn,*
> *And hunger is sharper than a thorn.*
> *And poison is greener than the grass,*
> *And the devil worse than Mother Eve was.*
>
> *So now, fair maidens all, adieu,*
> *This song I dedicate to you.*
> *I wish that you may constant prove*
> *Unto the man that you do love.*

"Thank you, blessed Lord," Adele breathed, watching the young man ride away. "I will remain constant and wait for the troubadour."

295

TWENTY-NINE

News of Abbot Suger's death reached Stephen's court in the fall of 1151, and news that Louis had annulled his marriage to his trifling queen, Eleanor, followed only a few months after. "I had wondered if such a thing were possible," Gislebert told Stephen as they pondered the news at dinner. "Louis never liked Eleanor, much preferring the company of his monks. She, on the other hand, preferred the company of scandalous knights and lovers who were less than modest."

"I heard it was her affair with one Raymond of Antioch that did her in," Queen Matilda offered. "Louis should not have insisted that she accompany him to the Holy Land."

"He could not trust her at home," Gislebert answered, shrugging. "I guess he could not trust her anywhere."

Stephen laughed and reached for the hand of his wife. "How unfortunate that our neighboring king made an unwise choice," he said, giving his wife's palm a gentle kiss. "He apparently did not realize that royal marriage partners can be taught to love."

"I don't know how he convinced the pope to annul the marriage," Gislebert wondered aloud. "Suger had always been quite insistent that the marriage should not fail."

"Suger is dead, the church is poor, and the campaign in the east cost dearly," Stephen said, raising an eyebrow in Gislebert's direction. "I'm sure 'twas more a question of *how much* Louis paid for the annulment of his marriage."

"Still, what has the marriage of a French king to do with us?" the queen asked. "Surely we will not consider this flighty French heiress for our son."

"Even though Eleanor is heir to all of southwestern France?" Gislebert queried, raising his glass to the queen's.

"Even though, indeed we will not," Stephen said, lifting his glass as well. "Let us drink to our Eustace's bride—may she be anyone but Eleanor of Aquitaine."

Three months later, the nobles and merchants of England snickered at the news that Henry, the nineteen-year-old son of Empress Matilda of Anjou, had married thirty-year-old Eleanor of Aquitaine. But in Stephen's court, no one laughed.

"Henry now holds not only his mother's possessions, but also his wife's," one of the king's counselors stepped forward and gently reminded Stephen. "All of Normandy, the southwest of France, the provinces in the northwest—"

"We know geography," Stephen snapped. "But does this increase Henry's power?"

"Indeed it does, for he can and will raise an army from among his new vassals. While he may not rise now to threaten us, my king, he will undoubtedly challenge your son."

"Eustace must be recognized by the bishops and anointed as the next king," Stephen said, slamming his fist down. "Tell the pestilent bishops that I'll drop my dispute regarding the papal appointments of vacant bishoprics. The pope can do whatever he likes, but he must recognize Eustace as heir!"

"Shall we take the message?" asked a knight, stepping forward. Stephen nodded, then gestured to Gislebert. "You, friend Gislebert, shall go to Rome with my escort and plead my case before the pope. Do not fail me, for England's future depends upon your efforts."

Pope Eugene III had laughed when Gislebert suggested that Stephen stood ready to concede to the desires of the church. "I know of Stephen's fears," the pope replied, the brilliant

white of his robes lighting the room. "And I refuse to intervene in this matter. God's will must be done."

Standing outside the king's hall at Westminster, Gislebert
chewed his knuckle and tried not to look as nervous as he felt.
He had utterly failed in his mission. How could he give this
news to Stephen? The king would not receive this news well,
for he grew older and more desperate every day.

Surprisingly, the king received Gislebert's news without
an outburst. "You have done well, Gislebert," Stephen
replied quietly, slouching in his chair. Great crescents of
flesh sagged under his eyes, and the king's head drooped forward as if he did not have strength enough to lift it. "We
shall continue to press my case with the English bishops
here. Perhaps they, in loyalty to our throne, will anoint our
son." The royal voice clotted with emotion. "But mean-
while, my friend, will you pray for our prince?"

"He is not well?" Gislebert asked, his pulse quickening.

"No." Stephen's lids drooped with weariness. "He and
his mother have taken to their beds with an illness, and the
doctors have bled them for days with no sign of improvement. Pray for them, Gislebert, and may God have mercy
upon us all."

Eustace and his mother died within a few hours of each
other, and Gislebert feared that Stephen would harm himself, so great was the king's grief. Stephen received the news
of their deaths in stony silence, then swept from the great
hall as his frightened counselors trailed behind. Gislebert followed, too, from afar but stood close enough to the royal
chamber to hear the king's gut-wrenching sobs as he cradled
his wife in one arm, his son in another.

The two were buried in solemn ceremonies at Westminster, then Stephen locked himself in his chamber and
would not come out. After six hours of unearthly silence
in the palace, servants knocked on Gislebert's door and
brought word that the king requested his presence.

The king knelt on the floor of his chamber by the bed,

his arms flung across his empty mattress. Stephen's face gleamed like chiseled marble. The proud head that had worn the crown in casual indifference was bowed with care and streaked with gray. "I am tired of life," the king whispered when Gislebert entered the room. "How can a man end his life with honor? How can a king?"

"A man cannot, and a king should not," Gislebert answered, walking carefully across the polished wooden floor.

Stephen's eyes, which had once sparkled with merriment and mischief, were dull and defeated. "I have been begging God to take my life," he said, the faint beginnings of a smile on his lips. "But God does not want me—neither do my people. Even the people of London grow tired of my failures."

"If you speak of the Holy Land, sire, all kings bear that defeat equally. Even now Louis of France—"

"I have personal failures as well," Stephen said. "The kingdom has suffered much on my account, and those who say I should not have been king—" He smiled as Gislebert moved to protest. "Oh yes, even a king hears the truth. They were right. I should have given Empress Matilda of Anjou the throne. Even now, I should give it to her son, Henry, for there is no one else to claim it."

"Will you surrender it?"

Stephen shook his head. "Once a king, how can a man be less? But God has forced me to see that Henry should rule England and Normandy, and I have paid for my pride and greed with the lives of my wife and son. But I will not surrender while I live, Gislebert, and you must aid my resolve to continue as king in manner and deed."

"My liege, I will do what I can."

Henry invaded the south of England within weeks of Eustace's death. Stephen mounted his war horse and led his knights to meet the invader, and when at last the two rows of knights met face-to-face across an English meadow, the ensigns of their sovereigns fluttering in the breeze, Stephen held out his hand and rode alone to meet Henry. Without bloodshed, the elder king met his young cousin and signed the Treaty of Wallingford, which decreed that Henry would succeed to the throne upon Stephen's death. Satisfied that he had won and that he did not have long to wait for the throne, Henry and his men turned south for France.

Stephen did not return to London but bade his counselors, knights, and Gislebert follow him to Dover, where he took a large house on the top of a hill overlooking the sea. Over the next year, Stephen set about the work of settling his life's affairs even as his kingdom adjusted to truce, order, and rest.

One by one, Stephen summoned his most faithful nobles and knights, and weeks passed before Gislebert was called to the dying king's bedside. The keening wail of a cold October wind rattled the windows of the small chamber where the king lay, but Stephen turned an almost sunny smile upon the troubadour. "For you, friend Gislebert, we have three gifts," the aged king said, struggling to sit upright against a mountain of pillows. "But first we wish to thank you for your friendship. You were the one man who came to us with nothing to gain but love. Did you never long for more land or more power as others did?"

Gislebert shook his head. "I have no taste for money or power, having never known them," he said simply. "But once I saw love, I coveted it so badly that nothing else in life seemed worth pursuing."

Stephen nodded. "Then we hope you find the love you seek. You have spent eight years with us, Gislebert, yet we have not forgotten your request or the mission that brought you to us. We release you from your vow to stay with us until death. You are free to go now with these three gifts."

A fit of coughing seized the king, and Gislebert respectfully paused until the king had regained his composure. "Three gifts, Your Highness?"

"Yes." The king took a deep breath and smoothed the

blanket that covered him. "We have been making inquiries and can now settle your account. First, we give you the knowledge that Jerome de Honfleur and his wife, Nadine, are residents again of St. Denis. For fear of our guards, Jerome did not dare cross into England. He has assumed control of Nadine's property in France. His English holdings have been confiscated as payment for his crimes against this throne. You will find Jerome and his wife, dear friend, in the house where you visited the lady."

Gislebert drew in his breath. Was it possible that his quest should end again at the house of Lady Jehannenton?

"Second, we shall give you an armed escort to exact your vengeance upon this knight. Louis of France has agreed to let you and your company pass through his kingdom, but you must leave before we depart this life. Upon our death, the knights will owe their allegiance to Henry of Normandy, and Louis will not allow Henry's knights to travel freely in his lands."

Gislebert accepted this news in silence, and the king reached under his blanket and pulled forth a length of cloth that he unwrapped. Enfolded in the cloth was a jeweled dagger; engraving shone upon the blade. Stephen lifted the dagger with both hands and offered it to Gislebert, who bowed and received it.

"He who wields this dagger does so with the blessing and forgiveness of the King." Gislebert read the inscription, then looked up at Stephen, his brows lifting in question.

"For your vengeance upon Jerome de Honfleur," Stephen explained. "My men will hold the blackhearted knave for you, and you have but to use this blade for your vengeance, and all will be settled. It has been agreed that no one will question you."

"This is a dangerous weapon," Gislebert said, regarding the dagger uneasily. "In the wrong hands—"

"That is why we entrust it to you," the king answered. "For violence is foreign to your nature, and you will be tem-

perate in its use. When you have finished your purpose, surrender the blade to a priest. All will be accounted for."

Gislebert clasped the blade to his chest and fell to his
knees before the king. "Why do you linger?" Stephen asked,
his voice softening. "Get you gone, Troubadour, for our
strength fails. The offer of armed escort will perish with our
royal life."

"I will not leave you," Gislebert answered, his compassion stirring for the man who lay in the bed before him. "I
will face my future alone and with your blessing, but I will
not leave you."

"Then God grant you grace, for you will need it," the
king answered, gratitude echoing in his words as his hand
fell limply upon Gislebert's shoulder.

THIRTY

Three weeks later Stephen breathed his last, and the royal knights stationed with him at Dover galloped away through the countryside with the news. "Hail King Henry!" The cries rang out from the village. "God save the king!"

Gislebert sat alone with the lifeless body of Stephen and pondered the future. All of England would surely rejoice at Henry's rise to the throne, but Louis of France might squirm in discomfort now that a rival held so many of his former French possessions, including his queen.

The thought of Eleanor as queen made Gislebert's stomach churn. From what he knew of her, he doubted her new marriage would weaken her affection for Jerome de Honfleur, a man she had once perceived as a friend and confidant. Could Gislebert safely exact his vengeance upon a man counted as a friend of the queen?

Gislebert gripped the handle of the dagger hidden in his surcoat and prayed that his courage would not fail him.

St. Denis

Perseverance must finish its work
so that you may be mature and complete,
not lacking anything.

JAMES 1:4

THIRTY-ONE

While England rejoiced at Henry's ascent to the throne, Gislebert mourned Stephen's loss. He remained at Dover long enough to oversee the removal of Stephen's body to London for burial, and on the gray day when the king's corpse was loaded into the wagon, Gislebert stood outside the house with a handful of mourners and devoted servants. The brisk autumn wind slashed and shoved against the small crowd, huddling them together.

"The way people are carrying on about the new king Henry," a rough soldier grumbled as he stood by the wagon that held the king's remains, "a body'd think Stephen never existed. They long to wipe him clean out of their minds."

"They are tired of struggle and ready for peace," Gislebert answered, clutching his fur-lined cloak about him as priests draped the shrouded corpse with the royal standard. "He may not have been a good king, but he was a good friend."

His eyes filled with tears as the wagon departed for London, and he blushed when a serving girl caught sight of them. "The wind," he explained crossly, dashing the water from his eyes.

When Stephen's funeral procession had passed out of sight, Gislebert returned to the house, cleared his small chamber of his few personal belongings, and mounted a horse from the stable. A bag of silver, a reward from the king, hung heavy at his waist, and his surcoat bulged gently at his breast

307

where two items had been carefully secreted: the jeweled dagger intended for Jerome and Nadine's psalter.

Wildflowers by the side of the road bent themselves in the fierce, steady wind that shrilled from the coast, and Gislebert found his melancholy mood lifting at the sight of them. After all, though the heaven was full of gray scud and winter would soon be upon them, still they had the courage to rise and bloom. *Nature never ceases,* Gislebert thought to himself. *Just as I should never cease to strive for my Nadine.*

He had wrapped the dagger and psalter in linen before placing them in his surcoat, and he had paused as he held the psalter in his hand. For eight long years he had greeted his love's portrait every morning, and every night before bed, he had kissed the crimson lips depicted there. Why did the colors now seem faded? Why did he find it difficult to imagine Nadine in any pose but this? and what of her voice? or her mannerisms? If God willed, he was only a few days away from holding a flesh-and-blood Nadine in his arms, and the thought made him tremble.

As he rode, he struggled to evoke memories of his love. Hadn't she tilted her head so and roughly rebuked him? No, that was Adele. Hadn't Nadine's voice been low and gentle? No matter how hard he tried, the voice, form, and gestures of his beloved eluded him. And only the impish memories of Adele remained fresh in his mind. "Why is it so difficult, my Nadine?" he whispered as the horse cantered smoothly southward. "You live in my heart. Why do you not live in my memory? Were our days together so few in number, or were they so precious that my memory has put a guard around them, lest in visiting that precious store, I deplete them?"

Gislebert smiled at the mystery of romance. There were no answers to love, for who could explain why and how one loved? The words of the old ballad rose in his memory, and he threw back his head and sang, his words carried away by the wind.

The troubadour laughed in sheer pleasure as he finished his song. As Adele had once reminded him, he had known thunder, hunger, the poison of treachery, and the devil himself in the guise of Jerome de Honfleur. But love would conquer all. And soon Jerome's treachery would be exposed and vanquished, and Nadine would be his lovely bride. He had waited all his life to find fulfillment; soon he would find it in the arms of his Nadine. The law of love demanded that it be so.

Lord Rainger and Lady Nicola were delighted to welcome Gislebert to their castle at Gisors, and the troubadour apologized for his dusty appearance as he greeted them in the castle's imposing hall. "Nonsense. Come in and be welcomed," Lord Rainger said, streaks of gray running through the hair at his temples. He gestured for Gislebert to take a seat in the casual circle of chairs near the fireplace. "Rest and refresh yourself. We hope you will spend the night under our protection."

"You look well," Lady Nicola offered, smiling gently. "A bit thinner, perhaps, but you have not changed."

"I had hoped I would look wiser," Gislebert replied, taking the seat Lord Rainger offered him. "I am, after all, thirty-six, and I have seen much since we last met."

"Thirty-six and yet unmarried?" Lady Nicola asked coyly, hugging herself in the chill with her slender arms. "How is that possible, friend Gislebert?"

Gislebert accepted the tall tankard of ale a serving girl offered him and smiled at his hostess. "I have been slow to take a bride," he acknowledged, "but I intend to do it within the month."

"Who is the lucky lady?" Rainger asked.

Gislebert nodded. "Still the lovely Nadine."

The smiles of both the lord and lady froze in alarm.

Gislebert frowned. "Is something amiss? Nadine is still alive and well?"

"She is alive—and the wife of Jerome de Honfleur," Rainger answered slowly, his voice like carefully chipped marble. "Are you certain you wish to marry this lady, Gislebert? What of her husband?"

"Her husband deserves to die."

Lady Nicola drew in her breath at Gislebert's abrupt answer, and Rainger scratched his thick beard. "I have heard the man is troublesome and ambitious," he admitted slowly, obviously searching for words, "but must *you* be the man to kill him?"

Gislebert casually waved his hand to disarm his hosts. "Do not fear, my friends; I would not bring danger upon this fragile body without thought," he said, giving them what he hoped was a winning smile. "I have devised a secure plan."

"What plan is this?" Lord Rainger asked, lowering his voice. "Jerome de Honfleur is a man of some importance and power, for his wife brought him wide estates and wealth—"

"Jerome de Honfleur also toyed with the affections of Louis's queen and flaunted the king's authority for the world to see," Gislebert interrupted. "The man is a base coward and has hidden behind a woman's skirts for the last time. I will go to Jerome and ask him to surrender for the trespass he committed against me years ago."

"He will never surrender," Rainger said. "He is a proud man."

Gislebert shrugged. "If he will not, I will plead my case before Louis of France and ask for the aid of his knights to apprehend Jerome. When the king hears my case and sees the implement of justice I carry from the hand of King Stephen, I do not doubt that he will aid my cause."

Lady Nicola's lovely face creased into a frown. Lord Rainger stroked his beard and sighed in contemplation. "You have reasoned well, Gislebert, but for one thing— Louis is a pious man, given to contemplation and tending toward forgiveness. What if his monks advise him not to give you aid?"

Gislebert smiled. "You forget, Lord Rainger, that for years I served Abbot Suger, counselor and confidant to the king. If ever a man despised Jerome more than I, Suger did. If I advise the king that Suger would agree with my plan of action . . ."

Rainger chuckled in pleasure. "I delight to know that men of God are often men of action," he said, motioning for a servant to fill his tankard. "Drink up, my friend, and take your rest for the day. Surely tomorrow will bring the most daring venture of your life."

"Still, I hesitate to think of you killing him," Lady Nicola spoke up, her pretty blue eyes troubled. "Murder will bring a stain upon your soul, Troubadour!"

"It will be done in the name of justice," Gislebert answered. He smiled and held up a hand. "I have learned that justice acts in her own way. Years ago, when my companion, Jonas, and I visited the Tower of London, a man attacked Jonas. The boy, a mere stripling, knocked the man into the Thames where he drowned. Was justice not done?"

Lord Rainger shrugged. "If the man intended grievous harm, I suppose it was."

Gislebert nodded in satisfaction. "Years later I learned that the man Jean de Honfleur was none other than the brother to this villain Jerome. If justice works her cruel irony to punish one brother for his misdeeds, shall she not do it for the other, as well?"

Despite the passion that burned in Gislebert's heart, Lady Nicola begged Gislebert to remain at Gisors through the Christmas holiday and much of January. Gislebert did not set out again for St. Denis until the worst of winter had blown over the countryside.

The road that led from the bank of the Seine to St. Denis had grown wider since the last time Gislebert had traveled it, and the small forest monastery and its related nunnery outside the city walls had grown as well. Gislebert did not pause at either of these two landmarks but kept his horse at a steady canter until he reached the imposing gates of St. Denis. An inscription on a pillar of the city gate

proclaimed, "St. Denis Cathedral lies within these consecrated walls and was dedicated to the patron saint of France
by Suger, in the year of our Lord 1144."

Gislebert chuckled as he read the inscription. The abbot
had been dead for three years, but still his influence surrounded the city.

Much of St. Denis had not changed. The outer rings of
the city were still littered with boxy little houses of mud and
timber, all revolving like poor cousins around the magnifi-
cence of the glorious abbey in the center of town. Single lines
of pious monks still crisscrossed the streets as they wandered
from their prayers to their tasks, and the courtyard of the
abbey still swarmed with masons and construction workers.

"Pardon," Gislebert called in French to a mud-smeared
worker as he dismounted, "what does the new abbot build?"

"More statues, to enlarge upon the glory of the other,"
the man replied.

Gislebert nodded, understanding more than the man
intended. The man certainly meant that new statues
enhanced the collection Suger had begun. But Gislebert had
a feeling that the new abbot, whoever he was, struggled to
compete with Suger's glory, which shone from every corner
of the cathedral.

He tied his horse to a hitching post and stepped through
the familiar doors of Suger's cathedral. He had entered a thousand times before, yet again he was struck by the unusual
amount of light and liveliness in the building. The cathedral's
brilliance, space, and embellished ornamentation stood in
stark contrast to the somber edifices of the English. Color
abounded in every direction; more than a hundred statues
were painted in violent, sometimes clashing, colors. Gislebert
half expected them to rise from their places and commence
whatever activity the sculptor's hand had forced them to con-
template for the ages.

The warm scent of candles brought back memories of
Suger, and Gislebert stopped before a colorful wall. The
inscription there read: "In honor of the Church which

nurtured and exalted him, Suger worked, rendering back to you your due, Saint Denis, martyr. He prays that your prayers will obtain for him a place in Paradise."

"I will pray, Abbot, but not for you today," Gislebert murmured. "I pray instead for my success with Jerome, for the king's cooperation, and for my Nadine."

He turned from the wall and made his way toward an altar.

THIRTY-TWO

Jerome turned the letter over and saw the familiar seal of Lady Nicola of Gisors. His dark face brightened as he thought of the delectable Lady Nicola. How enchanting she had been, with her blue eyes and slender form! An aura of untouchable dignity had surrounded her when they had first met, yet how easily that dignity had melted under his glance! His hasty flight from London became altogether pleasant with her—and other ladies'—attention. How gratifying to think that she still thought enough of him to write. He tore open the seal:

> *To Jerome de Honfleur, with warm regards from Lady Nicola of Gisors. Greetings:*
>
> *You should know, my dear Jerome, that a troubadour called Gislebert, of your past acquaintance, makes his way even now to your house with the intentions of revenge and murder. I have detained him for as long as I could so that you might prepare yourself for his arrival. This same troubadour, with his former companion, Jonas, conspired in the death of your brother, Jean, while in London. . . .*

Jerome frowned when he thought of the scrawny troubadour. Even if Lady Nicola's words of warning were true, there was no way that little wet bird of a man could do anything to harm Jerome de Honfleur. It might be amusing to watch the steadfast troubadour try, though. Of the many men who had risen to trouble him, Gislebert alone refused to stay defeated. He and his little friend had escaped in London. Gislebert had unfairly bested him in the contest for Nadine. Still, he, Jerome, had won, plucking the eager peach from the tree while the troubadour stayed home and sang to the moon. Nadine had given him lands, a name of ever-growing importance, three sons, and two daughters.

He had at last begun to feel satisfied, even though other, brighter ambitions stood before him. Louis's influence in the kingdom of France weakened even as Henry gained power in Aquitaine, England, and Normandy. And Eleanor's timely tributes to Jerome's coffers insured that he would soon have money enough to raise an army. Ever preferring peace over strife, Louis might be persuaded to relinquish the throne. If not, Jerome shrugged, the man could always be killed. Then he, Jerome de Honfleur, mighty and renown knight, would step forward into the vacuum of power. If only Jean could see him now!

Jerome's smile suddenly flickered and went out. There remained one other matter in Lady Nicola's letter: Had the troubadour and his companion really caused Jean's death? Jerome did not see how it could be, but Lady Nicola's testimony, plus the fact that they were at the tower when Jean disappeared, would surely be enough to convict them at a trial. This time Gislebert would not reappear to trouble Jerome again.

Some part of Abbot Robert's soul always chafed against the holy rule of obedience when duty required him to walk the gilded floors of Suger's cathedral, but today he conquered his rebellious spirit and accomplished his task without complaint. Though he could not see the ornate decoration of the magnificent cathedral, still he preferred to serve in the unadorned chapel of his small Cistercian abbey, where alms bought food for starving men and women instead of gold for the altar. Still, his order cooperated with the others, and the maintenance and construction of the massive cathedral required the services of nearly every monk in the province.

On this day, like many others before, Abbot Robert folded his hands inside the long sleeves of his robe and mentally measured his steps through the north choir aisle. Thirty-one steps, and he would turn right to walk through the ambulatory behind the high altar. There, twenty-three steps would take him to the south choir aisle, and thirty-one steps again would take him to the transept, where the fourth floor board squeaked.

Twenty-two, twenty-three. Behind the choir aisle, two monks whispered disobediently at the carrels, where they were supposed to be studying the monastic rule. Abbot Robert made a mental note of their voices. Although they were not of his house, he would see that they were reprimanded.

Twenty-four, twenty-five. His arthritic fingers ached, and Abbot Robert concentrated on extending them as much as he could within the privacy of his sleeves. Winter lingered in the air around him. He could feel its cruel cold in his bones even if he had not heard the howling wind outside. *You are getting old,* he thought, marveling that the simple act of opening his fingers could bring such pain.

Twenty-six, twenty-seven. The murmur of a voice at prayer caught his attention, and Abbot Robert immediately adjusted the angle of his approach so he would not disturb the man who petitioned God so earnestly.

Twenty-eight, twenty-nine, thirty, thirty-one. Turn. Something in the man's voice caught the abbot's ear, and he listened more closely. What accent was that? English, upper-class, nobility perhaps, but not quite—

The abbot stiffened in recognition. Adele's troubadour! He knelt even now outside the Lady Chapel.

One, two, three, four, five, six, seven. Abbot Robert stopped behind the high altar, out of sight, and waited for the troubadour to finish his prayer.

Gislebert recited every prayer and petition he had ever learned as a child, then gazed earnestly upon the face of the statue of Mary. Though he wanted to regard the stone maiden as the representation of the Blessed Virgin, still something in the statue caught his imagination and led his thoughts away from prayer. The eyes were amazingly full and well rounded, the smile gentle in its appearance and approach. Where had he seen features like those?

He mumbled other prayers for grace and mercy, then his eyes fell down to the statue's outstretched hand. Adele had always drawn hands that way, with the hand cupped as if asking for water, the thumb cocked gently inward. He groaned as the realization hit him. This statue had to be Adele's work! But when had she completed it?

Someone coughed behind him. Gislebert glanced back and saw the tall monk standing there.

"Holy Father," Gislebert said, his attention riveted by the statue, "whose handiwork is this? It has the look of statues done from sketches of Ade—of the boy called Jonas, but he died years ago."

"A gifted postulant at the nunnery wrought this statue," the monk replied, the rich timbre of his voice echoing in the vastness of the cathedral. "A postulant who will not take her vows because she waits for an unrequited love to claim her hand. Like you, Troubadour, she has waited patiently for love to find her."

How did this monk know him as *troubadour*? Gislebert looked more carefully at the monk who spoke and immediately recognized the blind eyes. "Abbot Robert," Gislebert said, apology in his voice, "I did not expect to see you here at the cathedral. Nor," he added, standing to his feet, "did I expect anyone to know me. I have been gone for—"

"Over eight years," the abbot finished for him. "You were missed, scribe Gislebert. Abbot Suger wished for you often as he struggled to put his affairs in order. What brings you now to the cathedral of St. Denis?"

"I am preparing my soul for the task before me," Gislebert answered simply. "Jerome de Honfleur must be called to account for his actions. Nadine is my lawful and rightful wife, so I plan to take her from the villain who stole her from me."

Abbot Robert held up a warning finger. "With what army do you plan to storm the house of Jerome?" he asked. "The man is not without allies of his own."

"With the cause of justice and, if need be, the king's army," Gislebert answered, his hand going protectively to the place in his surcoat where the dagger lay hidden. "And if Jerome will not surrender with honor, justice will be meted out with the dagger in my possession. King Stephen of England issued it to me, and the blade grants royal clemency for the one who uses it in a just cause."

"So you must murder in order to love?" the abbot asked, one brow rising in a question. "This is a strange love you bear, my friend. Before you consider this further, there is something I would show you."

With his unerring sense of direction, the monk led Gislebert through the maze of shrines and chapels in the massive cathedral. As they walked, Gislebert noticed with wry amusement that the blind monk knew his way more surely around the jeweled cathedral than Suger's own scribe did. "You walk as surely as if you had seen this beautiful place," Gislebert remarked as the monk shuffled along the narrow aisles.

"In my imagination it is more beautiful than this," Abbot Robert replied, opening his hand to indicate the priceless treasures that surrounded them. "What use have I for embossed altars, jeweled chalices, golden lavers, and vases of precious stone? Do you see Suger's jeweled cross, my son?"

Gislebert turned back to admire the tall cross, which sparkled in reflected light from Suger's stained-glass windows. "Aye, Abbot, I see it."

"In my mind it gleams not with jewels but with the priceless blood of my Savior," the abbot whispered, his chin quivering with suppressed emotion. "You see, Suger bought those jewels for much less than they were worth. He did not sacrifice to receive them. But my Lord Christ sacrificed his spotless life for my worthless soul, far too dear a price. That is what I see when I turn my head toward that cross, and I see something similar when in my imagination I behold this shrine of St. Denis."

Gislebert looked up. They had come to a new shrine, an ornate edifice that housed a small, oval relic that gleamed upon a black velvet pillow. Looking into the glass-enclosed cubicle, Gislebert gasped in astonishment when he recognized the crystal that Adele had placed in his hand for Nadine.

"The crystal!" Gislebert exclaimed. "Suger said he would give it a place of honor."

"It is now called the Saint Denis crystal, and people are greatly moved by its beauty," the abbot answered, but Gislebert barely heard, so distracted was he by the delicate engraving of the ovoid rock. The images of the crucified Christ and the women at his feet were like tiny figures of flesh and fabric pressed into glass.

"I call it the Jonas Crystal," the abbot whispered. "And I know it is beautiful."

"It is beautiful," Gislebert agreed, choosing his words carefully. Surely the warm and trusting tone in the priest's voice proved he did not know of Adele's shameful deception. "Did you give it to Jonas? He never told me."

"Its origin is not important," the abbot answered. "What matters is its effect upon people. I myself am humbled before this shrine, Troubadour, because in my mind I do not see a beautiful stone but a gleaming sacrifice of one life for another. A sacrifice given in the name of friendship . . . and love."

Gislebert stepped back and regarded the monk skeptically. The thought that Adele had given her life for the stone was intriguing, even unsettling. But how could that be? Was the old man losing his mind? Or was this one of the dastardly deals-with-the-devil stories that were often told by the peasants?

"I do not understand," Gislebert answered, trying not to let doubt edge into his voice.

"Do you think a poor child could procure such a relic without sacrifice?" the abbot asked, spreading his hands.

"Well, no," Gislebert answered, flustered. "But Jonas was—" he caught himself. "Uh, clever. You knew him as a boy, but . . ." Gislebert fumbled for words, then fell into silence. After a moment, he said quietly, "Jonas was not what I thought he was."

The monk only pressed his lips together for a moment, then spoke. "Did Jonas love you, Troubadour?"

Despite his resolve, the memory of Adele's desperate kiss came rushing back. Gislebert paused, glad the monk could not see the shame upon his face. "As friends love each other, yes, Jonas loved me."

"Jonas often told me that you would not leave him when he was ill," Abbot Robert went on. "So, as you are a selfless, honorable man, how can you seek the love of the wife of Jerome de Honfleur?"

"I am a man!" Gislebert cried, stamping his foot in frustration. "Men fight for what they are promised! Men strive to gain the women they love!"

"Does your love include killing the father of five children?" Abbot Robert countered softly. "Would your righteous anger kill the babes as well, Gislebert, if they stood between you and the attainment of your love?"

"Children?" It had never occurred to Gislebert that Nadine might have children. But she had wed Jerome; it was logical that they had produced *children*. The infants that suckled at her breast should have been Gislebert's. But no matter who had fathered them, surely they were as sweet and innocent as the babes at Margate Castle, the children who had inspired him to search for his own love, his own family.

"No," he whispered, confused. "I would never kill children."

"You would cast them off, then? If you have a legal right to kill Jerome, surely you have the right to cast his children from their mother—"

"No, I couldn't—"

"So you would take their mother and father and leave them as paupers, slaves, perhaps—"

"No, I can't!"

A stab of emotion cut through him, and in a breathless instant of release, Gislebert knew he could not kill Jerome de Honfleur. He was not a knight. Killing had no place in his nature. He could not take a father from Nadine's children. He could not cast them from the home where they lived. Surely God had guided him to this place to learn this lesson.

The old monk read his silence correctly. "Love does not murder or destroy, my son," he whispered in the stillness of the cathedral. "Love gives. Jonas acted in love when he surrendered his life for your happiness. His noble act gives him life, even today. You will act in love when you put aside this heinous act you have proposed. If you love," the old man nodded gravely, "you cannot act in hate."

"I would love," Gislebert cried, falling to his knees on the floor. "I am too weak to do otherwise." He fumbled under his cloak and pulled the dagger from his surcoat. "Take this, then, Father," he said, unraveling the length of cloth from the golden knife. He caught the monk's hand and placed it upon the dagger's shaft. "This blade is intended solely to rest in the heart of Jerome de Honfleur. If it shall not rest there, Abbot, may I trust you to melt it down to some better purpose?"

"Aye," the monk replied, taking the dagger from Gislebert. "Your heart has begun to see clearly, my son. But love is not weakness, it is strength."

"Is it?" Gislebert asked, looking up into the milky eyes of the monk. A strange mix of elation and regret filled his soul. "I love, so I spare the husband, but if I spare the husband, I have no bride. You tell me I am strong, but I am too weak to defend my own rights."

"You are a troubadour, a master of the laws of love, and yet the truth eludes you," the monk said, placing his free hand upon Gislebert's head. "Love is a choice, a decision the heart makes, but the heart sees only what it wishes. Choose to love again, my son, and walk where love leads you, for God is love. He who walks in love, walks with God."

"You told me once that God had plans to prosper my life," Gislebert said, recalling the old memory.

"'Plans to give you hope and a blessed future,'" the monk finished. "Words from the prophet Jeremiah. But there is more, Troubadour: 'You will seek God and find him when you seek him with all your heart.'"

Gislebert stared ahead at the ground, feeling that he knelt on the edge of a vast precipice. Without his quest for Nadine, what did life offer? How could he walk in love if not with Nadine?

"Walk in love," he repeated dumbly.

"Aye," Abbot Robert replied. "Do what love would do, see what love would see, and God will lead you to your blessed future."

Gislebert reclaimed his horse and rode through the city in a daze, his thoughts wandering first one way, then another. Had he truly been so caught up in false bravado? How had he imagined that he *could* kill Jerome? Even if the king's knights pinned the scoundrel to the ground in front of him, could Gislebert pick up the dagger and plunge it into the heart of his dire enemy?

In the searing light of the monk's words, Gislebert knew he could not. If he had gone to Louis and gained the king's help, even then he could not have killed Jerome. The attempt would have ended in utter embarrassment.

What, then, was he to do? "Walk in love," the monk had said. But how was that accomplished? Unbidden, an image surfaced in his mind: Adele, pale and trembling, offering the crystal to him. Her eyes, brimming with tears, as she declared her love.

But Adele was gone. Nadine was alive and waiting for him.

Let Nadine know of your love, his old nature suggested. *Visit Jerome and Nadine. Offer forgiveness to Jerome and understanding to Nadine. She must know that you spared her children. Nadine is surely weary of life with a scoundrel, and after hearing from you, she will leave Jerome de Honfleur and return your love at last.*

Gislebert smiled and turned his horse toward the former house of Lady Jehannenton.

The house had not changed much over the years. The tall wall around the house stood grayer with age, and a hedge around the garden had been replaced with a flowering bush now in gentle bloom. The gate Gislebert peered over was new, but it swung on rusty hinges that sorely needed repair. Two extra rooms had been added to the sides of the house— probably for the children, Gislebert guessed.

The cold wind of February blew past him, tingling the bare skin on his cheek. The wind moaned softly. There was no other sound save the wind and the incessant barking of a dog from the house across the road.

He gave the bellpull a single discreet pull and held his breath, studying the front of the house intently. A sound from behind startled him. Suddenly he stood surrounded by knights who rushed out from the house across the road. "What is your name and your business?" the first of them growled, clenching Gislebert's arm tightly.

"I am Gislebert, a troubadour, and I have business with the lord and lady of the house," Gislebert said, struggling to maintain his dignity.

"What business?"

"If you must know . . . ," Gislebert paused, hoping the knight would mend his manners, but the man's eyes burned with steely determination. "If you must know, I have come to offer forgiveness for a wrong committed years ago by Jerome de Honfleur. My intentions are entirely honorable."

The knight who held Gislebert's arm nodded to his fellow, who rang the bell again. In a moment, Jerome appeared, as handsome and untamed as ever. "Well, my old friend Gislebert," he called as he strode to the gate, his dark eyes snapping maliciously. "I heard you planned to pay me a visit. I also heard you planned to cut out my tongue."

"No," Gislebert protested, offering a weak smile. "Though that was my intention, I have come today to offer forgiveness, Jerome. I would not hurt your lady or your children by harming you."

"My lady?" Jerome curled his upper lip. "Ah, yes, my beautiful Nadine. I have sent her away, Troubadour, so we could meet alone. You have come here to kill me, so you said yourself, and these men are my witnesses."

"Aye!" the knights muttered their agreement.

"I also know that you and that little guttersnipe killed my brother in London. For this cause alone I should kill you, but for such a crime you should suffer and not enjoy a merciful death."

"*What?*" Gislebert paled. "That was an accident! The man attacked my friend and was defeated—"

"Save your breath, Troubadour. On this day you will stand before the king's counselor, and this night you shall spend in prison."

The four knights gagged Gislebert and bound his arms, then placed him in a waiting wagon. In the full splendor of a lordly knight, Jerome mounted his horse and led his men forward. "To Paris," Jerome announced, and a whip cracked over the team of horses that pulled the wagon.

They rode swiftly, and finally they approached a square, massive building of stone on the south bank of the Seine. A long bridge stood between the road and the fortress. "Petit Point," Jerome remarked, turning to the well-trussed troubadour. "Mark this place well, friend; it will doubtless become your eternal home."

A drawbridge gave the party access to the bridge, and the horses' hooves clunked noisily across the wooden structure, nearly obliterating the boisterous cries of the knights. Once they had reached the building, the knights hauled Gislebert out of the wagon.

In due time he stood before a judge in a bright blue robe.

"This man," Jerome announced, pointing with indignation at Gislebert, "came to my house this afternoon to kill me. Fortunately, I had been warned of his presence and his intention, and my loyal knights apprehended the murderer. I have also learned that he and his companion killed my brother, Jean de Honfleur, while in London."

"How came you by this information?" the judge asked, casting a suspicious eye upon Gislebert.

"The noble Lady Nicola of Gisors sent word to warn me," Jerome answered. "King Stephen had even promised this man a pardon for my murder."

"We do not recognize English sovereignty, especially from a dead king," the judge replied. "If murder was his intent, he shall be tried when the time is convenient. You— what is your name?"

The judge gestured toward a knight, who removed the filthy gag from Gislebert's mouth. Gislebert licked his lips and found his voice. "Gislebert of Margate, my lord. And I did not come with intent to murder, nor did I kill Jean de Honfleur. I came to St. Denis today to forgive Jerome de Honfleur, and a monk at the abbey can prove that I am innocent."

"Gislebert of Margate, you shall be bound over to the king's bailiff and installed in this place until we see fit to try your case," the judge said, writing upon a paper.

"But, I can prove—"

"You shall have your chance at trial," the judge answered, his eyes peering up at Gislebert in a warning glance. "Now go, and do not try my patience."

As he was led out, Gislebert heard the judge tell his gaoler: "Five days in La Fosse, then remove him to Fin d'Aise."

LE PETIT CHÂTELET

Love never fails.
1 CORINTHIANS 13:8

THIRTY-THREE

Why, Adele, won't you take your vows? Have we not proved ourselves in the eight years you have been with us?"

Madame Marie's delicate face shone with care and compassion, and Adele found it difficult to look directly at the abbess when she gave her answer. "I cannot, madame. Though the convent has given everything to me—"

"Has God not demonstrated his faithfulness?"

Adele nodded. "He has."

"Has he not healed the scars of your past?"

Adele reflected briefly. The sharp memories of her brutalized childhood were no longer in focus, for time and her friendship with the troubadour had taught her that not all men were cruel. The hardness of her heart had melted through years of prayer and almost daily confession of her shortcomings.

"My past," she said slowly, not looking directly at the abbess, "was terribly painful, as you know. But it lies behind me now, Madame Marie, and I look to the future with joy and hope."

"Then why not give that future to God?"

"I have given my future to God . . . but not to the convent." She bit her lip, speaking too hastily, and the warm glow in the abbess's eyes dimmed.

"I see you still love that troubadour," Madame Marie answered, stiffly pulling her hands into her sleeves. The abbess looked away, her veil cutting off Adele's view of her face. "Why, daughter, will you not give that love to God?"

"I have told you everything that is in my heart," Adele whispered, wringing her hands as she spoke to the abbess's shadowed profile on the wall. "You know I have trusted my life to God's hands and my heart to his wisdom. But I cannot promise to serve God in this place forever, for I truly believe that God will call me out yet again."

"You say God spoke to you. Yet he has never spoken to me."

"Not in audible words, Abbess, but in a clear, unrefutable sign. I know that I shall leave here, and I know I shall again meet Gislebert."

The abbess stiffened, as she always did at the mention of Gislebert's name, and Adele bowed her head, certain the abbess would never understand or forgive a woman who preferred the company of a man to that of God. But the abbess's next words were a surprise: "Would you be willing to test this sign of yours? Will you give your troubadour one year to return, and if he does not, will you acknowledge that your sign may have been coincidence or the wishful thinking of a yearning heart?"

An old and familiar defiance stirred in Adele's soul, and she raised her head to accept the challenge in the abbess's words. "One year?" she asked, mentally racing through the coming months. "Why not? I shall lay my petition before God, and if Gislebert has not come by the feast of St. John the Baptist of next year—"

"That feast is in the summer," the abbess answered, raising her hand in gentle reproof. "We will wait only until March of next year. If your troubadour has not come by then, I will urge you to confirm that God's will is that you take your vows and wed yourself to Christ."

"I agree," Adele answered, a lump rising in her throat despite her confidence in the future. She bowed before the abbess, then left the small chamber and went straight to the chapel. *Oh, God,* she prayed, prostrating herself before the altar, *did you really speak to me on that afternoon long ago?*

Did I really see that young troubadour? Or was the entire episode a dream invented by my lonely heart?

Stark, somber stone walls rose on Gislebert's right and left as guards escorted him down the narrow stairway that led from the judge's chambers to the cells of the prison known as Le Petit Châtelet. After the judge had pronounced sentence, Gislebert had been stripped of his cloak, purse, and his precious psalter, the only possessions he carried. Now he walked between two stocky gaolers whose huge hands and broad backs gave evidence of their peasant ancestry. As they descended into the windowless rooms and corridors below, Gislebert found himself gasping, for the air became increasingly foul.

"La Fosse for five days," the stoutest of the gaolers said, using the key at his belt to open the door at the lowest point in the stairway. "Pray we don't forget you, monsieur. No one has endured La Fosse for more than fifteen days."

The man swung the door open, and the guard behind Gislebert pushed the troubadour through the black space that yawned before him. He flew through the darkness in panic, flailing his arms and legs, and fell into putrid-smelling icy water that rushed over his head and choked him. His chest hit what felt like solid earth, and for a moment the force of the impact stunned him. Then every nerve in his body shuddered as he struggled to lift his head above water.

What was this dark place?

Gislebert forced himself to think as his lungs burned for breath. If a man could live here for fifteen days, this was not a bottomless pit. From far away he heard the muffled laughter of the gaolers, and he struggled blindly toward it. But his heavy, fur-lined surcoat weighted him down.

He thrust his feet out, hoping to find a solid surface, and brushed against something soft—a rat? He opened his mouth in a last desperate scream and water rushed in just as someone grabbed the back of his tunic and lifted him, mercifully, above the surface.

331

Gislebert released his pent-up terror and apprehension in one horrible yell as the door through which he had been thrown slammed shut with a terrible finality. The hand that held him loosened its grip, and his feet felt solid ground beneath him as he found his balance.

"There, there; La Fosse isn't worth all that," a man's soft and eminently reasonable voice called to him in French from the darkness. "The water is only thigh high, and a man should not drown on his first day."

Shuddering, Gislebert took deep breaths and tried to calm himself. But the air, rotten with the smell of decay, filth, and sewage, only burned his lungs and made him cough. The gentle lap of waves against stone echoed behind him; a high-pitched dribbling of water sounded ahead of him. "Who are you?" he asked, his breath rattling in his throat as he resisted the urge to gag from the stench. "I can't see you; I don't understand what this place is."

"Yes," his companion answered, switching to English after hearing Gislebert's accent. "And you were scared to death, weren't you? I'd bet my life you can't even swim."

"No," Gislebert shook his head and shivered. "I can't."

"Wouldn't do you any good in La Fosse anyhow," the voice went on. "A man drowns here because he's too tired to stand up, not because he can't swim."

"Drowns?" Gislebert's tension rose higher. "Why should anyone drown here?"

"Look around you, monsieur. There is no place to sit, no place to rest. Nothing to do but stand in water where the rats swim and the bodies of your departed cell mates float—after they bloat and rise to the surface, that is. Nothing to drink save the putrid water that holds you, nothing to eat unless you scoop the leavings from the water after the guards toss your dinner in—if they remember to come down here at all. This is La Fosse, sir. Welcome home."

Gislebert cast a hesitant look around as his eyes adjusted to his surroundings. One thin stream of light poured through a narrow drainage opening far above his head, and by the light from that small aperture, Gislebert could see that he stood in a large rectangular chamber, with walls that extended straight up at least three times his height. The walls, of cut stone, bore a skin of gray-green ooze.

There were three openings in the chamber: the high doorway through which Gislebert had fallen, now securely blocked by a heavy door with no interior handles, the barred opening through which water trickled in a vaguely musical stream, and a dark half-circle at the far end of the room, through which the water lazily spread itself into a tunnel beyond.

"Is that a way out?" Gislebert asked, waving at the far wall.

"Are you always so stupid?" the man gently rebuked. "The sewer gate is barred, and the iron grating around the passage bears the marks of frantic men who sought even to gnaw their way out. But no man escapes La Fosse, only the water . . . and the rats."

Waves of darkness passed over Gislebert, and he feared he would faint until the quiet splash of something behind him propelled him toward the man's voice. "Who are you, sir?" Gislebert called, gingerly making his way through the black water. He stepped on something solid that cracked beneath his weight; he shuddered and moved on.

He reached the wall and leaned against it, disciplining his mind not to rebel at the thought of the slime upon his tunic. He could see his companion now, a bearded man who stood stoically against the wall with his arms folded against his chest. Clad in wet rags that clung like a second skin to his skeletal body, the man had dark, wet hair that ran down his forehead and spilled over his shoulders like streams of black ink.

"I am called Dubois; I was a candlemaker," the man replied simply, "and I am here because I offended one Hugues de Bourgueil, a hunchback with a most beautiful wife. I made the mistake of announcing my appreciation for the young woman's beauty in public. The husband heard, I was arrested, and—" The man shrugged. "You see the result of my admiration for the lady."

"Had you no trial?" Gislebert asked, trying to find support against the slippery wall of the chamber.

"Trial?" Dubois threw back his massive head and laughed. "My friend, only nobles have trials, and only when their fellow nobles are absolutely hard-pressed. When I arrived in La Fosse five days ago, Salomon de Caus stood in these waters—a clever young man who had invented a means of forcing up water by a stream fountain. It was his misfortune to share his invention with an archbishop who thought his ingenious ideas evidence of possession by the devil. Here I found Salomon de Caus, and here he remains still, under these dark waters with those who have gone before us."

Gislebert's body went rigid, and he clenched his fists, afraid to move. Dead bodies were unclean, unholy, . . . and here he stood, surrounded by watery death and the stench of putrefaction. Vivid images filled his brain—rotten corpses under the water, bloated carcasses serving as a floating conveyance for rats, who would nibble the remains down to pieces small enough to pass through the barred sewer gate at the end of the room.

He closed his eyes and leaned his shoulder against the comforting solidity of the stone wall. "It is too much to bear," he whispered, and when he looked up again at his companion, the man's dark eyes seemed to be laughing at him.

"How can you be so—spirited?" Gislebert asked, feeling terror creep along his bones even as the water chilled him. "How can you just stand there. . . ."

The man's dark eyes turned suddenly serious. "My friend, you reside now in Le Petit Châtelet, and this is the worst of its chambers. No one will come through that door again until tomorrow, when we may get a bowl of scraps from the gaolers' tables. Few men ever walk out of here, and we are literally in the pit. There is no one to hear our screams, and no one to care." He shrugged. "I am spirited because I look forward to the next life and do not wish to linger in this one."

Dubois turned his back on the troubadour and walked a few paces away. Gislebert bit his lip, a dark suspicion rising within him. "I, sir, was sentenced to five days in La Fosse," he said, eyeing the man's thin back. "And you?"

"I am not as fortunate as you," Dubois answered quietly. "Five days I have been here, and perhaps I shall live to bid you adieu on your fifth day. But I am not to leave this place. It houses my body and soul now. In a month it will house only my bones."

Gislebert closed his eyes as compassion for the unfortunate candlemaker swept over him. *God, in your mercy, have tender pity on this man's soul . . . and remove me from this place.*

If he had to endure five days of this watery hell, he would steel himself to do it, and when he again saw the light of day, he would *demand* his trial. He would scream, he would fight, he would insult the king himself—whatever it took to make the gaolers listen to him and allow him a fair trial. Abbot Robert would be called, Gislebert's name would be cleared, and he would walk out of Le Petit Châtelet as a survivor.

"Like you, Adele," he whispered, suddenly realizing that his best hope lay in imitating the resilient spirit of the girl whose manners he had always deplored.

He stood firmly in place when daylight faded from the sewer opening high in the wall. He was still standing when the opening pinked with early dawn. His legs were numb from the chilly water that dripped from the sewer, and his body cried out with thirst, but Gislebert did not dare drink water populated by rats and dead men. "You must walk around to keep warm," Dubois told him frequently during the night. The motion of Dubois's walking stirred the waters in a circular current that Gislebert found disturbing, for it moved bits of floating refuse into a huge pile in the center of the room.

Yet Dubois continued his walking, moving around the unmovable Gislebert. "If the body of Salomon de Caus should nudge you, hold it fast, for it may save our lives," Dubois remarked more than once. Gislebert shuddered at the vague implication in Dubois's words and resolved that he would not move nor touch anything that had once lived.

As the light brightened on the second day, Gislebert shifted to adjust his position and found that his legs were numb. Off balance, he fell headlong into the waters, drenching his clothes and filling his mouth with offensive water. As Dubois laughed, he rose, shaking like a wet dog, sputtering in anger and humiliation. After that, he paced with Dubois around the walls of the room and tried not to think about the horrible pile of bones and refuse the current was depositing in the center of the chamber.

As they paced, Dubois's casual conversation amazed Gislebert. It was almost possible to believe they were two friends out walking on a summer's day. "How can you be so calm in this place?" Gislebert asked once, his own tension at a flash point.

Dubois stopped pacing and scratched his vermin-infested beard. "I have been at Le Petit Châtelet for over two years by my reckoning," he said, eyeing Gislebert steadily. "This is my way out, my friend. In a few days or hours, my waiting will come to an end. Then I will leave you to the troubles of the kingdom."

Dubois continued his pacing, and Gislebert quickened his pace to keep up. "I care not for the troubles of the kingdom," he answered. "My own troubles are burden enough."

"If you plan on rejoining the world, you should consider the politics of this day," Dubois answered, clasping his hands behind his back as he walked. "I hear many things here. The voices of nobles come down through the drain pipes in the dead of evening when all else is still. I have heard, for instance, that Jerome de Honfleur is setting up his own court to rival that of King Louis. An English knight held for six days in Fin d'Aise confessed under torture that Jerome is financed by Eleanor of Aquitaine."

Gislebert laughed grimly. "Why would Henry's queen give money to Jerome? He was once her lover, no doubt, but surely things are changed now that she is married to Henry of England."

Dubois shrugged. "I only know that Henry himself is said to encourage her support of Jerome. If Louis is engaged with struggles in his own kingdom—"

Gislebert finished the man's prediction: "Then Henry is not only lord of England, Normandy, Brittany, and Aquitaine, but soon all of France." Gislebert stopped pacing and struck his forehead with his hand. "If your words are true—"

"Why wouldn't they be?" Dubois growled, still moving ahead. "I am a candlemaker, not a liar."

"Did the gaolers tell King Louis?" Gislebert asked, hope rising in his soul. "If the king arrests Jerome—"

"The gaolers will say nothing," Dubois answered. "For they know the king will not be bothered with rumors; he is too busy erecting cathedrals and establishing abbeys. The gaolers here, even Clement, the king's counselor, never reveal information unless it is to fill their own purses. My guess is that they will blackmail Jerome himself with the information they obtained, and that does not bode well for you, my friend."

Gislebert leaned against the wall and pondered this new information. If the gaolers were blackmailing Jerome for this and whatever other schemes they had unearthed, their unholy alliance would guarantee that Gislebert would never be brought to trial.

"Jerome de Honfleur is my dearest enemy," Gislebert called out to Dubois, who continued his ceaseless pacing. "Unless he falls, I am doomed."

"Accept your fate then," Dubois answered, "as I have. My life is forfeit for a pretty woman and—" He tripped on something in the water and somersaulted forward through the water, springing up a few feet ahead of the place where he had fallen. "Watch out, friend, for here lies the remains of Salomon de Caus," he cried, pointing down into the murky pool. "Help me grab the body; we shall need it."

Gislebert winced but moved slowly toward the spot while Dubois thrust his hands into the water to retrieve the swollen remains of the genius Salomon de Caus.

THIRTY-FOUR

By the evening of the second day, Gislebert's legs demanded rest, and he sank to the bottom of the pool and struggled to hold his head above water. He was tall enough that if he reclined his head, his nostrils cleared the water. But if his mouth opened in sleep, water invariably rushed in and he awakened, sputtering and spitting. By the end of his second night, he had done everything he had resolved never to do—he relieved himself in the water in one corner, drank from it in another, and sat with Dubois on the rotting body of Salomon de Caus, for it afforded them an extra five inches of breathing space and an hour of sleep. They dared not sleep longer, for the cold water rendered them stupefied and senseless if they remained submerged for too long.

Dubois's voice grew steadily weaker during Gislebert's third day, and finally the candlemaker stopped his pacing and propped himself against the wall. "I came here, as I said, because I admired a pretty woman." He closed his eyes as he leaned against the wall. "For this sin I am willing and ready to die. But I would share my knowledge with you before I depart this life. I have spent time in nearly every room of Le Petit Châtelet, Gislebert, and hope that my experience will aid you. There are many rooms in this house, some worse than others, but in all there are certain dangers. In wet weather, or in winter's thaw, water will stream from all parts of your cell, and you are likely to be crippled with rheumatism. Keep moving, or you will be like I was, with pain so intense that I could not stand up for weeks."

Gislebert said nothing but nodded, and Dubois continued: "There is no additional clothing in Le Petit Châtelet, so if a companion dies, use what you can from his body before you call a gaoler." Dubois paused to wipe his running nose on his wet sleeve and went on with killing casualness. "On winter days you should use morsels of ice to quench your thirst—break them off the wall with the sole of your shoe, if your shoes survive La Fosse. If you have a window in your cell, don't be tempted to stop it up to block the snow or sun, or you will be choked by the wretched vapors from this cursed place."

Dubois's head drooped as he continued. "You will be stung by insects. The bad taste in your mouth will not leave you. You may be attacked by scurvy and will be unable to sit or rise. In ten days of scurvy my legs and thighs were swollen to twice their ordinary size. Under these rags, friend, my skin is black, my teeth are loose in their sockets, and I can no longer chew any food that has not been soaked in these filthy waters."

An awkward pause followed, and Gislebert searched his brain for something that might bring cheer to the wretched man. "Though death claims you, you gave your life for love," he finally whispered. "Is there a better cause for which to die?"

Dubois made a weak chuckling sound. "I give my life as payment for a rude and thoughtless act," he said, leaning his head back against the wall. "No, my friend, I did not love the wife of Hugues de Bourgueil, for how can love spring from a pretty face alone? In all my years I have never known love."

Dubois lifted his hand from the water and pointed toward the dark half-circle of the sewer gate. His head fell to his sunken chest, and Gislebert strained to hear his words: "Leave me now."

"No, I will stay here until you are stronger."

The candlemaker's head did not rise, but his hand jerked again toward the gate, and Gislebert recognized the effort and eloquence in that simple gesture. Obeying, he slipped away through the water until Dubois stood alone in the corner of the chamber. Gislebert looked through the dark bars of the sewer gate, staring at nothing. When he looked again for his companion, Dubois had slipped beneath the surface.

Adele recognized the tall form of Abbot Robert approaching on the convent road and nodded to the children who sat at her feet in the winter sunshine. "You may go," she said, raising her voice to be heard above their excited squeals. "I will see you again tomorrow."

Abbot Robert put out his hands to steady himself through the rushing sea of excited children, then he bowed toward the bench where Adele waited. "Bonjour, my dear abbot," Adele said, rising to take his hand. "I have news for you today."

"As I have news for you," the abbot answered, allowing her to lead him to the bench. "But perhaps you should share your news first."

Adele smiled and took her usual place at the monk's side. "Madame Marie has asked again if I would take my vows," she said, keeping her voice low lest any of the nuns wander through the convent garden and overhear.

"And you told her again that you would not?"

"Yes." Adele studied the wise face of the old monk who seemed to know her better than she knew herself. "But Madame Marie persisted, questioning my belief that the troubadour will return."

The beginnings of a smile played upon the monk's face. "And your faith is still unshaken?"

"That is my problem, Father, and my challenge. I agreed with Madame Marie that one year was sufficient time for God to bring Gislebert back to me. If the troubadour has not appeared by March of next year, I shall take my vows as a nun and spend the rest of my life in this place."

The monk pressed his finger to his lips as if holding in a secret, and the corners of his mouth rose in a smile. "Well, Father?" Adele asked, wondering why he kept silent. "Did I answer wisely?"

Abbot Robert nodded. "Very wisely, my child, for my news concerns this very matter. Five days ago I walked the aisles of the cathedral, and five days ago I spoke with a troubadour called Gislebert."

Adele felt a curious, tingling shock. "Gislebert is in St. Denis?" she asked, her spirit swelling with exhilaration. She brought her knuckle to her mouth and bit it to stifle the jubilant shout that threatened to burst from her.

Abbot Robert nodded an assent, and Adele's spirit threw off the genteel notions and manners she had learned at the convent. "Where is he?" she demanded, pulling joyously at the old monk's arm. "Does he know I am here? What did you tell him? What is he doing here? Where has he been?"

Abbot Robert threw up an arm in mock alarm, then he smiled and grasped Adele's skittish hands in his own. "The troubadour has been in England, serving King Stephen, and has returned to the shores of France to seek Nadine."

Adele let her head drop against the abbot's shoulder, unconsciously disobeying the convent's taboo against physical contact between nuns and priests. But the abbot paid no mind to her touch and continued. "He is a changed man, Adele, though not quite what he should be. He came to France with the intention of killing Jerome de Honfleur, but God revealed his truth in the cathedral, and the troubadour surrendered his weapon to me. He rode from the cathedral, content to leave Jerome and Nadine alone."

Adele found cause for both hope and despair in the abbot's last words. She raised her head and searched the monk's milky eyes for some further sign of assurance. "Does he still love Nadine? Does he know that I wait here? Why did he ride away? Where did he go?"

"He knows that a postulant at this abbey created a most

unique statue of the Virgin," Abbot Robert answered, raising an eyebrow. "He knows that this same postulant waits for her love to return. He himself remarked that the statue reflected the same skill and sensibilities as those done by the boy Jonas."

Adele clasped her hands in a gesture of prayer. *Please, God,* she prayed silently, *open the eyes of my blind troubadour and speak truth to his heart.*

"Where did he go?" she whispered, opening her eyes.

"I don't know, but I will endeavor to find out," Abbot Robert answered, putting out his hand to lift himself up from the bench. "And I approve of your arrangement with the abbess. Give Gislebert one year to come for you, my daughter, and leave the matter in God's hands."

Gislebert thought anything would be an improvement after the five torturous days of La Fosse, but the room called Fin d'Aise, or "the end of ease," was little better. Instead of water at his feet, Gislebert now suffered the torment of standing in filth and human refuse. Not only did rats make their home in Fin d'Aise, but the place also swarmed with reptiles and insects—roaches, snakes, lizards, and scorpions slithered or crawled throughout the room's cavernous depths. Men despaired over the simple act of breathing in this chamber of pestilences, for the air was so poisonous that the gaoler's torch could not remain lighted in it. Rest, the one thing Gislebert craved most after La Fosse, was nearly impossible until he adopted the habit of swatting away vermin in his sleep.

Twenty other men shared this vile chamber with Gislebert, most of whom were too ill to do anything but lie amid the filth and wait for death. When awake, Gislebert tried to stay active, remembering Dubois's warning, but even though he regularly paced from one side of the room to the other, his health failed day by day. Exercise and exertion exacerbated the need for air, and it was impossible to breathe deeply in Fin d'Aise. After a week, Gislebert wiped clear a portion of the floor and sat like the others, praying that God would soon bring either death or release.

During a conversation with a fellow prisoner, Gislebert learned a galling fact: The authorities who ran the prison were actually charging him a fee for his stay in Le Petit Châtelet. "You had a purse when you were brought in?" the wizened man next to him asked.

Gislebert nodded. "Not an overly generous purse, but over a hundred silver marks."

The man grinned and made a low, mocking bow before the troubadour. "Excuse me, my lord, but I thought myself in the company of a fellow pauper. You are a man of means, so why are you here? I myself paid six deniers for a daily bed in the Chaiâne room until my money ran out."

Gislebert gasped in astonishment. "You mean I don't have to stay in this pigsty?"

The old man shrugged. "Not if you can pay for better. One sou will buy you a bed of straw, three sous half a bed, five sous, a bed alone. But be warned, young friend—the better the room, the longer your stay at Le Petit Châtelet. Down here," the man pointed at the sludge-covered men around him, "the rent's cheaper, but we die faster."

"I do not intend to die," Gislebert answered, standing with what he hoped was a measure of dignity. "When the gaoler comes, I shall demand a better apartment."

"You'll get it, but only until your money runs out," the little man answered. "What will you do then?"

THIRTY-FIVE

Abbot Robert made discreet inquiries in the village throughout the winter and early spring, but no one had heard of Gislebert the troubadour. Except that he had the jeweled dagger in his possession, he might have been tempted to attribute the entire episode in the cathedral to the imaginations of an old man. But he had the dagger; the troubadour *had* stood inside the cathedral. The abbot dreaded each weekly visit with Adele when he had no news to give her. She had become obsessed in recent weeks, and on each visit she became more like the fiercely independent girl he once knew and less like a refined postulant one step away from becoming a fully professed nun.

One rainy June afternoon, just after the procession to celebrate the feast of St. John the Baptist, the abbot was called to the house of Sir Jean de Guise. The knight lay dying of a wound he received in a drunken brawl. As the abbot anointed the man's head and prepared to recite prayers for the dying, the knight grasped the monk's hand so tightly that the abbot thought his brittle bones would break. "Father, I must confess," the knight moaned. He began to rattle off a litany of sins that included stealing from the merchants, abusing his hunting dogs, impregnating a woman not his wife, and condemning an innocent troubadour to prison.

At the mention of the troubadour, Abbot Robert held the man's hand in both his own. "When did this condemnation take place?" he whispered, keeping his voice low so the mourners in the next room would not hear. "And who was this troubadour?"

"I forget his name," the knight replied, grinding his teeth as his life ebbed painfully away. "But it happened in January—just after the Feast of St. Agnes. Sir Jerome de Honfleur insisted that the man be taken straightway to Le Petit Châtelet, and we supported him before the judge."

"What was the man's crime?"

The knight groaned, and the abbot felt the man's hand shudder as his body stiffened. He murmured a hasty prayer, then repeated the question. "What was the man's crime?"

Jean de Guise relaxed, and the pain left his voice. "He was said to attempt the murder of Sir Jerome. But the charge was false—the man did not have a weapon on his person, and he was too weak to do Jerome harm."

Abbot Robert raised his face to heaven in thankfulness and began to recite the last rites as Jean de Guise drew his final breath.

"Gislebert the troubadour is in Le Petit Châtelet, in Paris," Abbot Robert told Adele in the convent garden on his next weekly visit. "The charge on his record is the attempted murder of Jerome de Honfleur and the murder of Jean de Honfleur. It is likely the troubadour is held there still. The door to that prison does not often lead men out."

"The charges are all lies!" Adele cried, leaping to her feet. "I must go to the prison and explain." The short veil of her postulant's headpiece flapped as a gust of hot summer wind blew across the convent courtyard. She was tempted to fling the veil off and be done with her charade. She walked, talked, and dressed as one betrothed to Christ, but while God did hold her in his hands, she could not believe he meant for her to be confined forever within the walls of this nunnery.

"You cannot go," Abbot Robert answered, his voice unusually stern. He put out a hand as if to steady her. "What good will you do, a woman alone in the streets of Paris? Your word will mean nothing against Jerome's."

"I have never been afraid of being alone."

"Haven't you?"

She did not answer, her silence acquiescing to the truth of his words. The thought of spending her life alone did, indeed, terrify her. She had run from her father to the troubadour, from the troubadour to the convent, and even in the convent she relied terribly on Abbot Robert. Although she trusted God, the thought of living with no companions except these nuns scared her beyond belief.

She lifted frightened eyes to Abbot Robert.

"I will go to Le Petit Châtelet," the abbot said in answer to her unvoiced plea. He stood to his feet with the aid of his walking stick. "I will go on the second day of every week, and I will find some way to reach the troubadour."

"It will take you the better part of the day just to walk to Paris," Adele protested. "Let me go, Father, for I am younger and am used to walking. You do not know the city and will have to ask for help, but I can find the prison straightaway—"

"Be silent," Abbot Robert answered, raising his hand in a no-nonsense gesture. "It is settled. I must do this for you, for I am concerned about the troubadour myself. I sent him away without telling him where to find you, and I will bring him back."

A familiar struggle rose in her heart, the conflict between her desire to reveal herself and the temptation to hide her true feelings from the man who knew her best. "Perhaps you were right not to tell him about me," she whispered, twisting her hands beneath her woolen scapular, the garment that hung over her shoulders as a visible reminder of the yoke of Christ. "He must seek me of his own volition, dear Abbot, not out of duty or curiosity. If he does not come in love, I do not want him to come at all."

"But he cannot come as long as he is imprisoned." The abbot's long fingers grazed her cheek, and he cleared his throat before speaking again. "You are wise, daughter Adele. Keep this wisdom about you, and pray that my journey will be fruitful."

THIRTY-SIX

Ten miles lay between St. Denis and the prison Le Petit Châtelet, and Abbot Robert began his long walk south before the sun rose. As he left the familiar surroundings of St. Denis, his senses heightened and his self-protective habits rose to the fore. His hearing warned him of approaching travelers; the feel of the road beneath his feet and the sun at his left hand kept him on course. Even the smells in the air guided him away from the tiny village he loved to the bustling city of Paris.

Perhaps Adele was right, he thought as he walked. *The journey might be too much for me to bear.* His hearing had dulled in years past, and he had only his walking stick to defend himself against any would-be attackers.

Fortunately, God smiled on him, and Abbot Robert entered Paris by the time he felt the sun baking his bald head. Surrounded by the usual hustle and bustle at the city gate, the abbot waved a hand to catch the attention of a passerby. A man stopped to offer help and was kind enough to walk the abbot to the drawbridge that stood before Le Petit Châtelet.

"The bridge is known as Petit Point," the man said, turning the monk so that he faced the bridge and the massive stone building that stood behind it. "A portcullis hangs between the bridge and the door. It is raised every morning to admit new prisoners."

"Thank you, my son," Abbot Robert said, holding fast

to the man's hand. "But how does one gain entrance to see
a prisoner?"

"Only with the permission of the gaolers or the king's
counselor who administrates the prison," the man answered.
"I don't think you'll be granted entrance, Father. They have
their own priests at the abbey here in Paris and are not likely
to admit another."

"Tell me, then," the abbot said, tugging on the man's
sleeve while he lowered his voice, "how does one get word
to a prisoner inside?"

Abbot Robert could sense the man's hesitation, so he
smiled broadly, hoping to assure the timid fellow that he was
not a spy. The abbot heard the man shuffle his feet in reluctance, and at last he spoke. "Sometimes the prisoners in the
upper floors toss letters wrapped around stones from the
windows to the bridge below," the man offered. "But they
have to be quick, or the patrols will find their letters. At
other times prisoners are permitted to exercise on the plat-
forms of the towers, and people in the street communicate
with signs or the waving of a handkerchief."

Abbot Robert nodded slowly and beamed in pleasure.
"And what does a blind monk do?" he asked. "Have you
any ideas, my son?"

The man hesitated again, then his words came out in a
rush: "If I were you, Father, I would walk every day on the
bridge. Though not seeing, you would be seen, and word
would pass among the prisoners until the man you seek
hears that you wait outside. Then he would try to get word
to you or would be comforted by your presence."

The abbot nodded. "Take me to this bridge, then, my
son, and God will bless you for your efforts on my behalf."

After waiting five debilitating months for an audience with
Clement, the king's counselor who ran Le Petit Châtelet,
Gislebert finally stood before the tall, thin man dressed all in
red. Clement held his nose without embarrassment as
Gislebert stumbled into the room and continued to hold it

as Gislebert apologized for his odor and explained his willingness to pay for a better room in the prison.

Clement listened, then nodded agreeably. "Go," he said, his nasal voice cutting through the silence of the room, "and take your stench with you. Gaoler, open the windows immediately!"

So in June, just as the heat of summer began to bake prisoners in the upper rooms, Gislebert was moved from the torturous Fin d'Aise to the Berceau, or cradle room—so called because of its immense arched roof.

Walking from the counselor's chamber to his new quarters, Gislebert was horrified at the other sights of Le Petit Châtelet. Women prisoners were kept in La Grieche, a large room where the inmates either cried piteously or cursed as he and his gaolers marched past their barred door. Beyond La Grieche, a small open window looked out into a courtyard thirty feet long and eighteen feet wide. In this squalid place, where tall walls forbade the circulation of fresh air, nearly five hundred prisoners stood shoulder to shoulder, with scarcely enough room to move.

"What have they done?" Gislebert cried as two gaolers led him past the courtyard toward a tower staircase.

"They are indigents," one gaoler muttered in reply, "arrested for nonpayment of debts."

The memory of the days when he and Adele had been penniless flitted across Gislebert's mind. But he had no time for reflection, for the guards pushed him up the stairs and down another narrow corridor on the next floor. Here heavy oak doors lined the hall like a row of blackened eyes. Small slits in the doors, no wider than three fingers of a man's hand, offered the only ventilation and light into six-foot-square cubicles, and Gislebert gasped as he peered through an open door where a surgeon tended a man half-dead. These were stoop-cells, more fit for dogs than humans. The low ceilings made it impossible for a man to stand upright in them. Five prisoners were housed in each of these stifling cells, and the heat from the open room smote Gislebert like a furnace blast as he staggered past.

The guards led him up another flight of stairs, and in contrast to the hell holes he had seen below, the Berceau stood as Le Petit Châtelet's definition of luxury. On the top floor of the prison, the large cradle room had three high windows that permitted light and air into the chamber. The arched roof allowed for reasonable ventilation, and as he stepped inside, Gislebert breathed freely for the first time in months. Rough straw mattresses were stacked against the wall, and clean straw lined the floor. Even this chamber reeked of urine and waste, but Gislebert noticed that his new companions had the common sense and decency to confine their malodorous necessities to one bare corner of the room.

His fellow prisoners looked up at him blankly when the guards pushed him through the doorway. But as soon as the key turned behind him, the men pressed toward him, ravenous for news. "From where did you come?" they questioned in frantic French. "What news do you bring from outside?"

"None," Gislebert answered, sinking wearily onto the floor. He coughed, phlegm rattling in his chest, and the men unconsciously backed away. Gislebert waved a hand. "I have been five days in La Fosse—"

"La Fosse!" someone exclaimed.

"And five months in Fin d'Aise. Now, though I shall pay most dearly for it, I intend to call the Berceau home."

A tall man in a tattered robe approached and bowed. Gentility surrounded him like a mantle. "Welcome, friend," he said simply. "We of the Berceau work together. If there is anything we can do for you, or you for us, we must make our wishes known. But before we press you into service, you must regain your strength. The scarcities of Fin d'Aise are well marked upon your frame."

A fit of coughing seized Gislebert, rendering him unable to answer, but he nodded his assent to the tall nobleman and closed his eyes in gratitude. Civility could exist even inside Le Petit Châtelet.

Within a week, Gislebert learned all their names: the Marquis d'Ancre was the tall nobleman who served as the unofficial leader of the group; stout Henry Du Bourg was the marquis' closest friend and acted as second in command of the small prison society. As the Berceau stood high above the other prison chambers, so these men were above the other prisoners in wealth and status. Through the unique codes of prison life, they knew a surprising amount about what went on in the dungeons and cells beneath them.

Gislebert was amazed at the ingenuity with which they solved the problem of communication within the prison. Messages were passed by raising the voice or speaking in unison to create a huge sound that echoed through all but the lowest dungeons of the vast stone house. Written messages were sent on scraps of linen or pieces of plaster torn from the wall. The drumstick of a fowl made a handy pen, and fresh blood provided an admirable ink.

Because they had the only window that actually looked out on the world, the men of the Berceau acted as eyes and ears for the entire house of Le Petit Châtelet. Clandestine communications frequently reached the nobles in the high prison room through sympathetic gaolers or the rumble of drainpipes or chimneys. The men in Gislebert's chamber felt it their duty to reach the outside world with whatever messages the prisoners had to offer.

Messages were sent with surprising efficiency by means of the windows. The three windows high on the walls could not be reached by a man, or even by a man on another's shoulders, but a tower of three men could easily peer over the windowsill or toss out a message. Henry Du Bourg allowed his broad shoulders to act as the foundation for the human platform. Laurent Testu stood upon Henry's sturdy shoulders, and the slender Charles of Bourbon acted as the top post of the human tower.

When Gislebert had regained much of his strength, Charles of Bourbon looked him over carefully and proclaimed that Gislebert would make an admirable window watcher. "You are tall, limber, and light," Charles announced. "You should practice with Laurent and Henry. There may come a day when we have need of you."

"What do you see when you look out there?" Gislebert asked, genuinely curious.

Charles grinned and ducked his head shyly. "Blue sky, the green waters of the Seine, and birds," he said. "Those sights alone motivate me to climb the walls with my fellows. But people gather on the bridge below, and their appearance is not accidental. For two weeks now, since the arrival of the Seneschal of Orleanais, his wife, the fair lady Diane, has walked the bridge, her face turned upward."

"A fair lady? Outside this place?"

Young Charles' face actually reddened as he nodded. "She is most beautiful, like poetry in motion."

Gislebert grinned. "You speak like a fellow troubadour, Charles. Perhaps I will climb your human tower and have a look at the lady myself. I have need of inspiration these days."

The other men laughed, and the flustered Charles changed the subject quickly. "Other bridge walkers include several women whose husbands are doubtless in the debtor's courtyard. Two nuns appear every day and make the sign of the cross incessantly. And every Monday a tall monk arrives after noon and walks for three hours, then disappears."

"A monk?" Gislebert asked, feeling a surge of sudden interest.

"Yes," Charles answered. "He is most unusual. A Cistercian, probably, for he wears no shoes or cloak, and I believe the man is—"

"He is doubtless here because the bishop of Autun was recently arrested," the Marquis d'Ancre interrupted. "The priests have not rested since the man deigned to visit our humble house."

As the other men laughed at the marquis' wit, Gislebert settled back on his straw mattress. It was too much to hope that Abbot Robert should make his way from St. Denis. No one would stand on the bridge for Gislebert, for Jerome had conquered him quickly and quietly. Not even Nadine would know of his fate.

He turned onto his side and buried his face in the stale mattress. His illusions of love had been stripped away by the harsh realities of prison. Through the agony of Fin d'Aise, he had seen Nadine clearly—as she had been on the day they promised to marry. He knew she did not love him. He knew now that she had left with Jerome willingly. She would not have borne Jerome five children, would not have continued with him or accepted his attentions, if she did not desire him.

He rolled onto his stomach and buried his head in his arms. Adele and Melusina had spoken the truth about Nadine's nature. But wherever Nadine was, whatever she was, he still loved her enough to forgive her.

THIRTY-SEVEN

The arched windows of the Berceau brought welcome fresh air in the autumn months but granted entrance to snow and biting cold when winter arrived. The prisoners of Le Petit Châtelet were provided no extra clothes, and Gislebert's ragged tunic and stiff surcoat offered little protection from the cold. Rendered inflexible with dirt, his leggings chafed his skin more than they warmed him, and his toes protruded from the tattered edges. As the temperature dropped, Gislebert often found that his feet were completely numb.

The Duc d'Epernon, a longtime resident of the Berceau who did little but sit and eat, died during a winter night. Before calling the gaoler, the Marquis d'Ancre had the Berceau prisoners draw lots for the leggings, tunic, and cloak of the dead man. Gislebert was delighted to win the man's cloak and tossed it over his own, uncomfortably aware that his fellow prisoners were probably consoling themselves with the thought that the cloak would eventually be offered again as a prize, especially if the troubadour's chronic cough persisted. But they were gentlemen, and those who did not profit from the demise of the Duc d'Epernon did not complain. Instead, they lay silently back on their mattresses as snowflakes came down through the windows and fell upon the naked blue body of the unfortunate duke.

Charles of Bourbon developed a fever the next day, and Gislebert looked up to see the Marquis d'Ancre standing before him. "We need you for the window," he said, jerking his thumb toward Henry Du Bourg and Laurent Testu, who waited expectantly at the wall. "Charles will not be able to climb today."

Gislebert wrapped his cloak about him and glanced up at the windows above his head. Charles of Bourbon had made scampering up to the window seem easy, but Gislebert did not know if he was capable of such acrobatic maneuvers. He looked around the room, hoping someone would volunteer to take his place, but the others were either too weak to climb or too heavy to stand on Laurent's slender shoulders.

Gislebert slipped off his shoes and walked to the wall where Laurent sat astride the solid Henry's shoulders. Laurent smiled in encouragement, then braced himself against the wall and stood upright. "Now, Gislebert," he called.

Gislebert gingerly placed his blackened foot into the stirrup Henry had created with his fingers. He counted to three, then braced himself against the wall and climbed upward, one foot in Henry's hands, the other on the wall, then one on Laurent's foot atop Henry's shoulder, the other in a higher crevice on the wall. Laurent reached out and entwined his fingers in Gislebert's long hair. For a moment Gislebert envisioned himself falling, his scalp remaining cleanly behind in Laurent's firm grip.

"My belt," Laurent instructed. "Move your left foot into the loop of my belt." Gislebert did as he was told, praying the entire time that he would not slip and break his neck. Laurent released Gislebert's hair and held his hand firmly, and Gislebert reluctantly placed his weight in the loop of Laurent's belt and inched his right foot farther up the wall until he was able at last to stand on Laurent's shoulders.

"Don't look down, and don't worry about toppling us, for we cling to the wall," Henry shouted up from below. "But go to the window and be quick!"

Gislebert shuddered and grasped the bars of the window, thankful they would support his weight if the men beneath him wavered. He looked out and gasped at the beauty of the sight before him: a wide gray sky, low-hanging clouds, waves on the water pressing forward by the winter wind. He had not seen the sky in nearly a year.

"Is the lady there?" Charles called from his sickbed below. "What color does she wear today?"

Gislebert strained upward to gain the proper perspective to look down on the bridge. "Yes, a lady walks there," he said, scarcely daring to speak aloud lest he disturb the men who held him aloft. "She wears a blue cloak trimmed in furs. The two nuns are there, too, making the sign of the cross in our direction." He looked down, giddy with discovery, and the sudden realization of how far up he stood caused him to jerk back to the security of the bars.

"Careful!" Laurent grumbled from beneath him. "Every move you make digs your bony feet into my shoulders."

"What else?" the marquis demanded. "Any sign of patrols? Might we throw down a message? The wine merchant in the seventh stoop cell asks that we contact his wife."

"No patrols," Gislebert said, still scanning the narrow bridge below. "But the monk is there—the tall monk in the robes of a Cistercian." He laughed softly. "I'll never understand why those monks walk without shoes in the snow—"

His thoughts were distracted when the monk reached the end of the bridge and turned again toward the prison house. He held a walking stick in his bony hand and tapped forward on the path ahead as if he were blind. Gislebert's stomach cramped in a sudden attack of nerves. *Abbot Robert!* The one man who could release Gislebert from prison! God had heard his prayers!

"I know this monk!" Gislebert called out, his voice ringing through the rafters of the tall ceiling. He thrust his head as far out the window as he dared. "Abbot! Abbot Robert!"

He could not tell if his voice carried over the whistling wind outside, but it seemed to him that the monk stiffened a bit and turned his head as if to hear better.

"Don't shout or you'll have the patrols out!" the

marquis warned. "Dictate a message, if you must, and throw it out on a stone!"

The men below stood ready to write, but Gislebert shook his head. "The monk is blind," he answered. "It would be no use."

"At least he knows you are here," Laurent spoke from below. "Now, if there is no other news, dismount, Troubadour. My shoulders ache from carrying you."

Abbot Robert paused in his long walk on the bridge. Had he heard a voice call his name in the bawling winds? Or were his ears deceived by the imagination and wanderings of an aged mind?

He walked again, slowly tapping his way along the bridge. The bitter cold knifed his lungs and tingled the bare skin of his head, hands, and feet, but he absorbed the pain, enduring it for Adele and for the blessed Savior who had borne much more. He endured it even for the unfortunate troubadour who had sought good and found evil.

The wind blew fierce and steady toward the prison house, and the abbot felt its gentle push at his back. Three more turns and he would go, two more forays with the wind in his face and once more with the howling beast at his back.

The clinking, metallic sound of the rising portcullis disturbed his concentration, and the abbot raised his head in the direction of the prison house. Someone was coming out. He mentally mapped out a path to the right side of the bridge so the conveyance could pass. But as he tapped his way across the bridge, he slipped on a patch of ice and lost his balance. Helpless, the abbot slid on his back across the ice-slicked bridge. Through his panic, his ears discerned the approaching sounds of a horse and wagon.

He finally stopped sliding and tried to rise to his feet, but sharp pains shot up through his right leg like cold needles. The sound of a horse's hooves drew closer. Frantic, he rolled desperately away from what he believed was the center of the bridge.

At the last instant, he knew he had miscalculated. The wind, which should have been in his face, blew at his back, and instead of rolling toward the safety of the bridge railing, he had curled himself directly under the approaching hooves of the horse.

"Eeegads! What was that?" the surgeon asked, peering over the heavy fur collar that blocked his view of everything below his horse's head. "That thump, bailiff, did you hear it?"

The prison bailiff reined in the horse and peered around the wagon at the bridge behind them. "We've hit a monk, Doctor. He lies in the road with his skull open."

The surgeon grimaced. "A monk, you say? We'll let the church handle it, I suppose. If his skull's open, the man's too damaged for us to do any good. Call a priest on your return, but get me out of here. Lord Halsey expects me."

"Oui, Doctor," the bailiff answered, cracking the whip over the horse's head.

Gislebert lay awake that night, scratching a letter upon a piece of linen torn from his tunic. He would find a way to get a message to the abbot, and what better way than the two nuns who faithfully came to the bridge? He would toss his missive to them, directing them to give word to the abbot, who could beg an audience with someone in authority. His nerves hummed with purpose as he scratched out his message in the moonlight, dipping the sharpened end of a chicken bone into a bloody, festering sore that had opened on his leg.

He reread his letter in the bright light of morning and awakened Henry and Laurent when he could contain his impatience no longer. "I have to send a message today," he said, indicating the strip of linen in his hand.

Laurent peered at Gislebert through sleepy eyes and jerked his head toward the window. "How do you intend to throw it out?" he asked. "How will you weight it?"

Gislebert frowned. He had concentrated so heavily on

writing the note that he forgot about weighting the linen so that it would fall straight onto the bridge and not be blown into the water. A quick glance around the room yielded nothing that would work. Finally Gislebert pulled off his worn shoe. "This will weight my letter," he said, yanking the rotten leather uppers from the heavy wooden sole.

Laurent took the sole and shook his head. "Your feet will regret this decision later this winter," he said. "You will have frostbite."

"I won't have frostbite if I'm not here," Gislebert answered, folding his frozen fingers into his armpits. "Now, please, climb up so I may send my message. The nuns will get word to the abbot."

Henry and Laurent assumed their usual positions, and Gislebert climbed up again, urgency speeding his steps so that he did not have time to worry about his precarious position. Once he was in place at the window and had caught sight of the two nuns, he nodded to the marquis, who tossed Gislebert's note up to him.

The nuns were too far away on the bridge, and Gislebert waved his hand in a wide arc, hoping to gain their attention. He thought he had succeeded when the dark-robed women began to move, but instead of coming toward him they separated and scattered to opposite sides of the bridge. Gislebert peered out in alarm. "There's a commotion on the bridge," he reported to the men below. "Several patrols and the king's counselor have come out with a priest. They have a pushcart, and the priest is chanting something, I think. He reads from a prayer book."

"A funeral," Henry grunted. "Someone has died."

"Someone important, else he would be tossed in the pits of the oubliettes and forgotten," the marquis added.

"Here is the body," Gislebert reported, watching the scene below with interest. "It is shrouded in cloth, and—"

A gust of wind stirred the cloaks of the men on the bridge and lifted the veil away from the body on the pushcart. Gislebert felt a chill of shock when he recognized Abbot Robert.

Gislebert watched in horrified fascination as the priest on the bridge stepped forward and replaced the veil. With one hand he held the veil in place, covering the dead man's gruesome wound, and the other he held aloft as he chanted a prayer. The men on the bridge nodded at the prayer's conclusion, and all made the sign of the cross. A patrol tilted the handcart over the edge of the bridge, and the shrouded body of the venerable old monk slid into the Seine.

Gislebert let his message drop to the floor of the Berceau as his dreams crumbled around him.

THIRTY-EIGHT

When Abbot Robert did not appear for his weekly visit, Adele prayed for his health. When he did not come the second week, she begged permission from the abbess to visit the forest monastery to comfort him. "Abbot Robert is not there," Madame Marie answered, her voice distant and chilly. "I spoke to a priest from the abbey this morning, and the abbot has been gone for nearly two weeks. They all suppose that he has died on one of his foolish wanderings, for he was old and weak."

Adele swayed on her knees, gripping the edge of the table in front of her to keep from toppling over. Could the abbot be dead? If he was, had he died on her errand? Tears of remorse sprang to her eyes, and she lowered her head so her superior would not see. "May I be excused?" she whispered, her voice clotted with grief.

Madame Marie nodded, sparing her words as she did her emotions. Adele fled to the chapel.

After an hour of prayer and soul-searching, Adele knelt before the abbess again. "Madame, I must go to Paris," she said, folding her hands quietly in front of her. "I must search for the abbot. I cannot rest until I do this."

The abbess lost her disciplined reserve. "Go to Paris?" she shrieked, in the same voice she would have used if Adele had asked permission to fly to the moon. "No, it is not done. We never travel alone—and never outside the community unless on a spiritual pilgrimage."

"I'm not one of you."

"You are of this house and due to take your vows in a few weeks," the abbess persisted, setting her lips in a thin line. "You may not go."

"I must go."

The abbess drew herself up to her full height. "You may not. The bishop will not allow it and will reprimand me if I let you out of this house—"

"I will be responsible to the bishop," Adele interrupted, raising her head in an attitude of defiance the abbess had never seen. She looked fully into her superior's eyes and measured her words carefully. "You will not be held responsible, Madame Marie, and if I find Abbot Robert, you will be much congratulated. When I have accomplished my mission, I will return here and fulfill our agreement."

The abbess set her jaw firmly and glared at Adele for a moment, then nodded brusquely. "It's the troubadour, isn't it?" she asked, her eyebrows flashing a warning signal. "You say you are willing to wait until God brings him to you, but you would chase him to Paris and throw yourself at his feet."

"I will not." Adele stiffened her spine, and anger made her tone harsher than she intended. "I will search for Abbot Robert for one week. At the end of that time, madame, I will return and wait the rest of the appointed year."

Madame Marie turned to the wall to consider Adele's proposition; when she turned back to Adele, the corner of the abbess's mouth drooped in wry amusement. She nodded and motioned for Adele to stand. "In one week, my daughter, you must return," she said, making a compact sign of the cross over Adele's head. "With your will of iron dedicated to God, my dear, you will make a most excellent nun."

Dressed in the postulant's dark woolen tunic, scapular, and short veil, Adele found that she was best able to keep warm by walking briskly. She reached Paris five hours after leaving the nunnery at St. Denis, and after making inquiries, she had no trouble finding the monstrous prison known as Le Petit Châtelet.

Standing at the drawbridge that led to the long bridge of Petit Point, she paused. How could anyone live in such a place, much less the sensitive troubadour? With its windows open to the cold and snow, was it possible that he still lived?

She bowed hesitantly to the two guards at the lowered drawbridge and ventured forth upon the icy span. Two nuns in full habits and winter cloaks stood there, making the sign of the cross toward the prison windows. Adele shyly stepped forward to meet them.

"Excusez-moi," she said, moistening her chapped lips with her tongue, "but I have come seeking a priest, Abbot Robert. He left his abbey two weeks ago for Paris and has not returned. He is tall and blind. Have you seen him?"

The two nuns looked at each other in silent communication, then the elder nun turned compassionate eyes upon Adele. *"Oui, mademoiselle,"* she answered, motioning toward the center of the bridge. "He died, just there, on the bridge. A horse and carriage . . ." She paused delicately. "There was an accident, and the priest was killed. The gaolers cast his body into the river the next day."

Adele clung to the bridge railing for support; only the iron discipline of the convent restrained her from wailing in agony. After a moment she managed a polite reply: *"Merci beaucoup, mademoiselle."*

For the rest of the day she stood at the railing in mute tribute to the abbot. In all her twenty-nine years, she had but two friends. Both were men: one was dead, and the other locked in this house of horror, if he lived at all. She froze in terror as a horrifying thought occurred to her: She was responsible, if the troubadour died, for both of their deaths. Gislebert had been arrested, in part, for the death of the man *she* pushed into the river; the abbot had died on her errand.

The abbot should have died in his sleep, blessed Lord, she prayed, arguing with heaven even as she struggled with her own guilt. *He should have died in his bed, not on a mission to help me. He was quiet and gentle, and did not deserve this violent death.*

The bone-numbing cold hardened her heart and her resolve. Although the wind tugged at her cloak and scattered her hair like a wild woman's, she did not stir from the spot until the sun had set over the gray-green gloom of the Seine. As the sun disappeared behind the western waters, the two nuns had compassion on her and took her to their convent for a warm fire and the comfort of a straw mattress.

"A new member of your elite society, gentlemen," the gaoler announced, thrusting open the door of the Berceau. "Welcome Monsieur Fouquet, formerly in the service of the renowned Jerome de Honfleur."

Gislebert sat upright on his mattress and scrutinized the newest inmate of their cell. A solidly built man with a hard jaw, tendoned neck, and deep chest, Monsieur Fouquet walked through the room with the attitude of a courtly gentleman inspecting inferior quarters.

"It is clear that *he* wasn't welcomed to Le Châtelet with five days in La Fosse," Gislebert remarked dryly to Laurent, who sat near him.

"Nor will he be," Laurent answered. "I know of this knight; he is far too valuable to Jerome to be confined here long. Jerome is most likely teaching the man a lesson in manners."

"What is his crime?" the marquis called to the grinning gaoler at the door. The dark eyes of the marquis bore the newcomer no love. "We are noble men, sir. Should we be on our guard against this man?"

"Not unless you have breasts and a soft belly," the gaoler jeered. "The man attacked the maid of Jerome's wife."

Fouquet moved to face the marquis with the sure grace of a forest creature, a snide smile cutting his long, mustached face in half. "Tell my master I am ready to serve whenever he calls," the man called to the gaoler, still staring insolently at the marquis. The bolt of the heavy door slid into place, and

Fouquet nodded to the marquis. "I will be released from here within three days, so do not trifle with me, noble gentlemen."

The marquis thought it dangerous to expose too many of their secrets to a man who might be released in only three days, so during that time the men of Berceau did not climb to the window nor send or receive messages. Instead they sat, ate, and watched in silence as their newest companion grew more irritable and moody with every passing hour.

On the fourth day, when it became clear to all that Fouquet was badly mistaken about his lord's intentions, the man's mood grew blacker than the grime on the filthy wooden floors. "She was just a serving girl and therefore worth less than Jerome's favorite hunting dog, *n'est-ce pas?*" he said. "Why, then, am I still here?"

"Perhaps your master has another reason for confining you," the marquis suggested. "What other reasons might he have in mind?"

Fouquet grew silent and said nothing until the next day, when he awoke and rushed toward the heavy door in fury. "I will not stay here another hour!" he yelled, beating furiously on the door while Gislebert and Laurent exchanged glances. "I know something that could make you all rich men! I know something Jerome wants kept silent!"

Accustomed to the mad ravings of prisoners, the gaolers ignored the man, but Gislebert found an opportunity in the man's desperate frenzy. Once Fouquet calmed himself, Gislebert approached and slipped a casual arm around the man's shoulders. "Tell me of this information you have," he whispered in a confidential tone. "Perhaps we can work together, you and I, for I am also here on Jerome's account."

Fouquet's eyes narrowed. "You? How long have *you* been here?"

"Ten months," Gislebert answered, feeling his way carefully. "And I may be here for ten years, as will you, unless you share this information you know."

Fouquet glared suspiciously at Gislebert. "What good will my news do you? You are as helpless here as am I."

"We are not as helpless as you might think," Gislebert answered, smiling confidently at the marquis.

Fouquet glanced skeptically at the marquis, then turned again to Gislebert. "Jerome plans to assassinate the king at the Feast of St. Andrew," he said, his words coming in a rush. "He has hired two archers to kill the king and the dauphin as they ride to the cathedral at St. Denis. The archers will not fail, and even if they are killed by the king's guards, Jerome will be free. He plans to claim the throne."

"The gall!" Henry exclaimed, slamming his fist into his open palm. "Would that I were free, I could—"

The marquis held up a restraining hand. "St. Andrew's feast," he said, his eyes gleaming. "Fouquet, what day were you brought here?"

"The twenty-third of November."

The marquis nodded. "You have been here five days, so today is—"

"The twenty-eighth," Gislebert spoke up.

"Two days," the marquis answered, his eyes turning to Gislebert. "We must get a message to the palace."

"A message?" Fouquet asked, bewildered. "How? The gaolers are deaf and dumb to my cries."

"Forget the gaolers," Gislebert answered, tearing another strip of linen from the weakened fabric of his tunic. "We have our own methods here in the Berceau."

Laurent smoothed the linen from Gislebert. Henry produced a sharpened chicken bone. Gislebert gnashed his own wrist with his teeth to produce the needed supply of blood. The marquis penned the message that Gislebert dictated, and then Charles bound Gislebert's wound.

When the message had been written and weighted, Henry and Laurent took their places at the wall and Gislebert prepared to climb up. Fouquet watched in amazement as the three men assembled their human tower, gaping in astonishment when the weighted message was tossed up to Gislebert at the open window.

"Who walks outside?" the marquis called from below.

Gislebert peered down at the bridge below. "Three nuns today," he called down. "I shall try to gain their attention."

The biting wind nipped the fingers of his left hand as he clung to a bar of the window, and Gislebert resolutely ignored the stinging pain as he leaned his chest upon the windowsill and cried out with all the strength in his slender frame. The wind seemed to snatch his words away, but as his eyes watered under the force of the chilling wind, he thought he saw the nuns' faces lift toward him. Two of the nuns did not move, but the third walked forward a few paces and bravely waved the corner of her cloak in reply.

"Le bon Dieu, she sees me!" he cried, wrapping the fingers of his right hand over the precious hunk of linen and wood. "May God guide my throw!"

He tossed his missive out the window and hung forward, scarcely daring to hope that his aim was true. A gust of wind blew from the west, and Gislebert held his breath, afraid that the bundle would fall into the river. But it continued on its steady course and landed with a thunk on the wooden deck of the bridge.

The young nun scurried forward and covered the piece of wood with her habit as a patrol guard stepped out of the gatehouse to investigate the mysterious sound. Gislebert saw her bow politely to the man. She must have made pleasant conversation, for the guard laughed and made a dismissive gesture, then turned away for the warmth of his gatehouse. Gislebert stuck his neck out farther—the girl stooped, picked up the missive, and looked up again at the high window.

He could not make out her features, so great was the distance between them, but he waved his hand in salute and saw her wave in reply.

"Hurry, the gaoler comes!" the marquis called from the doorway. Gislebert ducked back inside the window and scrambled down to safety. As the gaoler opened the door and brought in the baskets of bread and bowls of pottage that served as dinner, Gislebert caught the eyes of Monsieur Fouquet. In them shone the dark glimmer of respect.

Adele grasped the hunk of wood and linen in her hand and hurried from the bridge. She couldn't be sure if the tattered scarecrow in the window had been the troubadour, but the cry that first caught her attention had carried the sound of his voice. She nodded politely to the two nuns who stood at the end of the bridge, and the elder of them put out a hand to stop her. "Are you sure, mademoiselle, that you ought to read such a note?" the woman questioned gently. "Perhaps we should take it to our abbess, who will present it to the bishop. After all, these men are criminals."

"This note was tossed to me, not to the bishop or the abbess," Adele answered, thrusting the wood and linen inside her scapular. "I am entrusted with whatever duty this note requests."

She hurried off the bridge and waited until she was well away from the drawbridge and its attendant guards before unwrapping the linen from the wood. Written in French, and in a hurried hand, the message was written in dark red ink. Adele gasped when she realized that the ink was actually blood.

> *Greetings:*
> *I, Gislebert the troubadour, with Monsieur Fouquet, the Marquis d'Ancre, and our fellows in the Berceau at Le Petit Châtelet, do urge you to warn the king that Jerome de Honfleur has hired an assassin to kill the king and his heir en route to the Cathedral at St. Denis on the day of the Feast of Saint Andrew. It is our prayer and wish that you hasten to the palace with this news, never stopping for aid or help until you relay this message to his most gracious highness—*

Adele let the wood in her hand fall to the ground and raced toward the palace.

THIRTY-NINE

The gaoler's keys rattled at the door, and Gislebert and his companions stirred from their places and telegraphed silent warnings to each other. The hour was too late for dinner and too early for the admission of a new prisoner. What news did the gaoler bring?

The gaoler swung the door open and stood back as the king's counselor swept into the room, his rich red cloak fanning like a carpet behind him. "One of you tossed a message from this window to the bridge below," Clement announced, his eyes skimming the faces of the prisoners before him. "Who threw it, and who were his accomplices? Speak, or you will all spend the rest of your days in Fin d'Aise. Or perhaps you would prefer the oubliettes?"

Gislebert shuddered at the mention of the terrible subterranean pits, where sharpened iron points protruded from the walls to catch the flesh of those thrown into the cavernous depths. These despised pits did not officially exist on the gaoler's records. But whenever a prisoner disappeared from his regular cell, the gaolers had been heard to mutter that such-and-such a prisoner now rested "*in pace,*" or "in peace,"—a misleading euphemism for the horrible oubliettes, where prisoners were left to perish from hunger and pain.

Gislebert glanced toward the marquis, whose dark eyes gave nothing away. Then he looked at Fouquet, whose mouth hung open in abject terror.

"Speak!" the counselor demanded, his deadly bright

eyes searching the group for a weak link. "Or one by one, I will serve you to the oubliettes, beginning with you!"

His long narrow hand pointed at the fevered face of Charles, who lay flushed and weak on his bed. Charles shook his head and snorted in contempt for the counselor, and one of the gaolers moved forward to seize him.

"That won't be necessary," Gislebert said, standing to his feet. He moistened his dry lips, then raised his chin to face the counselor. "I threw the message."

An odd feeling of power coursed through his veins. He was so carried away by it that he bowed gallantly before the counselor, even doffing an imaginary hat. *This* was honor. This was why he left Afton and Calhoun at Margate. For all his life, including his time with King Stephen, Suger, and Calhoun, Gislebert had been nothing but a recorder of deeds, a vassal, an appendage to some greater man. But surely this was a heaven-sent opportunity to discover and endure the consequences of his own heroism.

If only Calhoun of Margate could see me now, Gislebert thought, sweeping his imaginary hat before the counselor's feet. He stood upright, laughing aloud, and Clement's narrow face reddened in anger.

"What was the message?" the counselor demanded. Gislebert merely raised an eyebrow and said nothing.

"How did you do it?" the counselor barked, and another voice answered in the stillness.

"I helped him," Laurent Testu said, standing to his feet. A moment later, Henry Du Bourg stood as well, and Gislebert looked at his friends and shook his head in regret.

"We three did it and no others," Henry said, his homely face arranging itself into a grin. "Do with us as you will."

"By all that is holy, I shall," the counselor muttered, jerking his cloak from his wake as he turned to leave their chamber. He gestured to the gaoler at the door and two who stood outside with their swords drawn. "Take these three men to La Fosse," he roared, striding from the room. "And charge them double for the pleasure!"

The king's seneschal studied the message again, then looked back at Adele. "You are certain of its authenticity?" he asked, his hooded eyes scrutinizing her carefully. "I cannot disturb the king with anything less than the truth."

"I know Gislebert the troubadour, and he is a truthful man," Adele answered, throwing her hands open. "He is being held in the prison unlawfully. Please, you must bring this matter to the king's attention!"

The seneschal debated, then motioned for her to sit down. "I will," he said, "but you must remain here. If these things are false, mademoiselle, it is you who will pay the price."

"I will pay it gladly," Adele answered, taking a seat by the fire. "Just hurry with the message!"

The water seemed a bit lower in La Fosse than Gislebert had remembered, but infinitely colder. His legs were blue with cold after only three hours in the putrid pit, and although he tried to pace around the chamber to keep up his circulation, exhaustion broke his spirit. In despair he hung his head, silently weeping. Laurent and Henry were faring no better, their faces pale and chalky in the dim light.

The three men leaned against the wall in quiet desperation. Once he had spent his tears, Gislebert looked over at his friends. "You should not have spoken," he said, wiping his face with the crusty sleeve of his surcoat.

Laurent managed a fleeting smile as he shivered. "I could not let a mere troubadour outdo me in gallantry," he said, rubbing his arms over his shoulders in a futile effort to keep warm.

"Nor I," Henry answered, his grunt echoing through the chamber. "Besides, you have bragged so often about how you bested La Fosse, we wanted to see if your words were true."

Gislebert accepted their lighthearted answers silently. He noted that the rats had disappeared—apparently the water was too cold even for their comfort. "I have heard that La

Fosse kills a man in fifteen days in the summer," he offered, turning again to his companions. "I wonder how long it shall take in the winter?"

"Mademoiselle Adele, His Royal Highness the Most Christian King Louis the Seventh summons you!"

Adele crept forward into the king's chamber and bowed low before the dignified man who sat upon the massive carved chair. Louis was younger than she expected and more simply dressed, but there was no denying the authority represented by the jeweled crown upon his head. "I have read and heard the report of the message you took from my prison," the king said, his eyes lightly flitting over her form. "It is only because of your religious vocation that I give you audience and heed your words, Mademoiselle Adele. Long ago I entrusted my soul to God and do not usually take care for my life, for God preserves it."

"Yet God has seen fit to use me and these lowly prisoners to warn you of danger," Adele said, choosing her words carefully. "Might we also be part of God's plan for the preservation of your life?"

The king inclined his head slowly. "You speak the truth, mademoiselle. Therefore I will heed your words."

"Will you arrest Jerome de Honfleur?" She sensed that she might have spoken out of turn, for the king raised a sharp eyebrow. His four counselors, who regarded the proceedings with dour faces, glared at her in profound disapproval.

The king stroked his chin with strong fingers. "I will wait until the Feast of St. Andrew and catch his mercenaries in the act of treachery," he said. "After the archers have been found and have confessed Jerome's name, then I will move to arrest this errant knight who has long given me trouble." A smile flickered across his face, and Adele thought for the briefest moment that the king *could* be handsome. "And what of your reward, Mademoiselle Adele? A purse of gold, perhaps?"

"No, Your Highness, I must return to my nunnery. I ask nothing for myself, but only for these men." She gestured toward the bloody warning in the king's hand. "I ask that they be released from prison, or else brought to a speedy and fair trial."

The king pointed toward a long-nosed counselor in a red cloak, and the man paled before the king's hand. "Clement, you administrate Le Petit Châtelet. You will see to it." He held up a warning finger. "But do not release the prisoners until the day of the Feast of St. Andrew—"

"But, sire—," Clement interrupted, his narrow face singularly pinched.

"Do not move them from where they are until that day," the king insisted. "We must not do anything to arouse the suspicion of Jerome de Honfleur."

November 29 brought low gray clouds over Paris, and as Adele trudged back to the nunnery at St. Denis, an odd sense of accomplishment covered her like a warm cloak. The king's life was saved. Gislebert would be released, and Jerome suitably punished. Her week had passed; she would keep her word and return to Abbess Marie. Was this not a circle of completion? Had she not accomplished all that God had set out for her to do?

Even though her mind congratulated her for her part in the week's adventure, still her heart stirred with the knowledge that the frail man in the high window had been Gislebert. Once again, he had looked at her and not recognized her. Once again she had run to do his bidding knowing full well that he would probably turn from her to Nadine. *Is this not a circle of stupidity?* her heart chided.

She had declared her love once and borne his contempt. Did she have the courage to face him again?

In the dark cavern of La Fosse, Gislebert and his companions stirred slowly, their limbs as heavy as lead. All three had shivered through the night, but now, Gislebert noted, their shivering had lessened even as their movements grew sluggish. As they walked and changed positions to ease the pain of the cold in their limbs, Gislebert found himself dizzy and drowsy.

"Don't sit," Laurent warned him, his slurred voice echoing in the room. "Your wet clothing will make you colder."

"I can't stand any longer," Gislebert said, slumping against the wall. I must sit down."

"Lean on me," Henry volunteered, making his way through the water to Gislebert's side. "Lean on me, and I'll hold you as you sleep. Later I'll lean on you, or Laurent. Together we can outlast this madness."

Gislebert had no strength to argue. He pitched forward like a rag doll into Henry's arms as unconsciousness claimed him.

Gislebert had no idea how long he slept or if he slept at all. Through a haze he dimly realized that the door to La Fosse had opened and that he was being dragged forth from the watery chamber. A pair of gaolers carried him to a small room where a fire burned brightly, and a buxom maid sponged warm cider down his throat as he lay by the fire with nothing but a thin sheet over him. "Drink, you will need your strength," someone murmured. Then he was propped on a stool while a maid scrubbed his arms, legs, neck, and back. Warm blankets were heaped upon him, and steaming gruel was set before him.

The stupor of sleep and exhaustion did not leave him until the king's counselor swept into the room. "Gislebert the troubadour, you will be released today," Clement said, his eyes regarding the troubadour with reluctant respect. "You have saved the life of the king, and for this he wishes to thank you."

"I?" Gislebert tried to focus his thoughts. "What of my companions?"

"The marquis, Fouquet, and the others will be released as well," the counselor added.

"And—Laurent and Henry?"

"They did not survive La Fosse," the counselor replied, turning to leave. "It is my understanding that their bodies supported yours during the night." His eyes narrowed as he studied the scrawny bare chest of the troubadour. "What sort of power do you have over men, sir, that makes them want to lay their lives down for you?"

Gislebert could not answer, and the counselor shrugged indifferently. "Well then, hurry, sir, for the king awaits to pay you tribute."

A maid stood before him with a new tunic, leggings, surcoat, and cloak. Gislebert wondered why she blushed and curtseyed before dressing him.

After donning robes and shoes finer than any he had ever known, Gislebert followed a guard from the inner chambers of Le Petit Châtelet to the vestibule. Outside the large receiving chamber, two of the king's mounted knights waited to escort him to the palace. He tarried alone in the room for a few moments, finding it difficult to adjust to freedom. An isolated part of his mind identified the escorts as gaolers, the palace yet another prison.

As he stood in the cavernous chamber, he went back in time to the day when he had been brought into this horrible place. The memory set his teeth on edge. *Jerome, you were my nemesis then,* he thought, picking up the strings of time that bound him to the dark knight. *But I hated you more for stealing Nadine than for sending me to this place.*

A commotion in the courtyard beyond disturbed the quiet of the vestibule, and Gislebert hung back against the wall, not quite ready to face another confrontation. Two royal knights entered, with Jerome held firmly between them, and Gislebert felt a rush of guilty pleasure. The swarthy Jerome caught sight of Gislebert only for an instant. He barely had time to roar an oath before he was whisked through the door and pushed into the corridor beyond.

Other guards entered, escorting men whom Gislebert supposed were Jerome's knights or the archers he had hired to kill the king, and finally, a huddle of distraught women followed, most of whom sobbed and wailed hysterically.

They would wait, Gislebert knew, until they had learned what was to become of their men, for often the law of the king confiscated the estates and property of criminals, leaving families destitute.

Gislebert felt his heart stop as he spied Nadine. She had aged little in the twelve years since he had last seen her. Her figure was fuller, but her red hair still flowed in lustrous tresses to her waist. Her creamy skin glowed pale in her distress, and her red-rimmed eyes drew him like a magnet. Before he knew that he had moved, he stood in front of her.

"Sir," she cried, not looking at his face but at the rich robe he wore, "I see by your dress that you are a man of some importance. If you have any influence with the king, please beg mercy for Nadine de Honfleur. If the king's wrath falls upon me now—"

"Nadine."

He whispered her name softly, like a prayer, and something in his tone made her lift her eyes. Recognizing him, her pale cheeks flooded with color, her lips sprang open in surprise, and she fell to her knees at his feet.

"Can it be you?" she asked, green flames dancing in her eyes. "How often I have thought of you, Gislebert the troubadour. How often I have prayed that I would see your face again."

"Truly?" Her smile dazzled him. Gislebert felt his none-too-steady head swim.

"I have loved you always," she whispered, her words for him alone. "See here—" Her hand paused at her bosom for a moment, then picked up a string of emeralds that had been hidden under her tunic. "I have worn your necklace always, since the first night we pledged to marry," she confessed, her eyes swimming up to his. "My heart has been yours all along, Gislebert, but Jerome took me, forced me to lie with him, and in my disgrace I thought you would never take me to be your wife."

Gislebert smiled as he listened. Surely he was dreaming! Nadine, the woman he had wished for and sought for years—it was inconceivable that she knelt at his feet now, only hours after the horrors of La Fosse. A sense of tingling delight began to flow through him, and her admiring gaze brought his dormant passion for her to life again.

She reached for his hand, and the touch of her palm against his sent a tingling up through his arm. "I have loved you since the time we first met, do you remember?" she asked coyly, her dark lashes tilting up at him. "Your own dear friend, the artist Adele, told me about you, and I wanted to know you so much better!"

Her words were breathless, her voice low and husky, and the combination made Gislebert's pulse pound. He backed away from her and fell onto a bench at the wall, laughing at his own helplessness. *I act as if I am drunk,* he thought happily, feasting his eyes on the vision of loveliness that still knelt before him. *Well, why shouldn't I be? Nadine does love me, and has all along. Adele was wrong, for she said that Nadine was vain and selfish—*

Then he stopped, his brain paralyzed as, unbidden, sudden memories flooded over him: Adele, returning empty-handed, with no letters from Nadine, no kind words for him from his love; Nadine, cool and aloof, as he offered his heart in love; Jerome, grinning slyly as Nadine blushed in pleasure at his attentions. . . .

His eyes flew back to Nadine's face, and he gazed at her, incredulous, understanding. *The lady was lying!* Nadine had never wanted to know him better, for she had never written in reply to his many letters. He recalled Melusina's certainty that she had gone willingly with Jerome when he took her away on the eve of her proposed wedding, and he knew now she had been right. Nadine could have sent Jerome away from the beginning, but here she was, dressed in Jerome's robes, fragranced with oils he had provided her, wearing gold rings engraved with Jerome's initials. She was mother to the knight's children, confidante to his dark plans—probably a conspirator to plans to destroy the king of France. And then another thought hit him.

"You knew Adele," he said, his words more a statement than a question.

Nadine gave him a rare, intimate smile, beautiful in its brightness. "I loved her like she was my own sister," she answered, creeping toward him on her knees. "So great was my love for you."

Gislebert leaned his head against the hard stone of the wall. *Your love for me.* The truth washed over him like a wave, and he began to laugh. He laughed until tears rolled down his craggy cheeks. All this time he had been seeking Nadine, thinking to find love in her, when at his side was the greatest love he would ever know. Adele was love. Not this vain, deceitful, beautiful woman who knelt before him. Adele had stood by his side, kept him alive in the woods, brought him the crystal when he so desperately desired a sign of true love. When he was low-spirited, she had lifted him up. When he was foolish, Adele had known how to inject reason into his vain ideas. She had seen him at his worst, and still she loved him. And finally she risked everything to tell him the truth . . . and he rejected her.

Gislebert put his hands to his head as he slowly submerged himself into memory. That night, that awful night when he had taken the crystal to Nadine, a truly loving woman had kissed him, a woman deserving of love and attention. And he had spurned her. Even then, her love had not faltered. Adele had loved him enough to give him the priceless crystal she had sacrificed to gain—how had Abbot Robert put it? She *surrendered her life.*

Gislebert let his hands fall to his sides. Abbot Robert . . . what else had he said? Gislebert's brow furrowed in concentration. Adele had disappeared on the day of his wedding, he had thought her dead, and yet . . .

His eyes widened, shocked realization gleaming in their depths. In St. Denis there remained a postulant who sculpted like Adele . . . it had been a postulant on the bridge below who had responded to his voice and yanked him from this prison. The troubadour laughed again as Abbot

Robert's words sang in his mind: *a gifted postulant who would not take her vows because* . . .

Shaking his head in wonder, he stood to his feet and swept past Nadine before he even realized that she still knelt on the floor of the vestibule. Her startled cry halted his steps. "Excuse me, madame," he said, going back and extending his hand to help her from the floor. "But I owe you an apology. Years ago I left the only home I had known to search for love. Yours was the first beautiful face I had ever seen, and upon you I pinned my hopes and dreams. It was unfair of me, for I expected you to be what you are not."

"I can be whatever you want," Nadine moaned, frantically pulling on his hands.

"No," Gislebert said, shaking his head as he helped her up. "You married the man you loved. Our vow of betrothal was broken long ago, and I release you from your promise to marry me. Go home to your children, madame, and may God's grace follow you."

"But," Nadine gasped, flustered, "what will become of me if Jerome—"

"I do not know," Gislebert answered, feeling a wave of pity and compassion for the woman in front of him. "But I must go." The troubadour's head felt clear, his heart free. He released Nadine's hands. "The king waits for me, and after that—" He laughed again, once more recalling Abbot Robert's words. The wily old monk had known everything!

He glanced down at Nadine and finished his thought. "A postulant waits in St. Denis for her love to return. I will not disappoint her."

His swollen feet itched with eagerness as the king knighted him and gave him a bag of gold as reward for his faithful service. Gislebert gently reminded Louis that others in the Berceau had also been instrumental in saving the king's life.

"They shall be rewarded as well," the king promised, nodding gravely at Gislebert. "Now, Sir Gislebert, where do you wish to go? I will prepare a wagon or a strongcoach for your transport, and grant you an estate in any part of my kingdom."

"*Merci*, no," Gislebert answered, wobbling unsteadily on one knee. "But I would appreciate a horse. I have urgent business in St. Denis, and my legs are yet weak. . . ."

The king gestured to two knights, who saluted. "These men will ride with you to St. Denis," the king said. "May I ask what urgent business draws you away from Paris so soon?"

"Love, Your Highness," Gislebert answered, bowing low.

Adele had just finished helping to clear away the serving bowls from the Feast of St. Andrew when the sound of pounding hooves approached, ending abruptly at the gate of the nunnery. A young nun hurried to answer the ringing bell. As a nun's composure required, Adele pretended that nothing unusual had happened when the young nun practically sprinted to fetch Madame Marie.

Adele lingered in the courtyard long enough to see Madame Marie answer the summons at the gate, but then Adele turned toward the front hall in case the abbess should walk past her with news for someone else. When she felt the abbess tug on her sleeve, Adele whirled around, knowing full well that her face betrayed more than she intended.

"A visitor asks for you," Madame Marie said, a trace of wonder shining through her expressive gray eyes.

Adele flew from the abbess and hurried toward the gate, pausing only once to pull her short postulant's veil from her head and smooth her hair. Her fingers trembled. Would her heart be broken yet again?

She opened the door. Gislebert stood there, in handsome robes and a lush cloak in colors only the king's weavers could produce. His eyes glowed at the sight of her, and his hands reached out for hers and drew her to him before she could catch her breath.

"My little Adele," the troubadour crooned into her ear as he pulled her close. "Can you forgive me for being the greatest fool of all that we met on our journeys together?"

"Oh, Troubadour, your foolishness is part of your charm," she said, pulling away to look into his eyes."

The troubadour threw back his head and laughed, his brown eyes sparkling with merriment. "I know," he cried, wiping a tear from the corner of his eye. "I was a blind fool, but I see everything clearly now."

She cupped her hands around his face, searching his eyes. They were alight, not with the dreamy gaze that the thought of Nadine had always envoked, but with the simple warmth and honesty they had always shared as friends . . . and something more.

"What brings you here, Troubadour?" she asked, scarcely daring to hope that he would say what she longed to hear.

Gislebert smiled and dropped to one knee in front of her, taking her hands from his face and holding them tightly. "Fourteen years ago I left Margate Castle to search for love and found it within three weeks of leaving. How blind I was! But now that God has taught me to see, I am driven to place my life in your hands. As your love, I would reply with my life to all imputations made against you. I would answer in combat all charges opposing you. I would rescue you if you were assaulted, search for you if you were lost, and redeem you if you were captured. If you were tested, I would stand beside you. If you were insulted or tortured, I would avenge you. If you were ever taken prisoner, I would post bail for you—"

"You are a fool, Troubadour." She knew her smile belied her words, and he stood to his feet, his heart shining in his eyes.

"No," Gislebert answered. "Of all men, I am the wisest. Despite my blindness, God has allowed me to find love in you, and I swear to love, honor, and cherish you without question and without hesitation for as long as I live. That, my dear Adele, is the price pure love demands, and it is what I will freely give—if you will accept me."

He opened his arms and she came into them freely, locking her arms around his neck. "I accept you," she whispered standing on tiptoe to whisper into his ear. "Just as you are, my troubadour, my friend."

Name	Pronunciation
Abbot Suger	Soo-'gair
Adele	Ah-'dell
Afton	'Af-tun
Ahearn	'Ay-hern
Calhoun	Cal-'hoon
Charles of Bourbon	Boor-'bohn
Corba	'Core-buh
Dubois	Du-'bwaah
Duc d'Epernon	Duke 'day Pear-nohn
Eustace	Yoo-'stahss
Fouquet	Fooh-'kay
Gislebert	Jheel-'bear
Henry Du Bourg	Onri doo 'Boohr
Jean de Honfleur	Jhon Dohn 'Flehr
Jean de Guise	Jhon Deh 'Geeze
Jerome de Honfleur	Jhay-rhóm Dohn 'Flehr
Lady Jehannenton	Ja-'han-nan-ton
Laurent Testu	Lohr-'on Tess-'tu
Lord Galbert	Gal-'bear
Lord Rainger	Rayn-'Jhay
Marquis d'Ancre	Mar-'kee 'Donk-ruh
Melusina	Melooh-'seena
Salomon de Caus	Sahla-'mohn deh 'Cohz
Vonette	Voh-'nett

Place	Pronunciation
Aquitaine	Ah-ckwih-'taine
the Berceau	Bear-'sew
Chaîne room	Shen room
Fin d'Aise	Fen 'Dez
La Fosse	La Fohs
La Grieche	La Gree-'esh
Le Havre	Le 'Ahv-rah
Le Petit Châtelet	Le Peh-'tee 'Shah-tah-lay

GLOSSARY

barbican—tower or gate

boon work—work done at the request or demand of a feudal
lord

borough—a medievel fortified town with special duties and
privileges

castle keep—the strongest and securest part of the castle

fief—an estate controlled be a feudal lord or king

gaoler—British variation of jailer

gruel—thin porridge

novitiate—the period or state of being a novice; a novice

oubliette—a small hole in the floor of a dungeon where a
prisoner would be dropped—and generally forgotten

scapular—a cloth covering worn over the shoulders and
falling over both the front and back; part of the
monastic habit

verjuice—the juice of crab apples or of unripe fruit,
usually sour

villein—a common villager

If you enjoyed this book, you'll want to read volume 1!

THE THEYN CHRONICLES
#1 Afton of Margate Castle   0-8423-1222-6
This rich medieval saga focuses on a peasant girl stolen from her family to become the earl's daughter.

Additional titles by Angela Elwell Hunt

CALICO BEAR   0-8423-0302-2
A warm bedtime story that reassures children of God's love for them in a changing world.

CASSIE PERKINS SERIES   Volumes 1–9
This bright, ambitious heroine teaches junior high readers about finding God in the challenges of growing up.

LOVING SOMEONE ELSE'S CHILD   0-8423-3863-2
A supportive, practical book for adults who are taking the responsibility to care for children not their own.

THE RISE OF BABYLON *Charles Dyer, with Angela Elwell Hunt*
0-8423-5618-5
Dyer shows how Babylon and present-day Iraq fit into Bible prophecy, pointing to Jesus as the source of true security.